REBEL
FAY

REBEL FAY

FAY

BARB & J. C. HENDEE

A ROC BOOK

ROC
Published by New American Library, a division of
Penguin Group (USA) Inc., 375 Hudson Street,
New York, New York 10014, USA
Penguin Group (Canada), 90 Eglinton Avenue East, Suite 700, Toronto,
Ontario M4P 2Y3, Canada (a division of Pearson Penguin Canada Inc.)
Penguin Books Ltd., 80 Strand, London WC2R 0RL, England
Penguin Ireland, 25 St. Stephen's Green, Dublin 2,
Ireland (a division of Penguin Books Ltd.)
Penguin Group (Australia), 250 Camberwell Road, Camberwell, Victoria 3124,
Australia (a division of Pearson Australia Group Pty. Ltd.)
Penguin Books India Pvt. Ltd., 11 Community Centre, Panchsheel Park,
New Delhi - 110 017, India
Penguin Group (NZ), cnr Airborne and Rosedale Roads, Albany,
Auckland 1310, New Zealand (a division of Pearson New Zealand Ltd.)
Penguin Books (South Africa) (Pty.) Ltd., 24 Sturdee Avenue,
Rosebank, Johannesburg 2196, South Africa

Penguin Books Ltd., Registered Offices:
80 Strand, London WC2R 0RL, England

First published by Roc, an imprint of New American Library,
a division of Penguin Group (USA) Inc.

First Printing, January 2007
10 9 8 7 6 5 4 3 2 1

ROC REGISTERED TRADEMARK—MARCA REGISTRADA

LIBRARY OF CONGRESS CATALOGING-IN-PUBLICATION DATA:
Hendee, Barb.
Rebel Fay: a novel of the noble dead / Barb & J.C. Hendee.
p. cm.
ISBN-13: 978-0-451-46121-6 (alk. paper)
ISBN-10: 0-451-46121-5 (alk. paper)
1. Vampires—Fiction. I. Hendee, J. C. II. Title.
PS3608.E525R43 2007
813'.54—dc22   2006018474

Set in Garamond
Designed by Ginger Legato

Printed in the United States of America

In memory of Dan Hooker,
who stood by us from the start.

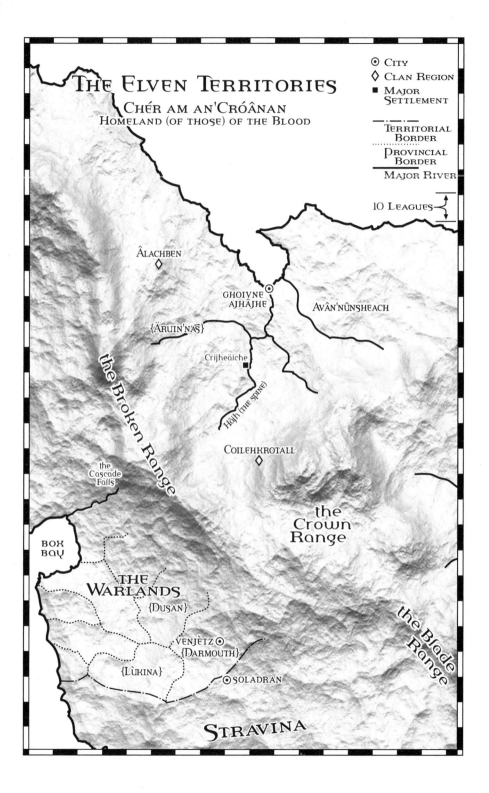

PROLOGUE

Eillean's heart grew heavy as she walked away from the city of Venjètz and into the night forest. Dressed in breeches, cowl, face scarf, and cloak, all dark-tinted, between night-gray and forest-green, only her movement would have betrayed her presence to any watchful eyes.

She did not care for sentiment, but lingering melancholy nagged her just the same.

Brot'ân'duivé walked silently beside her.

Tall for an elf, he stood almost a full head above her, yet he was proportioned more like a human. Both traits were common among his clan. His hair was bound back beneath his cowl, but a few silvery strands still wafted across his dark-skinned forehead. Faint lines surrounded his large amber eyes.

She had not asked him to come on this strange journey. Yet here he was.

They had traveled for nearly a moon from their homeland—what humans called the Elven Territories. Crossing the Broken Range and its western foothills, they arrived at the lake beyond Darmouth's keep. And for what? To bring a majay-hì pup to Léshil, a grandson she had only watched from afar.

Foolishness—and yet she had felt compelled.

With the pup now safely delivered to Cuirin'nên'a, her daughter, Eillean brushed her gloved hand against fir tree branches as she walked. She missed her people's verdant forest, and it was time to return home.

Brot'ân'duivé's cowl was up and a wrap covered his lower face, the same as hers. Not that it mattered. He too hid his emotions behind a passive mask. Perhaps their age and decades among their caste were responsible.

He was not that much younger than she, and she had walked this world for more than a human century. Not so old for an elf, though beyond middle-aged, but venerable for a life of service to the people. A life among the Anmaglâhk was seldom a long one.

"Why do this, if it troubles you so?" Brot'ân'duivé finally asked. "Why bring the pup for Léshil? Taking a majay-hì from our land will not sit well with our people."

Always direct—his most devious approach. No matter how well Eillean hid her mood, he often sensed it. It was in part why she had taken him into her confidence shortly after Léshil's birth.

"I stopped at the enclave where I was born," she answered quietly. "There were few faces left that I remembered. A female majay-hì had borne a litter in the settlement, and this one pup was not playing with the others. I picked him up and . . ."

"Now you have doubts?"

"Léshil must be strong . . . uninfluenced by ties beyond his training. It was why Cuirin'nên'a chose to bear a son of mixed blood, an outsider to any one people. I do not wish to soften him."

"A companion does not make one soft."

Eillean scowled slightly. "You sound like his mother, and I fear Cuirin'nên'a has too much love for the boy."

"As you have for her," he answered.

She stopped walking. "You are most irritating."

His calm eyes peered down at her over his face wrap's edge. "One emotion can serve to counter another. And you are still hiding from something more."

"We labor from within the shadows," she said. "Cuirin'nên'a cannot elude the risks she faces alone. She bred Léshil in her own body and now trains him to kill an Enemy we still do not know. All we have are Most Aged Father's fears and his mad obsession with crippling the humans. I am tired of waiting for something we cannot predict."

She paused with a small snort. "So I brought my daughter a majay-hì pup for her son . . . and do not ask me why again! Perhaps it may clarify this future none of us can—"

"It might," he said.

Eillean stalled at a sudden spark of warmth in Brot'ân'duivé's eyes. How did he always know the right thing to say . . . in the fewest words possible and in the most annoying way?

Emotion had no place in an anmaglâhk's life. It clouded judgment in choice and action when both might be needed quickly and without conscious thought. That was the difference between life and death in silence and in shadows. But Brot'ân'duivé always found a way to goad her.

Eillean stepped into Brot'ân'duivé's way, bringing them both to a sudden halt.

"Swear to me that no matter what comes—no matter what you must do—you will protect Cuirin'nên'a, and that her vision will be your vision. Swear to me that all she has done will not be for nothing."

Brot'ân'duivé put his hand upon her shoulder. It slid softly down her arm to her hand.

"I swear," he whispered.

Eillean had lost her bonded mate, Cuirin'nên'a's father, long years ago. His death shattered her, and she had barely clung to life. She was too old now for such things, and still . . .

She put her free hand on Brot'ân'duivé's chest and clutched the fabric of his tunic. She did not let go so long as she felt his hand in hers.

Who among the living—even the Anmaglâhk—could claim to have never been a fool at heart?

CHAPTER ONE

Chap fought for each breath the blizzard tried to rip away, and every step sank him nearly chest deep in the snowdrifts clinging to the cliff's path. Squinting against the wind, he flexed his paws to fight the numbing cold.

His fur and the folded blanket Magiere had tied across his body were thickly crusted, and his vision blurred if he looked up too long at the whitened sky. To his right, a deep gorge fell beyond sight, while on his left, the peak's steep face rose sharply, its upper reaches lost in the blizzard.

Lashing snow and hail had pelted his face for three days as he led his companions onward. This was the third storm since they had entered the winter-shrouded Broken Range over a moon ago. The map Wynn had procured in Soladran had guided them partway, but once beyond the Warlands' foothills, it was of little help.

Chap had crossed these mountains only once before, and in winter as well, as a pup. Leesil's grandmother, Eillean, had carried him in the company of the deceitful Brot'ân'duivé. Here and now, so many years later, Chap tried not to think upon his failure.

He could not find a passage through to the Elven Territories.

Chap flattened his ears. Each time he raised them, pelting flakes collected in the openings and sent an icy ache into his skull. Even that pain did not quell his panic. Rather, his fear grew as he looked back down the narrow path.

A dozen paces back, a short figure trudged toward him, half-obscured by snowfall blowing in the harsh wind. It was Wynn. Beside the small sage thumped the hulking silhouette of a burdened horse, either Port or Imp. Farther behind came two more figures with the bulk of the other horse.

And three questions still plagued Chap as he waited for his companions to catch up.

Why did Aoishenis-Ahâre—Most Aged Father—seed war among the humans? Why had the dissidents among the Anmaglâhk—Leesil's mother and grandmother included—created Leesil to kill an enemy they knew nothing about? Why had Chap's own kin, the Fay, now abandoned him?

More than a season past, he had left Miiska with Magiere and Leesil. Every day and league brought more questions he could not answer. All he had wanted in the beginning was to find Magiere and keep her from the hands of the returning Enemy. And Leesil had been his instrument to accomplish this. It was—should have been—a simple task to accomplish. Perhaps this life in flesh made him foolish and naïve, stunting the awareness he had shared among his kin.

Wynn's muffled form grew distinct as she neared, one mittened hand braced against Port's shoulder. Her cloak's hood was cinched around her face, and the wool blanket tied over her cloak was caked with frozen snow. A loose corner of Port's baggage tarp snapped and cracked in the wind.

The little sage stumbled and then collapsed.

Her knees sank in the snow, but her left arm jerked straight up, as if her hand were frozen to Port's shoulder. A cord tied around her wrist disappeared beneath the tarp at the base of Port's neck. It was all that kept her from falling facedown into the drift. She dangled there, legs dragging through snow, until Port halted under the extra burden.

Chap lunged down the path and shoved his muzzle into the scrunched opening of Wynn's hood. He licked furiously at her face, but she remained limp and slack-faced, as if not seeing him.

Dark circles ringed her large brown eyes, and her olive complexion had gone pallid. Food had run low, and for the last quarter moon they traveled on half rations. Wynn's chapped lips moved slightly, but her faint words were lost beneath the wind's howl.

Chap pressed his head into her chest and shoved upward. Wynn twisted, not quite gaining her footing, and flopped against Port's shoulder. Chap braced his shoulder under her hip, ready to force her to stand.

"Get up," a voice growled. "On . . . the horse."

Magiere stood at Port's haunch with Imp's reins clutched in her gloved hand. She held her cloak closed and looked from Chap to the young sage. Like Wynn's, her appearance was one more warning of the cost of Chap's failure.

Snow clung to black locks dangling free of Magiere's hood. A crusted tendril swung across her white face, but even her steaming breath could not clear the ice. And her irises were full black.

No other sign showed of her dhampir nature. No sharpened teeth, no elongated fangs, no feral anger twisting her features. Only her eyes showed that she held her darker side half-manifested.

Chap watched her change each dawn to remain strong enough to move on and watch over Leesil and Wynn. Each dusk when she let go, her exhausted collapse grew worse, and the next morning's rise took longer. Windburn marked her face, and it was disturbing to see stains of color on her ever-pale cheeks.

Magiere dropped Imp's reins and closed on Wynn. She grabbed the sage's cloak front with both hands. Wynn lashed out wildly with her free arm, knocking Magiere's hands away.

"No—too much!" she shouted, and her voice grew weak as she sagged. "I am too much . . . Port carries . . . already carries too much."

Magiere pulled Wynn into her arms, shielding the smaller woman from the blizzard. Around Port's far side, a third figure struggled past along the steep slope.

Leesil sidestepped across the incline, bracing one hand against Port's far shoulder. His calf-high boots were caked to their tops. At each step, the slope's white blanket cracked and chunks slid around his legs. Strands of white-blond hair blew over Leesil's face to cling to his cracked lips. He scanned the expanse over the gorge and settled angry amber eyes upon Chap.

Determination fueled Leesil in the worst of times. But since discovering his father's and grandmother's skulls displayed as trophies in Darmouth's crypt, it had become something else.

Chap had seen the warlord's death in Magiere's memories. And in Leesil's, he had felt the blade sink through the tyrant's throat to jam against the man's spine. From that moment, Leesil's determination sank into blind obsession beyond caution or reason. Any suggestion by Magiere to turn back and wait out the winter met with vehemence. Though he was as worn and weak as his companions, Leesil's fanaticism pushed all of them onward.

Somewhere in Imp's baggage, the skulls rested in a chest, where they were to remain until the moment Leesil placed them in his mother's hands. Cuirin'nên'a—Nein'a—was alive and waiting, a prisoner of her own people.

If they all lived to find her.

"Enough!" Leesil shouted at Chap, but the storm made his voice seem far away. "Find shelter . . . anything out of this wind."

Chap turned about, facing up the path and into the gale. For an instant, he forgot and lifted his ears. Snow filled them, and his head throbbed.

Where could he find shelter in these dead and barren heights?

The narrow path traced the steep mountainside, rising and falling over rock outcrops peeking above the drifts, but he had seen no worthwhile shelter or cover all day. The last place they'd stopped for the night was a half day's retreat behind them. They were too fatigued to reach it before dark.

Chap trudged up the path, wrenching chilled muscles. He rounded the next outcropping and stopped. In this lifeless place, he tried to sense Spirit from anywhere . . . anything. He reached out through the elements—Earth and frigid Air, frozen Water but no Fire, and his own Spirit. He called to his kin.

Hear me . . . come to me, for we . . . I . . . need you.

Cold seeped up his legs from stone and snow and frozen earth.

No answer. Their silence brought no more despair than he already bore, and his spirit fired another plea.

How many times must I beg?

He tried often enough. Once before, Wynn had flinched and swallowed hard, and Chap knew the young sage sensed his efforts. Her awareness of his attempts to commune with his kin, as Wynn called it, had slowly grown.

Chap had not spoken with them since the Soladran border. He had turned from the Fay in outrage and raced to the aid of fleeing peasants. After all the times they had harassed and chided him, not once since entering these mountains had they answered his call. He looked back to three silhouettes in the storm huddled near the horses' larger shapes.

I have brought them here . . . and they will all die here!

Wind across the hidden peak above issued a mournful whistle. It ended in a strange staccato of shrill chirps. It was the only answer Chap received. He lifted his muzzle at the sound.

A horse screamed under a rumble like thunder.

The upper slope's white surface appeared to move. Every muscle in Chap's body tightened.

He lunged back down the path, struggling through the snow toward the others. Panic sharpened with each bound. He closed the distance as the rumble grew abruptly.

Leesil vanished beneath a river of cascading snow.

The slide collided into Port, pouring over him as Imp screamed and backed away. Port's rump pivoted toward the gorge's lip and caught Magiere's back. Chap lost sight of her and Wynn as the avalanche spilled around and over them.

Wind and the thundering slide smothered Chap's howl. He staggered to a halt at the slide's rushing edge. Twice he tried to wade in, only to thrash his way back before the current could drag him over the edge.

Port's head and forelegs broke through the slide, snow spraying up around the horse. It seemed impossible that the animal held its place, and Chap saw no sign of the others. Port struggled up on the precipice's edge, thrashing head and forelegs in the deep drift, but he could not pull himself up.

The river of snow slowed, and Chap lunged in before it stilled completely.

He plowed toward the horse, probing the snow with his snout as he searched for anyone not forced over the edge. His nose rammed against something.

He smelled oiled leather and wool. A metal stud grated along his left jowl. He snapped his jaws into the leather as a voice carried from the gorge below.

"Magiere!"

It was Wynn, somewhere below yet still alive. There was no time to wonder how, and Chap heaved on the leather hauberk clenched in his teeth.

A gloved hand reached out of the snow and grabbed the back of his neck.

Chap's paws scraped upon stone beneath the drift as he backed up, hauling Magiere up from where she clung to the precipice by one leg and one arm. He did not let go until she was on her knees.

"Leesil!" Wynn called out, voice filled with alarm.

Leesil rose from out of the deep snow at the path's far side with a stiletto in each gloved hand. He had somehow managed to duck in against the slope and anchor himself with his blades.

Chap darted around Magiere to peer over the edge and into the gorge.

Port's haunches hung out in midair, and Wynn clung to his baggage. She was coated in white. The cord from her wrist to the saddle horn had snapped, and she had held on to baggage lashings. She dangled against Port's rump as the horse kicked wildly at the cliff's side, trying to find footing. Wynn's eyes widened at the sight of Chap.

"Help me!" she cried and tried to pull herself farther up.

Port whinnied in panic as he slid farther over the edge. His shoulders and forelegs sank deeper in the drift. More snow shifted, tumbling around him to strike Wynn's head and shoulders. One of her hands lost its grip, as wind slapped the loosened baggage tarp into her face.

Chap leaned down, snapping his jaws, but the sage was far beyond his reach.

"Leesil, get to Wynn!" Magiere shouted and dove for Port, grabbing the horse's halter.

But Leesil scrambled the other way, toward Imp at the snow-slide's edge.

"Hold on!" he shouted. "I'll be right there."

Imp whinnied, trying to hop free of the snow that had flowed in around her legs. Leesil snatched her reins, pulled her head down, and reached under the baggage tarp. He jerked something out and lunged back toward Magiere.

"I'm coming!" he yelled.

He carried Magiere's unsheathed falchion. When he reached her, he slammed it point-down through the snow with both hands. Magiere grabbed its hilt for an anchor as the wind ripped away her blanket.

Chap peered down helplessly as Wynn coughed out snow and clawed for a grip with her free hand. He dug furiously around Port's stomach to clear footing for the animal. The horse slipped again, and Chap scrambled away before he was clubbed by a forehoof.

Wynn cried out as the horse's belly scraped across the stone and frozen earth of the path's edge.

Leesil heaved on Magiere's waist as she pulled on the embedded falchion. She swung her left leg around it and sat down to sink waist deep in snow. She braced her chest against the sword to keep from slipping toward the gorge's edge and snatched the other side of Port's halter. The falchion's hilt ground into the chest of her hauberk as the backs of Port's forelegs locked against the path's edge.

The horse's quickened snorts shot steam at Magiere. His wild eyes were as unblinking as Magiere's, but her black irises expanded rapidly. She gripped his halter tightly, trying desperately to keep him from falling.

"Get Wynn," she said through clenched teeth.

The tears that always came with her change barely reached her cheeks before the wind whipped them away. Her lips parted, and her face wrinkled in a snarl around sharpened teeth and elongated canines.

Magiere's dhampir nature rose fully, and she heaved on Port's halter. The horse's creeping slide halted.

Leesil let go of Magiere and started to rise. The falchion against her chest began to bend. He quickly sank back down, bracing his legs, and threw an arm over her shoulder, holding her tightly around the chest.

"Climb!" Leesil shouted. "Wynn, you have to climb up!"

Chap clawed the path's edge, clearing a space for himself as he barked at Wynn. The young sage looked up at him in fearful confusion.

"Climb!" Leesil shouted again.

Chap barked once for yes.

Wynn grabbed the next lashing within reach. She pulled herself up and braced one booted foot against Port's rump. The horse kicked again at the cliff's face, and the strap in Wynn's first grip snapped.

She spun like a tassel in the wind and twisted over Port's side. Her back and head slammed into the stone cliff below Chap. Her remaining grip on the baggage lashing began to slip as her hand went limp.

Chap lunged out.

One clawed forepaw ground against Port's side. He snapped his jaws closed on Wynn's wrist, and tasted blood between his teeth as it soaked through her mitten. Wynn shrieked in pain, and Port whinnied.

Chap's forepaw began to slide down the horse's side.

A heavy weight fell on him from behind and pinned him across the cliff's edge.

Leesil's panting breaths filled Chap's ear as he felt Wynn's mitten and skin tear in his teeth. Leesil squirmed and pulled on Chap. The dog's chest scraped back over the edge until his forepaws were digging into the snow.

Leesil reached over the edge and grabbed the shoulder of Wynn's cloak to pull her up. Even when she lay beside them in the broken snow crying in pain, Chap was too terrified to release her wrist.

"Let go!" Leesil shouted.

Chap opened his jaws, and Wynn curled away from him, grabbing her wrist.

"Let go," Leesil repeated.

But he was not looking at Chap, and Chap's gaze flashed up.

Magiere held only Port's reins wrapped in her grip. The horse's struggles had broken her hold on his halter. A panic-pitched snarl twisted into growled words between her clenched teeth.

"No . . . no . . . more . . . lost!"

One rein snapped in half.

Port jerked farther over the edge. The falchion tilted sharply forward as Magiere was pulled hard against it. Port struggled wildly, rolling sideways against the edge, and the blade flattened completely.

Magiere drove her feet down through the snow to brace herself, refusing to let go of the remaining rein. And still she slid.

"Let go, damn you!" Leesil shouted, and thrashed in the drift to get up.

Chap lunged at Magiere. He snapped his jaws closed on the taut rein. The part that Magiere still held severed under his teeth. Before he could open his jaws to release the other half, his head wrenched sideways toward the gorge.

Chap saw white . . . the white-ringed terrified eyes of Port vanishing over the edge . . . the white of snow in the horse's face as he slid . . . the white blizzard air of the gorge below him.

A hard grip closed on his rear leg and jerked him back. Arms closed around him in a tight grip.

No sound echoed up from the gorge, at least none that could be heard over the wind.

Held tight in Magiere's arms, Chap heard a sound in her chest, like a low rumble smothering her whimper. He answered it with his own as he struggled about with his muzzle buried in her neck.

Somewhere above them the wind whistled across the peak. Three short bursts, sharp and quick. And then again.

Chap's ears perked and stayed there, even as the wind spiked into his skull.

He wanted to give Magiere a moment for grief. At a crunch of footsteps, he squirmed about to find Leesil half-dragging, half-carrying Wynn. Leesil lowered the sage beside Magiere.

Chap writhed free of Magiere's hold. The snow-slide had exposed part of the upper slope's face, and he climbed it for a short distance before stopping to listen.

The sound in the peak . . . it could not be the wind.

He stood there so long he wondered if he had heard anything at all, until . . .

Three short and shrill whistles of even length and spacing.

The blizzard's wind could not make such a sound—not twice. Had his kin finally answered his plea?

Chap tumbled and hopped halfway downslope, howling as he went. When Leesil looked up, Chap reversed, climbing two steps before barking loudly. He needed them to follow.

Leesil just stared at him. But when the whistles came again, his gaze rose to the heights above Chap. He scrambled to Imp and began slashing off her baggage as he shouted at Magiere.

"Get Wynn and follow Chap!"

At first Magiere did not move. Her irises were still large and black, and her teeth had not receded. She rolled onto all fours and glared upslope like a wolf searching for any member of its pack. Her black eyes found Chap, and her head swung toward the sage curled in a ball within a pocket of snow.

Magiere hoisted Wynn over one shoulder and stood up. She braced her free hand against the slope's partially exposed rock and took a step upward.

Leesil swatted Imp's bare rump, sending the unburdened horse down the way they had come. The horse could not follow them. He stepped in behind Magiere with whatever baggage he could carry.

Chap climbed toward the heights.

Magiere was near the end of her strength, even with her dhampir nature unrestrained. Wynn was injured, perhaps most by what Chap had done to save her. Even Leesil had given up driving all of them onward. A sudden doubt gripped Chap.

After a moon in these barren mountains, without one touch from his kin, why would they choose to help in this obscure way?

He grew wary of what he had heard, and what waited above in those heights. The more he pondered with each upward lunge, the more his doubt grew.

What choice was left? Either he found shelter, or those under his protection would perish.

Leesil lost sight of Chap above and stopped. Daylight was fading, and he scanned the slope, blinking against flecks of snow pelting his face. A reassuring howl and yip rolled down on the rushing wind, and Leesil turned to check on Magiere.

She still followed, one hand braced against the steep slope and the other gripping Wynn's legs where the sage hung over her shoulder. Her black irises had reduced in size, and were all that remained of her dhampir nature. She'd used up the last of both natural and unnatural strength.

Leesil tried to see through the storm to the heights. Chap had to find somewhere for them to hide, as Magiere had only moments left. He swung the small chest of skulls up on his shoulder over the saddlebags slung there. He gripped the one horse pack he had brought and dragged it upslope. A rock outcrop appeared above, and Leesil halted, panic rising.

It jutted out overhead, perpendicular to the slope. Long icicles crusted its edges. Leesil couldn't spot any passage onward but he heard Chap howl, and the sound rolled around him in the wind as he looked about.

Three paw prints showed in the snow beneath the overhang. They led to the right. The rest of the trail in the open had already vanished under snowfall. Leesil followed the way, looking upward as he passed beyond the outcrop's side.

Chap stood atop the stone protrusion and lowered his head over the edge, barking urgently. He turned a circle back from the edge and then returned.

Whatever the dog had found couldn't be seen from below. Leesil stomped down the snow, trying to make footing Magiere would need, and then heaved the chest and baggage up next to Chap. He turned back for Magiere and found her collapsed beneath the outcrop with Wynn on top of her.

"I'm done," she mouthed, and her eyes began to close.

"No, you're not!" he snapped, and heaved Wynn off of Magiere.

Wynn's whimper was barely loud enough to hear as she tried to grip her bloodied wrist and hold her head at the same time. She curled in a ball at Leesil's knees.

"A little farther," he insisted. "Chap's found something."

Magiere lay on her back with her eyes shut and mouth slack, taking long labored breaths. Each exhale sent up vapor that lingered around her white face beneath the outcrop's protection.

"Sleep . . . ," she growled at him. "Leave me alone."

Leesil's own fatigue overwhelmed him. It felt like relief, making the cold, noisy, white world seem far away. He felt warm and sleepy, ready to lie down next to her.

Chap howled from above with angry frustration.

Leesil snapped his eyes open, and the cold hurt his face once again. He leaned across Wynn and grabbed Magiere by her cloak front, catching the neck of her wool pullover as well. He jerked and nearly toppled himself as she rolled toward him.

"Get up!" he shouted. He tasted blood and knew he'd cracked his wind-parched lips.

Magiere's eyes rolled open as she glared at him. Her irises were their normal dark brown. She struggled to sit up, and then grabbed Wynn under the arms.

Leesil ducked out from beneath the outcrop. He climbed up on the ledge next to Chap and spun about to reach down. With Magiere lifting from below, they hoisted Wynn up. Chap darted away before Leesil could see where the dog went. When he turned in his crouch with Wynn slumped between his knees, he saw a narrow crack in the mountainside where the outcrop met the slope.

Chap poked his head back out of the narrow opening and barked.

Leesil grabbed Magiere's arm and pulled her up.

"I'll take Wynn," he breathed. "Get whatever baggage you can manage."

He knelt down, urging Wynn until the young sage straddled his back.

They climbed upward through the narrow crevice with Magiere in front. The footing was better, as the shielded path was reasonably bare of snow, but the tight space made the wind screech in Leesil's ears. And then a dark gash appeared in the mountainside.

Leesil couldn't see much around Magiere, until she vanished into the opening. It was jagged and ran at an awkward angle up the icy peak. The gash was far too narrow to enter with Wynn riding on his back.

Magiere reached out of the opening, and Leesil lowered Wynn so she could stand. The two of them threaded the staggering sage through the crack, and Leesil followed. Darkness swallowed them for an instant.

It took longer than expected for his half-elven eyes to adjust. Perhaps long days outside had made his eyes weary, where the world seemed brilliant white even at night. The first thing he saw was Magiere holding up Wynn against the side wall as she gazed deeper into the passage.

Its sheer walls slanted like the narrow opening, though it widened farther on, and its bottom was filled with rubble. Uneven footing at best, but the floor beyond seemed flat and manageable. Freezing winter winds and the light thaw of high summer rain had long ago loosened anything that might fall.

A strange rhythmic sound echoed softly around Leesil. It startled him until he recognized it.

Breathing.

He heard Magiere and Wynn breathing, now that they were all out of the blizzard wind. Then he heard claws scrambling over shifting stones. Light from the cave's opening caught on two crystalline eyes looking at them from down the dark passage.

Chap stepped into sight, huffed once at them, and then headed back into the dark.

Leesil rummaged through the saddlebag and horse pack but found neither of the lanterns. They must have been lost with Port. When he looked up, Wynn was trying to reach across into her left cloak pocket with her right hand.

"Crystal . . . ," she said. "I can . . . not get to it."

Magiere reached around and pulled it out for her. She removed her gloves and rubbed the crystal in her hands, but the responding light was weak.

"Too cold . . . ," Wynn added weakly. "Put it in your mouth . . . for a moment."

Magiere was too exhausted to even scowl. She slipped the crystal between her cracked lips and closed her mouth.

In the cave's darkness, her face slowly lit up. Pale features burned from within and her face became a glowing skeletal mask, too much like the skulls of Leesil's father and grandmother. The ghastly sight made him rise and reach for her.

"Take it out!" he snapped.

Magiere spit the crystal into her hand. Its light sprang up so strong that they all flinched. With the crystal in one hand, she prepared to lead the way after Chap.

"Wait," Leesil warned.

He pulled one of Magiere's extra shirts from the horse pack to fashion a sling for Wynn's arm. Then he saw the dark stains around the mitten cuff of the sage's left hand. He carefully peeled the mitten off.

Wynn's wrist wasn't bleeding anymore, but blood had smeared across her hand and up her forearm around where Chap's teeth had torn through her skin. Leesil hoped it looked worse than it truly was, but he wouldn't know until there was time to clean her up. He ripped off the shirttail for a quick bandage.

Wynn didn't flinch until he tried to tie the shirt's sleeves around her for a sling. He worried that her shoulder had been pulled from its socket, and he needed to keep her arm secured. She yelped, cringing away, and Leesil finished quickly.

"Follow Chap," he told Magiere. "We need to get away from the opening to someplace more sheltered."

Magiere scowled, as if all this were his fault, and glanced at Wynn slumped against the stone, breathing weakly. She carefully took Wynn by the waist and led the way with the crystal in her free hand.

Leesil heard Chap scrabbling ahead over the uneven floor, so he hoisted their few belongings. The deeper they went, the quieter it became, until the wind outside sounded far off. Along the way, Leesil noticed pockmarks of darkness high above that the crystal's light couldn't erase. There were smaller openings—cubbies, holes, and other natural cracks, perhaps even channels and smaller tunnels connected into the larger passage. But always at a height impossible to see into.

What at first seemed a cave at the passage's end, made from ancient shifting rock inside the mountain, became a series of subterranean pockets. One led to the next, ever inward below a connecting tangle of smaller cracks and fissures overhead. The air felt slightly warmer, or maybe it was just that they were out of the wind. The way narrowed, then widened, shortened then opened, over and over, until inside one tall cavern the crystal's light barely reached the stone ceiling overhead.

"It's so high," Leesil whispered, and then thought he heard something.

Cloth or some other soft substance dragged quickly across rough stone.

Every move they made echoed and warped off the walls, and Leesil couldn't be sure it wasn't just a trick of fatigue. He quick-stepped to catch Magiere's shoulder and called out to Chap.

"Here . . . we stop. Over by that wall there's a smooth slant of stone."

Magiere looked where he pointed and guided Wynn to their resting place. Leesil dropped their belongings beside them, but Chap remained poised at the cave's center.

The dog let out a low rumble, turning his head slowly. He scanned all around the chamber.

Something made Chap wary, and that was enough for Leesil to hesitate. He took a few steps out toward Chap, turning his own eyes upward to the hidden high places above.

"What is it?" he asked.

A long silence followed. Chap huffed three times to say he didn't know.

Leesil backed up to Magiere and Wynn, still watching all around.

Magiere had settled Wynn to lean against the horse pack. She stripped off the sage's blanket, shook away clinging snow, and laid it across the woman's legs. Leesil knelt down on Wynn's left.

"I have to look . . . feel your shoulder and upper arm," he said quietly, and pulled off his gloves.

Wynn didn't even nod. Perhaps she hadn't heard him.

Magiere sidled closer on Wynn's right, waiting tensely as Leesil unfastened the sage's cloak and short robe. He rubbed his hands together before his mouth, trying to warm them. As he pulled Wynn's shift open and slipped one hand in, Magiere slid her arm behind Wynn's back and held the sage tight against herself.

"Squeeze hard," she whispered, gripping Wynn's good hand. "Hard as you have to."

Leesil held Wynn's left arm with his free hand as he closed his fingers around the soft skin of her small shoulder. Wynn sagged and buried her face into Magiere with a soft whimper.

For all he could tell, Wynn's shoulder was sound. She had not winced when he'd first gripped her upper arm, so it was unlikely any bones had broken or cracked. He closed up Wynn's clothing and grabbed the crystal Magiere had left atop the skulls' chest. Setting it down before his knees, he unwrapped Wynn's wrist.

Once he'd rinsed away the blood with a bit of chilled water, the teeth marks in her skin didn't look so bad. He rewrapped the bandage, put the crystal back, and shook out his cloak and Magiere's.

Leesil reclined against the pack as Wynn settled and closed her eyes. With the sage between himself and Magiere, he covered all three of them with the cloaks and blanket.

Magiere watched him with something akin to a frown on her wind-burned face. Or was it disappointment? She finally closed her eyes.

"Go to sleep," she said, and a dull flush of shame washed through Leesil.

They were all in a desperate way, and Wynn had been injured yet again.

Leesil couldn't count the times he'd cursed at Chap for every blocked passage or dead end they'd run into. But his guilt was always outmatched by what drove him.

Somewhere beyond reach, his mother waited. As he laid his head back, his gaze fell upon the small snow-dusted chest.

Dusk fell as Chane huddled in his cloak within a makeshift tent, listening to Welstiel's incessant murmurs.

"Iced stronghold . . . show me . . . where . . ."

Chane cocked his head.

Dark hair marked with white-patched temples gave Welstiel the distinguished look of a gentleman in his forties. But over passing moons since leaving the city of Bela in Magiere's wake, the once fastidious and immaculate Welstiel had fallen into disarray.

Disheveled locks, mud-stained boots, and a cloak beginning to tatter made it hard for Chane to see the well-traveled noble he had first met.

Chane sneered. He knew that he looked no better.

"Orb . . . ," Welstiel muttered.

Chane tried to focus upon Welstiel's scattered words. He pulled the threadbare cloak tighter around his own shoulders.

Cold was a mortal concern to which he gave no thought, but he was starving. He longed for the heat of blood filling him up with life. Hunger grinding inside him made his thoughts wander.

Well past a moon ago, he and Welstiel had pursued Magiere and her companions through the Warlands and into the city of Venjètz. None of them knew Welstiel followed, and they believed Chane was gone, after Magiere had beheaded him in the dank forests of eastern Droevinka. Welstiel remained undetected, but Chane was not so certain that Magiere was unaware of his return to the world.

Welstiel purchased sturdy horses, grain for feed, and a well-worn cloak for Chane from a merchant caravan they happened upon. He also procured canvas, several daggers, and a lantern. From a distance, they followed Magiere, Leesil, Chap, and Wynn through the foothills and into the base of the Broken Range where it met with the Crown Range. On the twelfth dusk within those heights, Chane was preparing for the night's travel when Welstiel mounted and turned his horse east by southeast. Away from Magiere's path.

"We follow our own way—into the Crown Range. Magiere will find us when she has finished chasing Leesil's past among the elves."

His voice had been calm, but Chane knew better. He sensed resignation in his companion. No undead could enter the forests of the elves, or so Welstiel had once claimed.

Chane heard something that made him pause, and he urged his horse up next to Welstiel's.

Voices carried down the mountainside, not quite clear enough to understand. But his vision expanded to full range, and he caught movement far above. Magiere and her companions had set up camp below a granite spire jutting up from the mountainside. As their campfire sprang to life, Chane's grip tightened on the reins.

Wynn crouched near the sputtering flames.

Now Welstiel would have him just turn away?

Anger burned against Chane's hunger at this last glimpse of Wynn, still wearing his cloak. As far as Chane knew, Welstiel had never noticed this one telltale sign.

On the last night in Venjètz, Chane had carried Wynn from Darmouth's keep to safety. Welstiel knew as much, and Chane never denied it. Wynn remained unconscious the whole time, never seeing who carried her. But the others with her—one frail but sharp-eyed noblewoman and a strange girl child—would surely have told Wynn that he had been there.

And he had covered Wynn with his cloak.

The thought of her so far from reach, beyond his protection—especially among those bigoted elves—was unbearable. But Chane did not blame Welstiel.

He blamed Magiere.

Wynn would follow that white-skinned bitch down into every netherworld of every long-forgotten religion. Chane had once tried to dissuade her and failed. Nothing he did or said would stop Wynn. Now he had no home, nothing he truly desired, and little future other than to follow Welstiel in search of the man's fantasy—this . . . orb.

Welstiel believed some ancient artifact would free him from feeding on blood, though he was not forthcoming about how. From pieces Chane gathered, it would somehow sustain the man without "debasing" himself. But while Welstiel had once believed he could not procure the object without Magiere, he now planned to locate it himself and lure her to it, once she emerged . . . if she emerged . . . if Wynn ever left the Elven Territories.

The "orb" of Welstiel's obsession pulled Chane from the one thing that mattered most to him. Whatever source of information Welstiel found in his slumber, it had begun doling out tidbits again, like a trail of bread crumbs leading a starving bird into a cage. Yet the trail was incomplete. Perhaps purposefully so?

All Chane wanted was to find his way into the world of the sages, his last connection to Wynn. For that he needed Welstiel's promised letter of introduction. The man had more than once implied a past connection to that guild. So Chane followed him like a servile retainer. And then Welstiel turned irrationally away from Magiere . . . away from Wynn.

It made no sense, if Welstiel expected to pick up Magiere's trail later, for she would surely return—if at all—through the Broken Range. Something in Welstiel's dreams now pushed the man towards the Crown Range.

Now, Chane was starving, huddled in a makeshift tent and wrapped in a thin secondhand cloak, with no people living up this high to feed upon.

Welstiel's head rolled to the side, exposing his thick neck and throat.

The grinding hunger grew inside Chane.

Could one undead feed upon another? Steal what little life it hoarded from its own feeding?

It had been twelve days since Chane had last tasted blood. His cold skin felt like dried parchment. He could not take his eyes off Welstiel's neck.

"Wake up," he rasped.

The words grated out of his maimed throat. He slipped his hand into his cowl to rub at the scar left by Magiere's falchion.

Welstiel's eyes opened. He sat up slowly and looked about. The man always awoke disoriented.

"We are in the tent . . . again," Chane said.

Welstiel's lost expression drained away. "Pack the horses."

Chane did not move. "I must feed . . . tonight!"

He waited almost eagerly for an angry rebuke. Welstiel looked him over with something akin to concern.

"Yes, I know. We will drop into the lower elevations to find sustenance."

Chane's anger caught in his throat. Welstiel had agreed too easily. His surprise must have shown, for Welstiel's voice hardened.

"You are no good to me if you become incapacitated."

Welstiel's self-interest did not matter, so long as the prospect of human blood—and the life it carried—was real. Chane slapped open the tent's canvas and stood up beneath spindly branches of mountain fir trees. Welstiel followed him out.

Half a head taller than his companion, Chane appeared over a decade younger. Jaggedly cut red-brown hair hung just long enough to tuck behind his ears.

Snow drifted around him in light flurries across a landscape barren and rocky except for the scattered trees leaning slightly north from relentless winds. Chane hated this monotonous, hungry existence. For a moment he closed his eyes, submerging in a waking dream of nights in Bela at the sages' guild.

Warmly lit rooms were filled with books and scrolls. Simple stools and tables were the only furniture, though often covered in so many curiosities it was hard to know where to begin the night's journey into unknown pasts and places far away or long lost. The scent of mint tea suddenly filled the room, and Wynn appeared, greeting him with a welcoming smile.

Chane surfaced from memory and turned dumbly to saddling the horses.

Both were sturdy mountain stock but showed signs of exhaustion and the lack of food. Chane had begun rationing their grain as the supply dwindled.

Géorn-metade . . .

Wynn's Numanese greeting stuck in Chane's thoughts. She spoke many languages, and this was the tongue of her homeland. Chane glanced sidelong at Welstiel with a strange thought.

He knew next to nothing of Welstiel's past, but several times the man had said things . . . comments that implied the places Welstiel had traveled. How could the man have a connection to the Guild of Sagecraft abroad without the ability to converse with them?

"Géorn-metade," Chane said.

"Well met? What do you mean?" Welstiel stepped closer. "Where did you hear that greeting?"

Chane ignored the question. "You've traveled in the Numan lands?"

Welstiel lost interest and reached for his horse's bridle. "You are well aware that I have."

"You speak the language."

"Of course."

"Fluently?"

Welstiel held the bridle in midair as he turned on Chane. "What is brewing in that head of yours?"

Chane hefted the saddle onto his horse. "You will teach me Numanese while we travel. If I'm to seek out the sages' guild in that land, I'll need to communicate with its people."

Snowflakes grew larger, and the wind picked up. Welstiel stared into the growing darkness, but he finally nodded.

"It will pass the time. But be warned, the conjugations are often irregular, and the idioms so—"

He stopped as Chane whirled to the left, head high, sniffing the air.

"What is it?" Welstiel asked.

"I smell life."

Chap slowly paced the cavern, watching its dark heights. He smelled something.

Like a bird, but with a strange difference he could not place.

Perhaps a hawk or eagle took refuge here against the storm. The crystal's light did not reach high enough for even his eyes to see into the dark holes above. He approached the far wall, peering upward.

A thrumming snap echoed through the cavern.

An arrow struck in front of him and clattered on the stone.

Chap backpedaled, twisting about in search of its origin. He braced on all fours with ears perked and remained poised to lunge aside at any sound. About to bark a warning to his companions, he heard another sound high to his right.

Something soft . . . . pliant . . . smooth that dragged on stone, followed by a brief and careless scrape of wood. Then silence.

Chap growled.

"Come back here!" Leesil called in a hushed voice.

Chap remained where he was but heard nothing further. Whatever hid above and had called to him amid the storm, it did not care for anyone coming too close. And he no longer believed it had anything to do with his kin.

He inched forward, sniffing carefully at the small, plain arrow.

The strange bird scent was strong on it, especially on the mottled gray feathers mounted at its notched end. The shaft was no longer than his own head, and ended in a sharpened point rather than a metal head. He gripped it with his teeth, and the light-colored wood was harder than expected. It tasted faintly sweet, not unlike the scent of jasmine, and maybe cinnamon, reminding him of spiced tea Magiere served at the Sea Lion Tavern.

Memory. How strange the things that came to him—and the things that would not. Things he must have once known among the Fay.

Chap looked up to the cavern heights. Instinct and intellect told him there was likely no danger, so long as they left their hidden benefactor well enough alone. Still, he did not care for a skulker watching them from the dark. He loped back to his companions with the small arrow in his teeth.

He dropped it upon the edge of the layered blankets and cloaks, prepared to nudge Leesil.

Wynn rolled her head and half-opened her eyes. Chap stepped as close as he could, sniffing at her loosely bandaged wrist, the one he had injured trying to save her.

He peered at Wynn's round face by the waning light of the crystal atop the chest. She settled her hand clumsily on his head. It slid over his ear, down his face, and dropped limply against her side as her eyes closed again.

"It is all right," she said, and even weaker, like a child on the edge of sleep, "thank you."

Chap turned a circle and curled up at Wynn's feet.

He laid his head upon his paws, trying to keep his eyes open, and watched the heights of the cavern. He never knew whether fatigue or the waning crystal finally pulled him down into darkness.

CHAPTER TWO

Welstiel urged his horse through the dark, keeping up with Chane amid the scattered trees of the rocky mountainside. Occasionally, Chane slowed to sniff the night breeze.

Disdain tainted Welstiel's grudging respect for Chane's hunting instincts. He had suppressed such long ago, but given their present situation, the need for life to feed upon grew desperate even for him.

Since leaving Venjètz, Chane had reverted to the resourceful companion he had been in Magiere's homeland of Droevinka, securing supplies, setting proper camps before dawn, and hunting. Even his ambition to seek out the sages had renewed. Welstiel was pleasantly relieved, at least in part.

"Are we close?" he asked quietly.

Chane did not answer. He wheeled his horse aside, sniffed the air like a wolf, and then kicked his panting mount forward.

Welstiel followed with a frown. When they pushed through thin trees tilted by decades of wind, he caught a whiff of smoke. Chane's starvation might drive him to lunge the instant they found prey, but Welstiel had other plans.

"Stop!" he whispered sharply.

"What?" Chane rasped. He reined his horse in, his long features half-feral around eyes drained of color.

"Whoever we find, I will question them first." Welstiel pulled up beside Chane. "Then you may do as you please."

The sides of Chane's upper lips drew back, but his self-control held. He pointed between two small boulder knolls.

"Through there."

Welstiel smoothed back his hair. Despite his threadbare cloak, he still had the haughty manner of a noble. It was near midnight, and as Welstiel rounded a rocky hillock he saw a small flickering campfire. Two figures sat beyond its ring of scavenged stones.

"Hallo," he called out politely.

Their faces lifted. The flames lit up the ruddy dark features of an aging Móndyalítko couple. Unbound black hair hung past the old woman's shoulders with thin streaks of gray turning white in the firelight. She was layered in motley fabrics, from her quilted jacket to her broomstick skirt. The man tensed and reached behind where he sat. Dressed in as many layers as his mate, he wore a thick sheepskin hat with flaps over his ears.

Behind them stood a lean mule tied to a small enclosed cart not nearly so large as these wanderers usually lived in. What were they doing up here all alone? Welstiel smiled with a genteel nod and urged his horse to the clearing's edge.

"Could we share your refuge and perhaps some tea?" he asked, gesturing to a silent Chane. "We had trouble finding a place out of the wind. We can pay for the imposition."

The man stood up, an age-stained machete in his grip. His manner eased as he eyed the night visitors, who were clearly not roving bandits.

"Coin's not much good up here," he replied in Belaskian with a guttural accent. "Perhaps a trade?"

"Our food supply is low," Welstiel lied, as he had no food. "But we have grain to spare for your mule."

The old man glanced at his beast, which looked like it had not eaten properly in some time. With a satisfied nod, he waved the night visitors in.

"We have spiced tea brewing. Are you lost?"

"Not yet," Welstiel answered wryly. "We are cartographers . . . for the sages' guild in Bela."

The old man raised one bushy gray eyebrow.

"I know . . . mapmakers, wandering about in the dark," Welstiel replied. "We stayed in the upper peaks too long. Our supplies dwindled faster than anticipated."

The woman snorted and reached for the blackened teapot resting in the fire's outer coals.

"Hope these sages—whatever they are—pay good coin to track ways that few ever travel."

Chane remained silent as he settled by the fire. Welstiel knew these pleasantries were difficult for him at such close range, but Chane would have to hold out a little longer.

"And what are you two doing up here in winter?" Welstiel asked.

"Stole cows from the wrong baron," the man said without the slightest shame. "We know these ways, but the baron's men don't."

This blatant honesty surprised Welstiel, and it must have shown on his face.

The old man laughed. "If you were the baron's hired men, you'd hardly have waited for an invite."

Likely true. Welstiel glanced at Chane and noticed his hands were shaking. In the camp's flickering light, Chane's skin looked dry like parchment beginning to show its age. Neither Móndyalítko took notice of Chane's odd silence.

Welstiel hurried things along. He returned to their horses, took a grain sack hanging from Chane's saddlebag, and dropped it beside the fire.

"Take what you need," he said. "At dawn, we head down for supplies."

"We thank you," the old man said with a casual shrug, though it did not hide the eager widening of his eyes.

"Our employers asked us to locate any structures or settlements," Welstiel went on. "Way stations, villages, even old ruins . . . any strongholds high up. Do you know of any we should seek out when we come back?"

The woman handed him a chipped mug of tea. "There's Hoar's Hollow Keep. A lonely old place trapped where the snow and ice last most year 'round."

Welstiel paused in midsip, then finished slowly. *Locked in snow and ice.*

"You're certain? How many towers does it have?"

The woman frowned, as if trying to remember. "Towers? I don't know. Haven't seen it since I was a girl."

She stepped around the ring of stones and poured Chane a mug of tea. He took it but did not drink.

"Can you tell us the best route?" Welstiel asked.

"You'd do better to wait for the thaw," the old man answered. "It's a ways, and at least then most of the path would be clear."

"Yes, but where?" Welstiel's grip tightened on the mug, and he struggled to relax his fingers.

"Thirty leagues . . . or likely more, into the Crown Range," the woman answered.

Chane let out a hissing sigh.

"Hard going, so it'll seem longer," said the man.

"Just head southeast until you reach a large ravine," his wife continued. "Like a giant gouge in the mountainside. It stretches into the range, so you can't miss it. The passage is marked by flat granite slabs. Come to think, they might not be easy to spot in the snow. Once down through the passage, you'll see your stronghold, but it'll be blocked away by winter now."

Welstiel stayed silent. It was the only way he could contain a rising relief that had waited for decades. A chance meeting with two Móndyalítko thieves put the end of his suffering in sight.

Elation faded like the vapor of hot tea in a cold breeze. Was it chance?

Perhaps his dream patron relented from years of teasing hints. Perhaps those massive coils in his slumber took a more active role in his favor.

A season had passed since he had trailed Magiere into Droevinka, the land of her birth. Before her birth, in his own living days, Welstiel had resided there. Ubâd, his father's retainer, had waited there all Magiere's life for her to return within his reach. When she came and then rejected him, the mad necromancer had called out to something by a name.

il'Samar.

In hiding amid Apudâlsat's dank forest, Welstiel watched dark spaces between the trees undulate with spectral black coils taller than a mounted rider. The same coils of his dreams—his own patron—or so it seemed. And it abandoned Ubâd in his moment of need. Welstiel had watched as Chap tore out the old conjuror's throat.

He turned the warm mug in his hands as he studied the Móndyalítko couple. What he had seen in that dank forest left him wondering.

Were this il'Samar and his patron one and the same? If indeed his patron could reach beyond wherever it rested—beyond dreams and into this world—had it done so here and now? Should he trust such fortune appearing when he desired it most?

He had learned all he could from the old couple. He rose and leaned over on the pretense of opening the grain sack. The old man stood as well.

Welstiel drove his elbow back into the man's chest just below his sternum.

The old man buckled, gagging for air. Before Chane's mug hit the frigid earth, his fingers closed on the old woman's throat.

"Wait!" Welstiel shouted. He whirled and smashed his fist into the man's temple, and the aged Móndyalítko dropped limp, face buried in the grain sack.

The pulsing life force of the woman in his hands drove Chane half-mad. He jerked her head back until it seemed her neck might snap, opening his jaws and exposing elongated canine teeth.

She gasped in fear, but couldn't draw enough breath to scream. He bit down hard below her jawline, drinking inward the instant he broke her skin, desperate to draw blood into his body.

Welstiel rushed in and back-fisted Chane across the cheek.

Chane stumbled away. His grip tore from the woman's throat. She screeched once as his fingernails scraped bleeding lines across her neck.

He spun with his teeth bared as Welstiel struck the woman down and she crumpled next to her mate.

"I said wait!" Welstiel shouted.

Chane closed in slowly, enraged enough to rip his companion's throat out instead.

"There is a better way," Welstiel stated. "Watch."

Something in his voice cut through Chane's hunger, and he paused warily.

Welstiel held up both hands, palms outward. "Stay there."

He hurried to his horse and retrieved an ornate walnut box from his pack. Chane had never seen it before. Kneeling by the unconscious old woman, Welstiel opened the box and glanced up.

"There are ways to make the life we consume last longer."

Chane crouched and crept forward, forcing himself to hold off from savaging the woman as he looked into the walnut box.

Resting in burgundy padding were three hand-length iron rods, a teacup-sized brass bowl, and a stout bottle of white ceramic with an obsidian stopper. Welstiel removed the rods, each with a loop in its midsection, and intertwined them into a tripod stand. He placed the brass cup upon it and lifted out the white bottle.

"This contains thrice-purified water, boiled in a prepared vessel," he said. "We will replenish the fluid later."

He pulled the stopper and filled half the cup, then rolled the woman onto her back. Chane pressed both hands against the ground and fought the urge to lunge for her throat.

"Bloodletting is a wasteful way to feed," Welstiel said, his voice sounding far away. "It is not blood that matters but the leak of life caused by its loss. Observe."

He drew his dagger and dipped its point into the blood trailing from the woman's nostrils. When the steel point held a tiny red puddle, he carefully tilted the blade over the cup. One drop struck the water.

Blood thinned and diffused beneath the water's dying ripples, and Welstiel began to chant. It started slowly at first, and Chane saw no effect.

Then the woman's skin began to dry and shrivel. Her eyelids sank inward and her cheekbones jutted beneath withering skin. Her body dried inward, shrunken to a husk as her life drained away. When Chane heard her heart stop beating, Welstiel ceased his chant.

The fluid in the cup brimmed near its lip, so dark it appeared black.

Welstiel lifted the small brass vessel and offered it to Chane. "Drink only half. The rest is for me."

Chane blinked. He reached out for the cup, lifted it, and gulped in a mouthful.

"Brace yourself," Welstiel warned and tilted his head back to pour the remaining liquid down his throat.

For a moment, Chane only tasted dregs of ground metal and salt. Then a shock of pain in his gut wrenched a gag from him.

So much life taken in pure form . . . it burst inside him and rushed through his dead flesh.

It burned, and his head filled with its heat. He waited with jaws and eyes clenched. When the worst passed, he opened his eyes with effort. Welstiel crouched on all fours, gagging and choking.

Chane's convulsions finally eased.

"This is how you feed?" he asked.

For a moment Welstiel didn't answer, then his body stopped shaking. "Yes . . . and it will be some time before we need to do so again, perhaps half a moon or more."

He crawled to the unconscious old man and repeated the process. But this time, instead of drinking, Welstiel poured the black fluid into the emptied white bottle and sealed the stopper.

"It will keep for a while," he said. "We may need it, with so little life in these peaks."

For the first time in many nights, the painful ache of hunger eased from Chane's body. He rose up, his mind clearing. He felt more . . . like himself again, but he turned toward Welstiel with growing suspicion.

"How did you learn this?"

"A good deal of experimentation." Welstiel paused. "I do not share your bloodlust."

A cryptic answer—with a thinly veiled insult.

Welstiel picked up the abandoned kettle and poured tea into two mugs. He held out one to Chane. "Drink this. All of it."

"Why?"

"Does your flesh still feel brittle like dried parchment?"

Chane frowned and absently rubbed at his scarred throat. "Yes . . . for several nights past."

"Our bodies need fluid to remain supple and functional. Otherwise, even one of our kind can succumb to slow desiccation. Drink."

Chane took the mug and sipped the contents, annoyed that Welstiel lectured him like a child. But as the liquid flowed down his throat, the ease in his body increased. He retrieved the grain sack, but also untied the donkey and let it go.

Welstiel watched this last act with a confused shake of his head.

Chane kicked the fire apart to kill its flames and headed for his horse, glancing once at Welstiel as if noticing him for the first time.

They mounted up, and Chane led the way southeast until dawn's glow drove them once more into the tent and another day of hiding from the sun. He thought he knew most of Welstiel's secrets—or at least hints of them. What else of import did his companion hide?

Eyes closed in half sleep, Magiere rolled and reached out across Wynn for Leesil. Her fingers touched hard stone beneath a flattened blanket. She sat up too quickly, and Wynn rolled away, grasping the cloaks and blankets with a grumble.

"Leesil?" Magiere called in a hushed voice.

She teetered with exhaustion and her head swam in the dark. She tried to force her dhampir nature to rise and expand her senses.

No feral hunger heated her insides or rose in her throat. She'd held her dhampir nature in part for too many days, and now it wouldn't come in her exhaustion.

Magiere crawled around Wynn, feeling along the cave's rough floor until her fingers struck sharply against the side of the skulls' chest. She cursed, shook her hand, and followed the chest's contours until she touched the cold lamp crystal atop it. She rubbed it briskly, and it sparked into life between her palms.

Wynn slept rolled in Chane's old cloak beneath Magiere's own and the blanket. The makeshift sling had slipped off the sage's arm. She seemed in no serious pain or she would've fully awoken. There was no sign of Leesil—or Chap—anywhere in the slanted cavern.

Magiere's gaze fell upon something that made her tense, and she shifted to the bottom edge of their makeshift bed. Amid clinging strands of Chap's fur lay a small arrow. She picked it up, glancing warily about the cave.

Its light yellow shaft was too short for any bow and too thin for a crossbow quarrel. Tiny featherings bound at its notched end were a strange mottled white and almost downy at the forward ends. In place of a metal head, it ended in a sharpened point—or would have if it weren't blunted. Its last flight must have dashed it against something hard.

And it lay in Chap's resting place. Where had he found it?

Magiere tucked it in the back of her belt and rose to head up the way they'd come. The crystal's light spread wider and caught on something else.

Beside where she'd slept was a small mat of green leaves, each as large as her opened hand. They held a pile of what appeared to be grapes. Magiere dropped back to one knee.

Each fruit was the size of a shil coin, and dark burgundy in color, but they were not grapes. A green leafy ring as on a strawberry remained where each had been plucked from a stem. They looked more like bloated blueberries. There were more than she could quickly count, enough to overfill a cupped hand.

Magiere looked about, wondering how anyone could have approached while they slept, especially with Chap present. Then she spotted another pile near where Leesil had rested.

Where had they come from in these winter mountains?

Magiere checked Wynn one last time to be sure she rested peacefully. She considered waking the sage to eat or to ask what she knew of the berries. Instead she quietly picked up her falchion and headed for the opening to the path back outside.

She called out softly when she reached the next smaller pocket along the way. "Leesil? Chap?"

A rustling echo carried up the passage from behind her.

"Leesil?" came a voice, and it grew louder in panic. "Magiere . . . Chap, where are you?"

Wynn had awoken. Magiere hesitated between calling out and turning back, and finally retreated to the cavern so that Wynn saw she wasn't alone.

"Here," she said, "I'm here."

A distinct scrape and padding footfalls sounded from the passage behind her. She looked back to see two sparks in the dark passage that became crystal blue-white eyes.

Chap trotted out, silver-gray fur rustling and his tail high, as if he'd been out for a morning run. Leesil followed, carrying a torn horse pack and another set of saddlebags. His cloak's hood had fallen, and white-blond hair swung loose around his dark face to his shoulders. His oblong, slightly pointed ears showed clearly.

"Where in the seven hells have you been?" Magiere growled at him.

Leesil stopped, looked at her in bewilderment, and then held up the saddlebags. "Where do you think? I climbed back down and gathered what was left."

She paused, slightly embarrassed. Of course that was what he would do, but he might have thought enough to let her know.

"Next time, you wake me before you disappear! I told you—"

"That I'm not to leave your side," Leesil finished for her, "or you'll club me down before the second step."

For three slow blinks, his amber eyes glowered in cold silence. Magiere's anger melted toward the edge of despair. Was there anything left of the man she'd once resisted falling in love with? Or had he too been murdered in Darmouth's family crypt?

The barest smile pulled the corners of Leesil's mouth. Not quite the mocking grin he used to flash at her, but still . . .

"Were you worried sick about me?" he asked. "Afraid I'd been packed off by some prowling cave beast?"

A hint of the old Leesil reappeared—the one who'd teased her so often. The one she'd known before this journey of unwanted answers, their own dark natures, and too much death.

Leesil's smile vanished, as if he'd read her thoughts and couldn't face them.

"We should take stock of what's left," he said, and stepped past, heading for Wynn.

Magiere followed, feeling bruised inside. "How's the shoulder?"

"It is stiff, and it aches," Wynn answered, shifting her arm back into its sling. "But I can move it without sharp pain."

Wynn pulled back her hood, running fingers through her tangled, light-brown hair, and then winced.

"What's wrong?" Magiere asked too sharply.

"Nothing," she answered. "I have a lump like a . . . I banged my head when I hit the cliff, but I will be fine."

Wispy tufts of hair stuck out above Wynn's forehead. Chap circled around Leesil, sniffing at her wrist.

Magiere set the cold lamp crystal on the chest and crouched. She unwrapped Wynn's bandage to inspect her wounded wrist. Chap whined softly, and Wynn settled her good hand upon his head.

"That's good to hear," Leesil said. "Shouldn't be long before—"

"Did you find Imp?" Wynn asked.

Another long silence, and Magiere waited for it to end.

"No," Leesil answered. "I sent her down the path before we carried you here. It's still dark out, but the storm has faded. Hopefully she'll make it to the foothills."

Magiere dropped from her crouch to one knee.

They were only animals, Port and Imp, but they'd been with her for the better part of a long journey. She barely hung on to what she had left of herself—what was left of the Leesil she wanted. Anything more she lost sliced away another piece of her.

Chap licked at Wynn's cheek, and his ears perked. He turned around to sniff the cave floor beyond the blankets. Magiere was too lost to give him much notice.

She wanted to say something comforting to Wynn but couldn't think of anything. They had survival to attend to, and this place might offer hidden threats beneath its guise of sanctuary.

Chap barked sharply, shifting about until he faced all of them with his nose to the ground. Magiere realized what the dog had found. She grabbed the crystal and held its light up.

"Bisselberries?" Wynn whispered. "But . . . where? I have not seen such since . . . How did you find—"

"How do you know these?" Leesil dropped onto his haunches before the pile.

"These are bisselberries," Wynn repeated, then picked up one plump fruit, dropped it in the hand with the bandaged wrist, and tried to split its skin with a fingernail. "That is what my people call them, or roughly that in your language. We buy them at market to make puddings and jams for the harvest festival or special occasions. But they have to be——"

"Stop jabbering!" Magiere snapped. "How could they grow in winter mountains?"

Wynn scowled at her, still trying to split the berry's skin.

"They do not grow here. They only come from . . ."

Wynn's big brown eyes widened as she looked up at Magiere; then her breath quickened, and her voice vibrated with nervous excitement. "Elves . . . they only grow in the elven lands south of my country!"

Leesil spun to his feet, pulling stilettos from his sleeves. Magiere snatched her falchion and jerked it free of its sheath, as he turned about, searching the shadows.

Chap's rapid chain of barks echoed around the cavern.

Magiere spotted him off near the far right wall, opposite the opening they had come through.

"Stay with Wynn," Magiere told Leesil, and trotted toward the dog.

Chap dropped his head as she joined him. At his forepaws was a small hollow where the floor met the wall. She couldn't see far into it, but it seemed another passage below headed deeper into the mountain's belly. Chap huffed at her, head still low.

Another pile of berries lay on a mat of leaves near the hollow's far edge.

"No, don't!" Leesil snapped.

Magiere twisted about to see Leesil slap away a berry that Wynn tried to pop into her mouth. The sage looked up at him with shock.

"We are starving, you idiot!"

"Better than dead!" he countered. "We're not eating anything left by one of them."

"It's not elves," Magiere said as she returned. "Not that I can guess. Look at this."

She pulled the small arrow out, and Leesil's brow wrinkled.

"I found it on our blankets when I awoke," she added, "along with the berries near my head. Chap found more of those over there by another opening."

Leesil took the shaft, turning it in his hand. "Too thin for a crossbow . . . too short for any bow I know of, and it looks newly fletched. That other opening must be how . . . whoever got in here. Maybe another passage out to the mountainside."

Chap thumped Leesil's leg with his head, then stepped out a ways to the cave and looked upward. Magiere picked up the crystal, rubbed it harshly, and held up its brightening light.

Above them in the ragged slanting walls were other openings scattered about. Their irregular positions, sizes, and shapes suggested they were natural and hadn't been dug. Leesil headed for the far wall, eyes raised to one larger opening.

Chap rushed into his way with a snarl of warning.

"You found the arrow," Magiere said. "It came from up there? Did you see it hit?"

Chap huffed once for "yes."

"Wynn, dig out the talking hide," she called.

"She can't," Leesil said.

Wynn was already pawing one-handed through the pile of saddlebags, packs, and bundles that Leesil had scavenged. Her frown deepened.

"Where is my pack?"

Magiere knew the answer. She'd been the one to pack the horses the previous morning.

"It must've been on Port," Leesil answered. "Everything I could find . . . this is all we have left."

The little sage's eyes widened further, then narrowed at Leesil. "What? All my journals were in that pack, my quills and parchments . . . Chap's talking hide!"

Leesil turned away and wouldn't look at her.

"You sent most of your journals to Domin Tilswith," Magiere said, anxious to calm Wynn. "Before we left Soladran. You can rewrite anything of importance, and there's been nothing worth noting since we left the Warlands. The Elven Territories are still ahead, and that's what you've been waiting for most. We'll find parchment or paper—and I've seen you make ink."

"Of course," Leesil put in. "Soon as we're through these mountains . . . and a feather to cut a new—"

"If we get through!" Wynn shouted at him, and her words echoed about the high cavern. "If Chap finds a way. If we do not starve. If we do not die of exposure or walk blindly over a cliff into a chasm . . . because you could not wait for winter to pass!"

Any defense Magiere might have offered for Leesil was smothered in her own rising guilt.

They all knew from the beginning that if Leesil's mother still lived, she was imprisoned by her people. The elves wouldn't kill her, it seemed, so she would still be there no matter how long it took to find her. But from the moment Leesil discovered the skulls of his father and grandmother, he'd stopped listening to reason.

Magiere had argued with him, time and again, over waiting out winter. In the end, she always relented, and he pushed them onward. Now here they were without horses or adequate food, and beaten down with fatigue and injury. Wynn's words were aimed at Leesil, but they struck Magiere into silence.

"What about Chap's talking hide?" Wynn continued. "How is he to talk efficiently with me, now that it is gone?"

The talking hide was a large square of tanned leather upon which Wynn had inked rows of Elvish symbols, words, and phrases. Both she and Chap could read it, and Chap pawed out responses beyond his one, two, or three barks.

Chap shook himself and barked once for "yes," then poked his nose into Wynn's shoulder.

"He can still talk with us a bit," Magiere offered.

Wynn didn't answer. She took another berry, fumbling to peel its skin with her thumbnail.

Magiere was about to stop her, for Leesil's suspicion was half-right. They had no idea where this gift of food had come from or why. She glanced at Chap, ready to ask if the berries smelled safe. He huffed a "yes" before she spoke and headed off across the cavern floor.

With a sigh, Magiere set the crystal aside and took up a bisselberry of her own, pulling back the fruit's skin.

Leesil wandered off to the cave's far side and crouched to gaze blankly down into the hole Chap had found. He was so driven to keep moving, to reach the Elven Territories and find his mother. But Magiere knew they'd be lucky to even find their way back out of the range. She looked toward the hole he inspected and saw a flash of silver fur.

"Leesil, where is Chap?"

Magiere snatched up the crystal and her falchion as the tip of Chap's tail disappeared down the hole.

"Get back here, you misguided mutt!"

Chap crawled over the hole's lip and hopped down into a sloped tunnel, heading deeper inside the mountain. In the darkness he barely made out the passage, but scent guided him more than sight. He smelled something familiar. As much as that made his instincts cry a warning, he had to be certain of what he suspected.

The passage was rough and its ceiling so low that his ears scraped if he raised them. A few sliding paces downward, it dropped again a short way to the floor of a wider tunnel. The scent was strong, and Chap jumped down. His nose bumped a pile of plump fruits that tumbled apart, rolling off their platter of fresh leaves.

Bisselberries, Wynn had called them. What the elves of this continent called *réicheach sghiahean*—bitter shields—for their edible skin was as unpleasant as the inside was sweet.

He pushed on down the tunnel, and when it seemed he had gone too far without encountering another pile, he paused and sniffed the air. It took a moment to separate the scent behind him from anything ahead, but they were there, somewhere down in the dark.

More bisselberries.

Someone . . . something . . . had laid a trail for them into the belly of the mountain. This was too mundane to be the working of his kin. He could not determine the direction in which the passage ran—forward or back or even to the side through the so-called Broken Range. Where would they end up, even if the trail led out of the mountain at all?

Entombed in stone, a manifestation of the element of Earth, Chap called out through his Spirit one last time.

In this dark place, the silence of his kin made him sag. He stiffened and rumbled with outrage.

They would not come to him, and the survival of his companions—his charges—now depended on skulkers who would not reveal themselves. Behind the scent of fresh fruit and their green leaves, behind grime and dust kicked up by his own paws, was the other scent he had smelled upon first entering this place.

Like a bird and yet not. Faint but everywhere in the dark beneath the mountain.

Chap turned back, stopping long enough to pick up several bisselberries in his mouth to show the others. Hopefully it would not take long to make them understand. There was only one path to take, if they were to avoid starving or succumbing to winter.

Someone was trying to lead them through the inside of this mountain. Someone had called them in from the storm to find shelter.

Chap headed back toward his companions. He had to convince them to follow him into this passage . . . to trust his judgment once more.

CHAPTER THREE

Aoishenis-Ahâre—a title, a heritage, and an obligation.

"Most Aged Father" waited within the massive oak at Crijheäiche—Origin-Heart. As the centermost community of what humans called the Elven Territories, it was also home to the Anmaglâhk, a caste apart from the clans of his people. He had lived so long that even the elders of the twenty-seven clans no longer remembered scant tales of where he came from or why he had led his followers into seclusion in this far corner of the world.

The massive and ancient oak that was his home had lived almost as long as he. A dozen or more men with outstretched arms could not have encompassed its girth. One of the eldest in the forest, the hollowed chamber within its heart-root had been carefully nurtured from the living wood since its earliest days. It sustained him to fulfill future needs for his people's sake. And its long roots reached more deeply and widely than any other in the land.

Wise in the way of trees, Most Aged Father no longer walked among his people. His withered body clung to life by the great forest's efforts that sustained him through the oak. But he was still founder and leader of the Anmaglâhk. They in turn were the guardians of the an'Cróan—(Those) of the Blood, as the people properly called themselves.

Through the oak's deep roots, he reached out with his awareness through branches and leaves to wander and watch within his people's land. Through slivers of "word-wood" taken from his oak and placed against any living tree, he heard and spoke with his Anmaglâhk in far lands.

Now he waited beneath the earth in his root chamber. He waited for his most trusted servant, Fréthfâre—Watcher of the Woods—who lived by her namesake. He sensed her approach as she pressed apart the curtains across the doorway above, at ground level.

"Father?" she called. "May I come down?"

All anmaglâhk called him Father, for they were the children of his vision and his strength.

"Come," he answered weakly. "I am awake."

Her step light as a thrush, he still heard her descend the steps molded from the tree's living wood. She entered the earthen chamber around the heart-root and appeared at its opening into his resting place.

The hood of her gray-green cloak was thrown back, revealing long wheat-blond hair. Most of the people possessed hair as straight as corn silk, but Fréthfâre's tumbled past her narrow shoulders in gentle waves when she did not bind it back. Today it hung loose and tucked behind her peaked ears.

Her large amber eyes were unusually narrow, and her lips thin. An overly slender build gave her the illusion of height, though she was not tall compared to others. She was Covârleasa—Trusted Adviser—and thereby highly honored among the Anmaglâhk.

"You are well?" she asked, always concerned for his comfort.

Most Aged Father lifted a frail, bony hand with effort and gestured to the stacked cushions before his bower.

"Yes. Sit."

Fréthfâre crossed her legs as she settled. "Has there been sign of the human interlopers? Has Sgäilsheilleache sent word?"

"No, but they come. Sgäilsheilleache will bring Léshil to us."

He had sent Sgäilsheilleache—Willow's Shade—to lead a small band of anmaglâhk to intercept Léshil before that abomination entered their land unescorted. But there were more important things to discuss.

"You will assist me in presenting Léshil an offer," he continued. "One which no other should know."

Fréthfâre arched her feathery eyebrows. "Of course, Father, but what bargain could you make with such a creature? He is not one of us . . . and has polluted blood."

When Most Aged Father smiled, responding warmth flooded her eyes. She never saw him as the withered husk he knew himself to be. His dry white hair, too thin for his pale scalp, and the shriveled skin stretched over his long bones never troubled her.

"True enough," he acknowledged. "Léshil has human blood, and any human is not to be trusted. But he comes for his traitor mother—Cuirin'nên'a—and that is the reason I give him safe passage. Cuirin'nên'a could not have acted alone in her treachery, and we must find her conspirators. We will promise Léshil anything, even his mother, in exchange for his service. With such an offering, we secure his fidelity for as long as we need it."

Cuirin'nên'a's subversion pained Most Aged Father like an ache in his sunken chest. In the end, it had done her little good. After years of delay, Darmouth was finally dead. His province would rip itself apart, and the other tyrants of the Warlands would be at one another's throats trying to claim the spoils.

Since the birth of the Anmaglâhk in forgotten times, their service was revered by the people. Cuirin'nên'a seeded doubt and deception among their caste. It must be rooted out before it spread, even unto the elders of the caste. Or had it already done so? One more name lingered in his mind with that concern.

Brot'ân'duivé—Dog in the Dark—friend of the fallen Eillean, one of their greatest.

Eillean had stood for Fréthfâre when she had first come as a girl, barely past her name taking, to beg admittance to the Anmaglâhk. It seemed impossible that Eillean could be in question, but she had borne Cuirin'nên'a, a treacherous daughter, and lost her life in retrieving that wayward offspring. In turn, Cuirin'nên'a had borne a half-blood son.

Between these two women of their caste—faithful Eillean and deceitful Cuirin'nên'a—which way did Brot'ân'duivé lean?

Fréthfâre showed open surprise and pursed her thin lips. "Promise him anything, Father? Very well, but why depend on the half-blood? We have our own to uncover subversion—"

Most Aged Father raised one finger ending in a yellowed nail. "For our people . . . and their survival in fearful times to come, we must follow this path. Upon Léshil's arrival, escort him to me. Reveal nothing of what I have said. You are my hand outside of this oak . . . now I must rest."

Fréthfâre stood with a daughter's affection in her eyes. "I will bring food and tea later."

As she stepped to the opening of his heart-root chamber, she looked back at him. A gentle bow of her head accompanied the whispered litany of her caste.

"In silence and in shadows, Father."

He lowered his eyelids in place of bowing a head too heavy for his weariness.

"In silence and in shadows," he answered.

Most Aged Father slipped his awareness into the oak. He watched Fréth-fâre step out through the curtained doorway and into the daily life of Crij-heäiche.

A true daughter of his own blood would not have filled him with greater pride.

But he valued his caste and the clans of his people more. It was why he had brought them to this land so long ago. Here they remained safe, shutting out the humans with their flawed blood, ignorant minds, and weak spirits.

Most Aged Father took a heavy breath to smother ancient fear.

Yet the fear still coursed through him.

Lost were the track of years, decades, and centuries, but not the sharpest memories of a war that had swallowed his world. Nor memories of an unseen adversary called by many names. It had whispered in the dark to its puppets and minions, the perverted, the weak-willed, and those hungry for power without caring for its price. And in death and defeat, it merely slumbered.

It would return.

He knew this, believed in it with a horrified faith. He felt it like a worm burrowing its twisted way through the earth's depths. It had only to waken and show itself, in whatever ways it would, to wage a renewed assault.

This time, it would not have the human horde as one of its engines of war. Despite any ill-conceived deception by Cuirin'nên'a and her confederates, he would see to it. He would remove all instruments of this Ancient Enemy and leave it raging helplessly in hiding. His wisdom, his will, and his Anmaglâhk would shield their people.

Most Aged Father drifted into sleep—but, as always, a fitful one. Among all other dreams, one had come each night for centuries.

Broken corpses lay strewn across a bloodied land as far as he could see. Numb in heart and mind, he stood unmoving until the sight was slowly swallowed by dusk. Only then he turned away, stained spear dragging in his grip and his quiver empty.

Somewhere in the growing dark, he thought he heard something struggling to get up.

Wynn flinched each time Leesil mimicked any Elvish word she pronounced.

He would never become conversant by the time they reached the elves—if they reached the elves—but he insisted that she teach him. And she had agreed. A bad decision, upon reflection.

At least it passed the time, as they climbed ever downward through the mountain toward an uncertain destination. Chap had convinced them to follow him, and as they walked, Wynn suffered through the attempt to assist Leesil with his Elvish. What started as distraction from doubts and fears became a lesson in futility rather than language.

"Soob!" Leesil said again.

Wynn cringed.

"No." She tried not to sigh. "The ending is like the V in your language, but the lips close on its termination, like a B."

"So which is it?" Leesil snapped. "B or V?"

"Just"—Wynn started to snap—"listen carefully . . . *suv'*."

"That's not your Elvish word for your bisselberries," Leesil sniped.

Wynn gritted her teeth. "It is a general reference for any type of berry."

She carried his pack slung over her good shoulder. He paused ahead of her without turning and shifted the lashings holding the chest of skulls to his back, trying to resettle his burden.

Wynn did not like that vessel constantly before her eyes.

"Everything in Elvish," she continued, "has its root word to be transformed to noun, verb, adjective, adverb—and so on. But there are general terms for things of like kind."

"So, 'eat a berry' is . . . ," Leesil mumbled, trying to remember. "La-hong-ah-jah-va . . . soob?"

Wynn clenched her teeth. "Only if the berry is eating you!"

"Leesil, please," Magiere growled behind Wynn. "Enough! You're not going to learn it like this. Just leave the talking to Wynn, if . . . when we find the elves."

He glanced over his shoulder with the cold lamp crystal held high like a torch. Its light turned his glower into a misshapen mask that would frighten small children. Wynn did not care.

They had traveled downward for more than a day, perhaps two. And yet they had stopped only three times. She was cold and hungry all the way.

Leesil sidestepped a twisted angle in the passage, and a jagged outcrop caught his shoulder.

"Valhachkasej'â!" he barked.

Wynn stiffened, then grabbed the shoulder flap of his hauberk and jerked him about.

"Do not ever say that around an elf!" she snapped at him. "Or is profanity the only thing you can pronounce correctly?"

Leesil blinked. "It's something my mother said. You've heard me use it before."

"Your mother?" Wynn's voice rose to a squeak.

The last thing they needed was Leesil's ignorant expletives offending someone, especially one of those bloodthirsty Anmaglâhk.

"Smuân'thij arthane!" Wynn snapped at him. She pushed past as Leesil wrinkled his brow in confusion.

Chap waited out in front and stared at her with his ears ridged in surprise. He cocked his head, glanced at Leesil, then huffed once in apparent agreement with her outburst.

Wynn was too miffed to even feel embarrassed that Chap understood exactly what she had called Leesil . . . though it hadn't been half as offensive as his own utterance.

"Time for another rest," Magiere said.

"No," Leesil said, his expression cold and pitiless. "We keep moving."

She ignored him and unstrapped her pack to drop it with the saddlebags she carried.

In their early days, Wynn had never seen such a look on Leesil's face. Lately she had seen it too often. Hardness overwhelmed him from within whenever he was pushed any way he did not want to go. And he did not wish to stop this journey for anything.

Chap padded back up the tunnel and plopped down. Clearly outvoted, Leesil sighed and lowered the chest off his back.

Wynn dropped too quickly in exhaustion and got a sharp pain for it in the seat of her pants. She let Leesil's pack slide off her shoulder in a heap as

Magiere dug out what remained of their rations. The last of the bisselberries were nearly gone, and they had discovered no more such gifts along the way. Magiere held a few crumbling biscuits and a handful of venison jerky strips.

"That cannot be all of it," Wynn said.

Magiere uncorked a water flask and dropped down beside her. "We'll find more once we're out of this mountain."

Wynn divided the biscuits and tossed a jerky strip to Chap. He caught it with a clack of his jaws. Leesil muttered to himself as he inspected the chest's rigging. Wynn turned her eyes from the grisly vessel.

"What was that Elvish you just said?" Magiere whispered.

"It was . . . nothing," Wynn whispered back. "I was tired and irritated."

"Yes, I got that." Magiere rolled her eyes and bit into half of a dry biscuit, still waiting for a better answer.

Wynn dropped her head, voice hushed even more. "It means something like . . . 'thoughts of stone.' "

Magiere coughed up crumbs and covered her mouth. "Rock-head? You called him a rock-head?"

A flush of shame heated Wynn's cheeks, but the look on Magiere's face cooled it with surprise. She knew Magiere well enough to gauge her dark moods and acidic nature. The tall woman was often caustic even at her friendliest. But this expression was almost something new.

Was Magiere trying not to grin?

"I'll remember that one," Magiere whispered back.

"I heard that," Leesil growled.

He sat on the chest with his back turned to them, like some monstrous guardian statue perched the wrong way upon a castle parapet.

Wynn quietly ate her half biscuit and two berries. She pulled a tin cup out of Magiere's pack and poured some water for Chap. When she set the water flask down, it teetered on the tunnel's uneven surface, and she made a grab for it. She tried to settle it more firmly, but something grated beneath its bottom.

She felt the tunnel floor beneath the flask, and something soft shifted beneath her fingertips. When she took hold with a pinch, it felt light as a feather. She lifted it up into the light . . .

It was a feather.

Mottled gray, it was longer than her outstretched hand, with downy frills at its base. It seemed familiar, and that was unsettling, for she could not think why.

Where had she seen it before?

Chap's rumble startled her. He glared intently at the feather and then lifted his muzzle high to gaze about overhead. Wynn cast her own gaze upward and saw nothing but the uneven tunnel roof.

"There's a quill in the making," Magiere said, and reclined on the cold stone. "All you need now are ink and paper. Get some rest while you can."

She rolled onto her side, eyes open, watching Leesil perched upon the chest.

Wynn lay back as well with Leesil's pack as a pillow. She rolled over to face away from him and Magiere. Chap lay with his head on his paws, but he was not trying to sleep either. He studied the feather in her hand, but without the talking hide, she could not ask him why.

Cuirin'nên'a . . . Nein'a . . . Mother . . .

Memories flickered through Leesil's thoughts as he followed the others down the passage. He hadn't slept during their last pause, even after the crystal waned and went out. How long did he sit in the dark before waking the others to move on? It had been hard to meet Magiere's eyes when he finally shook her by the shoulder.

She might see him for what he really was. It hadn't been long since he'd realized it himself.

Guilt for long ago abandoning his parents didn't drive him anymore. Nor was it just sorrow in returning the remains of his father to his mother. Longing was still part of it, remembering a mother's gentle touch and firm lilting voice, and how these made his first life bearable for a while. But it had taken the memories that Chap stole from Brot'an in Darmouth's family crypt to make Leesil face much of the truth.

Darmouth had used him. And Brot'an had wielded him like the bone knife Leesil gouged deep into Darmouth's throat. If that moment had been the end of it, he might have put those bloody events behind him. He'd done it before.

But he began to see the pattern of his life, to understand the reason for his existence.

His life had been engraved by the scheme of a grandmother he never knew—Eillean. Even his own father must have had a hand in it, for Gavril had gone along with Nein'a's insistence. Leesil couldn't escape what he was—what his mother had made him.

A weapon.

He wanted to look her in the eyes and know the reasons for all she'd done to him, everything she'd trained him to be.

Wynn stumbled along in front of him. Beyond her, Magiere now led the way with the renewed crystal in hand. Somewhere farther on, Chap tried to sniff their way out, for the trail of berries had ended far behind them. Too far to turn back with no food left. Leesil hoped they had made the right decision following Chap.

The tunnel forked again.

Chap shifted anxiously between the mouths of the two passages. He sniffed the stone floor, staring down each in turn. The dog stood silent for so long that Leesil came out of his own dark thoughts, and then Chap trotted off down the right fork without looking back.

"I hope he knows what he's doing," Magiere muttered.

They moved on, and time dragged in this place without day or night. Leesil's shoulders ached from the chest's ropes biting into them. He'd sunk into himself once more when Chap suddenly stopped.

"What now?" Leesil asked, and peered around a too-silent Wynn.

Magiere felt cold inside standing behind Chap in tense silence. But it wasn't from the tunnel's chill. She resisted looking back at Leesil. He'd driven them hard with his desperation, but he drove himself even harder.

Their food was gone, and they'd been on half rations for longer than she could reckon. Their situation was dire, and they all knew it.

Chap lowered his head with a growl.

Magiere dropped her pack to the tunnel floor. She reached over her right shoulder and gripped the falchion's hilt where she'd strapped it to her back.

"What is it?" Leesil demanded in a hushed voice.

Chap let out a whine, then snorted as if some scent in the air had clogged his nose.

"Chap?" she whispered.

His ears pricked up, and he whined again, but it sounded more disgruntled than alarmed.

A light scratching carried up the tunnel from below.

"We are not alone," Wynn whispered.

Magiere drew her falchion, holding the crystal out with her other hand.

Beyond the light's reach, a pair of shimmers appeared in the dark. They bobbed up and down as the soft sound of claws on stone came nearer. The paired shimmers rose slightly from the floor. The dark shape of a small creature formed around them.

No larger than a house cat, its body was elongated like a weasel or ferret. A stubby tail, darker than its bark-colored fur, twitched erratically as it sat up on its hindquarters.

Around its eyes and down its pug muzzle spread a black mask of fur. Wide ears perked up with small tufts of white hairs on their points. Its strangest features were its tiny forepaws. Less like paws and more like small hands, they ended in stubby little fingers with short claws.

"Oh no!" Wynn breathed out.

Magiere had to look back. The astonishment on Wynn's features melted to loathing.

Chap shifted to the tunnel's side opposite the little beast.

"What is that?" Magiere asked.

"*Tâshgâlh!*" Wynn said. "And Leesil can swear at it all he wants!"

"Is it poisonous or something?" Magiere asked.

Wynn wrinkled her nose. "No, it's not—"

Chap growled, but he didn't close on the creature. He snapped his jaws threateningly and it dashed straight up the tunnel's side wall to the ceiling.

Magiere shoved Wynn back and held out her blade at the animal.

It clung there as if standing upside down on the tunnel's craggy roof. With one quick hiss at Chap, it turned its attention back toward Magiere. It began to coo at her, like a dove, and swayed slightly as its head bobbed with excitement.

Magiere carefully aimed the cold lamp crystal for a better look, and its black, glassy eyes followed the movement.

"Oh no, not on your mangy little life!" Wynn yelled, and ducked around Magiere to snatch the crystal. Then she scooped up a loose stone and threw it at the creature. "That is mine!"

Chap scurried back as the stone went wide, bouncing from one tunnel wall to the other.

The *tâshgâlh* hopped sideways across the ceiling, trying to regain sight of the crystal. Wynn pulled the glowing stone behind her back with a groan.

"We will never get rid of the little beast."

"What is it?" Magiere demanded.

"Its name means 'finder of lost things,' " Wynn answered. "A rather polite wording. They are nothing but incorrigible little thieves. It will follow us and dig through our belongings the moment we are asleep . . . now that it has seen something pretty that it fancies."

Chap jumped at the *tâshgâlh,* his barks filling the tunnel with echoes.

"You see?" Wynn shouted over the noise. "Chap knows the trouble they make."

"Quiet down, Chap," Leesil yelled.

The *tâshgâlh* darted back and forth across the ceiling, trying to stay out of reach but maintain sight of its coveted item. Chap kept barking as he lunged up one wall or the other. The little creature screeched at him, then raced along an arc down the tunnel wall and back the way it had come.

"How many of these things could be in the tunnels?" Leesil demanded. "And how do you know this animal? Magiere, will you shut that dog up!"

Magiere shot him an angry glance. When she turned to do as he'd asked, all she saw of Chap was his swishing tail as he took off after the fleeing animal.

"They do not live in caves," Wynn said. "They live in . . ."

Wynn spun about, staring wide-eyed down the tunnel. Before Magiere could demand a better answer, Wynn took off in a headlong rush after Chap.

"Wait! What are you doing?" Magiere called.

"They do not live in caves," Wynn shouted back. "They live in forests."

Magiere grabbed up her pack and slung it over one shoulder, preparing to run Wynn down before the sage added to her injuries in some stumbling fall.

"Forests?" Leesil repeated.

Magiere stared down the tunnel. The bobbing light of Wynn's crystal grew smaller as her voice echoed back up the passage.

"Elven forests!"

Chap raced after the *tâshgâlh*. The dark tunnel made it almost impossible to see his quarry, and he followed mostly by sound. The instant he had seen the little creature, he knew what its presence meant, but he had no way to tell the others. All he could do was terrify it enough to flee for its life.

The *tâshgâlh* went silent, and Chap skidded to a stop, listening. Then he heard its paws scraping on stone ahead.

He had seen its like twice when he was a pup in the elven lands. Majay-hì did not hunt *tâshgâlh,* for the little pests were a clever breed and easier prey was available. He could smell its fear of him, knew it wondered why he came after it, but this pursuit could not be helped. He knew it would run for the familiar safety of the forest.

Another scent filled his nose over the animal's musky fear and the passage's stale odor.

Pine . . . and wet earth . . . and warm, humid air.

Somewhere behind him, clumsy feet kicked rocks down the passage in haste. The *tâshgâlh* raced away ahead of him. Chap chased onward, and the scent of the forest grew stronger.

He could see the animal's stiff tail and pumping rear legs. And then light beyond it. An opening appeared, curtained by branches, but not enough to blot out the light of the sun.

The *tâshgâlh* jumped as it reached the passage's end, grabbing a tree limb. As the branch recoiled upward under the creature's weight, it swung out of sight.

Chap slowed to a halt just shy of the exit and stared at wet green pine needles glistening in sunlight.

It was still winter, but in the Elven Territories, the snow touched only the higher ranges.

He waited there, almost not believing that he had found his way through. For a moment he could not bring himself to step out into the world.

Chap breathed deep and filled his head with all the subtle scents of his days as a pup among his siblings. He was home once again, or at least the place where he had chosen to be born in flesh.

Wynn came scrambling up behind him. Her round eyes and olive-skinned face filled with relief at the sight of branches overhanging the opening.

"Oh, Chap," she said.

He stepped out with the young sage close upon his tail. Somewhere above in the trees, the *tâshgâlh* squawked derisively.

Morning had broken, with the sun just cresting the eastern horizon. But the trees still obscured the view down the mountainside. Chap pushed his way through the foliage dotting the small plateau onto which they emerged. When the last branch dragged across his back, he stood upon a rocky slope still partway up the mountain.

"We're on the eastern side of the Broken Range," Leesil whispered.

He and Magiere had finally caught up, but Chap did not turn his eyes from the vision spread out before him.

Down the sparsely forested ridge and stretching as far as he could see lay a vast forestland. Not as in Belaskia or Stravina, with spots of open plains and fields, nor the dank and dull green of Droevinka's moss-strewn fir and spruce trees.

It was vivid glowing green of multiple hues, even though winter was upon it and it lay nearly at the northernmost end of the continent. Multiple rivers flowed away from the range through the heart of a vast land, each a shimmering blue ribbon across a verdant fabric that rolled here and there with the hills beneath its surface.

The forest stretched as far as Chap could see. Somewhere beyond it to the northeast were the eastern ocean and the gulf bay no foreign ship had ever berthed in. He did not remember how large the Elven Territories truly were. But then he had not seen much of them as a pup before he was taken away.

"It seems to go on forever," Wynn said.

At the mountain's base, stepped slopes dropped gradually, and the sparse growth of the plateau built quickly to warm, bright foliage that reached for uncountable leagues.

Magiere stepped up beside Chap, but of them all, she appeared the least touched by the sight.

"Yes, so large it looks closer than it is," she said. "We're out of food, and we still have to make it down this mountain."

Chap looked up at her pale features marred by exhaustion. Where Wynn's showed relief and overwhelmed awe, in Magiere's face he saw some hint of fallen resignation. Then he glanced at Leesil, whose amber eyes sparked in the sunlight but were chill with determination.

A human, a dhampir, and a half-blood. He had brought them into a place where the word "unwelcome" was but a polite term for what awaited them.

Wynn's lips had parted to speak when a high-pitched chirp sounded above them. Chap looked up, but the sky was empty except for dark billowing clouds trapped upon the mountain peaks. The sound trailed into a string of slurred notes, erratic but strangely lyrical, and then it faded in the light breeze.

Wynn fished in her coat pocket. She pulled out the feather she had found. In the sunlight, it was mottled white.

"Where did you get that?" Leesil asked, as he had not seen the feather until now.

"I found it at our last stop in the tunnels."

Leesil took his pack off her shoulder and dug through it until he pulled out the small arrow. The trimmed feathers on its notched end matched the one in Wynn's hand.

Magiere only glanced at the feathers and then down the slope. "We need to get moving."

Chap turned along the plateau to find them a path. He barked for the others to follow him. For a moment, Wynn looked up into the empty sky then back toward the mountain's passage, hidden behind the trees. The feather was still in her hand.

CHAPTER FOUR

Descending the rocky mountainside took most of the day. As the sun passed to the west above the Broken Range, the forest surrounded Chap and his companions. He returned to the land of his birth.

Whenever a break appeared in the green canopy of needles and leaves, Wynn's gaze wandered to the mountain behind them. She insisted that the *tâshgâlh* might still follow them. Chap neither heard nor smelled it, but she was likely right. Those little bandits were persistent.

Chap nudged Wynn aside before she stumbled into a tangle of poison ivy clinging to an oak. She slowed, wavering on her feet, and Chap paused when he noticed that Leesil had halted as well.

Leesil glanced about as if searching for his bearings. With a shrug, he took a deep breath, prepared to move on, but Chap saw Wynn swallow hard with panic on her smudged face.

"You all right?" Magiere asked.

The question startled Wynn. "No . . . yes, I am fine, just . . . it is nothing."

Wynn shook her head and continued onward, but Chap watched her with concern. Now and then she stared through the forest, her wonder mixed with worry.

Chap stayed close as they moved deeper into the trees. He expected Wynn's normally incessant babbling to begin over all the subtle strange differences the forest held compared to those of the human lands. Her sage's curiosity was the main reason she had forced her own inclusion in this journey long moons ago back in Bela. But she remained silent and watchful, and more than once started at the sight of even the most mundane foliage or tree.

Chap had been just a pup when Eillean had carried him away from this place. Lush, oversized leaves and enormous red and yellow hyacinths hung from the vines in one grove. They all stopped briefly to replenish their water at a crystal-clear brook winding through scattered azalea bushes. A small flight of bees thrummed between the flowers until a hawk-wasp chased them off.

"It is almost warm here," Wynn said. "How is that possible?"

For once, Chap was relieved that the talking hide was lost. He did not wish for conversation now. He simply wanted to breathe the air and to *feel* the forest's life. Just for one more moment to forget the danger that lay ahead.

It was still winter, even here, but far warmer than the Broken Range or its chill labyrinth of caves and tunnels they had traveled. Here, winter would feel like early autumn to outsiders. He did not know why. Perhaps the elves had lived here for so long that the region itself responded to their nurturing presence and returned it in kind.

He hopped another brook. Wynn scurried to catch up and dug her fingers into the fur between his shoulders. She gripped him too tightly until he complained with a whine. She need not worry about losing him.

A wandering line of elms, silver birch, and willows led to a small open slope. On its far side rose an old cedar, its trunk stout and wide as a grain wagon.

"It's enormous," Magiere said. "I've never seen its like, even in the depths of Droevinka."

Chap sniffed the scent of clean loam on the breeze.

"We're here," Leesil half-whispered. "We actually found it."

They had all suffered for it. Now Leesil walked a vast foreign territory, with little notion what to do next or where to look for his mother. In truth, Chap was little better off.

He shrugged free of Wynn's grip, though she was reluctant to let go, and drifted back to lick Leesil's hand with a whine. Leesil was only half-elven, but could he feel the life that pulsed around them? If he let its current run through him, perhaps it would cleanse some of his burdens.

Leesil scratched lightly behind Chap's ear but did not look down.

Chap called up one of Leesil's distant memories of Nein'a leading a ten-year-old half-elf through the forest outside of Venjètz. The two moved in sync through the trees.

Leesil breathed deeply. "I know. We have to go deeper."

Magiere stepped close on Leesil's far side, brushing her shoulder to his. "Almost a dream of sorts . . . wasn't it? As if we'd never really find it."

He did not respond at first, but finally hooked his tan fingers into her white ones.

"Yes . . . no matter how hard we looked."

"But we're here," Magiere added.

"Have you learned to read minds now?"

The jest held only a hint of Leesil's old mocking humor, but Magiere still smiled and pulled him forward.

"Let's find your mother," she said.

He followed but turned his head both ways, as if looking for something and then frowned.

Wynn looked back at Chap over and over, to make sure he was still there. He trotted ahead to catch up to her. Her eyes wandered, but even as she passed black-stemmed amethyst flowers sprouting from dank tree branches, her wonderment was brief. Tiny hummingbirds of brashly mixed colors darted in and out of the large blooms.

Chap led them deeper into the trees, and the world shifted completely to rich hues pulsing in the somber light filtering down through the forest canopy. He pondered calling a rest while he hunted for food on his own; his companions were fatigued and hungry, but at the same time, he was wary of letting them out of his watchful sight.

"Did we pass those trees before?" Wynn asked, grasping his fur again.

Chap barked twice for "no" and took another step. He led them true with certainty. Within a day he hoped to reach the nearest river sighted from up the mountain.

Wynn's grip tightened and pulled him to a stop.

"I don't think so," Leesil answered, and glanced back at the cluster of elms.

Magiere released his hand, looking back along their path.

"We're lost!" Wynn whispered sharply.

"No, we're not." Magiere pointed to the old hulking cedar by the clearing slope, still within sight. "You can just see the line of trees back to the brook we crossed."

Her gesture pulled Chap's attention, and Leesil followed it as well, but his brow wrinkled with uncertainty.

"Yes . . . that's right," he finally agreed.

"No, it is not," Wynn said.

She turned a full circle, switching hands to keep hold of Chap. Twice she looked to where Magiere pointed, but her gaze flicked quickly about in confusion.

"It is not the same," Wynn whispered, and shook her head.

Chap was baffled. Even without scent he could backtrack their exact route by sight.

"Not the same?" Magiere asked. "Not like . . . the elven lands near your home?"

"No!" Wynn snapped. "I know those flowers—*blhäcraova*—and the birds feeding upon them are *vänranas,* but . . . but they are not where I saw them last."

Chap stared at the purple tree-flowers and garish hummingbirds. They were exactly where he had passed them.

"It changes," Leesil said quietly. "Sometimes . . . I think. The forest changes."

Magiere grabbed his arm. "Nothing's changed."

"I see where we came through." Leesil's uncertain gaze drifted back the way they had come. "But if . . . it's like I'm not sure until I look hard. And even then . . ."

Chap studied all of them. In his youth, he had encountered no elf with memories of humans in this land. The mere thought raised fear, even among the Anmaglâhk, who walked secretly within the human nations. He knew some of the forest's natural safeguards, such as the majay-hì, but was there something more? Perhaps there was a reason no outsider ever returned from searching for this place.

It seemed the impassible mountains were not the only barrier to entering the Elven Territories.

Chap studied the forest's depths. Something here addled the minds of his companions. It rejected those foreign to it, and each of his charges had human blood.

"What about you?" Leesil asked.

Magiere shook her head. "It all looks as it was."

A question occurred to Chap an instant before Leesil asked it.

"And why is that?"

Chap eyed Magiere, wondering at this strange inconsistency. Magiere looked to him, and he huffed twice, for he had no answer.

Leesil's lesser confusion, compared to Wynn's, could be attributed to his half-elven blood, but Magiere was as human as the sage. The only difference was her dhampir nature. But Chap could not see how that would make her immune. And if it did . . . such a twist left him deeply disturbed.

Dusk thickened among the trees and undergrowth.

"We must camp," Wynn said too quickly. "I do not want to walk this place at night."

Chap agreed. Before he barked approval, a flash of movement back near the massive cedar caught his eye. He growled.

"What?" Wynn asked too loudly.

Leesil jerked loose the holding straps of his punching blades as Magiere drew her falchion. Chap pulled free of Wynn's grip and inched back the way they had come.

From a distance, two of the cedar's branches seemed to move.

They separated from the others, drifting around the cedar's far side and into the clearing. Below them came a long equine head that turned toward the interlopers. Large crystalline eyes like Chap's own peered through the forest.

A deer would have been dainty next to this massive beast, though this was the closest comparison that came to Chap. Silver-gray in hue, its coat was long and shaggy. Two curved horns sprouted high from its head—smooth, without prongs, but as long as Chap's whole body.

He had never seen such a creature near the elven enclave where he was born.

Leesil pulled the crossbow off his back and quietly cocked its string, as Magiere handed him a quarrel from the quiver strapped to her pack.

The enormous silver animal stood motionless, staring at them through the forest. It slowly stepped an arc along the clearing's slope. Its crystal eyes never blinked, never strayed from watching them. It had no fear. Perhaps it did not know it was in danger.

Chap turned cold inside.

In the wild elven lands, this creature did not know of being hunted. He barked twice, as loudly as he could.

"Quiet!" Leesil ordered in a whisper. "We need food."

The animal did not start at the sound of Chap's voice. Whatever this creature might be, it appeared that neither elf nor even majay-hì hunted its kind. If they had, it would have fled at the sight of Chap himself, if not the others. And its eyes . . . the hue of its fur . . . so similar to his own.

Chap whirled about and lunged at Leesil with snapping jaws. Again, he barked twice for "no."

"Leesil, stop!" Wynn hissed. "Chap says no!"

"I heard him," Leesil answered, but remained poised with the crossbow aimed through the trees.

"Leesil . . . ," Magiere said.

He simply held the crossbow in place, fingers wrapped around the stock upon its firing lever.

Then the animal pawed the earth once, lifted its muzzle skyward, and a deafening bellow filled the air.

The sound rose up from its wide chest and out its open mouth and rolled through the forest.

Wynn sucked in a sharp breath, and even Magiere backed up a step.

Chap froze where he stood, not knowing what this meant. Then he bolted toward the creature, weaving through bushes and underbrush, until he slowed to stand beneath the cedar's branches.

The deer ceased its bellow, muzzle dropping from the air, and it studied him in stillness.

The scent of musk and something sweet like lilacs filled Chap's head.

It began wandering off the way it had come, but in a few steps it stopped. With long horns tilted to touch its own back, it lifted its muzzle high and bellowed again.

Chap ducked behind the cedar and raced back to his companions. A third bellow rang in his ears as he reached Leesil.

Leesil turned with the crossbow still raised, following the deer's passage. His eyes shifted once toward Magiere.

"That thing is making a lot of noise. And it would still make a decent supper."

Chap snarled at him.

Wynn stepped in front of the crossbow. "Put it away."

"He's joking," Magiere said, but cast Leesil a warning glance. "He's not going to shoot it."

The deer vanished into the forest's depths, but another bellow carried from farther off as Leesil lowered the crossbow.

"Let's put some distance between ourselves and that loudmouth."

Chap searched for any recollection of this strange being but found nothing among his memories. The deer's continued noise unnerved him, and he agreed it was best to get away from it. He started into a trot but immediately slowed so Wynn could take hold of him. He pushed the pace as fast as the little sage could manage.

Daylight was nearly gone. Somewhere behind them, the deer bellowed again—and again. No matter how far or fast Chap went, the next tone was no farther behind them. The deer was following.

A flash of steel gray darted through a teal-leafed bush ahead.

Chap dug his forepaws into mossy earth, and Wynn stumbled as he jerked to a halt.

The movement vanished in the deepening dusk behind a cluster of pale pines.

Not the deer, for it was too quick and low, and the ground did not tremble beneath large hooves. Chap heard claws cutting the earth as it flashed by.

He sidestepped, herding Wynn to the nearest tree. He settled himself, ready to charge anything that might rush from hiding.

Undergrowth rustled, and his head snapped to the left. Another movement flickered in the right corner of his vision, then another ahead. This time he caught a glimpse of fur, four legs, and glittering eyes. A scent drifted to his nose, but too thin as yet to recognize. A canine?

Chap slowly turned, watching darting forms circling around, out in the forest.

Across the way, Leesil half-crouched and blindly aimed the crossbow out into the trees. He jerked it quickly to the right. Magiere stood behind him with her falchion drawn.

"Light the damn crystal!" he snapped. "Now, Wynn!"

A head peeked out from behind a fir tree.

Chap growled before he could stop himself. He sniffed the air as Wynn's crystal lit up the narrow clearing. Something pushed its way through the teal-leafed bush into clear view.

Chap's tension melted in shock as he heard Magiere exhale.

"Majay-hì!" Wynn whispered.

Crystalline irises like sky-tinted gems stared at Chap from a long face covered in silver-blue fur. Its ears rose up to match his own, and Chap's breath caught.

At least five more circled in the forest around the intruders, weaving in and out of the vegetation. Like himself, they were long-legged, long-faced, and tall as hounds. Two were a darker shade of steel-gray, nearly as alike as twins. And one more was darker still.

His dark color, like ink brushed into his thick coat, made his eyes float in the dusk-shadowed space beneath a fir tree. He loped an arc to another overhang of branches, and the crystal's light caught the gray peppering in his muzzle.

The one peeking out from the teal-leafed bush dipped his nose, head cocked in puzzlement. He looked from Leesil to Wynn and wrinkled his jowls to expose teeth.

Chap answered with a low rumble and exposed his own fangs.

Leesil backed toward Magiere, crossbow still raised. "Chap?"

He had no answer, even if he could have given one. He had no idea what these majay-hì wanted or why they closed in. A glimmer of white darted from around the tree where the black-furred elder stood watching.

The female's coat was so pale it looked cream-white in the crystal's glow. A hint of yellow sparked in her irises. She was delicate and narrow-boned, and stepped so lightly that Chap wondered if her paws even left prints in the loam.

"Look," Wynn murmured, and the sight of the white majay-hì seemed to blot away her panic. "Like a water lily . . . I never thought others would vary so much from Chap."

"Don't get any ideas," Magiere warned. "They're not Chap . . . and I don't think they want us here."

Chap knew they were not like him, and not only in the way Magiere meant. They were only majay-hì—distant descendants of born-Fay from long ago and guardians of this wild land. They were like his mother and his siblings of childhood.

"Their faces . . . ," Wynn said, the edge in her voice returning, "the way they move. I do not think any are inhabited by a Fay. But can they still understand us at all?"

Chap took two steps toward the silver-blue before him. It backed into the brush, sniffing the air. A growl pulled Chap's attention to the dark elder beneath the fir tree.

A steel-gray and the white female circled him. As they passed each other, they touched or rubbed heads, one to the next. Chap reached out, trying to snatch any surfacing memory passing through their thoughts.

Jumbled images assaulted him, one after the other. Some repeated and the order disjointed further. He fought to grasp and sort them, but there were so many coming so fast. He caught only pieces . . .

The strange massive deer, and its urgent voice.

Racing toward its distant bellow.

A glimpse of an anmaglâhk in forest-gray attire.

Himself . . .

In the last flash that Chap grasped before it was buried in another cascade of sights, sounds, and scents, he saw himself through their eyes.

And these pieces of memory echoed from one among the touching trio to another.

Chap watched the majay-hì brush heads as the white and gray circled about the black elder.

Memories passed each time they touched. Not the random, scant surfacings of humans, but images passed willfully, one to the other.

Chap withdrew his awareness, shutting out the kaleidoscope that filled him with vertigo. It was too much to take in. But one image lingered as the silver-gray in the bush stepped forward.

An anmaglâhk in forest gray.

Chap backed away, looking again to the trio beneath the tree.

His eyes locked with the white female's. There were indeed flecks of gold within her chill-blue irises.

Chap's inaction left Leesil dumbfounded. He didn't know how much threat these dogs posed, and he expected some kind of lead from Chap.

All the majay-hì froze under another thrumming bellow in the forest.

Far out in the trees Leesil spotted the dim shape of the large silver deer. It stood posed upon a deep green hillock.

The majay-hì circled away into the forest like smoke thinning into the dark.

Chap stood rigid, ears pricked forward.

"Why are they are leaving?" Wynn asked.

Leesil had no answer. "We need to get out of here . . . find a place to camp."

Magiere's gaze remained on the trees where the majay-hì had vanished.

"What about food?" Wynn added.

Leesil had no idea where or how to find food, let alone what might be edible. This forest played with his wits, and even in daylight he had to concentrate just to see which way he had come.

"Camp first," Magiere said. "Then maybe Chap can come up with something."

Leesil sidestepped toward Chap, still watching the trees, and laid a hand on the dog's back. Chap was trembling.

"Can you find us another clearing?" Leesil asked.

Chap shook himself. He glanced about, circled around for Wynn to take hold, and padded off away from the sound of the deer.

A long arrow pierced the earth in front of Chap.

Leesil grabbed Wynn and jerked her back.

"Find cover!" he yelled.

With Wynn tucked behind him, he backed toward a moss-covered old log to his right. He heard a knock as something struck wood.

Wynn gasped. "Leesil!"

Another long arrow shuddered where it stood, embedded in the log. The shining metal head was familiar enough, like the bright-bladed stilettos his mother had once given him.

"Smother the crystal," he whispered.

Wynn closed the crystal in her fist, stuffed it into her coat pocket, and its light vanished.

Leesil couldn't see anything up in the branches, but he didn't wish to give their attackers the advantage of light. He heard something strike the earth to his rear, and then Magiere's voice.

"Damn it!"

Leesil didn't need to look for the arrow that had cut her off. "Get up against that tree, and don't move until we see them. We're open targets down here."

Chap rumbled from somewhere out in the darkness.

Leesil knew the dog was trying to sniff out their assailants. None of the three shafts had struck them but rather blocked any attempt at escape. He reached under with his left hand and undid the catch-strap of the stiletto on his right wrist.

A dark form dropped through the branches of the fir tree ahead of him. Leesil heard another to his right, and then again to the rear.

One came forward out of the shadows.

Leesil aimed the crossbow at its center mass, ready to fire and then drop it to pull his blades or stilettos. Figures took shape as they approached with quiet footsteps.

"I've got two," Magiere whispered behind him.

A rustle of brush pulled his glance. A fourth figure rose from behind the old log. The one in front stepped into plain sight.

Each tall and slender figure wore a wrap across the lower half of its face. They'd tied the trailing corners of their cloaks across their waists. All of their attire was a dark blend of gray and forest green. Two carried short bows with metal grips as bright as the arrowhead in the log.

Anmaglâhk.

Desperation filled Leesil. Four assassins had intercepted him and his companions before they'd finished one day's travel into this immense land. How could the Anmaglâhk have known, let alone found him so quickly?

He slowly twisted the ball of his foot on the earth, rooting himself for an ugly fight, one that he and Magiere probably couldn't win against four of them.

"Wynn!" he whispered. "Run!"

Leesil swung the crossbow one-handed, over Wynn's head to his right, and fired. The gray-green figure behind the log twisted away to the earth as the quarrel hissed by.

He released the crossbow from his right hand and snapped it like a whip. The hilt of the unclasped stiletto slid sharply across his palm. He snatched the blade's tip as it passed, his arm cocked back to throw.

"Léshil, stop!" A deep and lyrical voice spoke in clear Belaskian. "No harm will come to you and yours!"

Leesil halted in midthrow. The lead anmaglâhk raised empty gloved hands, palms out to him, and quickly spread them wide toward his companions.

"Bârtva'na!"

The one to Leesil's left cautiously lowered his bow, but kept his arrow drawn and ready. As the leader lifted one hand to his cowl, Leesil spotted Chap behind the elf. The dog crept in low and silent beneath the very tree the man had dropped from.

Leesil shook his head slightly, and Chap halted.

"We mean no threat to you," the leader said as he pulled back his cowl and, with one finger, lowered the wrap across his face.

Leesil sucked air through gritted teeth.

The man's narrow, deeply tanned face was unmistakable. His dark amber eyes were so slanted that their outer corners reached his temples. His nose was straight and sharp, like his cheekbones. He wore his thick, white-blond hair tied back at the nape of his neck, exposing his pointed ears. Everything about his appearance seemed elongated . . . and foreign.

"Sgäile," Leesil whispered.

Just last autumn, this one had come to Bela with an order to kill him, and then changed his mind. Sgäile was the one who'd first hinted that Leesil's mother might still be alive.

Before anyone spoke, Sgäile motioned to his companions. All removed their cowls and face wraps. Chap rushed in snarling, and Sgäile spun away, startled.

Chap circled around, placing himself between Sgäile and Leesil. Sgäile's companions' eyes went wide.

"He remembers you," Leesil spit out.

Sgäile glanced once at Leesil, then kept his amber eyes steadily on Chap.

Among Sgäile's companions were two men and one young woman with glowing white hair. She didn't linger as long as the others in studying Chap and turned her attention upon Leesil. While the others were still shocked by the dog's action, this female's feather eyebrows cinched together and open hatred wrinkled her angular features.

Leesil had never seen an elven woman besides his mother.

In spite of this one's expression, he couldn't take his eyes off of her. She didn't look anything like Nein'a. Her skin was darker and her features were almost gaunt in their narrow construction. He made out a prominent scar hiding beneath the feathering of her left eyebrow. Still, her white silky hair and peaked ears made his heart pound as he thought of his mother.

One of the men looked about middle-aged, perhaps even older than

Sgäile, though how many human years that meant was beyond Leesil to guess. Though taller than Leesil, he was the shortest of the males, with a rough complexion compared to the others.

The fourth was even taller than Sgäile and young. He looked no more than twenty by human standards and was the most stricken by Chap's savage entrance.

Light erupted behind Leesil.

Wynn stepped close beside him, her expression awash with fascination as she held up the crystal.

"What do you want?" Magiere demanded.

"Lower your weapons," Sgäile said, slow and soft. "Please, put them away."

The elven woman stepped closer to him but didn't sheathe her stilettos. They were longer of blade than any Leesil had seen, perhaps a third the length of a sword. She gestured with one toward Magiere and Wynn.

"Lhâgshuilean . . . schi chér âyâg," she hissed, and then pointed the blade toward Leesil. "Ag'us so trú, mish meas—"

"Tosajij!" Sgäile returned sharply.

She never looked at him but hissed and fell silent, her eyes still locked on Leesil.

Leesil didn't understand what either had said. Except for one word so close to what he'd heard from a young anmaglâhk in Darmouth's crypt.

Trú . . . Trué . . . traitor. He'd never have trouble understanding that.

Sgäile's half hints were the reason he'd come here. The reason he'd dragged Magiere and Wynn and Chap halfway across the continent. He wanted answers, and he kept his stiletto at ready. His own anger sharpened, and he stepped closer.

"We're not putting anything away," he said right into Sgäile's face, "until you tell us why you've come . . . and where my mother is."

The younger male had circumvented Magiere, coming up near Sgäile. His expression changed to nearly visible surprise at either Leesil's words or his tone, possibly both. He wasn't carrying a bow, but a boning knife appeared in his hand. From behind Leesil. Wynn spoke out in a long string of Elvish.

All four anmaglâhk turned full attention upon the sage with guarded surprise.

"You speak our language," Sgäile replied in Belaskian. "Yet strangely."

"Bithâ," Wynn answered.

The young female hissed something in Sgäile's ear.

"Do not let your grief breach our ways," said the older male with the rough face.

He stood off to the left but clearly spoke to the woman. She turned on him, but fell silent.

Leesil wondered what grief the elder elf spoke of.

"Where did you learn our language?" Sgäile asked, refusing to speak to Wynn in his own tongue.

"On my own continent," she answered. "There are elves south of the Numan countries."

"Liar!" the female snapped. "Deceitful, like all humans."

These were the first non-Elvish words she'd spoken. Magiere had kept her eyes on the older anmaglâhk to the left, but her attention shifted to the woman, and her voice crackled low like Chap's growl.

"How rich . . . coming from the likes of you."

She swung her falchion slowly around toward the woman. Sgäile raised an arm in front of his comrade, but it wasn't clear exactly who he protected or restrained.

Leesil was getting tired of all this. "You aren't going to keep us out of this forest. Where is my mother? Is she still alive?"

Sgäile's expression remained guarded, but a flicker of discomfort crossed his narrow face. "Cuirin'nên'a lives, I assure you."

Leesil quivered in sudden weakness, and the chest's rope halter seemed to bite deeper into his shoulders.

"We would never kill one of our own," Sgäile continued. "But she is a great distance off, and the forest will not long tolerate your companions . . . or perhaps even you. We were sent to guide and protect you."

"And we're supposed to trust you?" Magiere asked.

"No," Sgäile answered politely. "I offer guardianship . . . and the safe passage of Aoishenis-Ahâre himself." His gaze shifted back to Leesil. "Do you accept?"

Leesil's anger got the better of him. "Not by every dead deity that I can—"

"We accept your guardianship," Wynn cut in, "and that of your . . . greatgrandfather?"

Leesil turned bewildered outrage on Wynn. She remained calm and composed, facing only Sgäile as he returned a gracious nod.

"Wynn!" Magiere hissed. "What do you think you're doing?"

"What you brought me for," she answered flatly. "You do not understand what is happening, and there is no time to explain it all now."

"My caste is trusted by all of our clans," Sgäile added. "I will not allow harm upon you, so long as you are under my guardianship . . . and how else will you find Cuirin'nên'a but through us? She was once one of our caste."

Those last words taunted Leesil. Who else among the elves but the Anmaglâhk would know his mother's location? They had imprisoned her as a traitor, and it seemed this "great-grandfather" had authority over the whole caste.

"If she's still alive," Leesil asked bitterly, "did you leave her suffering in some cell all these years?"

The thought made him ill, for he blamed himself as much as the Anmaglâhk—as much as Sgäile. Nein'a had twisted Leesil's life to a hidden purpose, but he was the one who'd abandoned his parents eight years ago.

Sgäile's features twisted in revulsion, and his eyes flashed with anger.

"I did not leave Cuirin'nên'a anywhere! She is safe and well—and that is all I may tell you. I am a messenger and your assigned guardian. Aoishenis-Ahâre"— he glanced at Wynn—"Most Aged Father will answer your questions."

Leesil turned to Magiere; her white skin glowed in the crystal's light.

"I don't think we have a choice," he said quietly.

Magiere let out a derisive snort. "They're only concerned for themselves and their own goals! Every one of them we've met . . . they're all butchers who use the truth like a lie. They'll twist you around, Leesil, until you wouldn't know your own choice from theirs . . . until it's too late!"

Leesil flinched at her thinly veiled reference. Brot'an had tricked him into murdering Darmouth to start a war among the Warlands' provinces. But he still saw no alternative.

"Then believe in guardianship," Wynn said. "They would put their lives at stake to fulfill it. If you cannot trust them, then trust what I tell you. The way of guardianship is an old tradition and a serious matter."

Chap had remained silent and still all this time. His eyes held uncertainty and the quiver of his jowls echoed Magiere's distrust. As he crept around next to Wynn, he huffed sharply once in agreement.

"All right then," Leesil said with restraint. "As Wynn said, we accept . . . for now."

Sgäile nodded. "We will set camp through those trees. I will bring food and fresh water."

Wynn appeared to sag at those words, letting out all her fatigue.

Leesil sheathed his stiletto but had to nudge Magiere. She glared at him before doing likewise with her falchion, and then took Wynn by the arm with a frown at Chap.

"You two better be right."

Chap huffed three times for "maybe."

Magiere stopped short and her jaw clenched. "Oh, that's comforting." She moved on with Wynn after Sgäile.

Leesil fell silent. They'd just placed their lives in the hands of the Anmaglâhk. He hoisted the pack Wynn left behind, retrieved the crossbow, and followed, his eyes on Sgäile's exposed back.

In a short time and distance, Magiere sat upon a toppled tree stump before a small fire. She settled Wynn on the ground in front of her and covered the sage with a blanket. Wynn leaned back to rest against Magiere's legs.

The four anmaglâhk didn't appear to carry anything besides their bows and stilettos. She watched two of them disassemble the bows, unstringing first and then pulling the wood arms out of the metal grips. They stored the parts behind their backs beneath their tied-up cloaks. While Magiere was distracted by this, one of them had struck a fire, though she wasn't certain how this was accomplished so quickly.

Chap settled beside Wynn, his eyes always upon the elves, who moved off to gather by a far oak and argue in low voices. Leesil piled their packs and saddlebags with the chest of skulls and paced about the fire before crouching on Wynn's other side.

"Can you hear what they're saying?" he whispered.

Wynn nodded. "Bits and pieces—enough to catch the essence of contention. Their dialect is strange . . . older, I think, than the one I know."

Although no food had been provided yet, the chance to rest in warmth had revived the young sage a bit.

"I cannot quite determine their hierarchy," Wynn said with a shake of her head. "Sgäile is the leader, but perhaps only based on the mission he was given. They do not seem to use rank titles that I can pick out. The rough-skinned man is clearly the eldest, though I would guess Sgäile is perhaps fifty to sixty years old."

"Sixty years?" Magiere said too loudly, then lowered her voice. "He doesn't look more than thirty."

She knew most people would find Sgäile strikingly handsome—although she'd die before admitting that aloud. His white-blond hair was thicker than that of most elves, and he wore it neatly tied back. His face was narrow and smooth, with skin slightly darker than Leesil's.

"They live longer than we do," Wynn replied. "One hundred and fifty is a common age. Some live to be two hundred."

Magiere glanced sidelong at Leesil, who watched the conclave of assassins with fixed interest. By how many years would Leesil outlive her?

"The others are questioning Sgäile," Wynn continued. "Especially the angry woman."

"What about?" Magiere asked.

"They are unsettled by the task they were given, though the elder male supports Sgäile's adherence to the custom of guardianship. It seems safe passage for humans is unprecedented. None of them have even seen a human set foot in these lands."

Wynn cocked her head, still listening. "They are hesitant to question what this Most Aged Father has asked of them . . . but they are to take Leesil to him."

"I knew it," Magiere whispered. "Leesil, they're up to more than taking you to your mother."

He didn't answer. He didn't even look at her.

"I do not think Sgäile is lying to us," Wynn argued. "And this patriarch of their caste may have been the one to order Nein'a's imprisonment. If so, he is the one we need to see."

She tilted her head up to look at Magiere.

"The elder and the woman do not wish you or me to be taken farther. They do not want"—she stopped, eyes widening—"any 'weakbloods' in their homeland."

Wynn fell silent for a moment, listening.

"Sgäile refuses. He gave his word to Most Aged Father to offer guardianship to all with Leesil and deliver us to a place called Crijeäiche . . . 'Origin

Heart' . . . I think." Then she sucked in a long breath of air. "Oh, Leesil, you are considered dangerous, even by Sgäile . . . a criminal."

Magiere tensed. They'd had more than one run-in with these murdering elves in gray, who always found some way to put Leesil under suspicion.

The elves' debate ended as Sgäile stood up. He and the younger male disappeared into the forest. Magiere watched the two who stayed behind. They remained at a distance, and the woman turned her back, leaving only the elder man gazing stoically at the invaders gathered about the fire.

Sgäile returned sooner than Magiere would've guessed. He was alone and carried a bunched cloth of lightweight tan fabric. He approached and opened the cloth for Leesil. Within were more bisselberries mixed with bits of strangely wrinkled gray lumps.

"This will keep you until Osha returns from the stream." He turned toward Chap. "He will bring fish to roast."

Sgäile neither spoke nor looked at Magiere or Wynn. Leesil didn't appear to notice and took the offered food. He poked suspiciously at one gray lump.

"Muhkgean," Sgäile explained, then paused thoughtfully. "The heads of flower-mushrooms."

With a grimace, Leesil took a few berries and held the rest out to Magiere and Wynn.

Wynn snatched one mushroom head, popped it in her mouth, and chewed quickly with a deep sigh of satisfaction. Magiere took only berries.

"Osha . . . is this the young man's name?" Wynn asked.

Sgäile didn't answer.

"It means . . . 'Sudden Breeze,' " Wynn explained with her mouth still full. "A good name."

She yawned and drooped so heavily that Magiere had to separate her knees so Wynn leaned against the stump.

Sgäile remained silent. Regardless of this guardianship oath he'd taken, it was clear to Magiere that he was no more comfortable with the arrangement than his comrades were. Magiere placed a hand on Wynn's soft hair, thinking the sage grew weary beyond good sense.

"Soon as you've had some fish, you're going to sleep."

"Mmm-hmm," was all that came from Wynn, and she popped a peeled berry and another mushroom together into her mouth.

"Where did you find these?" Leesil asked, picking up the cloth of the berries and mushrooms. "We saw nothing like them in the forest."

Sgäile's thin white eyebrows arched. "The forest provides."

Leesil again offered the cloth bundle to Magiere. She shook her head. She wasn't about to touch one of the wrinkled gray lumps, and peeling berries seemed like too much trouble. And she didn't feel hungry.

This made no sense, considering she'd gone without food for as long as the others. Strangely, she wasn't even tired.

Sgäile walked back out into the forest, only to return moments later carrying six sharpened and forked sticks. He stuck three into the earth around the fire, so their forked ends slanted upward above the low flames.

Osha melted out of the trees. He carried three large trout hooked by their gills upon his fingers. He half-smiled at Sgäile and dropped to his knees by the fire.

The two elves' flurry of busy preparation was almost more than Magiere could follow. Three more sticks appeared, pointed on both ends. Osha skewered each fish from mouth to tail, then balanced the ends in the forked sticks Sgäile had planted. Soon, the trout began to sizzle above the flames.

Wynn murmured sleepily, closing her eyes, *"Am'alhtahk âr tú, Osha."*

Osha jerked his head up to look at her, studying Wynn's round face and wispy brown hair, but his expression held no malice. He went back to fanning the fire, then he sprinkled some powdered spice over the fish and a savory smell filled the air.

Chap sat up and whined. Magiere hoped he'd wait until the fish finished cooking before helping himself.

The other two elves finally approached, carrying large leaves, which they handed to Osha. All was quiet but for the crackling fire, and then Wynn's eyes popped open.

"Do all Anmaglâhk speak Belaskian?" she blurted out.

Leesil looked to Sgäile. "Well, do they?"

Sgäile frowned. "Some. . . . Osha is learning at present."

Groggy and exhausted, Wynn still seemed unaware that Sgäile avoided speaking to her.

"Wynn," the sage said to Osha, pointing to herself, and then to the others in turn. "Magiere . . . Leesil . . . Chap."

Osha blinked, glancing tentatively at Sgäile, then bowed his head briefly to Wynn.

"You placed a name upon a majay-hì?" Sgäile asked.

All the elves appeared unsettled by this. The woman hissed something Magiere didn't catch and turned away.

"Wynn, that's enough," Magiere warned.

"Should we not be introduced," Wynn asked, "if we are to travel together?"

Sgäile stood up in discomfort. Again, Osha glanced at him, clearly uncertain if he should speak. Then he pointed to the elven woman off among the trees with her back turned.

"Én'nish," he said.

"Én'nish . . . ," Wynn repeated sleepily, "the wild, open field."

Osha pointed to the elder man. "Urhkarasiférin."

"Shot or cast . . . truly?" Wynn tried to translate.

Osha scrunched one eye and looked up to Sgäile, who nodded.

"And Sgäile," Wynn added.

"Sgäilsheilleache," he corrected, the first words he'd spoken to any but Leesil since their earlier standoff.

"Willow . . . shade . . . ," Wynn murmured.

"Sgäile it is, then," muttered Leesil.

Magiere tried to retain the names. Hopefully, shortened ones wouldn't cause offense, not that she cared much if they did. To her relief, Osha finally lifted one trout off the fire, and all attention was diverted as he deftly slid it onto a large leaf.

He boned the fish, cut the fillets into pieces, and, using smaller leaves as plates, passed them around in no particular order. Sgäile worked on the next trout. He fanned a full fillet to cool it before placing it on a leaf for Chap. Urhkar picked up two servings and joined Én'nish off in the trees.

Magiere took small bites. She still wasn't hungry, even after three mouthfuls that smelled and tasted better than any fish she could remember. She continued to nibble rather than have Leesil or even Wynn make a fuss about her not eating. Once her own companions finished, she put a hand on Wynn's shoulder.

"Lie down and sleep."

The sage didn't argue. She scooted over to lie on the ground, but she stopped halfway.

"Oh, Sgäile, whoever keeps watch should take care. We encountered a *tâshgâlh* this morning. I have not seen it again, but you would know what they are like."

To Magiere's surprise, Sgäile spoke directly to Wynn with concern.

"A *tâshgâlh*? Where?"

"That little rodent?" Leesil asked. "We found it in a cave on the mountain. It didn't seem dangerous."

"But troublesome," Sgäile answered carefully, and gestured out into the dark. "The majay-hì should warn us, and Osha will stand first watch."

Magiere looked where he pointed. Here and there a shadow moved. She saw the shapes of the dogs among the far trees, some near enough that their eyes glimmered from the firelight.

Wynn lay down and pulled her blanket up, and Chap curled in next to her as always.

Both Sgäile and Osha stared with differing degrees of astonishment. Osha's mouth opened slightly as Leesil spread his cloak out on the ground and reached for Magiere. She lay down on her side.

Osha turned quickly and walked away. Sgäile followed without a word.

Magiere put her back against Leesil's chest. He pulled the blanket up and placed his palm on her temple, slowly stroking her head and hair.

"This isn't what I expected," he whispered.

What had he expected?

"We'll find Nein'a," she whispered back.

"I know. Go to sleep."

Magiere heard his breathing grow steady and deep. Once certain he'd drifted off, she reached over him for her falchion left leaning against the stump. She tucked it under the blanket next to herself with her hand on its hilt.

She lay awake for a long time, not tired enough to sleep, strange as that was. She listened but couldn't hear the elves above the forest's soft sounds.

Magiere finally closed her eyes and tried to drift off. . . .

She suddenly found herself walking the forest in darkness, alone, wondering how she had gotten so far from the camp.

Pieces of the night moved around her between the trees.

Here and there, half-seen shapes shadowed her. Their colorless and glittering eyes watched her, as if waiting for her to do something.

These were not majay-hì. They walked on two legs. And in her belly she felt their hunger. She smelled it, like blood on the damp breeze, and her own hunger rose up in answer.

The forest began to wither around her, until the stench of rot made her choke.

Magiere snapped her eyes open with every muscle ridged from the nightmare. It felt disturbingly familiar, as if she'd seen such a vision before. Lifting her head, she found the fire was now little more than glowing embers.

She didn't sleep for the rest of the night.

CHAPTER FIVE

By midmorning, Wynn's fear of becoming lost succumbed to awe as she walked the elven forest. Patchy lime-colored moss cushioned her footfalls as she followed the others. With all her ink and journals gone, it was heartbreaking to witness such diverse flora without a way to take notes.

Fresh food and a night's rest had revived her, and the pain in her shoulder had dwindled to an intermittent twinge, but her improved mood still wavered. This was a desperate search for Leesil's mother, and their guides were now the Anmaglâhk. These elven assassins were manifested dark shadows of the Leesil that Wynn had come to know in the Warlands.

Yet, she found them fascinating. Their ways were so different from the elves on her continent. She tried to mentally note everything about them for later records. Once she returned to her guild in Bela, she would write extensive work comparing the two elven cultures of the world as she knew them. And how stark the contrasts were or might yet be, for she had not met any elves here besides Sgäile's caste.

A temperate breeze rustled the foliage, and she pushed Chane's cloak back over her shoulders.

What would he think of this place? His interests lay in distant times back to the Forgotten History, and how societies evolved from unknown beginnings in the aftermath of the great war. He was always more interested in studying the past than the present.

Wynn pushed aside thoughts of Chane. He was part of her own past.

Sgäile led the way with his comrades following behind their guests. The pace was too slow for him, as he often paused after stepping too far ahead, but he made no complaint.

Wynn avoided looking back at Én'nish walking at the procession's rear. The woman was no less angry than in their first meeting. Silent and stoic Urhkar walked in front of his bitter comrade, and Osha came directly behind Wynn.

All four elves left their cowls and face wraps down. There was some significance in this, as secrecy seemed paramount to their ways. Perhaps they simply felt at ease in their homeland.

Leesil and Magiere walked ahead, behind Sgäile, and Chap trotted beside Wynn with his head turning at every new sight. His nose worked all the time, and Wynn often heard him sniffing as his muzzle bobbed in the air. She looked about at the lush flora, and more than once her boot toe caught on a root, stone, or depression when she was not paying attention to the trail.

Of all their escorts, Osha betrayed the most curiosity about the interlopers. He was so tall that when he stepped close, Wynn had to tilt her head back to see up to his chin. She felt awkward and rather too short. His hair was white-blond like Leesil's and hung loose to the center of his back. His somewhat horselike face was not nearly so handsome as Sgäile's, but it was pleasant. Although quiet, he was certainly the most polite of their guides.

They passed a large weeping willow with vivid orange fungus growing up its trunk's northern side. The color was so eye-catching that Wynn wandered absently toward the tree. Chap rumbled at her, following partway, but she ignored him in her rapt fascination.

"Osha, what is this?" she asked in Elvish, and pointed to the shelves of fungus. "The edges look like seashells."

Osha hesitated, looking to Sgäile as if awaiting instructions. He finally joined her.

"It is called woodridge," he answered in Elvish, and he put his hand against the fungus, closed his eyes for an instant, and then broke off a small piece to offer her. "It is safe to eat, though pungent until properly cooked."

His strange conjugations and declinations took time to comprehend. It reminded her of the oldest texts she had been permitted to browse at the elven branch of the guild on her own continent. It made some sense, for these elves had lived in isolation for centuries, while their counterparts of her world interacted with other races more freely.

Wynn put the orange lump near her lips and breathed in its scent. It smelled of wet earth. She snipped it with her teeth. A sweet sensation flowed over her tongue.

"Very good."

The taste thickened suddenly, bitter and pastelike. She swallowed, trying not to grimace, and smiled. Osha nodded in approval with perhaps a little surprise.

"Wynn, what are you doing?" Magiere called. "Did you just eat that?"

"Osha said it is safe."

Chap stood stiff and silent, watching the tall young elf, and then cast a glare Wynn's way.

She knew that look on his furry face. She did not care for his parental disapproval.

Wynn stuffed the hunk of woodridge in her pocket and hurried to catch up, as both Magiere and Leesil looked uncomfortable. She stepped back into the traveling line with the others.

Since Osha was the most amiable among his group, she continued questioning him in Elvish. His answers were short, but at least he answered—with occasional glances toward Sgäile, as if expecting admonishment. Sgäile remained silent, not once looking back.

Wynn kept her questions to the world around them, though she wanted to ask of the people here. Intuition told her not to do so. A few times Osha paused after an answer, about to say something in turn. Perhaps he had questions of his own. He seemed intensely puzzled or startled by the way she acted and spoke, but he never asked. They passed an oak so large that its trunk was far wider than Osha's height.

Wynn stared at it a bit too long. "How old is this one?"

"As old as the forest perhaps," Osha answered. "The trees are the bones and blood of its body."

At this, Sgäile looked back sternly. Osha fell silent, dropping his eyes as he stepped out ahead of Wynn.

She was uncertain whether to be disappointed or worried. Clearly Sgäile thought the conversation had gone on long enough. Hopefully she had not gotten Osha into trouble.

Leesil slowed, his irritation far plainer than Sgäile's.

"What is wrong?" she asked.

"How could anything be wrong?" he muttered. "I haven't understood a word all morning."

"Leesil . . . you brought me because I speak Elvish—and you do not."

He sighed, grudgingly. "I know, I know . . . but I didn't think it would be like this—not understanding anything that anybody said."

Wynn was not sure which would be worse—a Leesil completely inept with the language or one able to proficiently express his ire in Elvish. He remained silent a moment, then looked up thoughtfully at Osha in a way that made Wynn nervous.

"I'll ask him if he knows how far away my mother is."

Before Wynn could grab him, Leesil quick-stepped up beside Osha.

"A-hair-a too bith-a ka-naw, too brah?"

Osha's mouth gaped.

All four elves came to a sudden halt. Any tentative curiosity in Osha's long face turned to horror. He glared at Leesil, and a stiletto appeared in his hand.

Magiere dropped a hand to her falchion's hilt. Before she could do anything stupid, Wynn scurried in between Osha and Leesil. She turned on Leesil angrily but never got out a word before Én'nish thrust her heel into his tailbone.

Leesil sprawled forward as Én'nish drew her long stilettos. Wynn floundered out of Leesil's way, stumbling back into Osha, who caught her under the arms. She flinched at the sight of his blade appearing in front of her.

Leesil tried to roll, but the chest on his back hindered him. Even Urhkar was caught off guard as Én'nish rushed in. Leesil pulled his own stiletto as he spun around on his knees.

"Bârtva'na!" Sgäile barked at Én'nish and grabbed the back of Magiere's pack. "Stop this now! He does not know our tongue."

Én'nish slapped away Urhkar's attempted grasp and slashed at Leesil's face. He ducked and spun on one knee, swinging a stiletto on his pivot. Én'nish bent rearward at her midsection like a willow branch, and the blade tip cleared her stomach. She tried again to close on Leesil.

Chap rushed in and snatched her cloak from behind. He bolted around her side, twisting her in its cloth. In the same instant, Wynn lunged from Osha's support. Én'nish, intent with fury and shocked at a majay-hì hobbling her, did not see the sage coming.

Wynn swung, and her palm cracked loudly against Én'nish's cheek.

"This is your oath at its best?" she shouted in Elvish, and then gripped her throbbing hand. It was a challenge to Én'nish, and even to her comrades, for this violent breach of guardianship.

Én'nish turned upon the sage. When she raised one of her blades, Urhkar angrily grabbed her wrist. She held her place without resisting him.

Wynn shook with sudden fear as she turned and found Sgäile on guard beyond the tip of Magiere's falchion.

"Is this what the oath of guardianship is worth among your people?" Wynn asked.

"No!" he answered flatly, and his hard gaze turned on Én'nish. "You have our deep regret for this shame . . . it will not occur again."

Osha still looked offended, but his expression melted into shame as Wynn glared at him.

"Leesil does not know what he said," she explained. "It was a mistake, not an insult."

Osha nodded and sheathed his blade as Leesil did the same.

"Please . . . put up your weapon," Sgäile said. With an open hand he cautiously tilted Magiere's falchion aside and then closed on Én'nish. *"Ajhâjhva ag'us äicheva!"*

Én'nish spun away and stalked past all of them into the lead. Osha followed her with his eyes lowered as he passed Sgäile. Leesil stood baffled.

"What just happened?" Magiere asked.

Wynn ignored her, turning all her fear-fed anger on Leesil. "What did I tell you?"

"All I asked was how far to—"

"No, you did not!" Wynn clenched her fists. "You said his mother is 'nowhere,' and that he knew it . . . and you said it wrong, even at that. You called his mother an outcast!"

Magiere let out a deep sigh.

"Wait . . . ," Leesil started. "I didn't mean—"

"Shut your mouth!" Wynn shouted. "And never again speak Elvish to an elf!"

Leesil blinked. He looked down at Chap for help, but the dog just licked his nose with a huff.

"That would be best," Sgäile added quietly.

"Don't blame him," Magiere warned. "However he bungled his words, it had nothing to do with Én'nish."

"Yes . . . and no," Sgäile replied. "Én'nish is the daughter of Osha's mother's sister by bonding . . . similar to what you call marriage."

"So she takes it on herself to step in?" Magiere asked. "Because she's his cousin by marriage?"

"No, not precisely," Wynn added. "Relations are a serious matter among elves—and more complex than Sgäile can state in your language."

Magiere shifted toward Sgäile. "That had nothing to do with kin."

"She is . . . was . . . the *bóijt'äna* of Grôyt'ashia," Sgäile said pointedly. "The closest term you would know is a 'betrothed.' "

The name was unfamiliar to Wynn. She was about to ask when Sgäile turned sharply away to follow Osha.

Brief puzzlement passed quickly from Magiere's face and her gaze dropped as her dark eyes slowly closed. Wynn heard the creak of leather as Magiere squeezed the falchion's hilt.

"Who is Grôyt'ashia?" Wynn asked.

When no answer came, she looked down at Chap, but the dog's eyes remained on Leesil. Without acknowledgment, Chap quickly trotted after Sgäile.

Magiere wouldn't look up. She sheathed her falchion and strode after the others.

Leesil just stood there in cold silence.

"What did you do?" Wynn asked, not certain she wanted to know.

Grôyt . . . Grôyt'ashia.

Magiere had heard the name once before. It echoed in her head with Brot'an's voice as he had shouted it in Darmouth's crypt. She'd turned to see Brot'an's young accomplice and Leesil trying to kill each other. It ended with Leesil soaked in blood—again—as it spilled from Grôyt's split throat.

It hadn't been Leesil's fault. Not that death. But Magiere couldn't stop from wondering. How many women—or men—in Leesil's life path waited for someone who would never return?

It wasn't his fault. Not for what Darmouth had made Leesil do to survive . . . do for his parents' lives, and all because of what Nein'a made him. Magiere closed on Sgäile from behind.

"It was self-defense," she said quietly, so the others couldn't hear.

"I am aware of the events involved," he answered without stopping.

"You knew . . . and you let Én'nish come with you?"

"It was not my choice to make."

"No more dodging!" Magiere snapped, too loudly, and grabbed Sgäile's shoulder.

He spun about, jerking free before she could get a true grip. "You know nothing of an'Cróan ways," he warned, "with your simple-minded human . . ."

He stopped himself as his eyes wandered across her face and hair.

Magiere didn't understand the term he'd used, but she grew unsettled under his scrutiny.

She wondered if he noticed her appearance, maybe how it differed from other humans'. Or had Brot'an spoken to his kind of what he'd seen of her during their fight in the crypt? How much did Sgäile know?

"Then tell me a little," she said. "Make it simple for a . . . human, if you wish."

"You were offered guardianship because of Léshil," Sgäile said, once more composed and formally polite. "That will be honored at all cost. How the events in Venjètz are seen in the end will depend on what status Léshil truly has with our people . . . and perhaps our caste. It is not my place to speak. You will wait until he has spoken with Most Aged Father."

With visible restraint, Sgäile turned and stepped onward.

Magiere bit back another demand. Regardless of Sgäile's personal feelings, it seemed he would stand by his words and strange customs, obeying his superiors and doing what had been asked of him.

"And what are these an'Cróan?" she asked instead.

Sgäile slowed. "It is the proper name of our people, versus your human labels. Your short companion would say . . . Those of the Blood."

Magiere's stomach turned. Everything concerning Leesil came back to blood.

Chap walked behind Magiere as she argued with Sgäile. He reached for any memory surfacing in the man's thoughts.

Flashes of human faces surfaced in Sgäile's mind. He was well traveled, from what Chap caught. It was as if the elf searched for a comparison to Magiere's pale skin and red-stained black hair. Nothing came close, and

Sgäile remained perplexed. He did not know what Magiere was and saw her only as some oddly pale human.

There remained the issue of blood. Blood of heritage, of people, and blood spilled.

It was a tangle that even Chap found himself trapped within. Whether it unsnarled or cinched tight to strangle them all depended on how Leesil was viewed by his mother's people.

No matter how many memory fragments Chap gleaned from Sgäile, he could not clearly piece together all concerning this issue and the consequences of killing an anmaglâhk. But Chap felt certain that Sgäile would follow his people's ways with as much conformity and integrity as he could.

Én'nish was another matter.

Her thoughts were clouded with memories of Grôyt'ashia. They shared a like fire that had burned hot in their separate natures. She smelled of blinding anguish and hatred, even from a distance.

Another scent reached Chap as he trotted watchfully behind Magiere. Movement in the trees caught his eye—a flash of silver-gray.

All other thoughts vanished when he saw the majay-hì skirting the path. He watched for them—for one of them—as they wove among the trees, drifting in and out of sight.

The silver-white female appeared briefly and then vanished.

"It is all right, Chap," Wynn said. "Go run with them, if you like."

He had not even realized he had slowed to fall back beside her. He peered into the forest with rapt attention but remained at Wynn's side. A high-pitched chirp made his ears perk up.

It trailed into a song, like someone whistling too perfectly, and then faded. He had never heard any such bird in his infancy among the elves.

Wynn lifted her gaze, searching for what had made the sound.

"What kind of bird was that?" she asked, and turned toward Urhkar at the rear.

Urhkar stopped for a long pause, and Chap did so as well, as the man looked back the way they had come. When the elder elf turned around, his expression was astonished.

He did not answer Wynn's question. And when Chap reached for any memory surfacing in Urhkar's thoughts, he caught only a vanishing glimpse of full black eyes and wings of mottled white feathers.

* * *

Six days more, and Leesil still didn't know how far Sgäile intended them to travel. They encountered no other elves and few animals besides the majay-hì among the trees. He once had to pull Wynn back from going after a multi-hued dragonfly and a cloud of shimmering moths. There were a few common squirrels in the trees, and ones colored something like a mink.

And the infrequent song of some bird out of sight.

Wynn's warning about the *tâshgâlh* had unfortunately proven valid. They hadn't seen it, but small things were missing from their packs. Including a flint stone, the last tin of Wynn's tea leaves, and several coins, as they'd found their purse spilled on the ground one morning. Leesil took to sleeping with the chest of skulls near his head.

Clear streams were plentiful, and the Anmaglâhk produced two decent meals a day for them with little effort. One of them simply disappeared into the forest and returned shortly with necessities for breakfast or dinner. Fruits, nuts, and more ugly little mushrooms served as a light midday meal while they walked.

Every time Leesil thought of Wynn, he felt small and petty. She annoyed him, and he couldn't help it. She might be fluent in Elvish, as she often re-minded him, but what good was it? Sgäile barely acknowledged she existed, so the only elf Wynn spoke with at length was Osha, who didn't strike Leesil as particularly bright.

Each day was new torture as Leesil pictured his mother in some elven prison, though shame or anguish always mixed with resentment. Every time he asked Sgäile how many more leagues, the only answer he got was "More days . . . we will travel more days."

Leesil grew tired of it.

Magiere walked beside him, plainly uncomfortable and as distrusting as always. But more so now with the Anmaglâhk. She looked well enough, her black hair shimmering with lines of red in the sunlight, but he'd noticed how sparingly she ate, and at night she had difficulty sleeping. Each day she grew more tense, a nervous energy building in her.

He'd always viewed Magiere as someone who preferred the night—who felt out of place in the sun—but here, she'd changed somehow.

Leesil tried to remember the last time they'd been truly alone. Too long. Each night, guilt mixed with longing as he crawled beneath the blanket with her and pressed his face into the back of her neck. It was one moment when he forgot why he had come here and what he'd done to achieve it.

On this sixth day, Sgäile put his hand up, and everyone stopped.

"We near my home enclave, where we will spend the night with my family." His features tightened thoughtfully until he pointed to Magiere's falchion. "You are hu . . . outsiders, and bearing weapons might produce a dangerous reaction. I will carry them for you until we leave tomorrow."

"Not if I were already dead," Magiere growled at him.

Sgäile sighed, gesturing to Leesil's winged punching blades. "You have my word. We enter among my people, my clan. None have ever seen a human in this land. They will not take kindly to your presence. Less so, if you are armed."

"No," Magiere said flatly.

Én'nish backtracked to stand behind Sgäile. The corner of her left eye twitched.

"Savages!" she whispered to Sgäile, though she spoke in Belaskian for all to understand.

Leesil's eyes shifted quickly to Magiere, prepared for the inevitable flare of anger, but she was so quiet that it made him even more wary.

"Why did they send you?" he asked Sgäile. "Out of all of your kind, why you?"

Sgäile slowly swung his arm back until Én'nish retreated. "Because I am the only one you might trust . . . enough."

Leesil would never admit it to Magiere, but a part of him had begun to trust Sgäile—or at least the man's word.

"What if we keep our weapons out of sight?" he asked.

Magiere shook her head in disbelief. "You're not seriously considering what he asks?"

"They have their customs," Wynn warned. "And we are guests here."

Magiere turned to spit out a retort, but she didn't.

"No one else will touch your blades," Sgäile repeated. "And no one will touch you."

Én'nish uttered something under her breath. Leesil didn't care for her tone, let alone whatever she'd said. Sgäile held up his hand for silence and waited upon Leesil's reply.

For all Sgäile's calm manner, it was clear that unless Leesil and his companions agreed, they were not going one step farther. Leesil unlashed the sheaths of his winged blades from his thighs. Osha crept closer. Even silent Urhkar stepped around to a better vantage point. Én'nish kept her distance, though she watched intently.

Leesil handed his blades to Sgäile and followed with his two remaining stilettos, but he kept his wrist sheaths.

"What use?" Osha asked in clipped Belaskian, pointing to one winged blade.

Before Leesil answered, Sgäile uttered a short stream of Elvish with a lift of his chin toward Magiere as well. Osha's eyes widened.

"No," he said, then looked to Leesil. "It is . . . is truth?"

Sgäile fell back into Belaskian. "Pardon . . . I told Osha of your hunt for undead beneath your city."

Leesil remembered it clearly. He'd been half-crazed to take Ratboy's head. From Sgäile's perspective, it must have seemed bizarre indeed, considering why he'd tracked Leesil into those sewers beneath Bela. The Anmaglâhk hunted in silence . . . hunted the living.

The thought gave Leesil pause. In that, he saw himself—his past—once again halfway between worlds.

"May I?" Sgäile asked, gesturing to the strange weapon.

Leesil nodded, and Sgäile unsheathed one winged blade with a firm grip on its crosswise handle. He held it up, slowly rotating the weapon in plain sight.

Its front end was shaped like a flattened spade, tapering smoothly from its forward point along sharpened arcs that ended to either side of the crosswise grip. The grip was formed by an oval cut into the back of the spade's base. The handle was wrapped tightly in a leather strapping. The blade's outside edge continued in a long wing of a forearm's length, like a narrow and short saber that ended at one's elbow. Where the wing would have protruded a touch beyond Leesil's elbow, it was slightly short next to Sgäile's forearm.

In place of Sgäile's studious inspection, Osha looked suddenly confused.

"This dead-not . . . dead-not-dead," he said with effort. "We see . . . hear . . . not here, but hear stories small of other place . . . places. How you kill, if is dead?"

This talkative turn took Leesil by surprise, but it made sense. An unusual weapon captured attention from a caste of killers, even one as young as Osha.

Where some humans might think of undeads as only myth and superstition, Sgäile had stated the issue so plainly. The others accepted his word as fact.

Vampires might be rare enough in human lands, but Osha hinted at something else.

"What does he mean by 'not here'?" Leesil asked. "You have no tales or myths of undead?"

Sgäile seemed to consider his reply with great care. "No undead has been known to walk this land."

A direct though polite response, but Leesil caught the implication.

The undead—noble or otherwise—could not enter this forest.

"How kill not-dead . . . un . . . dead?" Osha repeated.

Leesil was lost in thought. "What?"

Magiere clasped her falchion's hilt, which made the young elf tense, but she didn't pull it. With her other hand she drew a slow, scything arc of fingertips across her throat.

Wynn sighed in disgust. "Oh, Magiere."

"Throat?" Osha asked.

Urhkar startled Leesil with a reply. "Not throat—neck. They take heads."

Osha's face paled through his dark complexion. Further off, Én'nish hissed under her breath. Sgäile spoke quickly to Osha. The young elf nodded.

"Forgive his reaction," Sgäile said. "Dismemberment of the departed is repulsive to us . . . but we understand the necessity."

"Have we finished with our debate over slaughter?" Wynn asked, disdain coloring her face.

Sgäile raised an eyebrow. He sheathed Leesil's blade and turned to Magiere, waiting.

Magiere didn't move a muscle.

"I don't like it any more than you," Leesil said. "But Wynn is right. It's their world . . . their way."

"All right!" she said. "Only because I can't see another way to find your mother. But don't get stupid on me. They're guards, not escorts, and they serve their own goals first."

Her blunt accusation jolted Leesil. In essence, she was right. The Anmaglâhk might look and even act somewhat like his mother, but he was a stranger here and didn't understand their customs, let alone the way they thought. But it changed nothing.

Magiere finally unbuckled her sword and held it out to Sgäile. He accepted it, and one feathery eyebrow rose a bit at its weight. He looked at her as if not quite believing she could wield it.

Wynn handed him the crossbow and quiver off Leesil's back. Sgäile gave these last items to Urhkar, who slung them over his shoulder. It made sense, as there were more arms than one person could carry efficiently, and Sgäile had promised to guard the blades.

Leesil took his rolled cloak off the pack that Wynn carried and handed it to Sgäile.

"Use this to bundle them . . . easier to carry and keep out of sight."

Sgäile nodded agreement. He was about to turn and lead on.

"Magiere!" Wynn said.

The little sage folded her arms and stared at Magiere's back. Stranger still, Chap gave Wynn a rumble, a displeased sneer, and a lick of his nose. She ignored him.

Leesil was lost. They'd handed over the crossbow, his blades and stilettos, Magiere's falchion . . .

For an instant Leesil considered saying nothing, but Wynn had already drawn too much attention.

"Give it up—now," he told Magiere.

How one woman could deliver so much spite from the corner of her eye still worried Leesil at times. It made him think of long-lost days in the Sea Lion Tavern, when she grew fed up with his antics.

Magiere reached behind her back and beneath her pack. She drew out the long-bladed dagger acquired before they'd headed into the Warlands.

Sgäile just opened the cloak bundle of weapons and waited. Leesil thought he caught a hint of humor in the man's eyes. Magiere tossed the dagger into the cloak.

"Come," Sgäile said, and gestured to his own companions. "The majay-hì may walk where he pleases, but you must stay inside our circle. Our people may become unsettled at the sight of you."

Én'nish remained in front, while Sgäile and Osha spread to the sides, with Urhkar at the rear behind Wynn.

They traveled only a short ways. Leesil caught odd changes in the trees when they passed through an area of dense undergrowth. Wild brush grew higher than his head. There were more oaks and cedars than other trees, with trunks wider than any he'd seen before.

Ivy ran up into their lowest branches, which were just within reach if he'd stretched upward with one hand. Their trunks bulged in odd ways that didn't seem natural, yet he saw no sign of disease. Foliage grew lush, thick and green overhead. In the spaces between trees, the underbrush gave way to open areas carpeted in lime-colored moss. Someone stepped out and turned away as if emerging like a spirit from the bloated trunk of a redwood.

As Leesil drew closer, he saw thickened ivy hanging from its branches. The vines shaped an entryway into the tree's wide opening between the ridges of its earthbound roots.

"Dwellings?" Wynn asked, but no one answered.

Osha fidgeted nervously. Sgäile was as tensely watchful as the first night he'd appeared in the forest. And both made Leesil worry.

They passed more dwelling trees with openings and flora-marked entryways. A tall elf peered through a bordering arch of primroses around the dark hollow in an oak. Leesil couldn't make out more than that he was male and would have to duck his head to come out. The large clay dome of an oven sat in an open lawn, smoke rising from its top opening. Several women and two men standing near it stopped, touched their companions, and turned one by one to stare.

Among them was the one Leesil first thought had walked straight out of a tree. He recognized her strange hair. She stood off from the others upon the moss lawn, and a break in the canopy captured her in a shaft of sunlight.

Soft creases in her skin, darker brown than Leesil's own, marked the corners of her large eyes and small mouth. She was slender and tall like his memory of Nein'a, but this woman's hair was like aspen bark, shot with gray that looked dark amid the white blond. Advanced age on an elf seemed strange.

Her narrow jaw ended in a pointed chin tilted down to a slender and lined throat as she fingered through whatever was in her basket. She hadn't yet spotted the new arrivals, but other elves began to gather.

They appeared at openings in the living dwellings or stepped through ivy curtains and around arches of vines and bramble plants shaped to divide and define the community's spaces. A teenage boy in nothing but breeches crouched overhead in an oak's limbs, his brown torso smooth and perfect.

Some faces looked calm and welcoming at first, until they spotted the outsiders walking between the Anmaglâhk. Others froze immediately, and fear was tinged with something more dangerous. All stared at Wynn and Magiere. Some even looked at Leesil uncertainly.

Unlike in the human lands, no one here would long mistake him for one of their own. He was short by comparison, his amber eyes smaller, and, though beardless, his wedged chin was too blunt and wide. And his clothing was nothing like theirs.

Chap pushed in to walk close to Wynn.

In a few more steps, their small group was surrounded by people at all sides of the community's center green. A lean man about Sgäile's age stepped out. Én'nish halted, but the man wasn't looking at her.

"Sgäilsheilleache!" he spit out.

Leesil couldn't catch the stream of Elvish that followed, but Osha stepped back, positioning himself closer to Wynn. Leesil didn't find this comforting as he studied the growing crowd of elves. Their dress differed noticeably from the Anmaglâhks'.

A few wore their hair bound in tails upon the crowns of their heads by polished wood rings. Their clothing was dyed mostly in shades of deep russet and yellow. They wore quilted and plain tunics and vests, and shirts of lighter fabric, some white, which shimmered where sunlight struck it. Tangled embroidered patterns marked collars and loose sleeves on a few. Though some women wore long skirts of rich dark tints, just as many had loose tan breeches and the soft calf-high boots favored by the men. Besides the one boy, no other children were visible. No one carried tools or anything Leesil counted as a weapon.

As conspicuous as he'd felt among humans, here it felt worse that he looked like an elf at all.

Stunned, frightened, or angry, several of the village elves were now spitting words at Sgäile. The air filled with their noise, until the clamor made it hard to hear Sgäile's replies.

"Wynn," Leesil whispered, "what are they saying?"

"They accuse Sgäile of breaking sacred law," she whispered back. "He assures them he acts for Most Aged Father, that we are under guardianship."

Osha put a finger to his lips and shook his head in warning. Wynn fell silent, and Leesil listened carefully, though he picked out few words.

When Sgäile mentioned Aoishenis-Ahâre, half those who argued with him fell silent, some in shock, but their initial anger returned quickly enough.

Leesil took a step forward, watching their faces. He hadn't expected Sgäile to be challenged this aggressively. Part of the reason he'd agreed to follow was so that Magiere and Wynn would have protection in this land. Now he questioned how far this guardianship custom could reach. Gradually, the voices lowered, and Sgäile appeared to convince the others to back away and let him through.

Leesil heard and felt something grate along the chest on his back.

The chest toppled away behind him as severed harness ropes fell down his front.

He whirled to find Én'nish behind him, a long stiletto in her hand as she grabbed for the chest's latch. So intent in watching and listening, Leesil hadn't noticed her slip around behind him.

Magiere saw the chest fall from Leesil's back. Én'nish dropped to a crouch, fighting with the latch.

"No!" Magiere shouted, and made a lunge for the chest.

Én'nish's hand shot out, flat-palming the inside of her knee.

Magiere crumpled before getting a grip on the chest, and Én'nish flipped the chest's lid before Leesil could pull it away.

The cloth bundle within tumbled across the ground, and the two skulls rolled into plain sight.

Someone gasped.

Exclamations followed that Magiere didn't understand. Pain flooded her leg and her heart quickened. Too many things happened at once. She watched helplessly as Leesil rushed for the skulls, to hide these last remains of his father and grandmother from prying eyes.

Én'nish kicked into the side of his abdomen. Leesil stumbled beyond reach, gasping for breath, and Én'nish began shouting in Elvish.

Wynn screamed out, "Nâ—no! Na-bithâ . . . it is not true!"

Osha pulled both blades, but he stood in confusion, as if uncertain who to attack or who to defend.

Magiere ignored the pain in her leg and scrambled up to rush Én'nish from behind.

A grip like a manacle encircled her wrist, and she was heaved backward. She swung hard at whoever had grabbed her and caught a glimpse of Urhkar's face as he ducked the blow.

He swept one leg against the back of her knees, dropping her instantly, and pinned her to the ground. Anger gave way to shock as she fought to get free. Urhkar bent her wrist hard, with her arm twisted around his grounded leg, and she was pinned facedown on the village green. He remained crouched over her.

"Stay," he said calmly.

"Get off!" she ordered.

He didn't even respond. Anxiety stronger than rage filled Magiere.

With one cheek against the moss, she tried to look for Leesil.

Chap darted in front of Én'nish, snarling and snapping. She backed away, and Wynn made a dive for the skulls.

"Én'nish told them you came to hunt elves!" she shouted to Leesil. "For trophies!"

Magiere's stomach clenched.

Leesil either didn't understand or didn't care as he grabbed Gavril's skull. Wynn beat him to his grandmother's and placed her hand on it. She burst into Elvish, voice full of fear as she shouted to Sgäile. The only word Magiere caught was "Eillean."

Leesil dropped to his knees, clutching at his grandmother's skull in Wynn's arms.

"Stop!" Wynn cried. "Be still, or they will kill you!"

Magiere bucked again, trying to pitch off Urhkar, but he was like a stone statue above her, unmovable.

Wynn's words didn't matter to Leesil—only the skull. He wrenched it from her, crouching with the remains of a father and grandmother wrapped in his arms.

Sgäile's eyes were wide, and Leesil thought he saw his own torments mirrored in those amber irises.

"Eillean?" Sgäile whispered, pointing to the elven skull.

Leesil quickly pulled it aside.

A woman in breeches and an old man in a robe stepped from the crowd, their expressions hard. Chap snarled and rushed out with wild howling barks, and they stumbled back in a startled retreat. The dog cut a wide circle around the green before all those gathered, rumbling with menace. Elven villagers were bewildered—a majay-hì turning on them to defend an outsider.

The village glen grew quiet but for uncertain whispers. The ring of on-lookers cast confused glances from Chap to Sgäile and then back to Leesil. His skin crawled with their fixed attention.

"You took her remains from the keep's crypt?" Sgäile asked.

It sounded strange in Leesil's ears—a fervent statement hinted within a question. Sgäile said something loudly in Elvish, and the words carried the same tone and inflection. Reactions from those around the clearing changed little. Some became wary and startled, while others glowered in disbelief.

"You brought her home to her people . . . yes?" Sgäile added.

The words barely registered. Leesil didn't care what they wanted. His dead were no one's business but his own.

"Answer him!" Wynn insisted. "He is trying to save your life . . . and ours!"

Én'nish growled something, and her voice rose to a near screech. Leesil twisted about.

Urgent anticipation twisted her sharp features, as if she'd finally cornered some animal long hunted. Fury rose in Leesil, but he remained still.

Tears began to run down Én'nish's eager face and drip from the wedge of her chin. Urhkar barked at her in Elvish. She snapped around at him, and twisted hope vanished from her face.

Urhkar had Magiere pinned, but his expression remained passively stoic. Magiere was barely able to lift her head from the ground, and her dark eyes locked on Leesil.

How long before he saw those irises blacken and her teeth elongate? He wanted it to happen, to see her tear into the elf.

Urhkar leaned down and spoke softly to Magiere. She ceased struggling, and he glanced beyond Leesil. The elder elf nodded sharply once to some-one, and then leaped backward, releasing Magiere. She scrambled about, fac-ing him as she rose, then backed slowly to Leesil.

"It's all right," Magiere whispered, crouching with one hand braced against the earth. "No one will take them . . . I won't let anyone take them from you."

The roar of rushing blood in Leesil's ears began to ease under her voice.

"Please," Sgäile pleaded, "tell them all . . . tell my people I speak the truth."

Leesil saw pain on the anmaglâhk's face—and fear.

"Érin'n," Sgäile whispered, " 'truth' . . . say it!"

Leesil didn't understand, but Sgäile's urgency crept into his muddled mind.

"Ay-rin-en . . . ," he said once, and then again with force.

Sgäile sagged in relief.

Magiere reached for the fallen cloth, but Sgäile picked it up first. He opened it, draping it over his open hands like an offering.

"You shame me," he said quietly, and dropped his gaze to Eillean's skull. "You should have told me. I would have . . . begged to carry her. Even for a little of the way."

Sgäile hesitated at the sight of Gavril's skull, but then he held out the draped cloth. Magiere snatched it away and laid it carefully over the skulls in Leesil's arms.

He quickly wrapped them, hiding them from all prying eyes and stood up only when Magiere coaxed him.

Some of the elves gathered around still looked angry, but others lowered their heads in rising sorrow. Leesil didn't understand why his grandmother's return and one Elvish word had caused such a change.

Magiere slid her arm around his shoulders, but she looked behind him toward Én'nish.

"You touch him again," she said coldly, "and I won't need a sword to take your head."

Leesil heard no answer from Én'nish, but she came into sight around his right side, circling wide as she approached Sgäile. Urhkar strode into Leesil's view and cut her off.

Without the slightest emotion on his face, the elder anmaglâhk raised an empty hand, palm outward. He waved it between them, as if brushing some annoyance from the air.

Anger drained from Én'nish's face. She flinched as if struck suddenly by someone she cared for. She backed away from Urhkar, turned, and fled from the clearing.

Wynn climbed to her feet as Osha tucked away his stilettos and hurried to assist her. When he offered his hand, the sage pulled away and wouldn't look at him.

"We should get out of sight immediately," Wynn said.

Chap still paced before the elves, glancing every so often at Leesil.

An elderly man in a quilted russet shirt pushed through the crowd. His unruly hair was darker than the others' and shot with steel gray. Chap turned on him with a snarl. The old man froze just inside the ring of onlookers but would not retreat.

"Sgäilsheilleache?" he called.

In an unguarded moment, relief flashed across Sgäile's narrow features. *"Foirreach-ahâre!"*

"Chap, stop! Leave him be," Wynn called; then she whispered to Magiere, "Sgäile called that man his grandfather."

Chap turned a hesitant circle back toward Wynn, his eyes still on the new arrival. The older man approached, eying the dog. He didn't appear angry or frightened, only a bit startled and worried.

Sgäile spoke rapidly in Elvish, and his grandfather's answers carried a tone of polite admonishment. Leesil wondered at what was said and looked to Wynn. The sage followed their words with fixed attention but offered no translation. Sgäile gestured Leesil forward and kept his voice low.

"Hurry. Come to my home. You will be safe there."

Leesil bit his tongue to keep from snapping. Sgäile had made this promise before, and his assurance had proved false. Leesil wondered how much worse things could get.

CHAPTER SIX

Wynn gasped softly as she stepped through a wool curtain and into an oak tree as wide as a small cottage.

Moss from outside flowed inward across the chamber's floor, though she could not fathom how it remained a vibrant yellow-green without sunlight. The oak's interior had grown into a large rounded room with naturally curving doorways and walls. The walls were bark-covered like its outside, but in some places bare wood showed through. Not as if the bark had been stripped, but rather that the oak had grown this way yet still lived and thrived. Tawny-grained wood shaped arches to other curtained spaces. Steps rose upward around the left wall and through an opening in the low ceiling, perhaps leading to further rooms above.

Ledges at the height of seating places were adorned with saffron-colored cushions covered in floral patterns of a lighter yellow. Through one archway Wynn saw a smaller chamber with stuffed mattresses laid out upon the moss carpet. Soft pillows and green wool blankets graced those resting places.

She ran fingertips lightly across the bark wall as Osha stepped in.

After what had happened in the village green, she no longer felt certain he could be trusted. He drew blades at the sight of the skulls, but not to protect those under guardianship.

Magiere swept aside the doorway curtain and looked about with little interest in the surroundings. Her study of the place was more a wary search for potential threats or perhaps other ways out. She finally stepped in, holding aside the curtain.

Leesil entered, still gripping the bundled skulls, and behind him came

Chap, who surveyed their surroundings much the same way as Magiere had. Sgäile carried the skulls' chest under one arm. Beneath the other he held the cloak-wrapped weapons. Last came Sgäile's soft-spoken grandfather, and yet there was room for all.

Osha stared at the bundle in Leesil's arms. He took a long breath, held it for a moment, and then exhaled.

"It is a blessing you speak our language," he said to Wynn. "When I saw those . . . and heard Én'nish . . ."

He did not look at her. Wynn assumed he was shamed by yet another violent breach of guardianship. And he should be.

Sgäile gently set the chest at the room's far side.

"I should not have been so quick in my thoughts," Osha added.

Wynn didn't answer. Sgäile laid the cloak-bundled weapons beside the chest and turned a hard gaze upon Osha.

"The day has been long," he said. "The remaining journey will be longer. You may take leave for food and rest."

A polite dismissal, but Sgäile's dissatisfaction was plain. Én'nish had been a growing threat, but Wynn had come to expect better from Osha.

Osha looked down at her, as if to say something more, but he quickly headed for the doorway. He gave a brief nod of respect to Sgäile's grandfather and left.

Magiere turned on Sgäile. "You gave us your word that we'd be safe, and it meant nothing."

"Please sit and rest," Sgäile's grandfather interceded. "Be at ease in my home, for none will trouble you here."

Beneath his thick elven accent, his Belaskian was perfect. Wynn stepped in, hoping to divert further conflict.

"You are not Anmaglâhk," she said to the elder elf. "How did you learn Belaskian?"

"He is a Shaper—specifically a healer," Sgäile explained. "And a clan elder. He has twice been on envoy, sailing to the human coastal countries. He also serves enclaves many leagues apart, including Crijheäiche, the housing place of the Anmaglâhk. I have taught him more of the language, at his request."

Sgäile stepped back and held his palm out. "This is my grandfather, Gleannéohkân'thva."

Wynn turned the long name in her head—Reposed within the Glen. Even she would have trouble saying it properly, and she hesitated to try. Enough offense had already been given on this journey by a slip of the tongue.

"Gleann?" she said hesitantly.

Dark flecks of brown within his amber irises gave them a strange allure. The thin, soft creases around his mouth made Wynn think of an old owl. Unlike Sgäile and his comrades, Gleann looked Wynn straight in the eyes, sternly.

A faint curl grew at the corners of his mouth. He placed one hand over his heart with a nod, but as he turned to Sgäile, one feathery eyebrow rose.

"What have you done?"

Sgäile fidgeted like a boy caught in mischief. "I must report on our progress. Would you ask Leanâlhâm to bring food for our guests?"

As the words left his lips, the doorway's curtain flipped wildly aside. A pretty elven girl nearly fell into the room in a rush, panting out Elvish.

"Grandfather? . . . Uncle! What has happened? I heard you brought—"

She sucked in a breath so quickly that it choked her and backed against the wall beside the door. She stared fearfully at Magiere.

Wynn guessed the girl at about sixteen by human or elven standards, for the early years of either's development were much the same. Leanâlhâm's hair was almost dark enough for light brown rather than the varied blonds of her people. Her eyes, with their large irises . . .

Wynn blinked and looked more carefully.

Leanâlhâm's irises were not amber—they were topaz, with a touch of green.

Two thin braids down the sides of her triangular face held back the rest of her hair. On second look, her narrow ears were ever so blunted at the tips, though not as much as Leesil's.

Wynn's gaze slipped once to Leesil, the only half-blood she had ever seen or heard of. But she knew this girl was not a full elf.

Sgäile took Leanâlhâm in his arms, pulling her into his chest as he whispered in her ear. Wynn would never have imagined such affection from the reserved leader of their escort.

"It is all right, Leanâlhâm," Gleann said, keeping to Belaskian, which suggested the girl spoke it as well. "Your cousin brought unexpected guests for dinner."

Wynn took a cautious step toward the girl. "I am Wynn . . . and pleased to meet you."

Only one of Leanâlhâm's strange eyes peered around Sgäile's shoulder. It shifted quickly from Wynn to Magiere, paused briefly upon Chap, and then held on Leesil. He returned her gaze, pivoting to face her.

"Leesil," he said, and then nodded toward Magiere, saying her name.

Leanâlhâm remained apprehensive, though she pulled back from Sgäile enough to study all the strange visitors. Sgäile released her and headed for the doorway.

"I will return. Please see to their needs." He paused and dropped back into Elvish. "Make a bath for them and find spare clothing while theirs are washed. The smell grows worse each day."

Smell? Wynn's jaw dropped. At least neither Magiere nor Leesil understood. None of them had bathed or washed their clothes in weeks. Sgäile left, and an uncomfortable silence followed.

"Food first," Gleann said in Belaskian. "Then baths. Leanâlhâm, go to the communal oven and see what is left. Try to bring meat or fish for the majay-hì. I will find our guests some clean attire."

Chap barked once at the mention of food.

"What's this about baths?" Leesil asked.

Sgäile restrained himself from running. Once out of the village and into the forest, he broke into a jog. He fought to quiet his thoughts, to regain stillness and clarity, but his mind churned against his will.

Finding a young pine, he dropped to his knees. He waited for his breathing to ease and took an elongated oval of pale word-wood from inside his cloak. He reached for the pine's trunk, the word-wood couched in his palm, but then paused and lowered his hand.

He needed a moment more.

Regret was not an emotion he tolerated. There was no room for it in the life of service he had sworn to his people. But no one had ever been asked to escort humans through their land.

Of those few who ever made it through the mountains, skirted the northern peninsula by sea, or came up the eastern coast from the south, even fewer lived to tell of it to their own kind. But Sgäile needed to know how his people would react before he brought Léshil to Crijheäiche—to Aoishenis-Ahâre, Most Aged Father.

Word would travel swiftly, and he had thought this best rather than to appear suddenly in Crijheäiche with two humans and a half-blood. And selfishly, he had wanted Leanâlhâm to see Léshil, to know she was not the only one of mixed heritage in this world. Just one moment in which she did not feel alone among her own kind.

He thought his own clan would respect his mission and stand behind him, even in this unprecedented task. He was Anmaglâhk. His caste was unquestioned. And his own clan honored by his service.

Pride . . . Like some youthful supplicant first accepted to the caste, he had let pride—and sentiment—cloud his judgment. He should have bypassed his home and never brought Léshil among his own clan.

He should not have jeopardized his mission for personal reasons. Yet every time he dwelled on Léshil, everything became unclear, not unlike that moment in the human city of Bela, when he held an unaware Léshil in the sight of his bow. How could any one person be so stained in contradictions as Léshil?

Murderer, son of a traitor, with no connection to his heritage . . . who willingly slept beside a human woman.

Léshil, grandson of Eillean, who took great risk in returning her last remains to her people.

And just how had he breached the Broken Range and walked into this land?

Sgäile had refrained from asking, no matter how the question nagged him. It would be viewed as interrogation. Gaining trust from Léshil was far more important—and Léshil had shown trust in relinquishing his weapons.

The last thing Sgäile had wanted was to force the issue in a fight between Léshil and his own Anmaglâhk. It would have ended in bloodshed, perhaps on both sides, and this was not what Most Aged Father requested. So he allowed Léshil time to travel with him and hopefully trust in his word. He had waited until the last possible moment to ask for those weapons.

No blood was spilled, though entering among his people had been far more dangerous than Sgäile had imagined. He had thought only the humans would rouse anger and fear among his people.

Én'nish had nearly cost him everything. And when Urhkarasiférin dismissed her from his tutelage, she fled in shame.

The revelation of Eillean's remains—or rather the way it had occurred—nearly ruined all Sgäile's silent efforts. What little trust he had gained from Léshil had been shaken.

Then there was the majay-hì. The one the humans forced a name upon—perhaps the one who had found a way through the mountains.

One of the old ones . . . the first ones . . . imbued by the Fay.

Sgäile knew the first time he looked upon the dog from a distant rooftop in Bela. It was why he had stayed his arrow from killing Léshil.

Awareness of the Spirit side of existence was not shared by many of his people. Those born with it, as he had been, most often became Shapers or Makers. Humans would call them "thaumaturges," a grotesque term for humans who worked magics of the physical side of existence. In Sgäile's youth, his grandfather encouraged him to follow the way of Shapers, whose careful ministrations guided trees and other living things into domiciles, or encouraged the healing of the sick and injured. He had not the patience for it, and no interest in the Maker's arts of imbuing and fashioning inert materials, such as stone and metal and harvested wood. His heart turned toward a greater calling.

Anmaglâhk.

His own Spirit awareness did not fade as it did in many who went untrained. It stayed with him through the years. He could feel the power of Spirit within the trees and flowers of the forest, if he stopped long enough to focus. What he sensed within the creature that ran beside the half-blood was so strong he knew it without effort.

No majay-hì had ever been seen outside elven lands. And none born in generations had left Sgäile so stricken upon first sight.

And such a one had joined Léshil.

Sgäile could not fathom why, but it was not to be ignored. It had meaning, even if he could not immediately understand.

He grew calm, more focused.

Among his people there were twenty-seven clans. People were born into one, and sometimes bonded—married—into another. Then there was the Anmaglâhk. Not a clan, but a caste of protectors among the people, they followed a founder from the ancient days. No one was born an anmaglâhk, and not all who sought admittance were accepted.

Sgäile had never doubted where he belonged. Never doubted he would walk in a life of service.

His breaths deepened, grew even. He lifted the word-wood to place it against the pine's bark and closed his eyes.

"Father?" he whispered, and then waited.

Most Aged Father's voice entered his thoughts. *Sgäilsheilleache.*

"I am here, Father, at the prime enclave of my clan. We are on our way to Crijheäiche."

And Léshil comes willingly?

"Yes . . ." He did not wish Most Aged Father to know that he was troubled. "And two human companions. He would not come without them."

They are of no concern.

"Our welcome here . . . was worse than I anticipated. The presence of the humans . . . or even human blood did not sit well. And another matter that worsened the—"

That is of no consequence. Bring Léshil to me. But perhaps keep clear of our people when possible. Yes?

"Yes, Father."

Sgäile hesitated, wondering if he should say more. . . .

The short human female understood all their words. The white-skinned one had strange black hair that simmered like fire-coals in the sun. Léshil carried the remains of the great Eillean. And they all traveled with a majay-hì like no other—except in the oldest of tales, remembered only in fables for children.

"Soon, Father," he said.

He hesitated once more. He would not call it doubt, as there was no place for such in anything that he did.

"In silence and in shadows," he added respectfully, and lifted the word-wood from the pine, stood up, and turned back toward the village.

Chap's restlessness grew with the dusk. Time spent with Gleann and Leanâl-hâm over dinner had gone quickly, and he found them pleasant. Perhaps trustworthy enough that his charges might sleep safely for the night. Leanâl-hâm brought him a rich broth with portioned chunks of roasted rabbit, and he licked the bowl clean.

Gleann's voice carried from beyond a curtained doorway at the rear of the main room.

"No, it is a natural hot spring guided through earth channels by our

Makers. It can be closed off, like this. When finished, lift the center stone in the bottom. The water will drain slowly away and nourish our oak."

"Makers?" Magiere asked, with her usual bite of suspicion.

A moment followed before Gleann answered. "Let us leave that until you are clean and comfortable."

Chap worried Magiere might aggravate their unusually friendly host. He trotted over and poked his head through the shimmering wool curtain.

He had seen bathing rooms before. Not all domicile trees had such. The enclave where he was born had warm springs nearby in the forest. Raspberry and ivy vines were nurtured into dividers, providing a half dozen private spaces there.

In this small room was something akin to a tub hollowed out of the moss and earth floor. It was lined in polished black stones tightly fitted together. Sunk into the mossy floor next to the tub was a helmet-sized metal basin. Its lip met with the tub's edge via a shallow trough the width of a paw.

Wynn took hold of a wide metal peg standing upright in the basin's center. When she pulled it, steaming water welled in the basin. As it reached the lip, it spilled through the trough into the tub.

"A miracle," she said smiling.

"It may be too hot," Gleann warned. "Mix in the cooler rainwater we keep in those vessels."

At the far wall sat several cask-sized containers. But these were solid wood, with smooth grain and round edges, not slats held together with iron bands. Each appeared molded from one piece of wood.

Gleann gestured to a pile of russet and yellow clothing on a ledge. "Dress when you are finished, and I will show you where to rest for the night."

He headed for the doorway, glancing at Chap as he passed through the curtain.

Magiere inspected the clothing with uncertainty, but Wynn pulled off her cloak.

"Magiere . . . what did Urhkar say before he released you?"

"It was in Droevinkan," she answered. "He said stop resisting . . . that I had to help Sgäile with Leesil."

"Urhkar speaks Droevinkan?"

"Too well," Magiere added, "for what's happening in my homeland."

Wynn didn't reply, but Chap understood where her thoughts wandered.

In the Warlands, two anmaglâhk—Brot'ân'duivé and the deceased Grôyt'ashia—had come to assassinate Darmouth in a time of unrest. Before this, in Soladran, he and Wynn had heard word that civil war erupted in Droevinka. In turn, Magiere feared for the life of her aunt Bieja, who still lived there. And so Magiere and Wynn wondered about an elf who spoke Droevinkan fluently—as did Chap.

But it was impossible that Urhkar had gone there and returned before Chap and his charges found their way here. Still, there were other anmaglâhk to consider.

Wynn stopped short of popping the first button of her old short-robe and frowned at Chap.

"Get out," she said.

Chap backed out with a snort. She had little left to hide after this long journey together.

In the outer room, Gleann collected polished wood bowls and platters from the felt mat where they had all gathered to eat. Leesil sat against the wall next to the chest. The bundled skulls were gone, so he had likely returned them to the vessel. He had remained silent during supper, shifting uncomfortably under Leanâlhâm's furtive glances. The girl was nowhere about, though Chap wondered at the existence of another mixed-blood besides Leesil.

The outer door's curtain lifted, and Sgäile entered. He paused, looking at Chap.

Chap twitched his jowl, though he tried to remain the courteous guest in this home. Sgäile dropped to one knee, giving Chap a start.

The man's eyes held quiet sadness.

Chap had tried in the passing days to catch any memory surfacing within Sgäile, but he had gleaned little. This one did not dwell often on even the very recent past, but an image flashed briefly before Chap's awareness. As if Chap himself reached out with a "hand" to the trunk of a young pine tree. He heard the word "Father."

Chap tried to grasp Sgäile's passing memory for more of the conversation, but it faded.

"Your companions should stay inside," Sgäile said to him, and it was easier to understand than the dialect that Wynn spoke. "You are free to go where you wish, as all majay-hì do."

Sgäile stood up and pulled back the doorway's wool curtain. Chap looked uncertainly to Leesil.

"They will be safe here," Sgäile said.

A part of Chap wanted to go, to lope through the forest of his youth and all it offered to soothe his senses.

"Don't be long," Leesil said.

Chap trusted Sgäile's word, but not his purpose. He crept past the an-maglâhk with a low rumble, and loped outside among the elven dwellings.

Most of the people had retired and only a thin line of smoke drifted up from the communal oven. A howl drifted in from a distance. Chap gazed out into the forest beyond the domicile trees.

He hungered for soft earth beneath his paws and wild grass whipping his legs as he ran.

All of Leesil's grief, Magiere's anger and doubt, and even little Wynn's fears were too much at times. Uncertainty wore upon him, for he no longer saw what the future might bring for any of them. If only he could put down his burdens and forget for a little while, but he could not afford one instant of thoughtlessness. He was alone.

Where were his kin? Why so silent? Why not chide him again, if he acted now in spite of their disapproval?

Memory of existence among the Fay had faded over the years. Perhaps it had never been complete at all. The flesh he wore could not house the wide awareness he had shared with them. But flesh had its advantages, or so he believed.

Chap's instinct cried out that Most Aged Father was poisonous, and Leesil should not be allowed anywhere near him. And yet . . . how else could they find and free Nein'a?

Leesil would not turn from this purpose. And if truth be told, neither could Chap.

He stepped between the house trees, hearing voices within, and cleared the last one to stand upon the fringe of the wild. The eerie cry came again, closer this time. A shimmer darted through the trees. And then another.

Two majay-hì burst from the brush and stopped at the sight of him. Both were dark steel gray with crystalline eyes, so alike in look they were nearly twins. One whined and then both darted back into the underbrush.

Chap took a few steps.

They spoke in memories. He had caught such the first day the pack circled in at the silver deer's call.

Was their way of communing . . . communicating . . . where his own memory play came from? Was this, mingled with his born-Fay essence, what gave him such ability? Could they give him one memory not so dark and heavy as his own?

A piece of night moved beneath a shaggy old cedar, and a pair of eyes glittered at him.

The grizzled pack elder took shape as he stepped out. Other majay-hì circled among the trees, and with them came a flash of white. She turned around a bramble and stopped, one forepaw poised above the ground as she looked at Chap.

Wynn had called the female's color that of a lily. The light touch of yellow in the female's eyes reminded Chap of the pistils of that flower.

She came close and sniffed his nose, and her own scent was laced with rich earth and damp leaves. Chap felt her nose trace up along his shoulder, his neck, below his ear. Then her head pressed in against the side of his.

A silver female shining in moonlight flashed in his mind.

A mother . . . the white female showed him a memory of her mother.

Chap recalled running with his siblings on the moss of an elven clearing.

Another memory not his own flashed. Cubs wrestled over who could stay atop an old downed tree, half-covered in lichen that flaked under their tumbling little bodies.

She had heard his memory, and answered in kind.

To speak like this without effort, to share memory instead of only seeing those of others . . . . It was as if he found his voice for the first time and heard those of others after a lifetime in silence.

Chap had never known this as a pup. Perhaps he had not stayed long enough to learn it before Eillean took him away to a young Leesil. Maybe it was a skill, like human speech, that came with maturity. His thoughts rushed to memories of Nein'a and her half-elven son trapped within the city of Venjètz.

The white female pulled back. She knew nothing of human cities and ways, and the image must have been unsettling. He whined and licked her face.

She did not appear disturbed. She yipped at him, wheeled about, and bolted partway into the forest. She stopped, looking back.

Chap released all but the earth beneath his paws and the rich scent of her fur and followed.

The dreamer rolled in slumber. Within his dream, wind rushed over his body and ripped at his dark cloak. He flew high over rocky cliffs painted in snow and ice.

He had never traveled like this before in his slumber.

In a deep canyon valley between mountain ridges like teeth rested a six-towered castle. Each of the tall towers was topped with a conical spire fringed with a curtain of ice suspended from its roof's lower edge. He wanted to pass over its outer wall and reach the courtyard, but did not. Instead, he lighted upon the crusted snow outside and sank deep as it broke beneath his feet.

Twin gates of ornate iron curls joined together at their high tops in an arched point. Mottled with rust, the gates were still sound in their place. Far beyond them, the castle's matching iron doors waited atop a wide cascade of stone steps.

Something moved upon those steps.

At first she seemed dressed in form-fitting white, with hair as cleanly black. As she took a first step down the stairs, it was clear she was naked. A shadow appeared to flutter above her right shoulder. It coalesced into a raven, which rustled its wings as it settled next to her head.

Her face was so pale it was almost translucent around strangely shaped eyes that . . .

The image vanished.

The dreamer stood in a stone hall with shelves all around filled with scrolls, books, and bound sheaves. Upon a table of gray-aged wood lay a black feather quill next to a squat bottle half-filled with ink.

At the hall's far end, another set of heavy doors were sealed shut with a solid iron beam too massive to lift.

The dreamer lost his aching hunger. His body desired nothing.

It is here . . . , his patron whispered all around him, though he saw no massive coils of black scales, . . . *the orb* . . . *the sister of the dead will lead you.*

He was wrenched from sleep and back into the cold world of the awakened.

"No!"

Welstiel's eyes opened fully to find Chane crouched within the tent, staring, his narrow face intense.

The sister of the dead will lead you.

A bitter promise. Welstiel had heard it one too many times.

"What's wrong?" Chane asked. "Why are you shouting?"

Welstiel sat up without answering.

They had ridden night after night, and their mounts grew thin and slow from dwindling grain. He feared that soon they would be on foot and wished to get every last step from the horses before the beasts collapsed and died.

"Pack up," he said.

Lingering bitterness faded. His patron showed him much more than ever before, but again in small pieces that did not quite fit together. He had seen an inhabitant of the fortress—perhaps one of the ancients? And he had felt the calm from the close presence of what he sought.

Welstiel's hunger to feed had died in that place within his dream, and now his hunger for what he sought grew in its place. So why did he feel so bitter upon waking?

The sister of the dead will lead you.

Magiere was the crux. Whatever his patron showed him, it was never quite enough to be certain of his destination—and always with the reminder that Magiere was necessary. Yet she was far off on another deviation with Leesil. Welstiel would find a time and place to bring her back under his control.

He smoothed his dark hair back. He would have to trust in his patron but also in himself, and practice a mix of effort and reserve. He stepped out as Chane began pulling down the tent.

"Why were you shouting?" Chane asked again. "You have never shouted quite like that before."

Welstiel's suspicion rose. "What do you mean?"

"You talk in your dormancy."

Welstiel remained passive, hiding anxiety. How long had this gone on, and why did Chane choose this moment to reveal such?

"What do you hear while I am dormant?"

"Nothing comprehensible, but never such an outcry." Chane became hesitant and changed the subject. "I wish to continue my lessons in Numanese as we ride."

Chane finished saddling his bony horse and swung up.

Welstiel followed suit. "Where did we leave off? I believe it was the common irregular verbs in past tense."

"Yes."

Lessons continued as they rode, but Welstiel's thoughts drifted often to the icebound castle, to the new scroll-filled hall, and to the calm stillness he had felt as he looked upon the iron-barred doors.

He started from his wandering thoughts, as he thought he heard a whisper on the cold wind.

The sister of the dead will lead you.

CHAPTER SEVEN

Hot baths were almost a vague memory, until Magiere slipped into one beside Wynn, listening to the sage's embarrassing groans of pleasure as they washed. Once finished, Magiere pulled on the elven clothing made of felt and raw-spun cotton. Her skin smelled of honey and fennel from the soap. Leesil had his turn, complete with grumbling about soapy water that hadn't drained completely for his own fresh bath.

Magiere spent the rest of the evening sitting cross-legged in the outer room with her hosts. Leesil sat on her left with young Leanâlhâm on his far side. The girl studied Leesil with brief glances, thinking she went unnoticed, peering at his ears, eyes, and the shape of his face—until suddenly aware of Magiere watching her. Magiere didn't really mind the girl's interest in Leesil, or shouldn't have.

Leanâlhâm was overwhelmed that someone else in this world shared her differences from her own people. Magiere understood being different, constantly reminded of it when anyone looked closely at her.

Still, Leanâlhâm kept staring at Leesil.

How had this mixed-blood girl survived in a land where Leesil wasn't even welcome? And how could she possibly be related to Sgäile?

Magiere turned her attention elsewhere, seeking any distraction.

"Tell us about these Shapers," she heard Wynn say to Gleann.

"Some of our people are born with a heightened awareness," Gleann began, and his gaze slipped once to Sgäile. "They sense what you call the Spirit element of things. Given time and training, they can become Makers or Shapers . . . and a few healers."

It seemed Makers worked lifeless materials. When Wynn called them thaumaturges, Gleann made an effort not to grimace. They called Spirit into inert substance where they sensed accepting emptiness, making wood, stone, and metal pliable for fashioning by will, hand, and tool. Not in pieces but as a whole, like the rainwater barrels in the washroom.

Shapers took a separate path, plying living things that still held their natural Spirit at its fullest. They guided, nurtured, and altered living growth, like the trees and other plants shaped over years into useful things. Some learned to make a tree or plant grow part of itself into a separate piece that still lived. Patience seemed an absolute for a Shaper. And among them were the few like Gleann, who turned to the care of the sick and injured. Flesh as well as living wood could be guided by those with enough skill and training, and healers learned herb lore, medicines, and more common skills as well.

Magiere followed most of this, though some of Wynn's questions left her baffled. Gleann often answered the sage in Elvish, and then returned to Belaskian with a less lengthy reply.

Gleann spoke Belaskian well, despite his strong accent, and he'd taught Leanâlhâm in turn. Strangest of all was that Leanâlhâm was a quarter human. His strong love of the girl was surprising, as their people despised and feared anything foreign.

"You called Sgäile your uncle," Wynn said to Leanâlhâm. "But your grandfather referred to him as your cousin?"

Leanâlhâm grew shy, mustering a response, but Gleann answered in her place.

"Her grandmother was my sister by bonding, having married my elder brother. I believe, by your culture, this makes her Sgäilsheilleache's . . . second cousin? But he is a generation older than her, so . . ." He shook his head in resignation. "Our familial titles and relations do not translate well into your language."

"But would not her maternal grandmother be human?" Wynn asked bluntly. "I do not understand how her mother was half-human. And what of her mother—and her father?"

Gleann's expression grew tight and closed. "It is a family matter we do not discuss often."

Magiere glanced at Leanâlhâm and suspicions began to form. A marriage didn't mean both parents were involved in the making of a child. Nor that the mother was a willing participant. Magiere's own mother had been given no choice in her conception.

"Tell us of crossing the Broken Range," Gleann asked quickly.

"It took nearly a whole moon," Wynn began, "before we found a way . . ."

Sgäile lifted his eyes from pouring herb tea and fixed on the sage. All Magiere's senses sharpened in warning.

"In a blizzard, we were caught in a snow-slide . . . ," Wynn continued.

Leesil shifted uncomfortably, bumping shoulders with Magiere. He too spotted Sgäile's rapt interest, and yet Wynn kept babbling.

". . . we lost nearly everything, and then Chap—"

"That's enough for now," Leesil cut in, a blink before Magiere did so herself. "It's getting late."

Sgäile's narrowing eyes shifted to Leesil. It was only a brief instant, but enough for Magiere to catch his too-eager interest.

How they'd found the Elven Territories was a story best kept to themselves. To Magiere's knowledge, no one before had ever returned from such a journey. Should they have a chance to use a way out of this land, she didn't want the Anmaglâhk to know it.

"Maybe some tea first?" she suggested. "To cut the weight of fatigue."

Gleann gazed among his guests with concern before returning to Wynn. "At least I can assist with your scholarly losses."

He rose and climbed the stairs to the upper level, disappearing from sight. Sgäile held out a baked-clay cup of herb tea to Magiere. She shook her head, and he passed it on to Leesil.

She didn't care for this herbal stuff, too different from the true tea that Wynn had lost to a skulking *tâshgâlh*. And she trembled inside, as though she'd already had too much real tea.

Gleann returned with a drawstring bag of olive-colored suede. He settled on the felt rug and opened it as Wynn curiously leaned his way.

Out came a roll of off-white single sheets with mottled grain from whatever plant fibers were used to make them. Next were pearl-white ceramic vials, which Gleann explained were filled with black, red, and green ink. Last came a strange form of quill.

Its dark wood shaft was long and narrow, but the bottom widened bulbously above the head. The quill tip was made of a metal Magiere recognized immediately. It had the same brilliant sheen of Leesil's old stilettos and those of the Anmaglâhk.

"No," Wynn protested, studying the gifts with painful eagerness. "This is too much."

"Take them," Gleann insisted with a chuckle. "Beneath the quill's head is a pocket of sponge-weed fibers. It will draw ink deeply, and needs to be replenished less often."

Wynn was still politely reluctant, but eyed the quill's bright metal head. "Such a stylus . . . I have nothing to trade for something so dear."

Gleann rolled his large elven eyes. "How else will you record your travels and what you learn?"

"Grandfather!" Sgäile's expression darkened in alarm. "I do not think that wise. Some might not want—"

"By 'some' you mean your Most Aged Father." Gleann snorted, but then paused before turning back to Wynn. "Be discreet and save these for when you have privacy."

Sgäile spoke low to Gleann, but the old man flicked the words away with his hand, and patted Sgäile's shoulder like a patronizing grandfather. Sgäile swallowed any further argument as Gleann slid the pile of gifts in front of Wynn.

"Thank you . . . ," Wynn said, "so much."

Any spell of the evening's lingering ease broke as Sgäile stood up abruptly.

"Now to rest," Gleann said. "Thank you for a most pleasant chat."

The outer doorway's curtain rumpled and its hem dragged across Chap's back as he stalked in. Grass seed and strands stuck out in his fur, and his paws were filthy. He glanced about, movements sharp and manic in a way that magnified Magiere's own nagging nervous energy. And still she didn't know why she felt this way.

"Look at yourself!" Wynn said, and wrinkled her small nose at the dog. "What have you been doing? You will not crawl onto my bed in such a state."

Chap's eyes cleared as he fixed upon her. He barked twice for "no" and, startled by his own voice, whined and repeated himself more softly. He circled around to curl up beside the bundled weapons and the chest. Magiere wondered what he'd been up to.

Gleann showed them to the adjacent room of floor mats. As he said good night, Leanâlhâm nodded to them, but her eyes were on Leesil. She turned quickly away and hurried up the stairs.

As Leesil pulled the room's curtain closed, Magiere saw Sgäile sit down against the wall near the front door. Leesil remained poised, as if about to leave the sleeping quarters. Magiere sighed, understanding.

"The chest is safe," she said.

Wynn sat on one of the three beds. "Sgäile would not let anyone touch them, I think."

Leesil let go of the curtain and settled on the bed nearest the doorway. Magiere knelt on the one in the center.

The soft mattress smelled of wild grass, and the pillow's strange fabric felt like silk. She dreaded the rest of the night, fearful that sleep wouldn't find her or that worse might come if it did. Her only relief was in being away from so many strange faces, though Leanâlhâm surfaced in her thoughts.

"How does she bear it?" Magiere said. "Living among people who will always see her as different?"

Wynn, halfway into her bed, pulled up a blanket. "Who . . . oh, Leanâlhâm? Perhaps . . ." She shook her head sadly and lay down. "I do not know. But her name means 'Child of Misfortune.' "

Magiere's ire rose, smothering her edgy state. She had her own meaning for such a label. Magelia, her mother, had been forced to give birth, and had died shortly after. What could be more unfortunate than that in bearing children?

And though Leanâlhâm had her grandfather and, oddly enough, Sgäile, the girl was branded with a name that marked her for life. Like Leesil's own mother, how much cruelty could these people heap upon their children?

Magiere lay beneath her blanket a long while. She heard Wynn's breathing slow and deepen. She watched Leesil until certain he'd drifted into fitful sleep, then closed her own eyes, trying to rest. The night became endless under the persistent quiver in her body.

She found herself standing in the dark amid the forest; then she saw a shadow shift among the trees, coming closer.

It stepped so softly that footfalls came and went beneath the rustle of branches and underbrush in the light breeze. When she looked about, she saw no other dark shapes that had shadowed her through the night so many times before.

Magiere heard and felt something skitter across her foot.

Leaning against her boot was a freshly fallen oak leaf, still green and satin. She stooped and reached for it. At the touch of her finger, a brown spot appeared on it.

The dry color spread through the leaf's veins as its tissue faded and dried until fully wilted. Decay set in.

She jerked her hand away, rising up. The leaf rotted, then crumbled and came apart. Its fragments scattered across the ground in the night breeze.

A deeply shadowed figure stood quiet and still in the dark between two oaks. Something glinted in its hand . . . a stiletto. Even at night her eyes picked up a sheen brighter than silver. The glimmer of elven eyes showed within the figure's raised cowl.

Magiere reached for her falchion, gripping the hilt without taking her eyes off the anmaglâhk, but she hesitated. Was it an anmaglâhk? His forearm was bare—except for a wrist sheath. At his shoulder, she saw the hint of leather . . . of a hauberk?

She froze before the silent figure facing her in the dark. Rings of metal were bound in a weave of leather straps on the hauberk's front.

"Leesil?" Magiere whispered.

The figure didn't answer. Only the blade's tip tilted slowly up at her.

She pulled the falchion, backing away. "Leesil!"

Magiere half-awoke from the dream and thrashed the blanket aside. She scrambled across the pillow and backed against the small room's wall, looking about in terror. Her dhampir nature rose and widened her senses.

Leesil shifted in his slumber, rolling over with a mumble. Wynn didn't stir.

Magiere felt the rough bark through the elven felt jerkin she wore. Its touch made her back muscles spasm. Her shudders settled inward and grew to a hum in her flesh.

She fell forward onto hands and knees, and then collapsed in a heap when her shaking arms wouldn't hold. She curled in a ball upon her bed. The tremors slowly subsided. She wanted to reach for Leesil, to wake him.

But it had only been a dream . . . one more nightmare that plagued her sleep since they'd come into this forest. And for all she'd endured, Leesil's burden seemed far greater here.

Magiere turned about to put her head upon the pillow. Try though she might, she couldn't rest quietly, nor think clearly. Her muscles would not unclench.

Leesil roused slowly the next morning from a restless sleep filled with unwanted dreams—of his mother, and of a young anmaglâhk's split throat, the man's blood soaking into his breeches. When he stepped out into the main room, Magiere was already up.

She sat on the moss next to the chest, with Chap sprawled out beside her as she stared blankly at nothing. A clay cup of steaming tea sat next to her, but it looked untouched. Their cloak-bundled weapons were gone.

Leesil looked about and found the bundle stacked by the outer doorway with the rest of their gear. There was also an extra pack of dark canvas he didn't recognize.

He should have known Magiere would hardly be sitting quietly if her falchion were missing. Before he was ready to deal with the day, their hosts were up and about, taking away any private chance to learn what troubled Magiere.

Leanâlhâm descended the stairs without a sound. She saw him, and this time smiled slightly before slipping out the front doorway. Sgäile crouched to tuck something in the new pack. Gleann came down and followed his grandniece outside, but the two quickly returned as Wynn came out rubbing her face with a yawn.

Leanâlhâm and Gleann each returned with a wooden platter of food. Sgäile took some as they passed and returned to fussing with the gear. Leesil didn't like him digging about in their stuff.

Gleann unrolled a felt rug upon the moss, and breakfast was served: wheat biscuits with nuts, more bisselberries, smoked fish, and a thickened hot porridge smelling of cinnamon.

While Leesil satisfied himself on the latter, Magiere sat quietly beside him and touched none of the food. He nudged her several times, but she shook her head. She didn't even react when Chap snuck in and snatched a whole fillet of smoked fish before anyone could stop him. Wynn scolded the dog, brushing off dried mud he'd left on the felt spread. She loaded a plate to set behind herself, just for him.

As everyone finished, Magiere stood. Sgäile looked her up and down. Whether he studied her or the new clothes she wore, Leesil didn't care for it.

"Your own clothes are clean," Sgäile said, "and packed. It would be best for all of you to wear what you have on for the journey."

What was he up to?

"Where's my armor?" Magiere asked sharply. "If you think I'm walking about without protection, waiting for another of yours to jump us . . . think again."

Sgäile held up his hands with a frustrated sigh.

"Your protection is my concern," he said. "From afar at least, your present attire will draw less attention."

Leesil just frowned. Magiere didn't look any less foreign in loose brown elven pants and a yellow jerkin. She might be tall for a woman, but she wasn't built like an elf. And he was pretty sure Wynn wore the clothing of an elvish youth, but the bottoms of her drawstring pants were rolled up to keep from dragging. Her clothes were too long for her short stature.

"I do not mind," Wynn offered. "These are quite comfortable, but I will take my own cloak."

Osha stuck his head in through the doorway curtain, long white-blond hair hanging across his shoulders.

"Prepared?" he asked in Belaskian.

Leesil didn't have time to wonder where the young anmaglâhk and Urhkar had been all night. No one answered before Sgäile continued.

"There is much to carry, and we travel with haste. If you would allow, one of mine can carry your blades. They will all be at hand if needed."

"What?" Magiere spit back. "We disarmed for coming into your village—and little good it did! You keeping our weapons wasn't part of the arrangement."

Leesil agreed, though he grudgingly wondered if Sgäile made a valid point.

"Let's leave it be," he told her, "at least until we're out of this place."

Magiere turned her nervous glare on him. She shuddered suddenly and then turned away.

"I think Urhkar would be best to carry them," Wynn added.

"No," Magiere said flatly. "Sgäile will carry them."

Her choice baffled Leesil, but only for a moment. The way she looked at Sgäile, she was almost daring him to agree. If it came to taking their arms by force . . .

Leesil understood Magiere's choice and grew nervous at what it meant.

Sgäile wouldn't let inexperienced Osha stand against them. If they came fast at the younger elf, he probably couldn't stop them both. Urhkar was another matter, from what Magiere had experienced last evening at his hands. But Sgäile himself?

Magiere hadn't forgotten why the man had come to Bela. If she came at him, she wouldn't be reserved in how she took from Sgäile what was hers.

Sgäile gave her a pronounced nod. "I will carry them. You have my word."

Leesil put a hand on Magiere's arm, then noticed Osha standing silently inside the doorway with his eyes on Wynn. The young anmaglâhk dropped his gaze with the barest hint of hurt on his long face. She hadn't suggested him as the bearer of arms.

Strangest of all, Chap hadn't moved or spoken up. He lay quietly behind Wynn, his eyes equally on Magiere and Sgäile. The dog had been the first to turn vicious at the sight of Sgäile appearing with the other anmaglâhk, but now he was merely watchful.

Leesil took a slow breath. Things were growing more tense by the day.

Leanâlhâm returned from taking away platters and bowls. She stopped in the doorway but didn't seem to note the mood in the room. She remained in place, blocking anyone's exit.

"I come with you, Uncle," she said.

Sgäile's expression flattened, and then turned incredulous. Leesil had never seen so much unguarded emotion on the man's face. Before Sgäile could speak, Leanâlhâm rushed on.

"We need beeswax and seed oil—for the candles and lanterns—and we are almost out of cinnamon . . ."

"Such things are available in closer reach," Sgäile said, his voice rising a bit too much. "Closer than where we are headed."

"It is a year since you took me to Crijeäiche. There are many craftspeople who gather there, and it is the heart of our land, is it not? Please, Uncle."

Sgäile's jaw twitched. He switched to Elvish, speaking sharply to the girl. Leesil didn't have to know the language to get the gist of it. He suspected Leanâlhâm's request had nothing to do with cinnamon or beeswax.

Gleann jumped in with a few words, and Sgäile's open frustration mounted. This festival of emotion on his usually passive face was almost amusing. But Leesil found himself agreeing. He didn't need some infatuated girl tagging along.

"Let her come," Magiere said suddenly. "We'll look out for her."

"Then it is settled," Gleann said.

"It is not settled!" Sgäile replied. "Grandfather, you do not understand what—"

"I will prepare you a list, Leanâlhâm," Gleann said. "Your uncle will help you find everything."

Sgäile gestured at Magiere and Wynn, speaking Elvish again in short, clipped words.

"That is no reason your cousin cannot accompany you," Gleann replied in plain Belaskian. "How could she not be safe traveling with two others of your own caste? Leanâlhâm, get your things, as everyone is now waiting on you."

Sgäile almost threw up his hands.

Leesil remembered Wynn's scant comments from their first night within the forest. The Anmaglâhk didn't have rank like soldiers. Seniority of experience aside, they obeyed the one chosen to lead a particular mission. It seemed family hierarchies were another matter, even among mature adults. Gleann was the household elder and had the last word.

Leanâlhâm rushed past Sgäile and up the stairs. By the time Sgäile uttered two more frustrated phrases to Gleann, the girl scrambled back down with a hastily cinched canvas bundle slung over her narrow shoulder.

Leesil groaned softly as he grabbed the skulls' chest and Magiere picked up her pack. Sgäile hauled the rest of the baggage out the door in silence, where Urhkar awaited.

Others of the village were already out and about. Most paused to watch from between domicile trees or across the village's mossy center space. Once loaded up, Sgäile led their procession quickly back out the way they'd come. Leesil didn't look about to see the reaction of those watching, but he noticed that Gleann followed along.

Once out of sight of the village, Gleann caught up to Leesil and stopped Magiere as well. He shooed the stoic Urhkar on ahead. Urhkar might have frowned, though it was hard to tell as he walked on.

Leesil offered his hand to Gleann. "Thanks for the welcome stay."

Gleann studied this gesture in puzzlement and slowly lifted his hand.

Leesil had to take it in his own before the man smiled with understanding of the parting gesture.

"Perhaps we'll see you again someday," Magiere added.

Gleann turned serious, almost hard. "I do not hope so. For if so, I fear events will have turned against you. Finish what you must in our land . . . then leave quickly."

He looked warily beyond Magiere at Sgäile and the others before he faced her again.

"My grandson has a true if misguided heart," he said, "so trust his word, but not always his judgment."

Magiere slowly held out her own hand. Gleann took it with a smile as if he'd said nothing at all—as if she were no more human than he. He walked back toward the village, with Leesil watching him in silence.

When Leesil turned away, he found Sgäile waving to them, so he tugged Magiere's sleeve as he moved on. No sooner had they rejoined the others than Leanâlhâm took up walking close behind on his right. The rest stepped ahead except for Urhkar, who trailed at the rear.

From far behind, Leesil heard the strange high-pitched song of a bird as on other days of their journey. And just as before, when he searched for it, he saw nothing.

As they crossed a grass field beyond the village enclosure, Chap veered off, looking into the trees. Leesil spotted movement as a rush of silver-gray scurried by on all fours. Then another, as the majay-hì appeared one by one out in the forest. None came closer.

Wynn stepped up behind Chap, and then something shook the leaves of a bush. A blur of silver-white burst into sight.

The white female hopped forward and stopped. She yipped and darted at Chap, then quickly dodged away.

"Go on," Wynn said to Chap.

Chap didn't look at her but rather toward Sgäile's back, and then he trotted off.

Unlike the other majay-hì, Chap always remained within sight. More often than the others, Leesil spotted the white dog roaming near him.

CHAPTER EIGHT

Four days passed without incident. The forest's monotonous sounds droned in Leesil's ears, but his mother was never far from his thoughts. Their routine was little more than breaking camp at dawn, trudging all day, and stopping only when dusk ended and night settled upon them. Every time Leesil asked how much farther they would travel, Sgäile only answered, "Days . . . more days."

Chap ran with the majay-hì, returning often to pace close to the procession, at which point Leesil noticed the other dogs vanished. But the last time this happened, the white female stayed in sight among the trees.

Osha tried steadily in broken Belaskian to coax Wynn into talking, as she ignored him completely when he spoke Elvish. Little by little she relented. If their conversation carried on too long, Sgäile halted it with a single look. But today, he was less vigilant, and the two continued, often slipping into Elvish. The longer Leesil listened to them shifting between tongues, the more he picked out words here and there. He wasn't certain what was a verb or noun, but perhaps one of two "root words," as Wynn called them, began to sound familiar.

"Wynn," he called out, "none of our stuff has gone missing since we left Sgäile's village. Ask Osha if he thinks we've lost that *tâshgâlh*."

She craned her head around at him, slightly troubled. "I already have. He said it may have found something more interesting in the enclave. The Coilehkrotall will not thank us."

"The Co-il-ee . . . the what?"

"Sgäile and Gleann's clan . . . people of the 'Lichen Woods.' "

"Well, they can't blame us. We didn't invite that overgrown squirrel along."

Though Sgäile didn't turn, Leesil saw the man shake his head as he continued onward.

"Osha, what are these?" Wynn asked as she pointed to a large clear space between two silver birches.

Leesil stopped beside her and leaned over to examine a strange patch of flowers. Normally, Wynn's fascination with plants bored him, but he had to admit these were odd.

The pearl-colored petals—or leaves by their shape—looked fuzzy like velvet. They seemed to glow under the bright sun filling the small space. Their stems and base were a dark green, nearly black where sunlight didn't touch them. Leesil crouched down as Wynn reached for one.

Soft booted feet appeared beside Leesil, and a dark-skinned hand grabbed Wynn's wrist. Leesil rose quickly, nearly knocking over Leanâlhâm standing too close behind him.

Osha shook his head, releasing Wynn. "No."

Leanâlhâm took Leesil's arm, trying to pull him away.

Magiere came up behind them. "What's all this about?"

Sgäile hurried over and looked down at the flowers. "You cannot touch these. They are sacred," he said pointedly. "Osha should have explained before you tried to approach."

Osha's jaw clenched. Clearly he was growing tired of being blamed whenever one of their charges broke some unknown rule.

"Sacred?" Wynn asked.

Questioning Sgäile was futile from Leesil's perspective, but it seemed an especially bad idea whenever he looked displeased.

"They are sacred," Sgäile repeated. "Do not disturb them."

He motioned everyone to start moving again.

For the first time, Leesil had some idea what it must feel like to be Wynn. Maybe he was sick of Sgäile's evasiveness, or maybe he just wanted a real answer for once. The notion was interrupted by a burst of chittering overhead that sounded oddly like laughter. To Leesil's surprise, the elves all looked up with brightened expressions. Wynn tilted her head back so far that Leesil thought she might topple right over.

"Now what?" Magiere asked.

The trees seemed to come alive with movement as small creatures jumped from one branch to the next, making the leafy limbs shudder as if they too were laughing.

"Good fortune," Osha said in Belaskian, his lilting accent so thick the words were barely recognizable. He called Wynn over with the wave of one finger, pointing above as he spoke to her in Elvish.

The little creatures tumbling and hopping among the leaves had arms and tails longer than their thin furry bodies. Their heads had flat snouts and wide mouths between rounded ears, making them look almost human. Soft cream-colored bellies and faces broke their overall rusty coloring and matched the tuft of light hair springing from the ends of their long, curling tails. Oddest of all, they had feet like long hands.

"Fra'cise!" Wynn smiled widely. "Osha says they are filled with the playful spirits of the forest and bring good luck to those they follow. They are similar to a type of monkey."

"A type of what?" Leesil asked, as he'd never heard of such a creature.

Wynn started to reply, then simply shook her head and went back to watching the antics among the branches. One *fra'cise* hung upside down by its feet and swung so wildly back and forth that Leesil started to get queasy.

"They don't look fortunate to me," Magiere said. "More like a *tâshgâlh* that's been sneaking someone's ale."

Leanâlhâm put her hand over her mouth to hide her smile. "These are not thieves, just playful ones of our forest."

The *fra'cise* didn't come closer. They continued to swing and chatter overhead. Then as quickly as they appeared, they were gone, lunging from one tree to the next and off into the forest.

Wynn's barrage of Elvish erupted so fast that Osha looked overwhelmed.

The appearance of these idiotic little animals seemed to cut away Leanâlhâm's wary shyness. She dashed out into the forest, following them and pointing ahead to the branches above. Wynn jogged after the girl, a little less gracefully in her oversized clothes, and they slipped from sight among the tree trunks.

Magiere took two steps after them. "Both of you get back here!"

From somewhere in the brush, Leanâlhâm cried out, "Sgäilsheilleache!"

Leesil lunged off the path behind Magiere. Then he remembered they were unarmed. He ran on with the chest slamming against his back. Magiere dropped her pack, trying to keep up with him.

Sgäile was already five paces ahead, running through the trees, smashing his way through underbrush around stout cedars and oaks.

Far off to the left, Urhkar outdistanced all of them. Osha came up quick on Leesil's heels as they broke the edge of a bare ground clearing with patches of long-leafed yellow grass.

Wynn and Leanâlhâm knelt at the center before two adolescent elven males, bare to the waist . . . or were they elves?

They were shorter than even Wynn, if she were standing. Their bodies and faces were marked with strange symbols in blue-black ink or paint.

They had the pointed ears, triangular faces, and amber eyes of elves but wore no shirts or boots—only loose breeches of rough natural fabric frayed off below the knees. Their wooden spears with blackened and sharpened ends were pointed at the women on the ground. One had an ivy vine wreath around his neck, and he stared at Wynn in horror. When he lifted his gaze to Magiere entering the clearing, his reaction grew to trembling outrage.

Sgäile froze at the clearing's edge. He raised a quick hand for his own comrades to halt. When Magiere didn't stop, he grabbed her by the arm. She turned on him, but he shook his head.

"Please stay," Osha whispered behind Leesil.

And more of these short elves appeared from behind all the trees around the clearing.

Some carried bows with arrows drawn. Like the spears, these ended in sharpened points without heads. A few carried cudgels of polished wood shaped as if made from gnarled tree roots. Most had wild hair pleated back or bound with cords of twisted wild grass.

Chap burst from the brush at the clearing's far right.

Two of the small newcomers leaped out of his path. One more ran up the side of a tree trunk and clung to its lower branches. None appeared worried by the dog's snarling, only startled as they watched him.

Chap worked his way toward Wynn, still rumbling with teeth exposed.

Urhkar stepped forward with both hands open and empty at his sides. He crossed the space slowly and placed himself before Wynn and Leanâlhâm. The first savage short one stepped back, and the second lifted his spear.

Sgäile barked one word of Elvish, and Chap stopped growling.

One of the pair facing Urhkar snapped something at him, nearly shout-ing, and Wynn cringed back, pulling at Leanâlhâm. The girl looked as frightened as the sage, but her eyes turned toward her uncle in confusion, as if she had no idea what was happening.

"Sgäile . . . ," Leesil whispered harshly, "do something, damn you."

Sgäile's eyes never left the scene before him. He rapidly placed a finger to his lips and that was all.

Leesil's frustration vanished in dull surprise—Sgäile was afraid.

Sgäile had too many people to protect, a mission to complete, and now Wynn had made things even worse. He could not allow violence to break out here but hesitated to speak.

Although Sgäile had authority over this mission, Urhkarasiférin was clearly the eldest among them. Such distinction was all that these people—the old race of this land—would respect as authority. Sgäile let him take the lead.

Then Chap glanced his way.

A memory of grief-enraged Én'nish rose suddenly in Sgäile's mind. He did not know why this came to him now, and he pushed it aside.

One of the diminutive pair before Urhkarasiférin was called Rujh. Sgäile had seen him before as a messenger sent to the an'Cróan by the man's own people—the Äruin'nas. They had been in this land long before Sgäile's people, or so it was said.

Rujh spat an accusation at Urhkarasiférin. "You break faith with the trees!"

The elder elf shook his head with steady calm. "No. We are in guardianship of these humans and act on behalf of Most Aged Father."

His words had no impact on Rujh. "Your aged leader has no right to such a choice. We do not answer to him or your kind. The forest's own law is above his wishes—and yours."

"We escort these humans to him for questioning," Urhkarasiférin explained. "We must know how they entered this land . . . before others follow in their path."

"The forest has its way to deal with such!" Rujh nearly shouted. "It has no need of your assistance. You defile it with no remorse, and it is offensive enough that we now find mixed-bloods walking here."

He gestured to Leanâlhâm and then to Léshil. Sgäile crept slowly inward, blocking Leanâlhâm from Rujh's sight.

"They have the blood in them," Sgäile insisted. "And the forest has not seen fit to reject them."

Rujh turned his head toward Sgäile, and frustrated reluctance filled his angry face.

"We accept those who have blood that should not be spilled, but the other two . . ." He pointed to Wynn and then Magiere. "If you will not kill them, then we will do it."

"Do not attempt to violate guardianship," Urhkarasiférin warned.

Rujh tilted his spear slightly toward Urhkarasiférin, but the elder elf did not move or flinch.

Sgäile's stomach began to tighten. No doubt Urhkarasiférin and Osha would follow his orders if violence broke out, but it was the last thing he wanted. They could escape Rujh's numbers, but getting Léshil and his companions out would be a harder fight.

Én'nish's face flashed again in Sgäile's thoughts. He pushed the image away. Why did he keep thinking of her? Then came a memory of Rujh appearing out of the forest at Crijheäiche.

It startled Sgäile. He could not clearly remember which occasion this memory came from or why he thought of it now. But it made him study the short man.

Rujh had spotted Léshil too quickly as half-blooded. Had he known before Léshil appeared?

A flash of Én'nish came again. It flickered in and out with the memory of Rujh appearing from the forest. Sgäile felt dizzy, and then he realized . . .

There were too many Äruin'nas here at once. Not a hunting party or even an envoy to one of the elven clans. They lived to the northwest, where the forest thickened against the range. How had Rujh known to come here?

Someone had sought out the Äruin'nas, or sent word to them.

Én'nish's blind anguish and hunger for vengeance went further than Sgäile had thought possible. Perhaps Urhkarasiférin should not have dismissed her from his tutelage but kept her close and watched.

Urhkarasiférin sharply backhanded Rujh's spear aside. "You are not a judge of the forest's natural law."

"Neither can your Most Aged Father take exceptions upon himself," Rujh answered.

"You will do nothing without the will of all blood," Urhkarasiférin warned, "that of your people and of mine."

"Have your clan elders agreed to allow humans to walk among the trees?" A ray of hope grew inside Sgäile. "Nor have they agreed to execute them."

"Speak when spoken to!" Urhkarasiférin snapped, and Sgäile clenched his jaw.

He watched Rujh's face. Only clan leaders decided such weighty issues for Sgäile's people. Rujh knew this, for it was much the same among his kind. The small man scowled.

"There is a judgment to be made," he said, and turned away. "We will meet at Crijheäiche . . . where all will hear of this matter."

Sgäile quickly reached down and pulled Leanâlhâm to her feet, her innocent face still full of fear.

"Up," he said to Wynn. "Everyone return to our path."

Magiere grabbed Wynn's arm and turned back with Leesil close behind. Urhkarasiférin took the lead as Sgäile pulled Leanâlhâm along. Not one of the Äruin'nas remained among the trees. They had all vanished from sight.

What fuel of lies had Én'nish used to kindle this fire in her hunger for vengeance?

"Do not stop and do not look back," Sgäile said to the others.

He knew where Én'nish would head next. The same place he must take his own group in order to shorten the journey. Traveling alone and unburdened, she would beat him to the river and passage down to Crijheäiche. Leanâlhâm's hand trembled in his grip.

"You are safe," he whispered, pulling her close.

An anmaglâhk's duty, by life oath, was to protect his people. Sgäile had one failing in this. Leanâlhâm's safety came before all others.

Chap trotted beside Wynn, longing for the lost talking hide and the privacy to use it.

He needed to speak with Leesil, and he did not know how else this could be done.

Chap had never met the Äruin'nas—had never even heard the word until it rose from Sgäile's memories. But now, Chap had things to tell . . . things he'd seen in Rujh's memories.

Én'nish, for one.

The instant he realized what the female anmaglâhk had done, he pulled upon Sgäile's memories, until he felt Sgäile reach a realization. But Chap could not shake off his puzzlement over the tone Rujh used when speaking of Most Aged Father.

In youth, Chap had known but a few of the Anmaglâhk. Most Aged Father was no elder of a clan, for Anmaglâhk were a caste apart and servants to their people, but their patriarch was still held in high esteem. His word carried the weight of a clan elder, if not its authority. His word held power among the elves. Was that now changing?

Brot'an and Eillean had believed they took great risks in defying Most Aged Father. The patriarch believed an Ancient Enemy would return, as did Chap's kin. It was the reason they had sent him to Magiere—to keep her from falling into the hands of those who searched for her.

But what of Leesil?

His own mother and grandmother had conspired to create him, to train him, in order to kill this same enemy Most Aged Father feared. The thought rankled Chap, and he growled.

Leesil was no one's tool. Why had Nein'a wanted a half-blood for the plans of her dissidents? And what did Most Aged Father really want with Leesil?

Chap steeled himself for what would come at Crijheäiche, and what he might have to do to protect Leesil, Magiere, and Wynn from all sides.

His thoughts were broken as the white majay-hì loped toward him from the trees. Wynn had once compared her to a water "lily."

Chap agreed.

Lily kept her distance, glancing hesitantly at those walking with Chap along a wide-open way through the forest. Whenever the breeze shifted Chap's way, he caught her earthy scent.

His thoughts tumbled through memories passed between them in the night outside the elven enclave. He wanted more of this—more of her. He wanted to run with Lily among the pack. Or without them.

Was this what passed between Magiere and Leesil? A depth of longing he had not felt since Eillean had taken him from his siblings?

Lily yipped once in a standing pause, watching him. He did not need touch, as the other majay-hì did, to see her memories. Images of leaves and brush and grass and trees whipping by in the night filled his head. He caught a flash of silver gray running beside her.

A memory of him.

Chap remained beside Wynn, but he often turned his eyes to Lily.

Past nightfall, Leesil sat staring into the campfire that Magiere stoked with more wood. Wynn sat on the ground and struggled with a hay-bristle brush Leanâlhâm provided. But try as the sage might, she couldn't get the last mat out of Chap's coat. The dog's restless fidgeting didn't make it any easier.

At a light footfall, he turned to find Leanâlhâm approaching. She crouched near him, her expression uneasy. Perhaps the encounter with the Äruin'nas still troubled the girl. It certainly troubled Leesil.

Leanâlhâm watched Wynn's efforts and Chap's scant tolerance with fascination. The girl obviously hadn't known what the sage intended with the brush.

Osha had gone in search of food, and Sgäile stood at the clearing's far side, speaking in low tones with Urhkar.

"Magiere, come and hold him down," Wynn called, and Chap tried to belly-crawl out of reach. "He is a mess, but he will not let me finish."

"You hold him, and I'll do it," Magiere said.

Chap saw her coming. With a rumble, he licked his nose.

"I saw that," Magiere warned.

"You lose again," Leesil said to Chap. This resulted in another tongue-and-nose gesture just for him.

Leanâlhâm leaned forward. "Why are you talking to the majay-hì?"

Before Leesil could think up an answer, Wynn pounced on Chap and grabbed his neck with both arms. Magiere dropped on her knees, pinning the dog's hindquarters as she took up the brush.

"Oh . . . you stink!" Wynn said, wrinkling up her face.

The sight of the two women wrestling the dog into submission, and getting as dirty as he, was almost amusing enough for Leesil to forget the day's troubles.

"No! Do not treat him that way!"

Leanâlhâm's thick accent made her words hard to catch, and she jumped to her feet indignantly before Leesil understood. She grabbed for the back of Wynn's coat, and Leesil shoved his arm in her way.

"He is a guardian of our forest," the girl shouted. "Let him go!"

Both Magiere and Wynn froze and stared at Leanâlhâm.

Chap's ears perked as he ceased struggling. He rolled crystalline eyes and huffed once in agreement with Leanâlhâm's outrage. It sounded a bit too pompous to Leesil.

A way off, Sgäile and Urhkar looked on, and neither appeared pleased.

"It's all right," Leesil said, pulling Leanâlhâm down on the log. "Chap's a bit of a pig. If we don't clean him, he gets unbearable . . . and he knows it."

Chap growled at him.

"Oh, be quiet!" Wynn snapped, and clamped the dog's snout in her little fingers. "Magiere, finish it."

"And if he didn't really like it," Leesil added, "he wouldn't make it so easy for them."

Leanâlhâm's face filled with hesitant wonder. "He . . . understands?"

Chap shook his snout with a grunt, nearly toppling Wynn forward into the dirt.

Leesil sighed. They couldn't hide Chap's unusual intelligence forever, but perhaps it was best not to answer too many questions.

"Done," Magiere said and got up. "It might have gone quicker if you'd kept your butt still!"

Chap wrinkled a jowl at her and slunk off to the clearing's far side. He flopped down to clean himself. Wynn picked herself up, brushing dirt from her breeches.

Leanâlhâm was still watching Chap.

Leesil studied her face. A small loop of her light brown hair was pulled through a wooden ring and held there over a crosswise wood peg. From there, her hair fell down her back in a tail. Her skin was a bit lighter in tone than his, which was strange considering he had more human blood. She turned to warm her hands by the fire, her expression suddenly too serious.

"You all right?" he asked.

She only nodded.

"If elves don't spill the blood of their own," he asked, "why did you cry out?"

"I have only seen the Äruin'nas a few times," she answered, "but never so many at once . . . and so angry."

This was the most Leesil had heard the girl say to anyone but Sgäile or Gleann.

"They wanted to kill your companions," she added, "humans, but . . . they hated me the same way . . . and you. The words they spoke . . . terrible things . . . before my uncle came."

Leanâlhâm went silent, staring into the fire.

"People say terrible things about me all the time," Leesil answered. "Don't let it bother you."

He heard a hiss, and looked up. For an instant, he thought Magiere's vicious expression was aimed at the girl. She stepped slow and steady in front of him, until she stood beside Leanâlhâm while facing away from the fire. Leesil couldn't see her face.

Magiere's fingertips gently touched Leanâlhâm's shoulder. The girl jumped slightly, but Magiere headed off across the clearing toward Sgäile and Urhkar.

What was she doing? Leesil was about to go after her before she stirred up another conflict.

"You are fortunate to have the right hair and eyes," Leanâlhâm said.

"What?"

"Your hair is light," she said. "And your eyes are amber. You look more like our people than I do, and you are half human. I am . . . I wish I had hair and eyes like yours."

Her words were sickeningly ironic. Leesil wanted to tell her that in his world, growing up, his hair and eyes cut him off from everyone but his parents.

"There's nothing wrong with who you are, Leanâlhâm," Wynn replied. She sat on a folded blanket at the fire's far side, fingers laced around her pulled-up knees.

"Leanâlhâm," Leesil asked slowly, "how did you come to be here?"

"I wanted to tell you that first night you came to our home, but my grandfather and uncle are always worried."

She watched the fire for a while, and Leesil waited in silence until she spoke.

"My grandmother was not only bond-mate to my true grandfather, the brother of Gleannéohkân'thva—or Gleann, as you call him. She was also under Gleann's tutelage to become a healer. I call him grandfather because he is the one who raised me. It is the closest word in your tongue for the title.

"My grandmother traveled with Gleann as needed, helping those who had no healer among their own enclave. Illness spread through another clan's settlements to the southeast, and they went to assist. Grandmother was gathering *basha* weed in the hills near the shore, which helps lower fevers. She was attacked . . . by human men."

Leanâlhâm paused and did not look at Leesil. "Do you understand?"

"Yes," Wynn whispered.

"She was badly hurt when Gleann found her and brought her home. In another moon, they knew she was with child. My grandparents did all they could to make certain their coming child would not be treated as an outsider."

Leanâlhâm's voice broke with a painful breath. Firelight glistened in the tears running down to the edge of her triangular jaw.

Leesil understood. Even if Leanâlhâm's grandparents had accepted and shielded their half-blood child, some among their people still wouldn't accept it.

"Grandmother died the night my mother was born," Leanâlhâm went on. "Grandfather was broken inside, as happens among many who are bonded. He left my mother for Gleann to raise. No one saw him again.

"My mother was . . . not right in her mind. She wept often and seldom left the enclave's dwelling trees. Except at night, when she might sit alone in the forest. It was difficult for Gleann, as he never found a way to make her feel like one of the people.

"By the time my mother was of age, Gleann was a most respected healer. A young man with the Spirit awareness came from clan Chiurr to ask that she bond with him—but only if Gleann took him under tutelage as a healer. I think Grandfather was desperate to see my mother have a normal life. He agreed to the bargain. But my parents' bonding was short and then broken by my father, as my mother did not change. He left after I was born and returned to his own clan. By then it was clear that he had never truly loved her, or he would not have been able to leave."

Leesil knew better. Love didn't always last—and sometimes it wasn't enough.

"Not long after," Leanâlhâm continued, "my mother disappeared one night. Some in the southwest say a woman was seen heading for the mountains. She evaded all who approached. Perhaps she found a place among humans."

Leesil waited for more, but Leanâlhâm went silent.

"You grew up alone with Gleann?" he asked.

She nodded. "Except for Sgäile, but not until after my mother left . . . and his last testing to be Anmaglâhk. He was then free to see family again and to live where he wished, though most of his caste live in Crijheäiche."

Leanâlhâm turned to face Leesil fully.

"Sgäile's grandfather was bond-brother of my grandmother's father, though he calls Gleann his grandfather in respect. Sgäile and I share blood. He is often away, but his acceptance of me weighed greatly. Sgäile never knew my mother, but he stood for me among our clan, and he is Anmaglâhk."

She nodded slowly, as if remembering something.

"He has traveled many lands, but other mixed-bloods are unknown. So you are the first half-blood he has ever met."

Osha stepped from the trees with two gutted and cleaned rabbits ready for roasting. He also carried a bulging square of canvas tied up by its corners. Leanâlhâm took a long breath and stood up.

"I should help prepare the meal, as it grows late and we are all hungry . . . yes?"

Leesil nodded to her. He had no notion what else to say, no matter how much they shared. Words would weigh nothing against the life she had led and the one he had lived. He glanced across the clearing to where Magiere faced Sgäile engaged in some talk he couldn't quite hear. Chap was with them as well. Leesil couldn't help studying Sgäile for a moment.

The man must have more immediate relatives than Leanâlhâm and Gleann. Yet he chose to call the dwelling of a mixed-blood girl and an eccentric old healer his "home" and these two people his "family."

Leesil didn't believe he would ever understand Sgäile.

Magiere approached in quick pounding strides. Sgäile's tension rose and he broke off his discussion with Urhkarasiférin.

After their confrontation with the Äruin'nas, it had taken a long and heated argument with this woman to keep her and Léshil from reclaiming their weapons. Apparently that debate was not yet settled.

"No more," Magiere growled at him. "Give me our arms . . . now!"

Sgäile took a long breath. "I understand your concern, but if you had been armed today, we might not have talked our way out. I gave you my word. You will be protected."

"You can't," Magiere insisted. "We saw that today. What if those people hadn't listened? I won't risk those I care for, whether I believe you or not. It's not about your word or keeping it . . . it's about failing, regardless."

Sgäile was not certain how much insult hid beneath her words. He had his ways and customs to follow with faith, and his oath of guardianship to fulfill, and arming this human woman would make neither easy to accomplish.

"You couldn't even keep Leanâlhâm safe," Magiere whispered.

Sgäile fought down rising anger. Her voice carried no malice, but his frustration made it seem so.

"Get me my weapon, or I'll get it myself," Magiere threatened. "Choose!"

Sgäile hesitated too long, and Magiere took a step toward him. A snarl rose up, and she halted.

Chap stood between them, braced in Magiere's path against her legs, but his crystalline eyes looked up at Sgäile.

"Get out of the way!" Magiere snapped.

The majay-hì only growled and would not move.

Sgäile felt a moment's relief that this Fay-touched creature shared his concerns. Then the dog trotted around him, skirting Urhkarasiférin, and headed straight for the bundle and pack that held the weapons and armor. Sgäile went cold inside as the dog sat down next to the arms and stared at him.

Did Chap not understand anything he had tried to make this ill-tempered human accept? Now the majay-hì appeared to side with her.

Ever since the time Sgäile went to kill a half-blood marked as a traitor, this unique being's presence had shaken all he believed concerning the ways of his people.

A memory surfaced in Sgäile's thoughts, of Magiere, her white face aglow, standing by her companions in the forest the night he and his brethren had come to take them. Sword out, she stood ready to defend them from whatever came.

The memory snapped away, replaced with one of a terrified Leanâlhâm huddled next to Wynn amid the Äruin'nas.

The majay-hì lifted its paw and shoved the pack over.

Urhkarasiférin whispered in Elvish. "What is it doing?"

Still Sgäile hesitated and glanced at Magiere. She folded her arms, waiting, as if the dog's action required no explanation.

How could Sgäile explain to Urhkarasiférin what he saw and felt? How could be justify relenting to the majay-hì's request?

Sgäile was bitterly forced to admit that Magiere might speak the truth.

They had escaped the rightful anger of the Äruin'nas, but it had come too close to bloodshed. Leanâlhâm had suffered for it, despite the final outcome.

Sgäile knelt before Chap with uncertainty. He unbound Magiere's heavy blade and lifted it with the rest of the arms still in the pack. He held out the sheathed sword, and Magiere wrapped her hand solidly around it.

Sgäile did not let go. His gaze drifted across the clearing to Leanâlhâm. The girl was assisting Osha in spitting rabbits to cook over the flames.

Magiere followed his glance and then turned her hard eyes back on him. "No one will touch her," she said. "That's my word."

Sgäile released Magiere's sword.

CHAPTER NINE

Wynn walked beside Osha with Leanâlhâm nearby as they passed through an aspen grove filled with low grass and patches of dandelions. Magiere trudged ahead in her studded hauberk, the falchion strapped on her hip. Leesil was fitted with his weapons and hauberk covered in steel rings. Wynn was still uncertain how Magiere had managed all this, but part of her was relieved when she saw the two gearing up that morning, until Magiere forced Wynn to strap on the battle dagger over her short robe.

The last time Wynn tried to use a weapon she had been beaten to near unconsciousness by two of Darmouth's soldiers. The sheathed blade thumping against her side was an unpleasant reminder. She tilted back her head and saw a thousand green leaves haloed by the bright sun. Ahead, she heard the sound of running water.

"We have reached the river people," Leanâlhâm said. "Our journey will be easier."

"Why is that?" Wynn asked.

Leanâlhâm smiled. "You will see. Sgäile will arrange passage down the Hâjh."

"The . . . 'spine'?"

"Yes. The river passes by Crijheäiche, the settlement of the Anmaglâhk, on its way to the northeast bay."

Wynn admitted that traveling by boat was more convenient, but it offered less of an opportunity to see this world up close. Still, she might get a thorough overview from the river's open way.

"Chap!" she called, scanning the trees. "Come back here, unless you wish to swim the rest of the way."

Sgäile turned his head with a warning frown, and Wynn fell quiet.

It was not hard to fathom his worry. Soon Sgäile would face another encounter with his people. Anmaglâhk he might be, but his social skills were as stunted as Magiere's. Unlike Magiere, this shortcoming appeared to concern him.

"Gather," he called out in Elvish.

Osha and Urhkar took parallel positions at the procession's sides. As the aspen grove thinned, Wynn drew a long breath. Through the trees she saw three broad vessels slipping past upon the wide Hâjh River.

The barges looked like massive flat-bottomed canoes as opposed to their square and flat human counterparts. Laden with twine-bound bundles and smooth, slatless barrels, they rode lightly like leaves in a stream. Two headed downriver, while the other passed on its way up.

Each had a central mast of polished yellow wood. Their sails were furled, but the bound fabric was brilliant white in the bright sun. Where their raised sides turned inward at the pointed bow and stern, single tines sprouted to either side of their hulls like straight, bare branches on a tree's trunk. Wynn could not guess what these were for.

Elves front and rear in the barges held long poles but seldom dipped these. The downstream vessels moved on the current, and although the one headed upstream traveled as smoothly as the others, behind its stern, river water churned softly, like the slow thrashing of a giant fish just below the surface.

"Wynn! Get up here!"

Leesil's harsh shout broke Wynn's enchantment. She had unwittingly stopped while staring at the barges. Leanâlhâm pulled on Wynn's sleeve, while everyone else stood waiting. Their entire procession had halted and not one of them looked pleased with Wynn.

She hurried to catch up as Leanâlhâm outdistanced her. Magiere firmly pushed Wynn out ahead of herself, and Osha sighed some exclamation under his breath.

Chap charged through the aspens, the white female on his heels. Wynn saw no sign of the majay-hì pack, and Chap's companion stopped short, hanging back to shift uncertainly among the trees. Before Wynn tried coaxing her closer, Sgäile urged all of them onward. Just ahead lay a settlement more diverse than that of Sgäile's clan.

A few domiciles were made of stout aspens bent toward each other overhead, with vines of spadelike leaves woven into walls between them. In the upper branches of an elm, wood platforms supported partitions of anchored fabrics as well as shaped vines. One tall building was made of planked wood, grayed with age and weather. Thin smoke rose into the air from somewhere hidden at the settlement's far end.

The elves worked at varied tasks, mostly to do with goods near the docks. Their clothing had more hide and leather than the people of Sgäile's home wore. Many wore their hair cut midlength or even short to the scalp. Dock-workers picked among barrels and bundles, taking stock of goods arriving or awaiting departure.

Few noticed the newcomers at first, but by ones and twos they paused and called or gestured to companions. Wynn saw displeasure and even hatred, as in Sgäile's enclave, but none showed initial shock upon seeing humans. This made her more anxious.

"Is this a center of commerce?" Wynn asked.

"Commerce?" Leanâlhâm said. "I do not understand this word."

"The way you purchase . . . acquire with money."

Leanâlhâm blinked twice. "Money?"

"The people trade," Osha explained in Elvish, "all knowing the value of a thing, by its make and the time and effort involved. We barter, but we do not have . . ." He stumbled and switched to Belaskian: "Money. And Anmaglâhk do not trade."

"Why not the Anmaglâhk?" Wynn asked, still baffled.

"Quiet," Sgäile said.

A darker-skinned elf in matching leather breeches and tunic-style shirt rose at the head of one dock from inspecting bales of cattail heads. He appeared neither hostile nor surprised, and Wynn suspected all here somehow knew they were coming.

Leesil and Magiere hung back as Sgäile approached, but Wynn crept a little closer to listen.

The leather-clad man scanned them all, with an especially close study of Leesil and then Magiere. His blond hair was cropped semishort and stuck out in bristles. Soft lines creased his brow as if he frowned too often, and his tan skin glistened with sweat.

"Sgäilsheilleache," he said. "You are always welcome."

"My thanks, Ghuvésheane," Sgäile answered.

It took Wynn some thought to discern the man's name—Black Cockerel. It matched his demeanor if not his appearance.

"I need passage to Crijheäiche," Sgäile said, "for seven and one majay-hì."

Ghuvésheane shifted his weight to settle on the other foot. "I cannot ask this of any bargemaster. Not even for you."

Sgäile's expression hardened. "Has one of my caste passed this way?"

Ghuvésheane nodded sharply. "Three days ago. A woman, traveling fast. She took passage on Hionnahk's barge, headed downriver."

"You must try for us," Sgäile insisted. "By request of Most Aged Father."

Ghuvésheane's eyes narrowed, and he closed them.

"Ask them," Sgäile said flatly. "Ask in the name of Most Aged Father. Who among you would refuse the Anmaglâhk?"

"Assisting your caste is not at issue," Ghuvésheane returned, eyes still closed. "As you well know."

Several elves down the docks stopped in their labors. Two came up behind Ghuvésheane, dressed akin to him. But they looked far more offended, as if Sgäile had asked something shameful—something he should not have asked at all.

"Is it not enough that you bring humans among us"—Ghuvésheane finally opened his eyes, his steady gaze shifting toward Leesil—"let alone a murderer and traitor?"

Wynn bit her lip against a blurted denial. Osha remained passive, but an echo of the dockworkers' embarrassment filled his expression.

Urhkar licked his lips as if they had gone dry. "That charge has not been validated."

Ghuvésheane remained unconvinced. "Perhaps not, but you still ask too much, and my answer is the same."

Neither Leesil nor Magiere understood what was said, but Wynn wondered what would happen if Sgäile was unable to procure passage.

A young and thin-muscled elf came up the shoreline. "I will take you," he said, ignoring Ghuvésheane. "No one need ask me." He glanced at

Leanâlhâm, as if he knew her. "We are still loading, but there is space near the front."

Dressed in leather breeches, he wore a goatskin vest with the leather side out and no shirt beneath it. He was barefoot and gestured to a small half-loaded barge down at the end of the next dock.

Ghuvésheane turned away with an exhale tainted with disdain.

Sgäile's jaw twitched as he nodded to the young bargemaster.

The exchange was peaceful enough, yet Wynn felt that it cost Sgäile more than all the rest of the journey combined. Much of their passage seemed to have taxed the anmaglâhk's pride.

They were shown to a space near the barge's front where cushions and fur hides were laid out. Wynn made more seats out of their blankets. By the time the barge pulled into the river, everyone was situated, and the settlement slipped away behind them.

Their host's name was Kânte—Spoken Word. Though the young barge-master seldom issued commands to his crew, two of four elves always stood post, one rear and one forward, while the other pair rested at the barge's stern, away from the passengers.

They floated down the Hâjh both day and night, and Wynn passed the time watching a strange world drift by on the shores.

Trees of various make, flowers of wild color, a small waterfall, a bright flock of birds never ceased to pull her attention this way and that. Two *fra'-cise* drank at the river's edge, until they saw the barge and began jumping and splashing in foolish antics. Parts of the forest grew dense and dim. Then the barge would pass a large meadow spilling its vivid green to the river's shore, where a herd of speckled antelope grazed. Once, Wynn caught a glimpse of a large silver deer with tineless antlers, the same as had bellowed at them the first evening in the forest.

But eventually she grew frustrated and then weary.

All the wondrous sights passed beyond her reach. Landfall was rare. They ate cold meals, with no fire but for the large lantern hung at the bow each night. The simple fare was plentiful—fresh or dried fruit and smoked fish. The river provided clean water for drinking and basic washing. But as Wynn continued to watch the shore slip past, she began to feel slightly dizzy.

Osha remained good-natured, though he sat day after day in the same position.

He explained that this barge was loaded with raw materials. Kânte would unload some in Crijheäiche, trading with skilled craftsmen in the community. He would then fill his barge with other materials or goods—pottery, spices, tools, fabric, clothing, and more—for the journey to the bay. Some would be traded with the people of the city there called Ghoivne Ajhâjhe— Front of the Deep—while the rest would be bartered with ships bringing goods and materials to and from other coastal communities.

While they spoke, a high-pitched yip carried along the riverside, and Chap looked over, whining softly.

The entire majay-hì pack bolted out of the forest to run along the reedy shore, paws splashing through the shallow water. Shades of silver-blue, steel, and inky gray moved in circles along the bank.

"Magiere, look!" Wynn said. "They are following us."

The white female barked once at Chap. He whined again, and Magiere reached down to scratch his head.

And still they floated onward four more days and nights.

Then as they passed an enormous sycamore with large roots reaching from the bank into the river, Wynn saw an archway in the base of its trunk. She almost missed it, mistaking its gray curtain for part of its bark.

"We are close to Crijheäiche," Leanâlhâm said.

Wynn went numb. She did not know what to feel—relief or anxiety?

"How close?" Leesil asked, craning his head around.

Leanâlhâm pointed to two broad elms.

Wynn saw more doorways as the barge drifted by. Soon, every other oak, cedar, and fir was larger than the last, and the spaces between them broadened.

Sgäile stood up when five long docks appeared on the shore ahead, with barges and smaller boats moored along them. Wynn caught a hint of joy on his face.

From what she understood, they would enter one of the largest communities in all the Elven Territories. But Sgäile did not appear nervous. Was he not worried about their reception?

He put two fingers in this mouth and let out a long whistle.

Kânte stood in the barge's prow and dipped his pole into the water. All four of his crew around the vessel did likewise, and the barge turned smoothly toward the docks. Where the docks met land, no trees blocked the view, and Wynn took her first glimpse of Crijheäiche.

The doorways in these trees were larger than those she'd seen elsewhere, and some trunks bulged to impossible size at their bases. She saw stalls of planked wood and shaped flora and colored fabrics. Inside these, occupants were busy at many kinds of work. One place appeared dedicated to the purification of beeswax. She heard rhythmic metallic clanks but could not spot anything like a smithy. There were fishmongers nearer the river, or the elven equivalent of such.

As the barge slowed in order to make harbor, a wild tangle of aromas filled Wynn's head. Beneath the scent of baked and roasted foods were rich spices and the powerful scent of herbs she had only known in the gardens of her guild on another continent.

For all the industry here, everything was still interwoven with the natural world.

Kânte set his pole to stop the barge as four anmaglâhk trotted through the open bazaar and down the dock. Their long hair of sandy to white blond blew free in the breeze. None wore his or her cloak tied the way the few Wynn had seen beyond this land.

At first, only a few other elves turned and stared at the new arrivals, for barges landing here would be a common sight. From a distance, Leesil and even Magiere appeared to escape scrutiny. Perhaps their elven clothing obscured their true nature until an onlooker peered more closely. But a few eyes widened at Chap. Apparently, a majay-hì riding a barge was not a common sight.

The first of the four anmaglâhk to reach the barge's side was young, with blunt but prominent cheekbones.

"Sgäilsheilleache, well met," he said in Elvish. "Fréthfâre hoped you would arrive by today."

He did not look at Wynn or Magiere. In fact, he seemed determined to cast his eyes anywhere but in their direction.

"Where is she?" Sgäile asked without greeting.

"With Most Aged Father," the young one answered. "I will tell her you have arrived."

"Has anyone seen Én'nish?" Urhkar added.

The young anmaglâhk became rigidly formal at the sight of him and bowed his head in a reverent fashion.

"Yes, Greimasg'äh. She arrived two nights ago."

That one strange word eluded Wynn. A "holder" of something? Perhaps a title, as it certainly was not part of Urhkar's full name.

Sgäile nodded. "Have the quarters been prepared?"

"Yes, of course," the young elf answered.

Sgäile turned to Leesil, switching to Belaskian. "My caste has prepared a comfortable place for all of you. Please follow, but first . . . you must relinquish your weapons once more."

Leesil snorted. "You want to get us out of sight? Then where is my mother?"

"In truth, I cannot say," Sgäile answered and looked away. "You will soon speak to Most Aged Father, and he will answer in good faith. Now please, your weapons."

Wynn unbuckled the dagger, uncertain whether or not she was relieved to be rid of it. She was about to hand it to Sgäile, but turned instead to Osha. He took it with surprise and bowed his head as he tucked it in his belt.

"All right," Leesil said, unstrapping his punching blades. "But I want to see this leader of yours, and soon. Today."

He held out his blades and his stilettos. Sgäile took them with a hint of relief in his eyes. Once again, Magiere was last to relinquish her falchion, but she handed it over without a word. Leesil placed his hand on the back of her neck, combing his fingers through her dangling black hair.

Throughout the community up the slope, and across the other docks, numerous elves in bright clothing went about their business. Wynn noticed the Anmaglâhk among them. They stood out like dark pebbles in a clear stream's bed.

Kânte picked up Leanâlhâm's bundle before she could do so and held it out to her. The gesture made the girl fidget nervously, and she would not look him in the eyes.

"You have my thanks . . . ," Sgäile said to the bargemaster, but trailed off, unable to say more.

Kânte raised a hand in polite dismissal. "No need. You always have my service."

He offered his hand to Leanâlhâm. This made the girl even more uneasy, but she took it as he helped her onto the dock. Leesil lifted the chest of skulls and slipped his arms into its rope harness. Osha and Urhkar handed baggage off to their newly arrived comrades.

As Wynn stepped from the barge behind the others, the first young an-maglâhk glared at Leesil and pointed insistently to the chest. When Leesil re-turned only a silent stare, the young one's expression hardened. Two of his companions dropped their baggage and closed in as he reached out.

Before Leesil could strike, Magiere stepped in front of him, shielding him from any assault. Sgäile shifted instantly between her and the others.

"No!" he snapped. "Move on!"

The young anmaglâhk looked at Sgäile as if he had committed some vi-olation. Osha, who had always kept silent behind his elders, startled Wynn with his harsh tone.

"He is bearer of the dead," Osha said in Elvish to the others. "Léshil, de-scendant of Eillean."

The young anmaglâhk before Sgäile blinked twice. He glanced once at Leesil and Magiere, both still poised for a fight.

"I beg forgiveness," he said.

"Attend your duty," Urhkar added flatly.

The four anmaglâhk quickly took up the baggage. Not one of them said anything more.

Solid wood of the dock and then sound earth beneath Wynn's feet were quite welcome, but Sgäile rushed them all onward. Perhaps he was not so confident of their reception; or he neared the end of his mission and longed for it to be over.

Wynn wanted to study this new place, to poke about the stalls and ob-serve how exchanges were made, but she found herself jogging half the time just to keep up. All around them, elves paused at the sight of Magiere's dark hair and pale skin—and Wynn's own short stature and round olive-toned face. The four anmaglâhk with the baggage split into twos, a pair walking at each side of their passage. No one questioned or challenged them for bring-ing humans into this place.

A way past the shoreside bazaar, Sgäile halted before an enormous elm. He pulled aside the door hanging and motioned them inside. Only Wynn, Magiere, Leesil, and Chap entered, and Sgäile remained in the doorway.

"Be comfortable," he said. "You are safe and my caste will make certain of it. But do not leave this dwelling without Osha or another I designate. I will send food and drink as quickly as possible."

Leesil stepped toward him, and his mouth was taut in anger. Before he uttered a word, Sgäile cut him off.

"Soon," he said, and his expression seemed troubled. "You will speak to Most Aged Father soon. But heed me, Léshil. Do not leave this dwelling until I come for you."

He released the curtain and was gone.

Magiere put her hand on Leesil's shoulder, then began pulling the chest off his back.

Wynn believed that Sgäile would keep his word, though Leesil's impatience was mounting. No words of comfort from her would do any good, so she looked about their new quarters.

The elm's interior was one room, though larger than the family space in Gleann's home. Soft cushions were stacked to one side along with a rolled-up felt carpet of cerulean blue. The floor was bare earth instead of moss. There were ledges growing from the tree walls for beds or seats with cream blankets of downy wool folded upon each. A wide curtain of gray-green, like the clothes of the Anmaglâhk, hung from a mounted oak rod across the room's back. Wynn pulled it aside and found a small stone tub akin to Gleann's.

"Our guest house has been well prepared," she said.

Leesil's amber eyes flashed as he turned on her. "It's a cell."

By early evening, Leesil paced the tree's interior, berating himself for his stupidity.

Magiere and Wynn were captives, and he had no one to blame but himself. A wooden tray piled with fruit and a water pitcher had been brought, but he didn't touch any of it. There was also a glass lantern, prelit, that sent an aroma of pine needles through their cell. Some of their baggage had been delivered—but not their weapons.

To make matters worse, Magiere watched him with that same silent tension on her face that she'd worn throughout their time in Venjètz. She sat vigil on him, waiting to see if he would lose himself again.

Chap was the only one who could walk out if he wished. No elf so far had interfered with the comings and goings of the majay-hì. But the dog just lay on the floor with his head on his paws.

Though Leesil seethed over their situation, it was mostly frustration. At least one of his companions might suggest something helpful. Were they any closer at all to finding Nein'a?

"What do you think happens next?" Magiere asked.

She sat on a wall shelf with one leg pulled up, and Leesil's frustration faded.

Magiere was just worried about him—about them all. She looked paler than usual, and the sleeves of her dark-yellow elven shirt were lightly marred from the journey. With her head tipped forward, black hair hung around her cheeks. He reached down and hooked her hand with two of his fingers.

"I don't know," he answered honestly. "Whatever comes, it'll depend on what this leader of theirs wants . . . this Most Aged Father. He put Sgäile through a great deal to bring us here, so I'd assume this meeting won't wait long."

"He wants something from you," Magiere whispered.

Leesil saw the vicious narrowing of her eyes and wondered if her irises flickered to black for an instant.

"Of course he does," he answered.

She watched him, probably wondering what reckless notion he had in his head.

"And that means he'll pay for it," Leesil added. "Perhaps he wants it badly enough to release my mother. It's been so many days since we left the mountains. I thought surely I'd find her by now . . . seen for myself that she's all right."

Magiere stood up suddenly, and Leesil flinched, expecting another tongue-lashing.

She slipped her arms around his waist. The studs of her hauberk clicked against the rings on his.

Chap got up with a warning rumble, and the doorway curtain swung aside as Sgäile stepped in.

"Come, Léshil," he said. "It is time."

"Alone?" Magiere said. "I don't think so."

The curtain lifted once more, and another anmaglâhk stood in the doorway without entering. Something about her put Leesil on edge.

She was slender like a willow, with thin lips and a narrow face, but her features were otherwise pure elven. Her hair was like the color of sun-bleached wheat and hung in slight waves.

This one wasn't as adept as Urhkar, or even Sgäile, at hiding her feelings. Her loathing of him was plain to the eyes. Leesil nearly felt it crawl on his skin like dry heat from a weaponer's forge.

It was different from Én'nish's personal and manic hatred. This woman took in the sight of Magiere touching him, and Wynn sitting on the ledge next to Chap, as if she would burn this long-nurtured tree just to cleanse it of any human taint.

"You will come," she said in Belaskian. "Now."

"He's not going anywhere," Magiere answered. "Your leader can come here to speak to him."

The look in the woman's eyes almost made Leesil back up and pull Magiere away. She said something to Sgäile in Elvish.

Sgäile stepped close to Leesil, leaning in and speaking softly. "Léshil, you must come. This is Fréthfâre, the hand of Most Aged Father. He cannot come to you, so Fréthfâre carries his . . . request that you come to him—as a courtesy. All will be made clear."

Leesil only half-trusted anything Sgäile said, for one could bend one's word without breaking it.

"And then I see my mother?" he asked.

Sgäile hesitated. "I cannot say. That is for Most Aged Father to decide."

Chap crossed the room in silence. He stared at this woman, Fréth, for so long that she finally looked down at him. A bit of uncertainty broke through her revulsion.

Chap lifted his head toward Leesil and barked once.

"All right," Leesil said. He ran his hand down Magiere's back. "Stay here and look out for Wynn."

Magiere grabbed his arm so tight it hurt. "No."

"Chap is coming with me," he said. "They won't . . . can't stop him from doing what he wants. I'll be back when I learn what this is all about."

She was frightened, and a scared Magiere was dangerous. Her fear pulled at him, but he couldn't stop now. If he let her keep arguing, fear would quickly shift to anger. He peeled her fingers from his arm and held her hand for a moment.

Fréth backed out through the curtain as if the sight disgusted her.

Sgäile pulled the curtain back again, waiting. As Leesil turned to leave, Magiere tightened her grip.

"You owe me a promise for a promise," she warned.

Leesil wondered what it meant until he glanced back to find that Magiere's eyes weren't on him. They were on Sgäile.

Sgäile glanced at Leesil and nodded firmly to her. "Always."

Magiere finally released Leesil's hand.

"I'll be back soon," he said, and slipped out.

He emerged on the outskirts of Crijheäiche again. Fréth had already moved off, and Sgäile urged him to follow. He couldn't help but notice how fluidly Fréth moved—just like his mother. She turned in the waning daylight to look down at Chap.

"Majay-hì?" she said. "In Crijheäiche?"

Sgäile spoke something brief in Elvish. Fréth's lips were pursed. His answer did not seem to satisfy her, but she walked on.

Leesil looked about, but there were no other dogs in sight. The majay-hì pack that followed the barge had only appeared now and then, always hesitant to come too close. Perhaps they had lived so long in a land where humans weren't tolerated that they were confused by those who walked with elves. But still, Fréth's question was odd.

Fréth led them away from the riverside, but they continued to pass through populated areas. Many amber eyes watched their passing. Some whispers reached Leesil's ears. He thought he heard someone say "Cuirin'nên'a." His gaze wandered so much that, when they came upon it, the oak tree seemed to rise out of nowhere in front of them.

Sitting in a wide mossy clearing, it was ringed by other domiciles a stone's throw away. Any one of them would have matched Gleann's home, but compared to the oak at the clearing's center, they appeared small and stunted. Its roots made the earth rise in ridges spreading out from its base. Its breadth would have matched six men laid end to end. It seemed impossible that it even existed. And its mass of branches and leaves rose beyond sight, nearly blotting out the sky.

Five anmaglâhk stood near it, and one stepped out, exposing himself to full view.

He was taller than Sgäile, with broad shoulders and a build that seemed too heavy for an elf. To Leesil, he looked rather like a human stretched to a height not of his race. But the man was purely elvish, from hair streaked with silver-gray among the whitish-blond to large amber eyes in a triangular face with—

Leesil stopped and planted himself firmly. Anger made his throat go dry.

Four scar lines angled down the man's forehead, jumping his right eye to continue through his cheek to the back of his jaw.

"Brot'an," Leesil whispered to himself. Memories burned inside his head.

In Darmouth's family crypt, Brot'an had whispered to him; he'd told him that the one elven skull among the warlord's bone trophies was his own mother's. Leesil had rushed Darmouth, ramming his curved bone knife through the warlord's throat, and then watched as the tyrant drowned in the blood flooding his lungs.

Brot'an had done it with nothing but Leesil's own guilt, turning it to anguish with a simple lie. Leesil had finished what this anmaglâhk had come to do—assassinate Lord Darmouth and start a bloodbath in the Warlands.

Leesil had taken one more life, just like the weapon he was. The one Brot'an had used.

Chap's rage mounted until it overwhelmed what he sensed from Leesil. Ears flattered, he pulled back his jowls and opened his jaws.

Brot'ân'duivé—Dog in the Dark. Deceiver!

Chap shook under taut muscles with fur rising across his neck.

Brot'an's white eyebrows knitted, bending the scars on his face.

It did not matter to Chap whether this one shared any feeling for Eillean. Brot'an had used Leesil like a tool and brought Nein'a back to be condemned and caged. This much and more Chap had learned when he had dipped into the tall elf's surfacing memories in Darmouth's crypt.

He should have never listened to Magiere—never let this man leave that place alive. He should have torn off Brot'an's scared face, there and then.

And now, here was Brot'an, waiting as Leesil came to the patriarch of the Anmaglâhk. How much had this assassin told his own kind of Leesil and Magiere?

The others near Brot'an moved a few steps toward Chap in surprise. One of them said, "Majay-hì?"

Chap reached out quickly from one to the next, searching for any surfacing memory. All he caught were images of majay-hì in the forest mingled with a few from various inhabited settlements.

He had learned from the memories of Lily and her pack that the majay-hì occasionally bore their young among elven communities. They wanted their children to be aware of and accustomed to the elves before they returned to life in the forest. Chap was uncertain why these four and even Brot'an found his presence here so baffling.

Then it struck him. Of all the forest packs these anmaglâhk had witnessed, none had ever seen a majay-hì in this place—in Crijheäiche.

Why?

He heard Fréthfâre's sharp voice but did not catch her words—all his attention returned to Brot'an.

Let instinct take all reason from him. Here and now, all he wanted was to tear into Brot'an.

But Chap held his ground. Where would that leave Leesil?

Brot'an stood his place with only a puzzled frown on his long, marred features. The four behind him took hesitant steps froward, two shifting to either side of Chap and just out of his lunging reach.

"Greimasg'äh?" one said, looking to Brot'an, but the elder elf gave no reply.

Chap had heard this word, though he did not know its meaning. At the docks, it had been used for Urhkar as well.

Sgäile dropped to one knee before Chap, holding his palms out.

"No," he said in Elvish. "No . . . violence . . . here."

He spoke with slow emphasis, as if to make certain Chap understood.

"Léshil, make him understand!" Sgäile added in Belaskian.

Brot'an's eyes shifted with keen interest at this strange demand. Chap held his ground.

"Is this the real reason you took my weapons?" Leesil asked, but it sounded more like an accusation.

"No," Sgäile answered. "But it is now just as good a reason. This is neither the place nor the way for whatever grievance you and the majay-hì have with Brot'ân'duivé."

Reluctantly, Chap agreed. He circled back around Leesil's legs, coming up beside him to face the others. Let the deceiver breathe for now.

As far as Chap was concerned, Brot'ân'duivé was dead, though the man did not yet know it.

An exclamation erupted from one of the other anmaglâhk. Chap followed the man's astonished gaze out between the domicile trees at the clearing's edge.

A white blur darted from one tree to another, reappearing halfway around the next trunk.

Lily peered out at Chap and looked hesitantly at the others.

Chap's rage softened at the sight of her. Without thinking, he yipped, hoping she would join him.

Lily shifted nervously. She took two steps toward him but then backed away, half-hiding behind a domicile tree.

Chap knew her reluctance to be near humans and often sensed her concern and puzzlement that he did so. But as he reached for any memories surfacing within her, an image of the central oak appeared in his mind.

Its doorway was but a dark hollow he could not see into, and the sight of it was coated in Lily's fear.

He turned his attention back to the Anmaglâhk as Brot'an raised an arm toward the tree and stepped out of the way.

"Go inside, Fréthfâre," he said in Belaskian. "Most Aged Father awaits." His face took on a more pleased expression. "Well met, Sgäilsheilleache. Your journey was swifter than expected. Come and tell me of it."

Sgäile hesitated. "I have taken guardianship for Léshil and his companions."

"And my word holds all others to your purpose," Brot'an said. "No one will touch him or his. You will come with me."

Sgäile seemed only half-satisfied, but relented. "Yes, Greimasg'äh."

Events were not playing out to Chap's liking, but he saw nothing he could do. He and Leesil were surrounded by their enemies for now. Fréthfâre headed for the behemoth tree, and he nudged Leesil forward, keeping himself between his companion and Brot'an.

Brot'an's head turned sharply and fixed upon a point at Chap's rear. Something sharp clapped on Chap's right hind leg. He whirled to snap but quickly stopped.

Lily held his leg firmly in her jaws. She tugged, trying to pull him, then let go and began barking wildly as she backed across the clearing.

Chap saw the center oak and its black hollow doorway in her thoughts. She wanted him to leave this place, but why? And how could he tell her that he could not do as she asked?

He barked twice at her and trotted toward the oak. Lily did not follow.

Fréthfâre pulled the doorway curtain aside, and Chap entered first into a large empty space within. The only fixture was a wide stairway of living wood to one side, but it led downward into the earth, not up as in Gleann's home.

Chap descended watchfully and emerged into a large earthen chamber. He stood in a hollow space below the massive oak. Thick roots arched down all its sides to support walls of packed dirt lined with embedded stones for strength. Glass lanterns hung from above, filling the space with yellowed twilight. In the chamber's middle was the trees vast center root. As large as a normal oak, it reached from ceiling to floor and into the earth.

Leesil stepped down beside Chap, his tan face paled by the sickly light. Leesil hated not having control, as did Chap, and they had long since lost hold of their own path.

Fréthfâre descended behind them as a thin voice filled the earthen chamber.

"Come to me . . . here."

It came from the wide center root.

Chap stepped through the earthen chamber, around the center root, and found an oval opening that at first had been too hard to spot in its earth-stained wood. Leesil hesitated, but Chap inched forward to peer within. He froze at what awaited them.

The oak's vast center root held a smaller room more dimly lit than the outer chamber surrounding it. And its inner walls appeared alive even in its stillness.

Hundreds of tinier root tendrils ran through its curved walls like taupe-colored veins in dark flesh. The walls curved smoothly into a floor of the same make, and Chap was reluctant to even place his paw on its surface. Soft teal cushions rested before a pedestal flowing out of the floor's living wood. The back wall's midpoint flowed inward as well to support it.

Wall and floor protrusions melded together into a bower . . . or was it more a crude cradle? Among the clumps of fresh moss therein, two eyes stared out from a decrepit form.

Once he would have been tall, but he now curled fetal with his head twisted toward his visitors.

Thin, dry white hair trailed from his pale scalp around a neck and shoulders barely more than shriveled skin draped over frail bones. His triangular elven face was little more than jutting angles of bone beneath skin grayed by want of daylight. Deep cracks covered features around eyes sunken deeply into their large slanted sockets. His amber irises had lost nearly all color. All that remained was a milky yellow tint surrounded by whites with thread-thin red blood vessels. Cracked and yellowed fingernails jutted from the shriveled and receding skin of his skeletal fingers. His once peaked ears were reduced to wilted remnants.

"Father," Fréthfâre said.

She stood away from Leesil, bowing to the ancient elf. The old one ignored her and studied Chap and Leesil.

"Majay-hì," he said in a reedy voice. "I have not had such a visit in long years." He raised a hand to Leesil with slow effort. "Come closer . . . my son. Let me see you."

Chap reached for the memories of Most Aged Father.

He saw nothing. Not one image rose in the old one's mind. Chap remained poised and focused as he entered behind Leesil, and Fréthfâre followed.

Leesil tensed beside Chap as he took his first clear look at their host.

"I see your mother in you," said Most Aged Father. "And I know she trained you in the ways of our caste. You are Anmaglâhk."

"Not in your oldest dreams," Leesil croaked, finding his voice. "Where is she?"

At that question, Chap caught the flicker of a glade in Most Aged Father's mind. Before it vanished, he saw a tall elven woman seated upon the grass. Beside her was a basket of moth cocoons, which she had been using to spin strands for raw *shéot'a* cloth.

Chap swallowed. Nein'a. But he caught no hint of where she was held.

"She is with us," Most Aged Father said, and lowered his hand. "She is a traitor to her people . . . to your people, Léshil. You are Anmaglâhk, so I have brought you here to help her."

"Stop saying that!" Leesil answered. "I am not your son. You're nothing to me. Release her, and I'll take her far from here, where she'll never trouble you again."

Most Aged Father nodded, his head rubbing the moss on which he lay. A stale scent like dust flooded Chap's nostrils.

"In good time," he said. "First you must do a service for your people . . . yes, you are of the people, and you would not turn your back on your own. Not on your kin and blood."

Leesil's voice rose. "Make some sense, old man! What do you want from me?"

Fréthfâre spun toward Leesil, as if she wished to strike him down. Most Aged Father remained calm and unaffected.

"There are others like your mother." A long silence followed before he went on. "She was misled—misguided—so she could not have acted alone. Your birth was a violation of our ways, but that is no fault of yours. But the idea of . . . a half-blood child . . . it could not have come from her. No, she was misled . . . yes?"

Chap saw a flash in Most Aged Father's mind—another woman, an anmaglâhk. The resemblance to Nein'a would be clear to anyone, though her face was harder, her eyes colder.

Eillean.

"My sole concern is to protect our people," Most Aged Father continued. "Now you are honored to serve them as well. Most of the Anmaglâhk are true in their hearts. But a few . . . just a few have fallen from our way, like your mother. They will see you as the son of Cuirin'nên'a. They will seek you out. Find them, Léshil—help me shield our people—and I will release Cuirin'nên'a to you."

Chap could not help looking up at Leesil. This offer was nothing more than a trade of flesh, the dissidents for Leesil's mother.

Sweat now matted Leesil's blond hairs to the sides of his face, but his expression was guarded.

"Let me see her first."

"No," Most Aged Father answered softly.

"Then you get nothing from me. I talk to her first . . . then you and I might come to an arrangement."

Chap could not believe what he heard.

Most Aged Father seeded violence among humans. Did the Fay know of this ancient elf hidden in this shielded land? And if so, why had they never spoken of him? So concerned with keeping Magiere from the enemy's reach, had they no interest in why Leesil had been born and trained?

And now Most Aged Father sought to use Leesil for his own purpose, and Leesil had half-agreed.

Chap stifled a growl.

"We are not bargaining here," Most Aged Father said. "But there is no need for haste. I have given you so much to think on. I understand that you need time to consider. In the end you will do what is correct for your people . . . as I do. Go now. I will call for you again soon."

"I'm not going anywhere." Leesil's voice rose with every word. "My mother couldn't possibly be a threat to you now. Your Anmaglâhk . . . they may look at you like some saint, but I'm not one of them. And with all those like Sgäile, following you blindly . . . what could you possibly fear from a few dissenters?"

As these words left Leesil's lips, a rapid barrage of memories emerged in Most Aged Father's mind and assaulted Chap's awareness. The room went dark before his eyes.

Out of the darkness came black scaled coils—circling and writhing.

Chap's legs began to buckle.

He heard screams as the battlefield took focus.

Bodies of elves and dwarves and humans of varied race lay mingled among those of other creatures that walked on two or four legs. All mutilated and left to rot beneath a dying sun.

Two seas of the living had crashed together on this open plain of rolling hills. The battle's remains were so mangled and mixed that Chap could not tell which direction either had come from. Broken armor and lances and every other thing were spattered in blood that had already begun to dry or soak into the earth. There were so many . . .

So many that Chap saw not a blade of grass for as far as his sight could reach.

The growing stench thickened until it choked him.

On the ground at his feet—for he saw elven boots of forest green suede, and not his own paws—lay the broken body of what the humans called a goblin. Two-thirds a man's height, these pack animals walked on two legs with cunning enough to use a weapon as well as their teeth and claws.

Wild spotted fur covered its apish body and caninelike head of shortened snout and muzzle. It had clothed itself in motley pieces of armor, likely stolen from the dead in previous battles. Foam-matted jaws hung open, and its tongue sagged in the dirt. Dead eyes with sickening yellow irises stared unblinking at Chap's feet.

A jagged rent in its throat exposed the ends of its severed windpipe.

Perhaps one of its own had turned on it in their frenzy for slaughter. There was strangely too little blood on the ground beneath it.

Dusk rapidly closed in on Chap.

At first he noticed stars along the horizon. Then they moved.

Not stars, but glints from some light . . . on black scales that writhed all around him . . .

"Chap!"

Strong hands gripped his shoulders until his forepaws almost lifted from the floor. Leesil knelt before him, glistening face wary and awash in concern.

"Chap, what's wrong?"

Chap lifted his head, his legs still shuddering, and looked over Leesil's shoulder. Most Aged Father watched him in suspicion. He whined and pushed his head into Leesil's chest.

"You are dismissed," Most Aged Father said. "Leave now. We will talk again."

Leesil carefully released Chap and stood up. "Until I see Nein'a . . . don't bother sending for me."

He turned and, with a brush of fingertips across Chap's neck, strode out for the stairs, not waiting for Fréthfâre to usher him out. Chap did not look back to the old elf as he followed on unsteady paws.

The great war was but a myth to some. What he had seen and felt in that flash of the old elf's memory left him shaken.

The humans called it the Forgotten History . . . or just the Forgotten. Some believed this war had covered the known world.

And Most Aged Father had been there.

Most Aged Father settled in his moss-padded bower, neither worried nor distressed. The meeting with Léshil had progressed as expected. After so long a life, there was little he could not easily anticipate.

Léshil would struggle in anger and denial, until he realized no other choice remained. He could not leave this land without permission. He could not stay indefinitely. He could not find his mother without assistance.

He would realize the truth soon enough and accept it.

Most Aged Father was patient. The names of the dissenters would be uncovered. They would join Nein'a, each in his or her own separate solitude unto the end of their days. And he would turn his full attention to the human masses once again.

Only one thing troubled him. He had not anticipated the majay-hì.

None of its kind ever came here. He knew their history better than anyone, for in the end days he had fought beside a few of the born-Fay, who had
come into flesh in the war against the Enemy. But their descendants never
neared this place. He felt no blame toward them. No matter their ancestry,
they did not understand why he clung to life for so long.

The Enemy only slumbered and would return.

It would always return.

But this majay-hì with Léshil had walked into his dwelling and looked
him in the eyes.

Most Aged Father would learn more of this one. He did not care for being
in the dark on such matters. In his long years, he'd learned that nothing ever
happened without purpose.

But the conversation with Léshil had exhausted him. He placed withered
hands against the wood of his home, his life's blood. Slowly, the forest's life
flowed toward him. In recent years, it took more to sustain him another day.
His moments of strength and vitality shortened ever so slightly.

His Anmaglâhk thought him omniscient and eternal. They honored his
sacrifice for remaining among them rather than joining their ancestors in
rest. They believed his presence could reach to all living things that thrived
and grew from the earth. But this was no longer true.

He could reach out through the trees and hear words spoken anywhere in
this land, but long distances now took great effort. And remaining aware of
just one place at time was all he managed. It drained him quickly.

Today it was necessary. Today he must hear what was said between Léshil
and his companions.

Some time had passed, and likely Fréthfâre had returned Léshil to the
quarters prepared for him and his companions. Comfortable quarters but
lacking in any luxury or pleasing distraction that might make waiting easier.
Lacking enough to keep Léshil always on edge and wanting to leave.

Most Aged Father closed his eyes, his feeble hands still resting upon the
bower's living wood, and reached out through the roots of the trees. Through
the wood and leaves of a domicile elm, he heard Léshil's voice.

CHAPTER TEN

Magiere watched the light wane below the doorway curtain's hem as dusk settled in. All she could do was wait and listen, but she heard no footfalls outside.

Where was Leesil?

She paced their one-room quarters, glancing at the curtain each time she drew near it. Even if she got by Osha or whoever stood post outside, she had little chance of finding Leesil. And she no longer had her falchion or even the dagger she'd made Wynn carry.

The strange vibration in her bones returned. It had faded to an almost unnoticeable level once they'd boarded the barge. Here in this place of the Anmaglâhk, it built in her flesh once again. It made her even more anxious to take Leesil and run from this land by any passage they could find.

She finally sat and watched Wynn writing out one enlarged Elvish letter after another upon a piece of Gleann's paper.

"This will not be as quick as the talking hide," Wynn said with frustration. "Chap will have to spell out every word. Another hide would be better, or something less fragile than paper."

"At least we can to talk to him," Magiere said.

For once she took comfort in Wynn's sudden bursts of chatter. Wynn carefully scribed and blew dry two pages of symbols and pulled out another blank sheet.

"I did not expect their dialect to be so different," Wynn said, "until I heard these elves speak. It is no wonder Chap and I have problems communicating . . . beyond his frustration with language. If only I could dip into that messy head of his, in the same way he sees and uses other people's memories."

Magiere didn't answer. No one had come to their quarters after Sgäile took Leesil away. She hardly considered him or his companions to be friends, but it was strange that not even Leanâlhâm had looked in on them.

"Do not start pacing again," Wynn said. "If the elves wanted Leesil dead, none of us would have made it this far . . . nor would Sgäile have gone through so much to guard us. Our bodies would have vanished like any other curious human who came looking for this land."

How blunt the little scholar had become. A far cry from the soft-spoken sage Magiere had met back in Bela.

"I know," Magiere said. "It's just that lately Leesil has been so—"

"Erratic, pig-headed, idiotic, obsessive—"

"Yes, yes, all right," Magiere interrupted. A far cry indeed.

Wynn smirked slightly, her strange new stylus scratching out the next symbol. Just how many letters were there in Elvish?

Magiere hadn't bathed, wanting to be ready the instant Leesil and Chap returned. But she did change her clothing, tossing aside the elven attire for a pair of dark breeches and a loose white shirt. It was warm enough to leave off the wool pullover, but she had strapped on her hauberk again. It made her feel more secure—more like herself.

She closed her eyes. When all of this was over and done, perhaps Leesil might find his old self again. The one she'd fallen in love with so reluctantly at first. And if he didn't—she still couldn't see any day ahead of her without him.

The doorway curtain wafted inward, bulging up from the ground, and Chap slipped in under its hem. The curtain swung aside, and Leesil entered right behind the dog. Magiere was on her feet before the fabric settled into place.

"Are you all right? Did you see your mother?"

One look at his face answered both questions.

"What happened?" Wynn asked, and set aside paper and quill.

"He wants a bargain with me," Leesil answered flatly, and Chap issued a low rumble. "Most Aged Father wants the names of every anmaglâhk who might have a connection to my mother. If I get him those names, he'll release her."

Of all unsettling possibilities, this wasn't among the imagined worries that had run through Magiere's head.

"What makes him think any of his butchers would talk to you?"

"Because I'm Nein'a's son." He looked up, eyes sad and distant. "But he's lying. No matter what I do, I don't believe he'll release Nein'a—or us. You should've seen him. . . ."

His eyes squinted and his mouth tightened as though he'd tasted something stale and bitter.

"Why go to such lengths?" Wynn asked. "By bringing you here, he has clearly alienated his people, even some of his caste. He must be desperate."

"Who better to hide from the Anmaglâhk than an anmaglâhk?" Leesil retorted. "I think he's already exhausted his own means. I'm guessing my mother's refused to tell him anything in all these years. And I think he suspected my grandmother, but she's beyond his reach now."

"Chap, careful!" Wynn snapped. "I am not done. . . . You are slobbering all over the pages!"

Chap was pulling Wynn's papers off the ledge seat, and Wynn couldn't keep up with him. He dropped them on the ground, separating the sheets with his nose, and began pawing the Elvish symbols.

"Ancient Enemy," Wynn translated.

They'd heard this from him before outside of Venjètz, when he'd tried to explain that it was Eillean's skull, not Nein'a's, that Leesil carried. And that Neina, Eillean, and perhaps even Brot'an, had some hand in a conspiracy surrounding Leesil's birth and training.

Chap continued, and Wynn shook her head in puzzlement. "He spelled out . . . 'il'Samar' . . . or as close as he could."

The name snapped a memory in Magiere's head.

She and Chap had closed on Ubâd within a forest clearing near the abandoned village of Apudâlsat. Enormous spectral coils of black scales had appeared in the dark between the wet, moss-laden trees.

"That's the name Ubâd cried out before . . ." Magiere couldn't finish.

Looking at Chap with that memory in her head made her shiver. The dog had gone into a frenzy at the sight of those coils, which had seemingly come to Ubâd's plea. They didn't answer the old man, but instead spoke to her, Magiere, in a whispering hiss of a voice.

Sister of the dead . . . lead on.

And then Chap had torn out the necromancer's throat.

"What do you know about this?" Magiere asked of Wynn.

"It is definitely Sumanese. 'Samar' is obscure, meaning 'conversation in the dark,' or something secretly passed. And 'il' is a prefix for a proper noun . . . a title or name."

Wynn shook her head with uncertainty and perhaps a taint of fright.

"Back in Bela, Domin Tilswith showed me and Chane . . . a copy of an ancient parchment believed to be from the Forgotten. I cannot remember the exact Sumanese wording, but it mentioned something called 'the night voice.' Perhaps . . . from what you told us of Ubâd in that clearing . . ."

Magiere wasn't listening anymore. The name that Ubâd had cried out echoed in her mind. And then came a piece of the vision that her mother's ghost had shown to her.

Her so-called half brother, Welstiel, walked alone in the courtyard of their father's keep. As Magelia came upon him, he whispered to himself in the dark . . . or in answer to a voice no one else heard.

Chap struggled with how much he should tell them—and how to manage complex ideas with only a few sheets of large Elvish letters. The idea that Most Aged Father had been alive during the ancient war seemed too much for the moment. There was no telling what Leesil, or even Magiere or Wynn, might do in this strained moment if they knew.

Leesil and Wynn were little help with their tangled debate and speculations, and Magiere seemed lost within her own thoughts. For now, it was enough that they learned of an enemy that was known by many names in many places—and that Magiere was never as far from its reach as she might assume. Chap knew better.

As he was about to bark for their attention, the room blurred slightly before his eyes. It was more like a waver in the living wood of the wall. Then it was gone an instant before he fixed upon it.

Chap shook his head and looked about. Nothing had changed, yet he had felt something. Elation and then anxiety rose in him.

Had his kin finally come? But surely not in the presence of others, especially those in his charge?

They would not reveal themselves so explicitly to mortals. He sensed no echo within his own spirit that marked their presence and shook off the strange sensation. There was nothing here, and he was being foolish. Even so, the disruption left him restless. He padded to the outer doorway and stuck his head through its curtain.

Osha looked down curiously at him from the doorway's far side. Chap ignored him, and searched the trees.

There was no sign of Lily, and she had not been waiting when he emerged from Most Aged Father's home. Something about this place—and that one great tree—frightened her. It frightened all the majay-hì, and they would not come near. Lily had only come to try to drag him from it.

He heard a soft whine and raised his ears.

The barest hint of creamy white showed beneath a bush of lilacs beyond one domicile tree. Between its lower branches, two crystalline eyes stared back across the open space at Chap.

Lily hid where she might not be noticed. For all her fear of this place, she had come back and silently watched for him.

Chap glanced up at Osha, but the young elf had not noticed her. He wanted to run beside Lily through the wild forest and let nature's ebb help him decide what course to follow.

He knew he should stay and help his companions consider this shackling bargain with which Most Aged Father tried to bind Leesil. Magiere and Wynn were also in danger here as unwanted outsiders. And in some way, great or small, this was all bound together by the hidden whereabouts of Nein'a. Chap's companions desperately needed to gain some element of power here.

Nein'a's location was the crux of it all.

If they only knew where she was imprisoned, that would remove a good deal of Most Aged Father's hold on Leesil.

Chap heard Wynn half-shout behind him, "This is futile! We will not figure this all out tonight."

"It's all we have to work with," Leesil growled back. "And I'm tired of waiting."

"Stop it, both of you," Magiere said. "Leesil, come take a bath and let it rest for now. I can't even think anymore."

Chap looked out to Lily hiding among the white lilacs. He caught her memories of the two of them running with the pack—and alone by themselves.

Unlike her, Chap could read and even recall and use another's memories within line of sight, but he could not send Lily his own without touching her. There was something he must tell her . . . something she and her pack needed to help him do.

He had no time to tell his companions and have them argue over it.

Osha still watched him, so Chap turned away from Lily as he slipped out.

He trotted down toward the riverside bazaar, hoping she would circle through the forest and follow. When he cut between a canvas pavilion and a stall made of ivy walls, she was waiting for him.

Lily slid her muzzle along his, until they each rested their head upon the other's neck.

Chap rolled his face into her fur and recalled Lily's own memories of her time with her siblings under the watchful eyes of her mother. He sent his memory of tall Nein'a and a young Leesil together.

He was not as adept as her kind with this memory speech, and his limitation was frustrating. He had "listened" in as Lily and one of the steel-gray twins did this. Memories came and went in such a quick cascade. Whenever she spoke to him, the images were slow and gentle in simple sights, sounds, and scents. She understood he needed time to learn their ways and always showed him patience.

Chap repeated the parallel memories of mother and child. This time, when he called the one of Nein'a and young Leesil, he pulled away Leesil's image, leaving Nein'a alone. He then recalled Lily's memories of her pack hunting in the forest, and did his best to mingle it with his own memory of the tall elven woman.

The last image he sent was one stolen from Most Aged Father—a memory that had now become his own. Cuirin'nên'a, in a shimmering *shéot'a* wrap, sat in a glade clearing beside a basket of cocoons.

Lily grew still beside him. She sent him no memory-talk. She nudged his muzzle with her own and took off, out of the settlement and into the forest.

Chap raced after as Lily cut loose a howl. Somewhere in the distant trees, the pack answered.

"Where's Chap?" Wynn called out.

She sat alone on her ledge bed with the occasional splash coming from the bath area at the room's rear.

"At least one of us can get out of here for a stretch," Magiere grumbled from behind the curtain.

Wynn was a bit uncomfortable with Magiere and Leesil back there together, with only that gray-green fabric providing privacy. And with all the arguing over Most Aged Father's bargain and Chap's few troubling words . . .

She climbed to her feet. "Why would Chap slip out without telling us?"

"Who knows?" Leesil called back. "Stick your head out and call him, but don't go wandering about."

Wynn left the two of them to talk—or whatever they did in there. She pulled the outer doorway curtain aside and looked out, but Chap was nowhere in sight. Neither were Sgäile or even Osha. She stepped out for a better view.

There were no elves in sight, and Chap was gone. Both worried her.

Wynn took a few more steps, looking up and down the lane of cultivated trees. To her far left she could just make out the silent and still remains of the dockside bazaar.

"Chap?" she called in a harsh whisper.

Chap rushed into a gully behind Lily. Ahead, the pack waited by a tiny stream. The black-gray elder lifted his head from lapping water gurgling over stones.

Chap had not expected the pack to be so near, but they must have gathered to wait on Lily. As he approached beside her, the majay-hì circled about with huffs and switching tails, one by one touching heads as they passed her or him.

Spry bodies surrounded him with warmth. One yearling colored much like himself charged playfully and butted Chap with his head. Chap shifted aside.

He rejoiced in their welcome, but urgency kept him from languishing. He was neither certain how they could help nor how he could ask. Lily seemed to understand but would the others? On impulse, he pressed his head to hers and again showed her the stolen memory of Nein'a's hidden prison.

Lily stayed against him, listening until he finished, then darted away.

She brushed heads with the large black elder. An instant later, the male turned and touched a passing steel-gray female, the other twin. The rest joined in, and Chap watched the swirling dance of memory-talk as it passed through the pack.

The elder's crystal blue eyes turned upon Chap.

The old one tilted his gray muzzle, and then hopped the stream and scrambled up the gully's embankment more fleetly than his age would suggest.

Lily trotted back to Chap and pressed her head to his. He saw a memory of the two of them resting beneath a leaning cedar after a long run. It seemed he was to wait—but for what?

Chap's frustration mounted, still wondering if the pack truly understood what he needed.

A rolling, moaning howl like a bellow carried through the forest. It came from the direction where the elder had disappeared.

Lily brushed Chap's head with a memory of running as the rest of the pack charged off. He followed her up the embankment and through the woods. When he cleared the close trees, he saw the elder.

The black-gray majay-hì stood on a massive cracked boulder jutting from a hillside of sparse-leafed elms. The pack remained below, and he appeared to be waiting and watching for something. The elder glanced upslope over his shoulder, and Chap stepped back from the boulder's base to see.

Branches of a hillside elm appeared to move as if drifting through the trees. Two eyes high above the ground sparked in the half-moon's light and came downslope into clear sight.

Head high, the silver-gray deer descended, coming up beside the grizzle-jawed old majay-hì. Its tineless curved antlers rose to a height no man or elf could reach. The shimmer of its long-haired coat turned to pure white along its throat and belly. Its eyes were like those of the majay-hì, clear blue and crystalline.

The deer slowly lowered its head with a turn of its massive neck.

Lily nudged Chap, pushing him forward.

Chap did not understand. Was he to go to this creature?

She shoved him again and then darted around the boulder's side. She stood waiting, and Chap loped after her. Before he caught up, Lily headed upslope, and he followed. At the height where stone met the earth slope, she stood aside and lifted her muzzle toward the silver deer.

Chap hesitated. What did this have to do with finding Nein'a?

Lily pressed against him. Along with a memory echo of the tall elven woman he had first shown her, Lily showed him something more—a memory of the pack elder touching heads with one of these crystal-eyed deer.

Chap froze as the deer swung its head toward him.

He could not have imagined this creature might communicate in the same way as the pack. A tingling presence washed over him as he peered into the deer's eyes.

It felt so vague . . . like one of his kin off at a distance. And yet not quite like them.

The majay-hì were descended from the first born-Fay, born into flesh within wolves. Over many generations, the majay-hì had become the "touched" guardians of these lands.

But there were others, it seemed, as Chap had almost forgotten.

Within this deer, the trace of its ancestry was stronger than in the majay-hì, the lingering of born-Fay who had taken flesh in the form of deer and elk.

Chap crept forward to stand below the tall creature—this touched child of his own kin. It stretched out one foreleg and bent the other, until its head came low enough to reach his. Chap pressed his forehead to the deer's, smelling its heavy musk and breath marked by a meal of wild grass and sunflowers. He recalled the memories of Nein'a that he had shared with Lily.

The deer shoved Chap away, nearly knocking him off his feet. It stood silent and waiting.

What had he done wrong?

Lily slid her head in next to his, muzzle against muzzle. Images—and sounds—filled his mind.

A majay-hì howling in the dark. An elven boy calling to another. Singing birds, jabbering *fra'cise*, and the indignant screech of the *tâshgâlh* he had trailed out of the mountain tunnels.

Chap grasped the common thread. The deer wanted a sound. He approached as it lowered its head once more.

With the image of Nein'a in the clearing, Chap called forth a memory of her voice . . . and that of any who had ever spoken her name.

Nein'a . . . Cuirin'nên'a . . . Mother . . .

Wynn scurried around a domicile tree closest to the forest's edge. She still did not know why there was no one on guard outside, and she could not find

Chap anywhere. But as she turned to go back before being discovered, she heard footsteps.

She ducked low into hiding behind a tree, hoping whoever it was would just pass onward. As she leaned carefully out, she never made it far enough to see.

Wynn's vision spun blackly on a wave of nausea.

Her legs buckled, and she slumped down against the tree's base, clinging to its bulging roots as she covered her mouth and tried not to gag. Bisselberries and smoked fish rose in her throat from the evening meal, and the combined taste turned sour.

The loud buzz of an insect or crackling rustle of a leaf in the wind filled her head.

There were no insects and not even a breeze around her in the dark.

Wynn had not heard these in her mind for more than a moon. The last time was at the border of the Warlands.

Somewhere out in the forest, Chap now called to the Fay.

It had all started with a ritual in Droevinka, when she tried to make herself see the Spirit element that permeated all things. She had been trying to track an undead for Magiere, and then could not end the magic coursing through her flesh. Chap had to cleanse the mantic sight from her. But on the border at Soladran, it began to return in unexpected ways. She heard the buzz of leaf-winged insects whenever Chap communed with his kin.

Wynn swallowed her food back down, trying to quiet her gagging breaths. She braced for the onslaught of Chap's kin answering back in a chorus of leaf-wings that would make her head ache and the world whirl before her eyes.

It never came. Only one leaf-wing buzzed in her mind. The sound began to shape into . . .

Nein'a . . . Cuirin'nên'a . . . Mother . . .

A chill ran over Wynn's skin.

Words? They came in the Elvish dialect of this land. Beneath those were the same echoed in Belaskian and in her own tongue of Numanese. One voice spoke in many tongues at the same time, all words with the same meaning. Again, no chorus answered back.

Who did Chap call out to? Had he found Leesil's mother so close by? He would never try to commune with her—it would not work. To Chap's own knowledge, Wynn was the only one who had ever eavesdropped on him while communing with his kin. And she had never heard words before.

The buzz faded from her mind, leaving only a lingering ache.

But she had clearly heard those words.

There was no time to ponder another disturbing change in her unwanted gift. Chap was out in the forest, seeking Nein'a, and Wynn could not let him go on his own. How did he think he would speak with Nein'a, even if he found her prison?

Wynn braced on the tree's trunk and worked her way to her feet. She looked out into the wild and panic set in.

She could not navigate the forest without someone to lead her. It did not want her . . . a human. Even traveling with the others, it had tried to make her lost. Leesil, with his half-elven blood, had to concentrate to escape the forest's influence.

For once, Wynn wished the burden of mantic sight would come. But unpleasant as it was, it only came to her erratically. Once, it had overwhelmed her while she was alone with Chap, her fingers deep in his fur.

Wynn forced down fear until she reached calm. She closed her eyes, recalling all the sensations she had felt in that moment alone with Chap. She sank into memory until it blocked out all else.

Chap had sat before her, staring into her eyes. The room turned shadowy beneath the overlaid off-white mist just shy of blue. It permeated everything like a second view of the room on top of her normal sight, showing where the element of Spirit was strong or weak. Chap was the only thing she saw as one image, one whole shape.

His fur glistened like a million hazy threads of white silk, and his eyes scintillated like crystals held before the sun.

Wynn opened her eyes, and her food lurched up her throat once more.

Blue-white mist permeated all things of the forest. She felt so sick inside that it dampened any relief at her success.

Wynn stepped into the forest, and the trees began to look the same all around.

She turned too quickly, searching for the way she had come. The world spun in a dizzying blur. Breath pounded from her lungs when she hit the ground on her side, and she struggled up to her hands and knees.

"Only the mist . . . see only Spirit," Wynn whispered.

She tried to ignore the trees' true shapes and focus only on the permeating glimmer of Spirit in all things. Nausea sharpened, but as she turned her head, a sense of place became clearer.

Wynn saw glimmering silhouettes of trees and bushes, one overlaying the next into the distance, like silent blue-white ghosts in stillness. And beyond was a cluster of bright spots far off.

They moved, circling about each other like fireflies in the night. Three were higher above the rest, and one of those was larger than the others. A fourth glimmer separated from the largest one and shone in a sharp brilliant white.

Chap.

Wynn knew it was him. She scrambled on all fours to the nearest tree, pulled herself up, and stumbled toward him as her beacon.

Fully dressed again, Leesil pulled the bathing area's curtain aside enough to step out.

The press of Magiere's body in the hot bath still lingered on his skin. He loved her, but would she still love him when she realized he was only a thing to be used for killing? How long before she could no longer face what he really was? He would have to let her go, if that was her choice.

Knowledge of the pain yet to come felt like almost an illness in his body.

He wondered why she kept shaking slightly while immersed in the hot water.

He'd asked if she was all right. She hesitated, saying it was nothing more than all this mess they were in. Leesil knew better, but battling with Magiere was too much to face. He'd rather have one more quiet moment in her arms.

She wasn't sleeping well either, and ate too little each day. Yet she showed no more fatigue than himself, perhaps less.

"There has to be some way to get around Most Aged Father," Magiere said behind him, pulling her boots on.

Leesil wasn't really listening. Bowls of cold vegetable stew and a pitcher of water sat to one side of the room's floor. Wynn's scribbled sheets still lay on the ground where Chap had left them.

"Where's Wynn?" he asked.

"Probably at the door, looking for Chap," Magiere answered, and pulled the bath curtain fully aside. "She won't be satisfied until . . ."

Magiere looked about the empty room, lips still parted in unfinished words. Her breath drew in sharply before she snapped, "That little idiot!"

Leesil headed straight for the outer doorway. He swatted the curtain aside and looked out. There was no one on guard. Or had Osha gone with Wynn to look for Chap?

Magiere stepped past him as he looked off through the domicile trees. Then he glanced down toward the distant dockside bazaar. Among the structures there, from canvas tents entwined in briar and roses to the rising platforms in one wide walnut tree, there was no sign of Wynn or Chap.

Leesil heard footfalls coming his way.

Osha walked along with a soft smile as he studied an open cloth in his palm. Nestled in the cloth were small brown and cream lumps. He picked one and popped it in his mouth, not even looking up.

Leesil ignored the young elf and called out, "Wynn . . . Chap?"

Only then did Osha raise startled eyes.

"Stop!" he said, quickening his pace. "Stay. No leave."

"Where were you?" Leesil snapped.

Stunned at the demand, Osha quickly closed the distance to Leesil.

"I bring sweets," he began, stumbling over his Belaskian. "Honey cooked on nuts . . . for to give comfort. All you will like."

Leesil wanted to slap the nuts from the witless elf's hand. While this young whelp abandoned his post for dessert, Wynn had slipped off after Chap . . . wherever that dog had gone now.

"Get Sgäile," Magiere growled at Osha. "Wynn is gone . . . get him now!"

Osha shoved Leesil aside and peered into the tree. He turned about, panic-stricken, and pointed at Leesil as he backed away.

"Stay," he said, then turned at a run.

Leesil noticed lights all about him, spilling from doorways as curtains were pulled aside. Here and there, elves peered out at the noise. One or two even stepped from their homes.

Magiere wasn't looking at them, and Leesil saw her irises blacken. She shook visibly, though it wasn't cold, even for night. She was letting her dhampir nature rise enough to widen her night sight and search between the settlement's trees and brush.

"We have to find Wynn," she whispered, "before any of these people catch her wandering about."

"Just wait," Leesil warned. "We're no better off if we do the same as her."

"And what if she followed Chap into the forest?"

"Again, we're no better off," Leesil argued. "Even I have to think hard not to lose my way out there."

"I don't," she snapped at him.

The harsh reminder made him wonder over her strange symptoms of late.

"That's where she is," Magiere said, lifting her chin toward the open forest beyond the domicile trees. "She followed Chap . . . out there."

"She's not that stupid," Leesil replied. "Curious to a fault, maybe, but she knows she'd just get lost."

"Not if she caught Chap quickly enough." Magiere's anger intensified in her features. "He went looking for the pack . . . yes, and she just had to see the majay-hì for herself. I could kick that curiosity right out of her skull!"

A tall form came running through the wide trees.

Sgäile sprinted up, wearing a long white gown to his bare feet. Deep green oak leaf patterns were stitched around the split collar. His hair hung loose and wild around his long face, as if he'd just risen from bed. Osha came behind him, looking again like he was in serious trouble.

Accompanying them were two anmaglâhk Leesil hadn't seen before, both in the full dress of their caste.

"Do you know where your companion might have gone?" Sgäile asked immediately.

"We're not sure, but—" Leesil began.

"Get my weapons," Magiere cut in. "She's out there . . . in the forest."

Sgäile ignored her demand. "Why? A human would not last long, alone in our land. She will lose her way immediately."

All this delay frustrated Leesil. "She may have gone after Chap . . . if she thought he was headed for the other majay-hì."

Sgäile's lingering patience broke. "A pack will not tolerate a lone human wandering out there."

For an instant, Leesil was speechless.

"I kept your supervision to a minimum, wishing not to make you feel like prisoners." Sgäile glanced once at Osha, who flinched. "I trusted that all of you would have sense enough to follow my instructions. That is now finished."

Sgäile whipped about, growling at the two anmaglâhk. He turned on

Osha again as the pair stepped around him, one toward Leesil and the other closing on Magiere.

"*Tâshgheâlhi Én'nish!*" he snapped. "*Mé feumasij foras äiché âyâgea.*"

Osha took off running.

"What about Én'nish?" Leesil asked.

Her name was the only word he picked out. The anmaglâhk closest to him shoved him back toward the tree's doorway, and Leesil set his footing in resistance.

"I merely wish to know her whereabouts," Sgäile answered. "Go inside and stay there!"

The instant Sgäile's other companion reached for Magiere, and the only warning Leesil got out was "Don't—"

She slammed her fist into the elf's face with such speed that he lurched over backward, one foot slipping up from the ground. As his back struck the earth, he rolled away in retreat, coming up unsteady and so shaken he nearly lost his footing again. Blood ran from one narrow nostril and the side of his mouth.

The one near Leesil shifted his weight, a stiletto already in his hand.

"We're going after Wynn," Magiere said to Sgäile, her breath coming long and hard. "With you . . . without you . . . through you. What's your word worth now?"

Leesil didn't like how she was handling this, but it was too late to stop her. All he could do was back her up. If Én'nish was loose and heard about Wynn, what might she do for vengeance if she couldn't get to him?

"You should've watched that murderous bitch," Magiere warned. "If she gets anywhere near Wynn . . ."

"It'll end any hope of agreement with your patriarch," Leesil added. "I'll have no part of the search for his dissidents."

Sgäile's attention shifted instantly to Leesil—in open confusion. Could it be that he didn't know of the bargain Most Aged Father tried to strike? Was he even aware his own caste wasn't as unified as he believed?

"We can get on with it," Leesil continued, "or we can have it out right here. But it'll cost you to keep us back . . . if you can."

Sgäile stood in angry indecision, eyes shifting between Leesil and Magiere.

Leesil slowly reached for Magiere's arm. She jerked away but settled back, waiting. He just hoped she kept her self-control, as he had one more thing to attend to.

He ducked inside and retrieved the chest containing his father's and grandmother's remains. He slipped into its rope harness and returned with it mounted on his back.

Sgäile hissed something at the bloodied anmaglâhk facing Magiere, and the man trotted off into the night.

Leesil caught two of Sgäile's words, but his thought was interrupted as Sgäile spun back and stared at the chest.

"I'm not leaving it out of my sight," Leesil said. "I won't have anyone touching them while I'm gone."

Another flash of tension rippled across Sgäile's features. Even Magiere grew quiet and still.

Of the words Sgäile had spoken to Magiere's opponent, one was Urhkar's full elven name, who still held Leesil and Magiere's weapons. At least that much had been settled, and it appeared Sgäile had sent for their arms.

But the other word Sgäile spoke, another elven name . . .

Leesil grew angrier by the moment.

Three anmaglâhk jogged down the lane between the trees. The first was Sgäile's returning messenger. The second was Urhkar, looking none too pleased, and he wasn't carrying the bundle of weapons. The third and last of the trio . . .

Leesil flushed with heat, and the air turned cold upon his skin.

Bro'tan.

The deer lifted its head from Chap and stood to full height. Its long ears rose, each turning of its own accord. After one step, its head swung northeast and it became still again. Both ears turned that same direction.

Chap followed the deer's gaze. What was it listening to?

The deer clopped off along its chosen path. The pound of its heavy hooves vibrated through the boulder. It headed into the trees.

The dark pack elder huffed to his kin and turned to follow the deer. All the other majay-hì scurried upslope around the boulder. Lily licked Chap once across the face and loped off behind them.

Chap stared after them. What was happening? Did they know where they were going? There seemed little to do but follow, and then a voice cried out from below.

"Chap . . . wait!"

He turned as the pack froze on the hillside. He ran out to the boulder's lip and looked down.

Wynn teetered into the clearing. In the moonlight, her face glistened with a thin layer of sweat, and she dropped to her knees.

Chap lunged off the boulder's side, claws digging into the earth. What was this foolish little sage doing out alone in the forest? Somehow, she had snuck out and trailed him without getting lost. As he rounded the boulder's base, he heard a deep rolling growl.

The elder majay-hì came around the boulder's far side toward Wynn, his jowls pulled back from yellowed teeth. Snarls grew one upon the next as the pack spread around the clearing. Their crystalline eyes locked on the sage crumpled to the earth. Chap turned to face them, and the elder made an arcing inward charge to get around him.

Chap lunged around Wynn into the elder's path, snapping and snarling. The elder slowed, coming in a pace at a time with his shoulders rolling.

The pack tightened its circle.

Chap could not face all of them at once. Only Lily held back, watching from his right, and the silver yearling paced sideways in uncertainty. Lily suddenly bolted in, shoving the young one aside, and headed straight at Wynn.

Numb shock ran through Chap as he whirled to face her. He had no wish to fight Lily.

She slowed, creeping forward, and lowered her head, sniffing.

"Please . . . Chap, please," Wynn moaned. "Take it away!"

Lily shook her head, sneezed, and whined deeply.

Chap's eyes widened as Lily circled around, placing herself between Wynn and the other half of the pack. Chap backed up to Wynn, trying to think of some way to assure her that at least Lily meant no harm.

Wynn rolled on her back, squinting, and shielded her eyes from him.

"Please . . . take it," she whimpered, "from my eyes."

Her hand lowered to her mouth as she gagged. Her irises shrank at the sight of him—as if he were too bright to look upon.

Chap felt his breath turn thick and stifling in his chest. Wynn was not pleading for him to remove Lily.

Her mantic sight had risen. The little fool had somehow used it to find him and made herself sick again! He did not have his kin to call upon for aid in cleansing her.

Chap ground his paws into the clearing's floor, binding himself to the forest through Earth, Air, and his own Spirit. He leaned down and nosed Wynn's small hand aside, and ran his tongue firmly over her closed eyelids.

He could taste it. Rampant energies running like a disease still within her, which emerged to alter her sight. He swallowed them into his body, and forced them through his flesh, down into the earth . . . out with his breath to dissipate like vapor.

If only this were the end of it.

Wynn dropped her hand with a limp thud upon the ground. She sighed a long breath and swallowed hard.

The last thing Chap needed was someone to watch over in the forest. And worse still, a human wandering the territory of the majay-hì. Wynn had to go back—but would the pack wait for him to return? That was, if he could return Wynn unseen, and not end up fighting the whole pack just to get her out of this clearing.

"Where do you think you are going?" Wynn asked in a weak voice.

Chap was half-ready to snarl at her—witless girl.

Wynn sat up, and her eyes widened at Lily standing so close. She reached out her hand, but Lily backed away one step. Then Wynn noticed the pack surrounding them.

"Chap?" she said, scrambling to her knees.

He had no time to scold her. What he needed was a quick way to put the pack at ease.

Chap circled watchfully around to Lily's side. He touched his head to hers and called up a flurry of memories of every time and place he had shared with Wynn.

Lily pulled away with a grunt and shook herself. She eyed him for a moment, and then hopped off a pace and paused to stare at Wynn. With a whine, she trotted to the steel-gray male nearby and their heads grazed.

The male jerked away with a snarl as his twin sister inched close behind him. Lily butted him in the side and growled back, then turned to his sister.

The pack began mingling, touching heads as they passed each other. Their growls became broken with huffs and whines, and Chap saw it was still not enough. Perhaps there was nothing that could balance against human interlopers.

Chap barked for Lily's attention. When she returned, he gave her memories of Wynn brushing out his coat. He clung to the sensation of the sage's small fingers running through his fur.

Lily pulled away. But she turned her long head to Wynn, stretching out to sniff at the sage. Chap ducked his head under Wynn's hand, squirming to make it slide down his neck.

"What are you doing?" she said. "Stop playing around. This is serious!"

Oh, how he wanted a voice, just to tell to her to shut her mouth. He waited with his eyes on Lily.

She inched closer, and Wynn leaned away in fear. When Lily put her nose right in front of Wynn's face, the sage lifted a hesitant hand.

Wynn lightly touched the bridge of Lily's snout and slid two fingers over Lily's head.

A deep snarl filled the clearing.

The elder glared at the three of them—a human touching two majay-hì. He turned away with a clack of his jaws and headed back up the slope. Soon all the pack drifted after him, all but the steel-gray twins, who held back a moment to study the trio curiously.

"What is happening?" Wynn asked.

Lily pulled out from under Wynn's hand and trotted a short way across the clearing. She stopped to wait. Chap grumbled and jerked Wynn's sleeve. He had little choice but to take her with him.

"I heard you," Wynn said. "I heard you calling . . . for Nein'a."

Chap looked up into her worried face.

He had called up Nein'a's name for the deer, and somehow Wynn had caught it amid her mantic state. She had mistakenly heard something unintelligible the last time he had communed with his kin. But not words.

Chap let out a deep sigh. He had no time for this.

Another aberration had surfaced from Wynn's meddling with magic and the sickness it had left within her.

How much more trouble was this little woman going to be?

*   *   *

Wynn ran after Chap and the majay-hì as fast as her short legs could carry her.

She guessed that Chap had somehow learned of Nein'a through the pack, but how far off was Leesil's mother? Would Most Aged Father want Nein'a close to Crijheäiche——close to other Anmaglâhk? Or would he put her where she could never interact with them or any of her people?

The inky old majay-hì in the lead was out of sight, and the others were getting well ahead. Wynn had counted seven in the pack besides Chap but now saw only three. Chap lagged behind, slowing again and again for her, and the white female hung back as well. Beyond her were the two dark gray ones identical in their markings.

Without mantic vision, Wynn had to keep one of them in sight, or she would succumb to the forest tangling up her sense of direction. But her throat was already ragged and dry. She stumbled to a halt, bending over, trying to catch her breath.

"Chap!" she panted. "Chap, wait!"

He circled back, fidgeting anxiously.

"I can . . . cannot keep this pace," she panted.

The white female let out a howl that startled even Chap. The cry faded, and she drew a breath to offer another one. The pair of steel-grays returned immediately, and the leader and the others appeared shortly after.

Wynn watched the dark old male stroll toward them with head low and lips quivering beneath a threatening glare. Chap might have convinced the white female, but the pack leader barely tolerated her. Beyond him, a young silver male made a great show of mimicking the elder's displeasure.

Chap spun toward the white dog, and they touched heads. She loped off to the elder and did the same. He jerked away and snapped viciously at her, but she curled her own lips in response and would not retreat. Chap trotted up behind her, leaving Wynn nervously alone.

A lanky silver male with a light blaze down his chest raised his head and snorted at her.

Chap remained still as the white female slid her head along his and paused. An instant later, she began to howl again.

It came out like a moaning bellow that carried through the trees. The dark elder snarled.

Chap circled back to Wynn, his glower all too familiar. Like the time she confessed to overhearing him when communing with his kin. He cocked his head, studying her with parental displeasure.

"I am not the one who snuck off first," she grumbled at him.

Chap let out a rolling exhale, like a growl without voice. He twisted paws into the ground as if securing his footing.

Wynn's stomach lurched.

The chattering crackle of a leaf-wing filled her head. This time the strange way it shaped was clearer than the last.

You . . . ride . . . keep up . . .

Wynn went slack-faced, even with nausea twisting her stomach. She only caught those few words, but she held her breath and blinked.

The leaf-wing vanished from her thoughts, and Chap lowered his muzzle, almost mournfully.

Perhaps neither of them truly believed she had heard him the first time. Now it was certain. It might have been a wonderful new thing if not for making her sick every time . . . if not that it was one more wild symptom of what she had foolishly done to herself in Droevinka.

Chap lifted his muzzle toward the white female, and the flutter of a leaf-wing rose again in Wynn's head.

. . . Lily . . .

Wynn remembered the first time she saw the white female as the pack surrounded them upon entering the forest. She had said the dog's color looked like a water lily.

. . . yes . . .

Wynn held a hand out to Chap's companion, and the white majay-hì remained poised and still. She carefully touched the female between her ears, and the dog lifted its nose into her palm.

"Lily," Wynn repeated.

Lily spun about, staring through the trees with raised ears.

A large silver form stalked through the underbrush and walked slowly through the pack. The dogs dispersed out of its path, but the dark leader still rumbled. Wynn felt the tall deer's thudding hooves beneath her own feet, and the vibration grew as it approached.

Chap's multitongued words rose in her head: *You will ride.*

Wynn had to tilt her head back to look up at the deer's muzzle. Its large head was crowned by two tineless antlers longer than Chap's body. The crystalline eyes above her were so large they made her cower.

"Oh no." She backed away. "No—no—no!"

The deer swung toward Lily, stretched one foreleg and bent the other, and lowered itself until the two touched heads. Then the animal folded its legs and lowered its white belly to the ground.

"You cannot be serious!" Wynn exclaimed. "What about a horse . . . or pony . . . anything else?"

Chap growled and huffed twice for "no." This time, it was not his voice in her head that made Wynn queasy.

"All right," she said uncertainly. "All right."

CHAPTER ELEVEN

"How long has she been gone?" Brot'an asked in Belaskian.

Leesil didn't care to answer. He didn't want Brot'an's pretended help. He didn't want the tall elf anywhere in sight—especially not trailing after them through Crijheäiche as they hurried in search of Wynn.

"We don't know," Magiere finally answered. "Not long . . . we hope."

Leesil could tell she was still spiteful that their weapons hadn't been returned.

Urhkar was already out in the forest, trying to find any trail left by the sage. Sgäile said majay-hì packs preferred to range the forest's depths in their leisure, so he was leading their search inland, away from the river. They all were in agreement that Wynn was likely far beyond the settlement's bounds. A human spotted wandering the community would have caused a disturbance.

They rounded a wide oak with a gnarled trunk, and Sgäile pulled up short. He held up his hand for everyone to stop.

A female elf, tall and impossibly thin, stood on the oak's far side before its curtained doorway. By what little light spilled out around the curtain, Leesil saw her filmy eyes as she raised one thin brow in calm puzzlement. She was elderly, dressed in a long maroon robe beneath a matching cloak. Pure white hair hung around her sunken cheeks as she leaned heavily upon a staff of rippled wood.

The old woman squinted at Leesil, studying him with silent interest.

Sgäile gave her a bow and turned away to move on.

"Who was that?" Leesil asked.

"Tosân'leag of the Avân'nûnsheach . . . the Ash River clan, known for their scholarly pursuits. They make fine paper and ink, such as my grandfather gave your companion." Sgäile hesitated, and then added, "Clan elders have been arriving for days. Word of your presence has spread. Humans have never been given passage in our land before. We must find your companion before they hear she is missing."

"And before Én'nish does," Magiere said under her breath.

Or before Wynn stumbled alone into a pack of majay-hì. Leesil only hoped Chap and the sage ran into each other first.

As they walked, Leesil saw more wide-bellied and gnarled oaks than in the few other parts of the settlement he'd seen. At night it wasn't easy to get a good look at Crijheäiche, but they'd been walking for a while and still hadn't reached its inland end. They passed many of the tree homes, but none of the canvas or otherwise handmade structures.

After a while, the domiciles thinned, and the forest ahead thickened beyond a clearing. When they stepped into the break in the trees, Leesil stood on the edge of a wide and shallow depression covered in low-trimmed grass.

The surrounding oaks weren't homes, as they had no openings, though their trunks were large enough for such. Their lowest branches were half the diameter of the trunks. They reached out level to either side and appeared grown together, forming living bridges from one tree to the next and encircling the depression. Leesil couldn't guess the purpose of this place, and Sgäile pushed on around the encompassing oaks.

A shadow moved upon one bridge-branch nearest the open forest. Sgäile slowed, and Leesil moved up beside him.

Sgäile stood in silence and watched the silhouette with narrowed eyes. The shadow dropped to the ground as two more stepped out into view. The trio approached.

All three were dressed as Anmaglâhk, but the one leading was shorter and slighter than the others.

Brot'an spoke in clear Belaskian. "Return to quarters. We have no need of your assistance."

"With respect, Greimasg'äh," the lead figure answered. "I join this pursuit at the request of the Covârleasa."

Her voice was thick with an Elvish accent.

Brot'an exhaled harshly, and Sgäile's shoulders sagged just a bit.

The trio came closer, and Leesil clearly made out the sharp features of Én'nish within her cowl. Her eyes remained on him as well.

Magiere inched forward. "What is she doing here?"

"No one can deny her," Sgäile admonished, with barely suppressed frustration in his voice.

"She acts on behalf of the Covârleasa," Brot'an added. "The 'selected and trusted adviser' of Most Aged Father . . . Fréthfâre."

"And you're going to let her come with us?" Magiere demanded.

Leesil didn't understand the bizarre command structure these Anmaglâhk followed, but he was sick of it. Were they expected to hand over the search for Wynn to this vengeance-driven woman?

Brot'an's passive gaze remained on Én'nish. "She will not interfere in a task not given to her."

Én'nish looked up at Brot'an in hesitation. In spite of his calm tone, his words sounded like a pointed reminder of her place.

"Yes, these visitors are most certainly Sgäilsheilleache's responsibility," Én'nish answered.

She nodded to Brot'an with respect. Her two companions did likewise. Whatever their twisted rules, Brot'an appeared to hold sway over all present.

"Get rid of her," Magiere demanded.

"Remember your place . . . human," Brot'an replied quietly, the last word selected with care but spoken with no malice. "You are a guest here by exception. If not for your companion's imprudence, we would all be at peace this night."

"Let it go," Leesil whispered to Magiere. "For now."

Privately, he wondered at how Fréth, and likely Most Aged Father, had learned so quickly of Wynn's disappearance, and why Én'nish was the one sent to intercept their search.

Brot'an stepped past Leesil and out ahead. Én'nish and her companions moved from his path. Sgäile followed more slowly, ushering Leesil and Magiere forward, keeping himself between them and Én'nish. They caught up to Brot'an, and Leesil looked over his shoulder as Én'nish and her followers fell in behind Osha. The young elf breathed a bit too deeply for so little exertion, and his eyes wandered nervously.

Leesil heard a chirping whistle.

They reached the far side of the tree-ringed depression, and Brot'an stood before the forest proper with his hands cupped around his mouth. He let out a birdlike series of chirps, waited a moment, and then issued another shrill call.

A longer whistling chirp answered him from the forest.

"Urhkarasiférin has found a trail," Sgäile said, as Brot'an took off at a run into the trees. "Stay close, and do not wander."

Most Aged Father lingered in that place between consciousness and slumber. He had listened to Léshil and his companions in their quarters, but the effort wore him down. He withdrew his awareness as their conversation waned and Léshil went off to bathe. But he had learned things about each—their personalities, their fumbling grasps at plans, and their nature for deception. Magiere disturbed him in particular.

She was filled with a strange agitation. She warranted more consideration and observance until he was done with Léshil. So much complication arose from humans. The world was polluted with their chaos and frailty.

Most Aged Father was so weary he did not hear Fréthfâre's footfalls until she entered his private chamber in the great oak's heart-root. She bowed. As always, he was pleased by her presence.

Until she rose up with dark concern plain on her face.

"There is trouble with the humans," she said, settling upon one teal-dyed cushion of *shéot'a* cloth. "I do not believe Sgäilsheilleache has firm control over them."

Her criticism of a fellow anmaglâhk was disturbing. Most Aged Father valued all the Anmaglâhk, but he took greater pride in a few, such as Fréthfâre. Sgäilsheilleache was another, with his fierce devotion to his people and his strict sense of justice. Most Aged Father had known from the first time he set eyes on Sgäilsheillache that the boy was Anmaglâhk. Barely thirteen years old, he was only two moons past his name taking when he submitted himself for acceptance to the caste. He showed no fear at the prospect of training.

Taking Fréthfâre as Covârleasa had been a choice of careful consideration, and Most Aged Father valued her counsel. But he still expected good reason for her words against Sgäilsheilleache.

"One of the humans with Léshil—the small one—has gone missing," she said. "The majay-hì in their company has vanished as well. The human is believed to have gone into the forest, or so Én'nish reported. Sgäilsheilleache has gathered a hunting party to go after her, but he took Léshil and the pale woman with him. I have sent Én'nish with two others to join them."

Most Aged Father could not speak. He tried to sit up and failed, and the effort cost him.

"How long?" he demanded.

"Sometime after nightfall. I am not certain."

He was too tired for this foolishness. Of all his children, Sgäilsheilleache and Fréthfâre had done this. One unable to control the humans and the other compounding this new complication. Én'nish, who grieved the loss of her future mate, was the last who should be given any purpose involving Léshil.

Most Aged Father had been concerned when Sgäilsheilleache chose Urhkarasiférin to help escort Léshil. Én'nish was under the elder anmaglâhk's tutelage, and by caste law, the student always accompanied the teacher. Now that Urhkarasiférin had dismissed her, Én'nish was best kept far from Léshil—until Most Aged Father was done with him.

"Father?" asked Fréthfâre. He had been silent too long.

"Do not speak," Most Aged Father admonished her. "The humans are devious beyond understanding. Give me a moment to seek anomalies in the thread of life."

He had so little strength left, but it was unavoidable. He closed his eyes, worming his awareness through the forest's roots in the earth and into brush and tree and flower wherever he passed.

Nothing came to him at first, and then he felt the majay-hì. A pack loped at a fast pace behind one of the Listeners, the great silver deer, sentinels of the forest. Outrage rose in Most Aged Father.

The little human woman rode upon the deer's back.

The pack traveled purposefully, on a steady course as they wove through the forest. He followed them, slipping ahead to tree or bush whenever they outdistanced the present place of his awareness. The line they ran began to seed him with fear.

How could they know of such a destination?

Among the pack was the one majay-hì who had entered his home with Léshil.

Most Aged Father's eyes snapped open, and he tried to sit up.

"North," he cried out. "Catch Sgäilsheilleache and his charges at all costs. You will turn them back! Now!"

Fréthfâre spun up to her feet, startled by his tone.

Clan elders had been arriving for several days. Talk and rumor suggested they questioned his wisdom in allowing humans into the land for the first time. He could not let word of this wayward human's actions reach them as well.

And he could not allow any to reach the place they were headed.

"Go!" he cried out, his voice scratching the air. "None of them must reach Cuirin'nên'a's glade."

Sgäile burned with shame as he led the others through the trees. The fault was his alone.

He would never blame another serving under him—not even the naïve and immature Osha. It had been his own choice to assign the young elf as watchguard.

Osha had come later to service than most Anmaglâhk, and in the following five years, the young man had failed to attract the tutelage of a teacher among their caste. He remained a novice of only basic skills. Still, Osha wished to be of service, and Sgäile empathized with a desire that would not yield to any obstacle.

He had left Osha to watch over Léshil's quarters, and that decision resulted in the worst night of his life. Én'nish had been sent by Fréthfâre before Sgäile could resolve the crisis—which meant Most Aged Father knew everything.

It took no great feat of intelligence to guess how word had reached Most Aged Father. Én'nish must have been watching and waiting for an opportunity.

Sgäile grew sick to his stomach as they broke into a clearing where a large boulder protruded from a hillside. Halfway beyond the boulder's ledge top, Urhkarasiférin crouched upon the slope of thinly leafed elms.

"A pack was here," Brot'ân'duivé said, and Sgäile followed his gaze to the soft ground covered in paw prints. "And someone with small, human feet."

"Wynn?" Léshil asked.

Magiere stepped beyond Sgäile, pacing the ground with deep breaths.

"No blood," she said.

Sgäile was relieved, and then suspicious. Perhaps Chap had kept Wynn safe. But how, in the dark, had Magiere known no blood was spilled here? Léshil also watched her with wary concern. Én'nish hung back by the tree with her companions.

"Come," Sgäile said, and headed upslope. As he approached Urhkarasiférin, the elder anmaglâhk pointed through the elms to the northeast.

"At least seven . . . maybe eight majay-hì," he said. "Along with the woman . . . all making speed."

"And following a *clhuassas*," Brot'ân'duivé added.

"What is that?" Magiere asked.

"One of the large silver-gray deer you have seen," Sgäile answered, and said no more. The less humans knew of such things, the better.

Leesil knelt down by the split hoof prints, larger than any deer-sign in human lands.

Sgäile rarely saw even subtle distress in Urhkarasiférin's passive expression. But the man tightened his lips with a slight scowl and breathed sharply out through his nose.

"North by northeast," he said.

Brot'ân'duivé already stared off through the trees along the path the pack had taken.

"What's out there," Léshil asked, "and why would Chap or Wynn try to follow them?"

"They are not following," Brot'ân'duivé corrected. "They are traveling with the pack . . . being taken . . . to Cuirin'nên'a."

Such a blunt statement stunned Sgäile. But if Léshil came with them, he needed to know the truth of the situation. It was only right and fair to prepare him, as the shock could cause discord later.

Léshil rose quickly from the deer tracks, his eyes on the path ahead. He took off down the trail.

"No," Brot'ân'duivé shouted, grabbing for Léshil.

Magiere slapped Brot'an's hand aside with a menacing glare and followed in Léshil's footsteps.

Sgäile was at a loss. He could not allow anyone near Cuirin'nên'a, though he understood why Brot'ân'duivé had told Léshil where the pack headed.

He hoped they could catch the human woman before she and Chap reached Cuirin'nên'a.

It would be hard to turn Léshil aside, and harder still if he were in reach of his mother.

At least Brot'ân'duivé was with them—and that was some comfort. Sgäile would need his wisdom and calm counsel.

Én'nish tried to step around and head up the trail. Before Sgäile intercepted her, Brot'ân'duivé cut her off.

"You may follow," he said, "but do not forget that guardianship belongs to Sgäilsheilleache. Do not interfere."

Urhkarasiférin, about to head onward, cast only a passing glance at the woman. But Sgäile had another concern. He reached out to stop Urhkarasiférin, touching the elder's shoulder.

"I left Leanâlhâm alone," Sgäile said. "Please stay with her, and tell her I will return when able."

Urhkarasiférin gave only the slightest cock of his head to betray his surprise. He was the elder of the two of them, yet only involved at Sgäile's request. The elder anmaglâhk nodded and headed back toward Crijheäiche.

Sgäile turned to catch up with Osha close behind him. He heard Én'nish and the other two following. For the first few steps, it struck him as odd that Fréthfâre or even Most Aged Father would send another trio of the caste to follow him in tracking down one small human.

He pushed the thought away and ran on.

Chap loped beside Lily, growing tired and sensing the same in her. At times, thickened brush between the trees made passage difficult. Wynn clung to the deer's back with nothing to grasp but the animal's coat of long hair. She bent forward against its shoulders and neck, trying to hang on.

The ink-shaded elder slowed without warning, and all of the pack pulled up around him. They dispersed among the undergrowth, and a few dropped to the ground panting, pink tongues lolling out of their mouths.

A rest had been called, and Chap was no less grateful than the others. Lily lay down on the forest floor, but Chap trotted over to Wynn and barked once. She still clung to the deer as it shifted from hoof to hoof.

Wynn looked so small upon the animal's back, no larger than a child might appear upon a full-grown horse. Her hair was tangled and her oval face smeared by clumps of kicked-up earth. She had no cloak and shivered in her light elven clothing.

Chap barked again, and Wynn lifted her head. She slid her far leg over the deer's haunches and tried to slide off its back. She ended up dropping to her rump when her feet hit the ground. Chap whined and pressed his head against her shoulder.

She was too weary and stiff to even put a hand on his head. Instead she crawled on hands and knees behind him as he returned to where Lily lay panting.

The pack lay in groups of two and three to share warmth. Wynn settled next to Lily, and Chap stretched out before both of them. Wynn reached out slowly and stroked Lily's back. Lily raised her ears once but did not object.

"She is beautiful," Wynn finally said. "All your kind are beautiful."

Chap looked into her weary face. He hoped for her sake—and his—they would not travel much farther in this manner.

"I thought that all of them would be like you—born-Fay," Wynn added as she closed her eyes and lay back. "I did not know they would be so far removed—yet still like you."

He belly-crawled over to press his body against her. Winters here were far milder than beyond the mountains, yet the nights could be cool.

Chap found a strange moment of peace, considering what was at stake in this swift journey. With Wynn nestled between Lily and himself, it was good to lie on the earth of his birthplace. His eyes began to droop.

The first long baying rang through the night.

Several majay-hì stirred and got up as Chap opened his eyes. The sound rang out again, and he recognized it. The deer that had carried Wynn was still among the pack, yet this bellow came from farther off.

The deer lifted its head and issued an answering call. It turned and stalked toward the pack elder as Lily climbed to her feet. She joined them as the deer bent down to touch heads with the elder. Chap was too tired to try dipping into the exchange of memory. But when Lily returned to press her head to his, she whined in agitation. The flash of memory snapped Chap fully awake.

Gray-green-clad elves ran through the forest.

He could not see their faces clearly, for the image Lily gave him was not specific. Just anmaglâhk running in a line with purpose.

Why would she show him this? The answer came quickly to him. The Anmaglâhk were coming after them.

Wynn was still curled on the ground beside him. She had barely stirred at the deer's bellow. Chap ground his paws into the earth.

We are pursued.

Wynn thrashed over, grabbing her head. "Do not do that! Not unless I know it is coming!"

She sat up with a grimace and put a hand over her mouth. She looked at him as if he had poured a foul liquid in her mouth while she slept.

"What . . . what did you say?"

Chap repeated himself, and Wynn flinched slightly this time.

She looked back the way they had come. "How far?"

He barked three times rather than send more words to assault her. He had no idea how close the Anmaglâhk were.

He ran to the gray deer and barked once. Several of the majay-hì dashed on ahead, and if nothing else, Wynn knew they were on the move again. The deer stepped near a downed tree, and Wynn did not wait. She climbed onto its back and clutched its neck, and their race renewed. Chap took off beside Lily as the deer lunged ahead through the forest. The pace was now driven by urgency more than hope.

CHAPTER TWELVE

Wynn clung to the deer's neck, gripping its coarse hair until her fingers ached.

The majay-hì were relentless, and the pack ran all night. Wynn did her best to endure, but her legs cramped from gripping the deer's too-wide body.

She hoped dawn was not far off and kept her eyes down as much as possible. Each time she looked up, something ahead seemed as if she had just seen it behind, or to the side, or as if she'd never seen it before. Everything appeared foreign and unfamiliar in the night.

The dark forest pressed confusion into Wynn's mind. Trees flashed by like shadows. The only constants were the deer beneath her and the pack around and ahead of her. She clung to the sight of them against being overwhelmed and lost.

Wynn had no idea what they would find at the journey's end. If she and Chap came upon some elven prison, how would they gain entrance? But if—when—they reached Nein'a, Chap would definitely need her. As far as Wynn knew, Leesil's mother was unaware of Chap's true nature. Wynn would be needed to speak with her. How else could Chap relate that Leesil was among the elves and intended to free her?

She tried to shift her aching legs, but they were spread too far across the deer's wide back. Her backside was growing numb.

The black-gray pack leader slowed and the others with him. The deer's gait decreased to a steady clomp, and Chap circled back to walk below Wynn.

"Are we close?" she asked. "We must be close. It has been so long . . ."

When she looked ahead, the forest had thickened across their path. As the deer carried her closer, the pack spread out to the sides.

Birches of ever-peeling bark grew close together. Their branches intertwined one into the next beneath thousands of leaves. Through their tangling masses, elm and ash trees rose, exposing their tops above. Below, brambles and blackberry vines glistened with thorns and filled the spaces between the trees' trunks.

Everything was silent, without even a breeze or the vibrant creak of a cricket.

Wynn looked off to her left. The tangled woods stretched out into the darkness. When she turned the other way, the trees ahead appeared to have shifted to different positions among the strangling underbrush. When she turned left again, a clump of saw grass had sprouted through the thorny tendrils of a blackberry bush.

Had it been there, or had it appeared when she was not looking? The top of a cedar spread above the birches, dark and still, and she did not remember seeing it before. Was the forest toying with her again?

Wynn looked hopelessly about but saw no way through. Why had the pack or even the deer come this way, if this old growth barred the path? The way this wall of vegetation climbed and burrowed through itself was not natural.

The pack elder paced before the dense growth, and the other dogs trotted aimlessly about, arching necks and raising ears as they peered into it. The deer rolled its shoulders and shifted nervously beneath Wynn's thighs. It snorted and shook its antlered head.

These animals were as puzzled and disturbed as Wynn was. They had not seen this before.

The elder paced left along the wood's border and then suddenly lunged into it.

Wynn heard the rustle of leaves and bending vines from within the dense woods. The sound grew to a thunder of creaking branches and thrashing leaves. She grabbed the deer's coarse hair tightly as it back-stepped from the raucous sound.

A chokeberry bush ripped apart as the dark elder leaped out. Berries scattered in his wake like small black pellets. He stumbled, favoring one foreleg, and turned to stare back at the barrier. The rest of the pack circled hesitantly.

Lily turned right and darted for a birch of peeling bark, its lowest branches tangled in climbing blackberry vines.

"No!" Wynn cried out.

Chap went after Lily, but not before she tried thrashing her way into the thorny vines. She quickly retreated, never getting deeper than her shoulders.

Wynn shivered anxiously.

Chap remained on the barrier's edge as Lily arced around behind him. He rumbled softly in frustration. They could go back but not forward.

Wynn wondered if these woods were a safeguard, blocking trespassers from reaching Nein'a. But then how could a prisoner be fed and cared for? Or had Nein'a been left here to die, long ago? Had the elves lied to Leesil just to bring him within reach?

Chap's growl rose to a snarl and startled Wynn as nausea hit her. Soft buzzing grew like a birch leaf skittering about within her skull.

Fay . . . my kin . . . now they choose to return.

Wynn slipped from the deer's back. Nausea became vertigo, and she dropped to her knees, struggling under the chorus of leaf-wings.

The last time she had heard this was at the northern gate of Soladran as Chap communed with his kin, the Fay.

Chap quickly brushed heads with Lily and then bolted into the open forest behind them. Wynn tried to get up, hand over her mouth, to stumble after him, but Lily raced around to block her way.

Before Wynn cried out to Chap, his single leaf-winged voice crackled in her mind.

I am here . . . show yourselves, my kin . . . I demand it!

Chap ran blindly through the trees, searching. But not with eyes and ears and nose.

His spirit expanded in rage, reaching in all directions, until he felt them as he had upon staring into the dense barrier woods.

That warped growth should not be there. He had seen this in Lily's memory flash. No majay-hì had ever encountered such a tangled mesh and it was coated with the tingle of Chap's kin.

They tried to stop the majay-hì—stop him—from reaching Nein'a.

Show yourselves! Answer me . . . now!

His coat rippled under a breeze whirling downward from the night sky. It increased to a strong wind, encircling him as it ripped up mulch. He pulled up short amid a hushed chatter of branches and turned a tight circle with a low rumble. The wind settled to a breeze once more.

Chap stood in a small clearing loosely walled by sycamores and beeches grown tall from roots sunk deep into the earth. Their branches interlaced like the limbs of sentinels holding hands, and movement within them made those limbs sway slightly.

He would not cower before them.

Why interfere now, when you have been silent . . . so useless? Why return after abandoning me for so long?

Branches behind him shook softly, and he wheeled about. Leaves rustling in the low whirling breeze shaped to a chorus of voices in his mind.

Further and further you stray from your path . . . your purpose . . . to keep the sister of the dead in ignorance and away from the Enemy.

Chap rumbled at one birch. A bend in its trunk looked too much like a figure seated in judgment. His shoulders tightened as he half-crouched to lunge.

Leesil is necessary to my task . . . our need. But his suffering serves no purpose. So why bar my way? Why can he not free his mother?

A long vine of red hyacinth rustled.

Return to your task. . . . Return to the sister of the dead. . . . Leave this land and keep her far from her maker's reach.

That was no answer. In what other place could Magiere be farther from the Enemy's reach?

The hyacinth rustled more softly.

You have told your mortal charges far too much. So much that they might well turn upon a path that would end this world. Tell them no more, and take them from this place.

Chap's rumble grew. All Leesil wanted was freedom for his last remaining family. To be with his mother once again. Yet Chap's kin became obsessed with inaction.

And why could he not remember . . . more?

Bits and pieces learned in his mortal life still did not fit together. He did not retain enough awareness from existence among his kin to bind those pieces and fill in the gaps.

The branches shuddered around him.

You have taken flesh and lost our full awareness. Trust the path . . . trust in us. In flesh, you cannot understand all things.

Chap wavered in silence. He had relinquished eternity to follow the will of his kin. Once he must have known and agreed with their purpose, but now he could not remember why.

There must have been a reason . . . one that he had forgotten.

Wynn controlled her vertigo and tried to rush around Lily. Each time, the dog shifted or barked in warning and would not let her pass.

A chorus of a thousand shuddering and crackling leaves erupted within Wynn's head.

You have taken flesh and lost our full awareness. Trust the path . . . trust in us. In flesh, you cannot understand all things.

Wynn collapsed, wracked with dry heaves. She stared into the shifting dark trees on hands and knees, shaking uncontrollably. She heard the Fay communing with Chap.

His snarling howl rolled through the forest.

Wynn turned toward Lily. "Oh please, just get out of my way!"

Lily cocked her ears. Wynn crawled to a nearby cedar and clawed up its rough bark to her feet. The others of the pack ranged around her, but none came near. They only watched her and Lily in puzzlement.

Before Lily could react, Wynn lunged around the cedar's far side toward the sound of Chap's cry.

Chap quivered as his howl faded from his ears. Why did his kin treat him like a servant who owed blind obedience?

He had been one of them—one with them. He saw no possible harm in a son finding the mother who birthed and raised him. Nein'a did not want to see harm come to this world any more than the Fay, even though she had raised a son in her own caste's ways for her own purposes.

Chap's shudders faded, and he paced a slow circle, studying the sentinel trees. No voices came on the low rustling breeze. But they were still there—still waiting for him to acquiesce.

This had nothing to do with keeping Magiere from the enemy.

Why do you fear Leesil reaching his mother?

*   *   *

Chap's question rang in Wynn's head.

She spun around, lost once again with nothing to guide her. She had not taken one step. Yet if her eyes turned away for an instant, a vine, that patch of moss, or even the bare spot of earth to one side appeared to have moved.

Take the sister of the dead and leave. Go back to the human realms and never return to this land.

Wynn shut her eyes and threw her arms around an aspen trunk to keep from falling. The leaf-wing chorus drowned all other sensations. But she heard wind rustling branches not far off.

She opened her eyes, turning her face toward the sound, but Lily stood blocking her way. Wynn remembered Chap briefly touching heads with the white female. He had somehow told Lily to keep her behind.

"You must let me pass," Wynn whispered, uncertain how to make Lily understand.

Chap had communicated somehow with this dog. With Wynn's new ability to hear him and perhaps even communicate with him, she wondered if she might do the same with Lily.

She inched forward, trying to pick up any thoughts from Lily. She did not believe Chap could read her own verbal thoughts—when they communicated, she spoke aloud, and he projected words into her mind.

"Lily," she said. "Can you understand me?"

Lily stared at her intently, but the white dog seemed only to be acting as guardian, and Wynn heard nothing in her mind as she did with Chap.

Wynn closed her eyes, this time trying to reach inside Lily's mind. There must be some way to connect and express her desperate need to reach Chap! But she felt nothing and saw nothing. Lily was not like Chap.

They could not speak to each other.

Wynn grabbed for Lily. The dog hopped away and spun about to face her again. Lily's shift was in the same general direction as the sound of chattering branches.

Wynn might not be able to navigate the forest—but Lily could. The dog betrayed Chap's path in every attempt to keep Wynn from following. Wynn tottered forward and grabbed for Lily again.

This time Lily did not hop away. She turned with ears perked to look through the trees. Wynn settled her hand on Lily's back.

A shudder ran through the dog's slender body, but her attention remained fixed toward the sound they both heard.

"Chap," Wynn whispered and pushed Lily forward. Had the dog heard Wynn use that name enough to know it? Wynn repeated it, again and again.

Lily took one step, her crystalline eyes focused off into the forest, and whined.

Wynn could see Lily was afraid, but she shoved the dog forward.

Lily stepped slowly at first, weaving from tree to tree and peering around each before moving on. Wynn followed the white majay-hì as her only guide.

Chap's awareness sharpened to the presence of his kin. Within leaf and needle, branch and bark, and the air and earth, he felt their presence—their strained anticipation.

He let them wait.

Finally the breeze snapped sharply. The rustle of leaves was laced with the clatter of branches.

The elven mother is not important. Take your charges from here, and keep them in ignorance. Regain your faith in us.

Again no answer for Leesil's concern—and too much denial of Nein'a.

Even if Leesil fulfilled this blind scheme of his mother and her dissidents, why would Chap's kin not want such an Enemy to fall?

In his mind, he found no memory of his kin's concern for Leesil—only for Magiere.

From the moment of Chap's birth, he had known what to do concerning Magiere, and that a half-blood boy would be the means to that end. But he knew nothing of this hidden and evasive concern over Leesil and Nein'a.

Taking flesh was not the cause of this.

It was not the failing of his mortal mind to keep what he would have known among his own kind. Something more had happened in the infinitesimal instant between his place among his kin and being born into this world.

Why will you not speak of Leesil?

Only silence.

Why can I not remember this?

Unseen small creatures scurried among the branches and made dark spaces between them flex like mouths with lips of leaves and needles.

*You are flesh, frail and faltering. Your heart and earthly senses weaken your
purpose. It is little more than what we feared.*

Chap cringed—but not from their admonishment. He remembered the
first part of this journey as he had tried to lead Leesil to his mother.

In the deep winter of the Broken Range, in cold and hunger, Chap's kin
had ignored his pleas for aid. Only the high-pitched whistle of an unknown
savior had led him and those in his care to the caves. His kin had done nothing to save them. Even with Magiere at risk among the elves, these an'Cróan,
the Fay had remained silent.

Now they showed themselves only to bar Chap's way to Nein'a.

What better way to keep Magiere from the hands of the Enemy than to
allow her to die?

Whether in those mountains or among a hostile people, it would simply
be her fate and none of the Fay's doing.

How badly his kin wished to keep Leesil from his mother. Would they
allow Leesil to die as well, so long as it served some purpose Chap could not
remember?

And why could he not recall the answers? Such vital knowledge could not
have just slipped from him.

Chap closed his eyes. His spirit screamed like a wail that shook his body.

Betrayers . . . deceivers . . . you took this from me!

His own kin. They had cut his memories like a blade severing flesh and
bone. They had ripped out pieces of him, tearing away any awareness they
did not want him to have.

All in the moment he had chosen to be born.

Chap opened his eyes and cast his gaze about the clearing, looking for
something to rend and tear.

He froze at the sight of Wynn clinging to a tree beside Lily.

The sage's olive-toned face was a mask of horror, and streams of tears ran
down her cheeks as she stared at him.

Wynn heard the entire exchange. In communion with his kin, even some of
Chap's inner words to himself had chattered softly in her head.

He was supposed to be one of them—a Fay.

Through him, Wynn had come to believe that whatever they truly were, they worked for a worthy purpose. Chap had been sent to save Magiere—and Leesil as well, in some way.

But the Fay had used Chap. They had left him and all those with him to die. Even her, as she dangled over that gorge, half frozen in a blizzard, while the others tried to save her.

The wind died instantly into chilling silence.

Chap's voice rose like a shout in Wynn's thoughts.

Run!

Chap bolted straight at Wynn as the air churned with growing force.

She had been listening—a mortal eavesdropping upon the Fay.

Mulch and twigs swept up to join leaves torn from above in a growing, spinning circle of wind. Debris pelted Chap from all sides, obscuring his sight. He fought to stay on his feet and keep Wynn and Lily in sight.

She is an innocent!

No answer came.

Lily snatched the leg of Wynn's breeches and pulled on the sage. Wynn toppled to the ground, shielding her face as sheared-off branches battered against her.

Chap heard an aching creak of wood and the tearing of earth. Within the crackle of snapping branches, his kin shouted in outrage.

Abomination!

He shook off their malice and then realized it was not aimed at him. A birch tree at the clearing's edge teetered toward Wynn.

Earth around its trunk heaved upward. Deep roots tore free, slinging sod and mulch in the air. The birch tipped and arced downward, ripping through the branches of other trees as it fell directly toward Wynn.

As Chap tried to run toward her, something dark and long whipped at him in the corner of his vision. He swerved and ducked.

Wynn grabbed Lily's neck and scrambled with kicking legs. Dog and sage rolled away in a tangle as the birch's trunk slammed to the earth. The impact sent a shudder through the ground. Lily yelped and Wynn cried out as both vanished beneath the tree's leaves and flailing limbs.

He charged for the downed tree with the wind's roar filling his ears.

Something heavy and hard lashed the whole side of his body. The world flashed in a painful white . . . and then black.

Chap's vision cleared, and he lay slumped on the ground. Leaves, stripped from the birch's branches in the wind, churned in a vortex that filled the clearing.

Around the downed tree's base, dark forms writhed.

Its roots moved. Wide and sluggish where they joined the huge knot at the tree's trunk, their tapering bulk bent and curled like earth-stained serpents upon the ground. Two wormed their way along the trunk and into the bulk to the birch's leaves.

Chap had so fully focused on the toppling birch that he had not seen its roots come alive. One of them must have struck him down. He squirmed on the ground, trying to get up.

Wynn screamed from somewhere beneath the birch's remaining leaves.

Wynn heard Lily struggling to escape, but she could not see the dog among the cloud of leaves and branches pinning her to the ground. She tried to roll off her back and crawl out.

Her left leg snapped straight, and her back flattened against the ground.

Something curled and twisted up Wynn's leg, and her breath began to race. It crushed inward around her calf. Wynn screamed out in pain under its grinding pressure.

Leaves dangling against her face turned blue-white as her mantic sight surged up.

Lily's howl pierced Wynn's ears, and a chorus of leaf-wings roared in her skull.

Abomination! Sick thing that spies on us. Your taint rises in your flesh.

The grip on her leg jerked hard, and Wynn slid across the ground. Leaves and branches lashed her face and arms. The near-blue mist of Spirit permeating the leaves turned to a blur. She clutched desperately at branches only to have them bend and snap in her hands.

Wynn hooked her arm around the base of one branch and held on. The ache in her knee spiked into her hip as her whole body was pulled straight. A snarling and thrashing rose among the leaves above her.

Before Wynn's eyes, the mist of Spirit moved within the tree's bark.

It burned with a brilliance she had seen before, but only when she had looked upon Chap with her mantic sight.

Flowing blue-white wormed back and forth through the wood, as if alive and willful.

You hear us . . . listen to what is not for a mortal to know. Now you see us, yes? And you should not!

Leaves above Wynn's head split apart. A head glowing with blue-white mist shoved through at her face. Wynn almost lost her grip in fright, until she saw crystalline eyes.

One of the majay-hì snatched her tunic's shoulder with its teeth.

Chap heard Lily howl and then saw Wynn's legs emerge from the branches near the tree's base. A root was wrapped tightly around her shin and knee. Chap righted himself and staggered toward her as the pack bolted out of the forest from all sides.

Three dogs dove into the tree's bulk as the dark elder spun out in the clearing. He wove back and forth before the thrashing roots. Chap called to his kin.

Stop! You are discovered, but harming a mortal will change nothing.

Clinging dirt scattered from the roots as they rose in the air. One came down hard, rolling along the ground toward Chap.

He scuttled aside as the root lashed the earth, and mulch sprayed across his body.

The dark elder rushed in. His jaws snapped sharply over the root's narrow end and severed through it.

Chap's panic washed away in growing rage. His kin would not listen to him, and they tried to take Wynn. All because she had heard them and caught their deception, as he had. Lily hopped free from the birch's leaves, and two majay-hì followed after her.

One root rose high into the night. It lashed over backward into the mass of the downed tree. Leaves exploded upward under a clatter of snapping branches and a screeching yelp.

The root gripping Wynn coiled and jerked, and the sage spun out across the clearing. The shoulder of her tunic was torn open.

Three of the pack had gone in after Lily and Wynn, but only two had come out.

Chap rushed toward Wynn as his anger burst forth at his kin.

Now you injure your own children who took flesh long ago? It is you who have lost your way!

Wynn lay stunned as the root coiled up her leg, reaching for her torso. Its tip passed her chest, reaching for her throat, and Chap seized it, biting deep.

He ripped hard, shredding it with his teeth. Another root arched upward from the tree's base, and he whirled to grip Wynn's tunic.

The root arced downward as Lily appeared beside him. She took hold of Wynn beside him, and they both lunged backward, jerking the sage away. The root cracked down on bare earth, sending a shudder up Chap's legs.

He rushed into the open clearing before the tree's exposed base. He ground his paws through the scattered leaves and rooted himself amid the whirling wind.

No more will suffer for your hidden schemes.

He felt the elemental surge of Earth and Air, the moisture of Water within them, and even Fire from the heat of his own flesh. They mingled with Spirit from his own body as he closed on his kin.

Wynn tumbled across the ground. Then a crash filled her ears and thunder shook through the earth beneath her. She rolled over to find Lily beside her and saw Chap bolt out into the clearing.

She cowered for an instant at the sight of the tree's roots writhing in the air. Beyond Chap, the pack elder and two more majay-hì made quick darting passes as they taunted the roots. Each dog was two overlaid images in Wynn's mantic sight. Within their silver-gray forms glowed Spirit of blue-white mist. But not the tree and its roots—and not Chap.

The whiter essence of the Fay moved like shifting vapors within that dark-stained wood. And Chap was the only singular form Wynn saw.

One whole shape, glowing with brilliance. His fur glistened like luminous threads of white silk in the moonlight, and his eyes scintillated as if holding a light of their own.

And the light of him began to burn.

Wynn did not know what he was doing, but her eyes started to sting. She grabbed Lily with both hands to hold the dog back.

Trails of white mist rose from Chap like vapor in the shape of flames. Wynn squinted against the pain of his light, but could not take her eyes off of him. He stalked inward, low and tight, toward the base of the tree.

The pack elder and his companions pulled up short. They backed away with their eyes on Chap. The roots in the air quivered in hesitation, and then one cracked downward.

Wynn stopped breathing as it fell directly upon Chap.

In a burning blur, he leaped out of its path. The root hit the earth, and Wynn felt the impact beneath her. Before it could coil back again, Chap threw himself on it.

Through the white mist of his form, she thought she saw his jaws close upon the arching root.

And the light of his body flashed.

Wynn cringed as if stepping from a pitch black room into full sunlight. A thousand leaf-wings crackled inside her head. She heard only screeching blind panic and no words. Chap's lone voice rose above them.

I will tear you . . . rend you . . . I will swallow down your severed pieces into nothing!

Wynn clung to Lily as her sight slowly returned. Swirling colored blotches marred everything in the night. She barely made out Chap's muted form pacing before the birch's base.

But Chap was the only thing moving.

If you come again for me or mine . . . I will come for you!

Slowly Wynn's sight cleared more and more. Her mantic vision gone, all she saw in the moonlight was Chap standing tense and watchful.

The gnarled ball of the birch's base towered before him, but its roots extended in stillness as if the tall tree had just toppled. No hint of wind stirred the stray leaves fluttering to the ground.

Chap stood rigid, as Wynn crawled toward him on hands and knees.

His kin were gone.

Chap felt the vibrancy slowly fade from his body. He had turned on his own kind. He could taste them like blood in his mouth.

No, not his kin. Not anymore.

He wanted no more of them. They cared nothing for the lives they toyed with in silent schemes for a world they claimed was theirs. They would sacrifice those he had come to care for—all for some purpose they would not share with him.

In their vicious complacency, they cut him apart and left only those pieces that served them best.

Gentle fingers threaded through the fur on his back and up his neck.

Wynn knelt beside him, her face scratched and dirty. One abrasion on her hand and a shallow cut in the side of her forehead left smeared blood on her skin. She looked small and frail.

"I am sorry," she choked out. "I meant no harm . . . no offense. I worried for you, when I heard what they said . . . what you said."

He looked in her brown eyes. She had nothing to be sorry for. What was happening to her—her sight, the way she now heard him—was not her fault. He only wished he understood why it was happening or how to stop it.

Lily crept in, leaning around Wynn to sniff at him cautiously. The rest of the pack stayed at a distance and would not come near.

Had they seen him turn on his own kin? Did they look at him now as some being they did not recognize, which hid within a deceptively familiar form?

Only the inky black elder stalked through the open clearing. His gaze stayed on Chap until he was close, and then his grizzled muzzle lifted toward Wynn. He trotted quickly off into the branches of the fallen birch, but at least he no longer growled at the sage in disapproval.

Lily stretched out her muzzle, sniffing Chap again. He lowered his head. How would she now see him?

The warmth of her tongue slid up his jowl and across the bridge of his nose. But relief made him suddenly weary.

"You are not alone, Chap," Wynn whispered. "That will never happen."

A long mournful howl rose from the downed birch.

Chap lifted his head, and he, Lily, and Wynn looked to where the elder had slipped between the branches. When the pack had come, three had gone in after Lily and Wynn.

But only two had emerged.

CHAPTER THIRTEEN

Chane turned his horse around a jagged stone outcrop. He followed Welstiel each night southeast into the Crown Range as directed by the old Móndyalítko couple. At any moment, he expected one of their mounts to drop.

The beasts moved slower with each passing dusk. Welstiel did not appear to notice and pressed on relentlessly.

On a few evenings they had awoken trapped within the tent by heavy snowfall. Chane dug them out, but once it was so severe they spent the night inside. Not a pleasant night, for any delay aggravated Welstiel.

Tonight was cold but calm, and Chane reined in his horse as Welstiel suddenly halted to look up at the stars.

"How much farther?" Chane asked.

Welstiel shook his head. "Until we see signs of a ravine. What did the woman say—like a giant gouge in the mountainside?"

"Yes," Chane answered.

For half the journey, Welstiel seemed lost in thought. The last time Chane had heard the man talk in his sleep was the morning he awoke shouting; since then, Welstiel's dreams had grown infrequent. He had also nearly ceased any pretense of grooming. Dark hair hung lank down his forehead, and his once fine cloak continued deteriorating. Chane's was no better.

"I should look for a place to set up the tent," he said.

Welstiel just stared at the night sky.

Chane urged his mount onward, searching for natural shelter. It was some relief to be alone for a moment, as he believed Welstiel might well be going mad.

The man's state of mind grew worse each night, though at times he was as lucid as the first time Chane met him. They passed the time with Chane's lessons in Numanese, not perfectly enjoyable, but it broke the silent tension and kept Welstiel's wits from wandering. And Chane now spoke Wynn's native tongue in short but complete sentences.

Welstiel had made sure they would not starve, but feeding through his arcane methods was hardly satisfying. How a Noble Dead could settle for such bland and unpleasant sustenance was beyond Chane.

Chane's thoughts often slipped to the memory of a stimulating hunt: the taste of flesh between his teeth and blood on his tongue, and how his pleasure sharpened with the fear of his prey. Welstiel's method might last longer, and was necessary under their circumstances, but he appeared to prefer it. Chane would never understand.

He dismounted and trekked up the rocky slope to an overhang below a sheer face of granite. It would do for the day. He could tie off the canvas on the overhang's projections, weight the bottom edge with stones, and create a makeshift chamber. The extra room would be a small luxury, so he returned to his horse and began untying the rolled canvas.

He paused to scan the firs with their sparse branches and listen to the last of the night, but he heard only the coarse wind gusting across the mountainside. He dreaded another dormant day, locked in by the sun with Welstiel, only to emerge into another night of icy winds on an exhausted mount. Language lessons were his only respite.

Chane closed his eyes indulgently, his thoughts drifting forward. . . .

In Malourné, across the western ocean and the next continent, lay the founding home of the Guild of Sagecraft. Educated men and women would walk old and sound stone passages in robes of light gray. What libraries and archives they would have, tables full of scrolls, parchments, and books, all lit by the glow of cold lamp crystals.

He saw himself there.

Red-brown hair clean and combed behind his ears, he studied an ancient parchment. Not a carefully scribed copy, but the original, unearthed in some far and forgotten place.

The familiar scent of mint tea drifted into his nostrils. He looked up to see Wynn walking toward him, carrying a tray. She offered a soft smile only for him. Her wispy brown hair was woven in a braid down her back, and her olive skin glowed in the crystal's light.

She set down the tray with its two steaming cups. He wanted to smile back, but he could not. He could only drink in the sight of her face. She reached out and touched his cheek softly. The warmth of her hand made him tremble. She sat beside him, asking him questions as her eyes roved the parchment. They talked away the night, until Wynn's eyelids drooped little by little as she grew too sleepy. In that still and perfect moment, he lingered between watching her sleep and carrying her to her room.

Chane's horse neighed wildly. He opened his eyes at the first growl, and the vision of Wynn vanished.

Downslope between the wind-bent trees, wild dogs approached. He had neither heard nor smelled them while lost in wishful fantasy.

Six dogs, their eyes on him and the horse, snarled as they wove closer through the sparse foliage.

Most were black with hints of brown and slate gray, but each bore patches of bare skin where their fur thinned from starvation. Yellow eyes were glazed with hunger, and their ribs showed beneath shrunken and sagging skin.

The horse tossed its head and tried to retreat, sending stones tumbling downslope.

Chane snatched the reins and reached across the saddle for his sword slung from the saddle horn. He wondered how the dogs survived this far up with so little to eat. He closed a hand on the sword's hilt, and the two closest dogs charged for the horse's legs. Chane ducked away from the bucking mount as the lead dog sprang.

Its forelegs hooked across the horse's shoulders, and its teeth clacked wildly for a grip. The second dog charged from the front, snapping at the horse's legs. The horse screamed and reared. Before Chane could swing at either dog, another snarl sounded from behind him.

A skeletal dog was in midleap when he turned. He sidestepped and swung.

His longsword bit halfway through its neck.

The animal hit the slope and slid, smearing earth and rock with spattering blood. Another dog collided into Chane's back, and he toppled facedown.

Teeth closed on the base of his neck as his horse screamed under the growls of other dogs.

Chane released his sword and rolled, pinning the dog beneath his back, but it did not let go. He felt his skin tear as he wrenched his elbow back. The dog's jaws released with a gagging yelp at the muffled crack of its ribs. Chane turned onto his knees, pinned the dog's head, and shattered its skull with his fist.

His horse was down. Four remaining dogs tore savagely at it, and the mount's weak cries reduced to gasping whimpers.

All the dogs suddenly stopped and fell silent. Their bloodied muzzles lifted in unison.

Welstiel stood beyond them, the reins of his horse in hand. His expression was marred with livid disbelief.

"Why did you not stop them," he demanded, "instead of rolling about yourself like some rabid mongrel?"

"I was stopping . . . ," Chane answered in his nearly voiceless hiss. "There were too many to get all of them quickly enough."

"You are Noble Dead," Welstiel said with disgust. "You can control such beasts with a thought."

Chane blinked. "I do not possess that ability. Toret told me that our kind develop differing strengths—given time. That is not one of mine."

Welstiel's disgust faded, and he shook his head. His resignation made him look older.

"Yes . . . it is." He studied the dogs and then Chane's chest. "Do you still wear one of your small urns?"

Chane grasped the leather string slick with his own black fluids still running down his neck. He pulled it until a small brass urn dangled free of his shirt.

Welstiel stepped closer and the dogs remained still as he passed. "Leave one alive to take as a familiar. It can track ahead and perhaps aid in our search."

He turned away, glancing once at the dying horse with a weary sigh.

It was a sound Chane always found strange to hear from an undead, even when he did it himself. They breathed only when needing to speak, and a sigh was but a habit left over from living days.

"We'll walk and use my horse for the baggage," Welstiel said. "Collect what remains of your horse's feed, and roast its flesh to store for your new familiar."

Chane picked up his sword. It all sounded sensible and rational, but the scent of blood was thick around him. His hunger stirred, though he had no need for sustenance.

Dog and horse—lowly beasts—but the mount had served Chane, and the pack only sought to survive. He understood that, and it left him strangely disturbed as he skewered the first dog with the tip of his blade. Even at its yelp, the others just stood there, waiting to be slaughtered.

He did not pick or choose and merely killed the dogs one by one within reach, until the last stood cowering before him. He closed his eyes and imagined once more . . .

A quiet place in the world where Wynn's round face glowed by the light of a cold lamp crystal. Her eyes drooped in sleep over the parchment, and he reached out for her. . . .

Wynn returned with Chap and Lily to the barrier woods. The silver deer was gone, but the remainder of the pack ranged about.

Her face and hands stung from scratches, and her left leg ached, but she limped along. These injuries seemed paltry compared to the majay-hì found broken and dead beneath the birch's branches. The steel-gray female had come for her as the Fay tried to drag her out to her death. Now her twin brother wandered listlessly among the trees, barely in sight of the others.

Of all things Wynn had faced, from vampires to Lord Darmouth and his men, the Fay's sudden wrath terrified her most. It was so unexpected.

Before discovering Chap, she had considered the Fay to be little more than an ideological personification of the elemental forces that composed her world. In knowing Chap and coming to believe in what he was, she had thought the Fay benevolent if enigmatic, much like him.

They had killed a majay-hì because she had heard them and learned how they had used Chap.

The world now made far less sense to Wynn.

Chap stepped up to the brambles filling the trees of the barrier woods. He ground his paws into the earth. Wynn did not need mantic sight to guess what he did.

She had seen the silken vapor of spectral white fire rise around Chap as he faced his kin. When he turned on them to defend her, his body had flashed and blinded her for an instant. His kin had fled in fear.

He annoyed her so many times with his doggish behavior, slovenly and gluttonous habits that made it difficult to remember what he was. When he chomped a greasy sausage, she did not see how anything descended from the eternal could be so . . . disgusting.

But he was Fay—and now outcast. Perhaps traitor as well to his eternal kin, though they deserved no better.

Chap clamped his teeth upon a bisselberry vine, and Wynn watched in chilled fascination.

Round berries receded to flowers and then to small buds among the vine's broad leaves and long thorns. Leaves shrank in size and thorns shortened as both faded into light green stems. The vine's branching parts withdrew as they shrank in size.

Wynn watched its wild maturity turn back to infancy as the thorny plant grew younger and smaller. It receded into the earth from whatever fallow seed it had sprouted.

"You reverse the course of life?" Wynn whispered.

Chap stepped into the hollow left by the vines, and the leaf-wing whispered in Wynn's head.

Only to take my kin's touch . . . what they leave of their will upon the world . . . as I took the pieces of them reaching for you.

She had grown accustomed to picking meaning from his multitongued voice, though it still made her stomach roll. The inky elder followed Chap inward. Wynn stepped in with Lily, and the other majay-hì came behind.

Dawn grew to day as Chap led them, tunneling through the barrier woods. Wynn watched in awe as again and again he bit and licked its altered life into retreat. The sun had nearly cleared the treetops when the last bramble curled away before Chap. Wynn stepped out behind him through a patch of enormous verdant ferns with fronds reaching up taller than her head.

She emerged at a clearing's edge where the ground was covered in soft emerald grass. Here and there patches of darker moss were thick and spongy. At the center was a domicile elm as wide and massive as any oak or cedar in Crijheäiche. Beside its curtained opening sat a stool and a basket filled with white lumps. A small brook gurgled across the clearing several paces beyond the tree.

At the water's edge, a slender woman perched upon a wide saffron cushion. With her back turned, she did not notice the visitors.

Bright sunlight turned her hair nearly white, and its long glossy tresses hung forward over one caramel-colored shoulder. The folds of her shimmering wrap were pulled down, and she was naked to the waist. She washed with a square of tan felt in one narrow hand.

Wynn thought she saw lighter scars in the skin of the woman's back, as if she had been clawed by an animal long ago.

As the majay-hì wormed around Wynn and into the clearing, Chap hesitantly stepped across the green.

The woman paused and turned just a little. White-blond hair slipped from her shoulder and swung down her back almost to the cushion. She set down the felt and pulled up her wrap. Chap barked loudly and ran forward, and the woman whirled to her feet, even taller than Wynn had first guessed.

Wynn had seen elven women both here and on her continent, but none like this one.

Her face was triangular like all elves', though its long angles swept in soft curves down to a narrow jaw and chin. Her skin was flawless but for the scars Wynn had seen. White-blond eyebrows swept out and up above her temples like downy feathers upon her brow. A long delicate nose ended above a small mouth a shade darker than her skin.

Her almond-shaped eyes were large, even for her own kind.

She did not seem quite real.

"Chap?" the woman said.

He scurried to her side and rubbed into her legs a bit too hard. She crouched down and lifted an uncertain hand under his muzzle. Chap twisted his head to drag her palm and long fingers over his face.

This was Leesil's mother—Nein'a—Cuirin'nên'a, as her own people called her.

Wynn found it difficult to see her as one of the Anmaglâhk, spy and assassin, let alone a traitor to her caste or people. And Nein'a did not appear to be imprisoned.

She finally looked up at Wynn. An instant of surprise passed over her fine features before she turned with narrow-eyed suspicion to study the surrounding trees. The majay-hì spread across the green, sniffing about, and their ease in her glade seemed to calm her.

Wynn approached cautiously, uncertain how she would be received.

Nein'a stood, looking down upon the sage.

"How does a human come here?" she said in Belaskian. "And where did you find this dog?"

Beneath cold demand was an unsteady quiver in her voice.

"I came with Chap," Wynn said, "as did Leesil. He is here among your people, trying to find you . . . and free you."

Nein'a blinked once as her expression flattened. "That is not possible. He would not be allowed among the an'Cróan . . . no more than you would, girl!"

Wynn had not expected such cold and sharp words from her, though Nein'a had been alone for a long time.

"Chap brought us through the mountains. Sgäile came to escort us by the request of Most Aged Father. I swear to . . ."

At the patriarch's name, fear washed through Nein'a's beautiful face. It was quickly replaced by something coldly vicious as she peered again into the trees around the clearing.

"Get out!" she snapped at Wynn. "Do not bring Leesil here. Take him from this land while you still can."

Wynn was shocked into silence until Chap's voice scratched in her mind. *She must come now, before pursuit catches us all.*

Wynn stepped closer to Nein'a. "Come with us. Chap and I can hide you. I will get Leesil and Magiere from Crijheäiche, and we—"

"Leesil is among the Anmaglâhk?" Nein'a cut her off. "You are all fools . . . rabbits who crawl into a den of wolves! How did you even find my prison?"

Before Wynn could sort out answers, her stomach rolled at Chap's words. *No more time for this—we leave now!*

Wynn swallowed down nausea under Nein'a's wary gaze and then gestured at Chap and the other majay-hì.

"He brought me . . . and they led him. They can bring us back. But you have to come. There are others pursuing us, and we do not know how close they are."

Nein'a looked away. "What makes you think I could leave . . . not having done so in the long time I have been here?"

"Of course you can leave," Wynn insisted. "There are no walls, and Chap knows the way."

He barked once as his leaf-wing voice began to rise again.

"I heard you the first time!" Wynn snapped at him. "Keep quiet for a moment!"

Nein'a frowned at them both.

Wynn had no time to explain, and all Nein'a heard was Chap's agitated bark in reply.

Nein'a shook her head. "I am cut off, girl. I can no more walk the forest than you. It rejects me. If I step beyond the clearing, I am lost . . . wandering until I am quickly retaken and returned to his place. Do you think I have not tried?"

Wynn did not understand this. Every elf she had met was at home in this great forest and none suffered the confusion it pressed upon her.

"Trust me, or at least Chap," she urged. "He can lead us back."

Lily remained close by. In two steps, Chap brushed heads with her and tossed his nose toward the tall ferns. Lily yipped and the pack elder echoed her. All the majay-hì began to gather.

Nein'a watched them, but her large eyes kept drifting warily about the clearing, as if searching for some assurance. She sighed and scratched Chap's head.

"I have nothing to lose. But not so for you, girl, when we are caught."

"Just keep your eyes on Chap and the others. The forest cannot make them shift in your mind like it does with its own flora."

Chap led the way with Nein'a following, and Wynn fell in behind with Lily as the majay-hì swarmed around them. They stepped through the giant ferns and down the channel that Chap had created in the barrier woods.

"It took us all night to reach you," Wynn said, "but Chap and the pack know where to go. We still have a long trek ahead."

Nein'a did not answer, and seemed overly disturbed by the barrier woods, as if she had never seen it before.

Wynn tried to understand what the woman must feel, trapped alone for eight years. It would take longer than a few steps for Nein'a to accept she was free.

Another patch of tall ferns appeared ahead, blocking the path. Wynn didn't remember ferns at the passage entrance, only its exit into the clearing. But she put her faith in Chap's clearer perception as they stepped through the fronds.

Wynn stood on the clearing's edge with Nein'a's domicile elm at the green lawn's center.

Nein'a huffed. "Now do you see?"

"Whenever you try to leave, you just end up back here?" Wynn asked.

"No . . . ," Nein'a answered. "I have thrice wandered, lost in the outer forest, only to be captured again. This is the first time I returned directly to my prison. But I have never before had anyone try to lead me out."

Wynn was not listening closely. She was too preoccupied, spreading the tall ferns with her hands to peer back down the passage through the tangled woods.

"I did not know the forest had thickened outside," Nein'a continued. "It has been years since I last tried to leave. Perhaps it is a new safeguard placed by Aoishenis-Ahâre . . . since my son's return."

The title caught Wynn's attention. It was not Most Aged Father but the Fay who had raised the barrier woods. And Nein'a's misconception suggested something more.

Most Aged Father had some hand in cutting the woman off from the forest, leaving her susceptible to its bewildering influence. If that were so . . .

Wynn grew more wary and mimicked Nein'a's study of the surrounding trees. How much influence did Most Aged Father wield over this land, let alone its people?

Most Aged Father wormed his awareness through the forest. He drifted from tree to bush to vine as he followed Fréthfâre. Though he watched her run hard through the night without pause, he worried that she would not catch Léshil in time.

He slipped ahead and came upon Sgäile and his procession, pushing on with just as much speed. Most Aged Father clung to his calm, watching as they ran past. His awareness caught for an instant on the one called Magiere.

Before this woman's arrival, countless decades had passed since he had looked upon any human. Of those he remembered, not one breed matched her white skin and black hair. There was something wrong about her—more than just the flawed nature of a human.

The sun had risen, glinting off the crimson shimmers in her hair.

Most Aged Father raced on, but his awareness halted in a cedar strangled by blackberry vines growing all the way up into its branches. A lingering prickle within its living wood stung his mind.

Many years had passed since a majay-hì or a *clhuassas* had come close enough to his home for him to feel their difference from the forest's mundane creatures. They shied from him, and even sensed his presence slipping through the forest's growth. But here in this tree, in these newly grown brambles, he felt it . . .

The same lingering touch as in the descendants of the born-Fay. What did this mean?

Most Aged Father drifted within the barrier woods, as if the very walls of his own home had been altered while he had slumbered. His panic mounted.

Footsteps approached in the outer forest. He slipped away, burrowing inward toward Cuirin'nên'a's clearing.

The farther north they ran, the more desperate Sgäile became.

He had never seen the prison glade of Cuirin'nên'a, though most long-standing anmaglâhk knew its location. A select few chosen only by Fréthfâre went regularly to check upon Cuirin'nên'a's needs. At the inception of her internment, some expressed concern for her well-being in isolation. Most Aged Father assured them that he would be aware of her needs—or if and when more was required for her. Fréthfâre held firm to limiting contact, and none but those she chose ever went to Cuirin'nên'a.

At the start of this pursuit, Sgäile did not believe Wynn and Chap could reach her before they were caught. The majay-hì might, but not with a small woman slowing them down. Then he had seen their tracks halt, and Wynn's boot prints vanished amid the hoof marks of a sentinel deer.

That a human rode a *clhuassas,* like some servant animal, was sickening. The sun had risen, and Sgäile knew the prison glade was not far off.

Someone called out from behind him.

Brot'ân'duivé was the first to halt and turn. As if summoned by Sgäile's heated thoughts, Fréthfâre came at a run up the path behind them.

Haggard and panting, she stopped near Én'nish and her two comrades. Fréthfâre's face dripped with sweat that matted her hair against her forehead.

"Turn back . . . by word . . . of Most Aged . . ." she gasped out, hands braced on her knees. "Do not go farther!"

Sgäile tensed in confusion. "I have oath of guardianship to fulfill, and the retrieval of a human wandering our land."

"No one goes near the traitor," Fréthfàre insisted.

This was the second time in Sgäile's life that he was ordered to violate the ways of his people. The first had been when he was sent to kill a half-blood, also marked as a traitor.

None of his people, the an'Cróan, would willingly spill the blood of their own. But the Anmaglâhk obeyed the direct wishes of Most Aged Father. Only the presence of a majay-hì and the half-blood's ignorance of his own people had justified Sgäile's disobedience.

Brot'ân'duivé spoke evenly. "Why would Most Aged Father force this upon Sgäilsheilleache's and those he has chosen to share his purpose?"

"What now?" Magiere spoke up.

Through his fatigue and strain, Sgäile had forgotten that neither Léshil nor Magiere understood Elvish.

"We have been ordered to return," he answered in Belaskian, "by Most Aged Father."

Anger spread on Magiere's sweat-glistened white face. Léshil took two steps down the path toward Fréthfàre.

"I don't serve your master," he said. "Go back on your own!"

"Wait!" Brot'ân'duivé snapped, and stepped between them.

"Get out of my way!" Léshil demanded.

Magiere turned from Fréthfàre, but Sgäile was not sure if her eyes were on Léshil or Brot'ân'duivé.

"Why am I forced into shame?" Sgäile demanded, keeping to Belaskian in the hope that it might distract his angered charges a little longer. "You trap me between caste and people with no way to serve both."

"Nothing is greater than service to the caste," Fréthfàre returned. "That is our service to the people. In silence and in shadows . . . obey!"

Én'nish stepped closer to Fréthfàre, a new eagerness washing over her sharp features.

"No," Brot'ân'duivé commanded.

Én'nish's two companions—and Osha—stood with attention shifting between Brot'ân'duivé and Fréthfàre. Like Sgäile, they were at a loss as to who had the greater authority here between Most Aged Father's trusted counselor and a revered master among the Anmaglâhk. Én'nish's allegiance was clear. Fréthfâre remained certain of her position, and her words were only formally polite.

"You disagree with our father, Greimasg'äh? You question my place as Covârleasa?"

"Yes," Brot'ân'duivé answered. "When it is used against our people."

Sgäile did not know what to do when he heard this. Brot'ân'duivé had not only rejected Fréthfâre's position, he had denounced it—and that of Most Aged Father. Sgäile found himself in an untenable situation and wanted no part of this.

Fréthfâre stood to full height. "Careful, Greimasg'äh . . . you are not so highly honored as to change caste ways at your whim."

"And what purpose do those ways serve?" Brot'ân'duivé returned. "They serve our people, first and foremost. Guardianship was an old tradition before the first supplicant bent knee before Most Aged Father. Break the ways of our people, and what is left for us to protect?"

Fréthfâre remained unconvinced, but Brot'ân'duivé cut off any rebuttal.

"Take this before the elders, if you wish. Even now they gather at Crij-heäiche. It is for them to decide—not you or I—if the people's ways shall be altered. Would not Most Aged Father agree, as first servant to the people?"

True as this was, Sgäile was still reluctant. Én'nish closely watched Fréthfâre's silent frustration, waiting for the Covârleasa to counter Brot'ân'duivé's words.

Brot'ân'duivé stepped to the path's side, and his passive gaze fell upon Sgäile. The elder anmaglâhk held out a hand to the open trail ahead.

"We follow in service to your purpose."

Sgäile turned his gaze from Brot'ân'duivé to Fréthfâre and back again. He did not know which of them had put him in the worst position. He stepped past Léshil, and the others followed, including Fréthfâre.

Not long after, Sgäile paused again. Paw prints led both ahead and off into the forest on his left. Brot'ân'duivé studied the split trail. There were signs that the pack had turned into the trees and back again, but why?

"It is your purpose and your choice," Brot'ân'duivé said to him.

Sgäile took a slow breath. "We move on and leave this deviation for our return."

He headed on in silence, and a short way down the main trail he slowed in caution.

"Is this . . . ," he began in Elvish, for he did not want Léshil to hear.

"Yes," Brot'ân'duivé answered. "But it has changed."

The forest gathered upon itself in a wild and impenetrable tangle, except for one open passage that cut through the dense barrier.

"Well?" Léshil asked. "Is this it?"

Sgäile did not know how to answer, and Brot'ân'duivé had gone silent again.

"Fine!" Léshil snapped, and stepped into the path through the woods.

Sgäile followed. In spite of deep concerns over Léshil locating Cuirin'nên'a, he could not stop this search. They had to find Wynn at any cost and bring her back.

At the end of the long path, he stepped through tall ferns behind Léshil.

A pack of majay-hì bustled about a lawn of grass and dark moss surrounding a single domicile elm. There stood Chap between Wynn and a tall elven woman in a shimmering white wrap.

Despair washed through Sgäile as he met the glower of Cuirin'nên'a. Wynn had been found, and his guardianship restored, but Sgäile had failed Most Aged Father once more.

Leesil thrashed through the ferns and halted, rooted to the ground. He stopped breathing. Wynn and Chap stood in the clearing, but he didn't really see them.

He only saw his mother, the perfect lines of her face, her tall and lithe stature, and eyes that could swallow all his awareness. He felt as he had looking down from the mountainside upon the vast elven forest—relieved and overwhelmed all at once. He had struggled and fought—and killed—for this intangible moment.

A flicker of terror passed through his mother's eyes at the sight of him.

In Leesil's youth, she had seldom shown open fear—and never at him.

Magiere came up beside him, but Leesil couldn't take his eyes from Nein'a. "Mother?"

Someone grabbed his shoulder

Leesil knew it wasn't Magiere. Anger rose as he glanced back to find Sgäile restraining him.

Brot'an shook his head. "We are here now, and nothing can be done for it."

Sgäile's mouth tightened, but he stepped back as the others came through the ferns. Fréth's narrowing eyes turned on Brot'an.

Leesil moved slowly forward, and Nein'a—Mother—turned her face aside. Perhaps all the years alone made her cringe with sorrow. The thought almost stopped Leesil from going on. He shrugged off the rope harness and brought the chest around into his hands.

One steel-gray majay-hì started and then lunged away from the surrounding woods. It spun about to stare into the trees, pacing.

Chap flinched and warily watched the steel-gray dog. The white female beside him hopped in closer to push at Chap with a whine. The other majay-hì grew more agitated in their movements.

It was the dogs and not Leesil that made Nein'a lift her face. Fear returned as she watched them. Her expression darkened when she peered among the trees, as if searching out some hidden threat.

Leesil slowed under the growing weight of guilt. Long imprisonment had affected his mother's mind. He kept on, stopping only when close enough to reach her.

Unbidden memories came of long hours training with her, the meals they had shared, and how she checked on him in his room when she thought he was asleep—and of a sad father who had done all this as well with unexplained reluctance.

Leesil wanted to confess his sorrow and guilt for abandoning her, for his father's death . . . for everything. But the words wouldn't come.

"Mother . . . ," he finally said, "I'm taking you out of here."

Nein'a didn't reach out to put a hand upon his cheek, as she had long ago.

"Leave," she whispered with a slow shake of her head. "Get out of this land . . . if you still can."

Leesil's voice failed. He had come all this way, risked the lives of Magiere and Wynn and Chap—and her only response was to tell him to go?

Nein'a's large eyes shifted to Brot'an as the man approached. Leesil saw pleading in her gaze, and Brot'an's passive expression softened when he looked upon her. Leesil's stunned outrage was lost in chill anger.

Nein'a briefly spoke to Brot'an in Elvish, but the name "Léshil" was easy to catch. A silent Wynn looked up in dismay at Nein'a; this was enough to tell Leesil that his mother had asked Brot'an to take him away. He couldn't bear any more of this.

Leesil dropped to one knee and flipped open the chest, lifting the cloth bundle from within. He separated the cloth's folds and thrust out the skulls like a spiteful offering.

"I took them from Darmouth," he said sharply. "I went back looking for you and Father."

Nein'a's breath turned shallow as she reached out a hand. The closer it came to the skull of Leesil's father, the more her long, slender fingers shook.

"It is him?"

"Yes," Leesil said. "And your mother . . . though I was told it was you."

He cast a hateful glance at Brot'an, daring the tall elf to even try to explain. Brot'an offered no reply by word or expression.

"It is Eillean . . . and Gavril," Leesil said. "I brought them to you . . . for whatever last rites you see fit."

Nein'a's fingers slid to her mother's skull. Leesil had rarely seen her cry, but tears dropped down her caramel cheeks in silence. They seemed to drag her down into some strange sickness, and guilt flooded through Leesil again for his harsh words.

Nein'a took the cloth with both skulls and cradled them.

"Leave here at once," she whispered. "You cannot stay."

It was a long cold moment before she looked up and saw the others behind Leesil. Low, sharp Elvish erupted from her lips. The words sounded much the same as what she'd said to Brot'an, though this time Leesil caught Sgäile's longer elven name. She wasn't making a request, but a demand.

"You're coming with me," Leesil said. "I'm not leaving without you."

"I cannot," she whispered.

"It is true," Wynn said cautiously. "The path simply returns her, and anyone with her, back to this clearing. Chap and I have tried."

The sage's face and hands were covered in small scratches and scrapes. Leesil should've been angry for all the trouble she and Chap had caused, but then, they had found his mother.

"Enough!" Sgäile commanded. "We return to Crijheäiche. Léshil, come."

"No," he whispered.

He stood within reach of his mother—and she was alive. Her insistence that he go didn't matter. If anyone thought he'd simply walk away, they were dangerously mistaken.

At quick footsteps from behind, Leesil caught the barest cinch of Brot'an's scar-cut eyebrow.

Leesil back-stepped and spun out of reach.

As Sgäile tried to close the distance, Magiere snatched his cloak at the neck. Sgäile swung back with the edge of a flattened hand. It caught Magiere across the throat, and she fell back gagging.

"Stop this," Brot'an shouted. "Both of you cease!"

Osha stiffened at Brot'an's order, but the others didn't listen. As Sgäile turned his determined attention back toward Leesil, Magiere thrashed around on the grass.

Leesil saw her irises flood black.

"No," he whispered, panic-stricken. "Not now. . . ."

Magiere kicked into the back of Sgäile's leg.

Sgäile buckled, dropping to his knee. Fréthfâre and Én'nish's two companions descended on Magiere. Leesil tried to rush in.

Én'nish dodged in his way, a long-bladed stiletto in each hand.

Anxiety overwhelmed Most Aged Father. The little human woman had reached Cuirin'nên'a. When Léshil and the others arrived, all his careful plans evaporated.

He heard Cuirin'nên'a's repeated refusals to come away with Léshil and grew even more frustrated. Her words would only make Léshil lose hope, and without that, he would become more difficult to manipulate. It was clear that Cuirin'nên'a would sacrifice any tie to her son to protect him.

Most Aged Father writhed as the means to ferret out her confederates shriveled before him. She was a cunning one. He had hoped long isolation might make her desperate enough that Léshil could be used against her. Or his attachment to his mother could be used against him.

The only relief came at Sgäilsheilleache's urgent attempt to remove Léshil from the encounter. The longer Léshil faced his mother's denial, the greater the risk he might turn from any lingering desire to free her.

The pale woman grabbed for the back of Sgäilsheilleache's cloak.

Most Aged Father's frail heart began to race.

Magiere's eyes locked on Nein'a the moment she stepped into the clearing. Less than a year past, Leesil had told her of Nein'a and Gavril. How many years before that had he drank himself to sleep, hiding from nightmares of a past he couldn't bear and a guilt he couldn't escape?

And here was Nein'a, finally, yet she offered little welcome to Leesil. Magiere barely heard what was said as she waited for the easing of Leesil's pain.

It never came.

Leesil deserved more than this. It didn't matter what he'd done. There had to be more than the denial of a cold-blooded mother.

The low thrum in Magiere's body, which she'd held down for days and nights, began to make her shake. When Sgäile closed on Leesil from behind, it lunged up her throat like hunger and filled her head.

She snatched Sgäile's cloak from behind.

Her throat clenched when he struck. She fell back and lost sight of everyone.

She hit the ground, and hunger devoured the pain in her throat. The sun blinded her for an instant when her vision widened. She writhed around to glare at Sgäile's back, his hair now brilliant white in her sight. Then she saw Leesil's glimmering amber eyes fill with anguish. He stared right at her.

Magiere kicked the back of Sgäile's knee as the first tear ran from her burning eyes.

No one was taking Leesil from here until he got what he came for.

Her jaws began to ache the instant Sgäile buckled. When she slapped her hand to the ground to get up, someone pulled it from under her. Anger mounted as her face struck the moss and she lost sight of Leesil.

Magiere twisted on the ground and a flash of gray passed above her. Chap slammed into Fréth with a snarl, and Magiere's wrist jerked free of the woman's grip. She pulled her feet under herself as one of Én'nish's companions came at her. Magiere lunged from her crouch and slammed her hand into his midsection.

Her hardened nails bit through his tunic, and she grabbed his collar with her other hand. Turning, she dragged him in an arc as she rose. Gray-green fabric tore in her grip as she flung him into the clearing's border trees.

Where was Leesil?

Urgency shivered through her and she wanted to rend anyone who touched him. The bright sun made the world burn and blur in her expanded sight. Something struck her lower back.

Moss tore under Magiere's boots as she ground her feet in resistance.

What was it—this thing that tried to stop her from finding Leesil?

Magiere turned on it.

She saw a gray-green cowl around an astonished tan face. Her anger turned manic as it backed away. She lunged at it.

Leesil twisted aside as Én'nish slashed her right blade at his face. Her left stiletto thrust instantly for his gut.

He speared his hand downward and slapped away the blade, and it passed harmlessly off his side. Her lunge brought her close. Leesil twisted sharply right, driving his left elbow at her face.

Én'nish ducked, and her parried stiletto slashed across Leesil's midsection.

He heard it skitter across the rings of his hauberk. He felt its tip catch in one laced ring at his left side.

She shifted behind the blade to thrust with all her weight, and Leesil spun quickly, trying to turn out of her path.

The tip held and tore through. Leather split.

Leesil felt no burn of pierced skin, but he heard the tinkling of metal. One of his hauberk's steel rings dangled against the round guard of Én'nish's blade.

Leesil grabbed Én'nish's wrist below that dangling ring, and his gaze caught on her amber eyes so close to his face.

Another time and place—another woman with a knife—had looked at him with the same desperation. All because he'd killed someone she loved.

He raised his other arm on instinct, and Én'nish's free blade slashed his forearm.

Leesil shifted weight into his rear foot, prepared to throw a shoulder into Én'nish and take her to the ground. His rear foot jerked from the mossy ground and a soft-booted foot struck his hip.

Without footing, Leesil flipped sideways. A grunt erupted from him as his back hit the ground. When he rolled to his feet, Brot'an stood in his path. But the scar-faced elf wasn't looking at him.

"Enough!" Brot'an ordered. "Both of you!"

He held a wide and low stance with his right palm out at arm's length. But not toward Leesil. A half dozen paces beyond Brot'an's hand lay Én'nish.

She was curled on the lawn, holding her chest and gasping for breath. One of her long stilettos lay at Brot'an's feet.

Chap ground his forepaws in Fréthfàre's stomach as he snarled into her face. The woman went rigid on her back staring up at him. But Chap faltered at Magiere's hissing screech.

She lunged into one of Én'nish's companions. Tears ran from her eyes around a mouth wide with sharp teeth and fangs.

Magiere had lost all control in front of the Anmaglâhk.

She sank hardened fingernails into her target as Sgäile closed on her back.

The other majay-hì circled away from the conflict, but the pack elder lifted his grizzled muzzle. He stared intently at Magiere, and his jowls wrinkled.

Chap grew frantic. He had no more time to keep Fréthfàre pinned.

Lily paced behind the elder, looking into the trees where Magiere had flung her first opponent. That anmaglâhk had not gotten up.

Chap could not turn from Fréthfàre to touch heads with Lily. All he could do was reach for her own memories. He dipped into Lily's mind, calling up her sight of Fréthfàre standing before Most Aged Father's massive oak, and added the memory she had shown to him in fear—the dark opening in that tree. He repeated these in an alternating flurry and hoped she understood.

The pack elder charged at Magiere with an eerie howl, and Chap bolted toward Magiere and those closing on her.

Magiere rushed the anmaglâhk drawing his blades and drove one hand at his throat. Instead of slashing at her, he ducked into the brush beneath the closest birch. Something snagged Magiere's hair, jerking her head back. Her legs buckled under someone's whipping leg.

Her knees hit the ground. With her head pulled back, she looked up to see Sgäile, his grip tangled in her hair. He sucked a sharp breath at the sight of her face.

Magiere swung a hand upward to claw his astonished features, but Sgäile fell away beneath a snarling silver-furred bulk. Magiere toppled sideways as Sgäile's grip tore from her hair. Her hand slapped firmly against the base of the birch.

Shock ran through her and every muscle clenched tight.

A wild rush of nervous energy flooded her limbs from that brief touch and filled her up with its intensity.

Magiere jerked her hand away, rolling to her feet. Sgäile struggled under Chap's assault, but the dog wheeled around, charging the other way.

He was hunting—like her—and Magiere's hungry gaze traced the path to his target.

A dark-furred dog rushed at her, its gray-peppered jowls pulled back from yellowed teeth.

Leesil heard Magiere's feral screech as she reached for one anmaglâhk with Sgäile coming at her from behind. Chap took Sgäile down but not before Magiere toppled. When she rose, shuddering as she snatched her hand from a tree, Leesil saw her face.

Her teeth . . . the tears . . . her irises so full black they nearly blotted out the whites of her eyes. He started to run for her.

Brot'an stepped in his way, and Leesil threw himself at the tall elf.

"Leesil . . . no!" his mother shouted.

Brot'an's palm slammed against Leesil's chest, driving the air from his lungs. But it wasn't enough to stop him.

Leesil fell on Brot'an, and they both hit the ground. He tumbled away as Brot'an tried to grab him. When he reached his feet, Wynn raced by him, clutching something in her arms. She threw it, and only then Leesil saw the large, grizzled majay-hì charge Magiere.

Bits of fluffy white nodules spun from the basket Wynn had thrown. It hit the charging dog in the shoulder. The impact startled the dark majay-hì. It spun away, and Chap barreled into the dog. Both wheeled around each other in snapping growls.

Osha finally flew into motion, running after Wynn.

Leesil sidled around Brot'an, trying to reach Magiere, but he backed into someone else.

He pivoted, cutting upward with a fist at whichever anmaglâhk was behind him. He saw a flash of shimmering white before his wrist was snatched.

His mother twisted his swing aside, throwing him off balance. Leesil righted himself in panic at what he'd almost done.

Nein'a glared at him. "What have you brought among us?"

Leesil floundered in confusion until his mother raised her head. Her gaze fixed upon Magiere.

Most Aged Father's awareness flitted around the clearing from one tree to the next. Watching from within an elm, all he perceived left him overwhelmed, including the strange majay-hì assaulting his treasured Fréthfàre. Then his awareness fell upon Magiere.

Far from the glade and deep within his massive oak, Most Aged Father curled into a twitching ball. No one heard his whimper.

He saw the pale woman with her bestial face slap a hand against one tree. He felt the forest's life shudder under that touch. It hurt, as if a piece of him had been bitten away.

Ancient memory writhed in the back of his mind. In sickening fear, he slipped his awareness around the clearing toward the pale monster.

All of Magiere's rage turned on Sgäile.

"Undead!" he hissed, and a blade appeared in his hand.

She saw only one more obstacle to reaching Leesil. Her jaws widened but no words came out. A rustle of movement sounded in the brush behind her at the clearing's edge.

Sgäile held up his hand, but not at her, and he snapped some command in Elvish. He never took his eyes off her, and his horror fed Magiere's hunger.

"Stop! All of you. Stop this now!"

Brot'an's deep voice carried through the glade. Magiere twisted her head around, tensing at the threat. Behind the tall elf stood Leesil, his wrist gripped tightly in his mother's hand.

Osha had Wynn pinned in his arms.

"Magiere . . . enough," the sage shouted. "Please . . . get control of yourself."

Fréth knelt nearby, mouth ajar at the white majay-hì blocking her off. Just short of them, Chap crouched in the way of the larger dark dog. The rest of the pack began to circle in.

Magiere's head began to ache as the hunger shrank into the pit of her stomach. The more it receded, the more she started to shake. As if she'd swallowed too much drink . . . too much of Wynn's tea . . . or too much food, too much . . . life.

She stumbled back, and her heel caught in a bush. She toppled, falling against a tree trunk, and slapped her hand against its bark to steady herself.

Another shock ran deep into Magiere.

The world went black before her eyes. In that sudden darkness, strange sounds and sights erupted in Magiere's head.

CHAPTER FOURTEEN

Curled in his tree's bower, Most Aged Father gaped in pain.

The pale-skinned monster touched the birch the instant his awareness slipped into it.

He felt the tree's life slipping away into her flesh. He felt it as if she touched his skin, feeding upon him, and memory welled up to wrap him in suffering.

Another like her had come for him in the dark . . . long, long ago. . . .

Sorhkafâré—Light upon the Grass. That was his true name back then.

He had dropped weary and beaten upon a stained wool blanket, filthy from moons of forced marches. He did not even care to have his wounds tended and lay in the darkness of his tent.

Only two of his commanders had survived the day. He had lost more officers upon that field than during all of the last moon. Someone called to him from outside his tent but he did not answer. Hesitantly, the voice came again.

"The human and dwarven ranks are too depleted for another engagement. They must fall back."

The enemy's condition was unknown. With his eyes closed, Sorhkafâré saw nothing but the sea of dead he had left on the rolling plains. The fragile alliance had been outnumbered nearly five to one on this day.

Again he did not answer. He could not look at the faces of the living, and even if he opened his eyes, he couldn't stop seeing those of the dead.

The enemy's horde had pressed north along the eastern coast of the central continent. At dawn, he had received word that Bäalâle Seatt had fallen to an unknown catastrophe. The dwarven mother-city in the mountains bordering the Suman Desert had long been under siege. Scattered reports hinted that neither side had survived whatever had happened there.

The enemy's numbers seemed endless. And all that remained in the west to stop them were Sorhkafâré's forces, the last to keep the enemy from turning inland toward Aonnis Lhoin'n—First Glade—the refuge and home of his people.

He heard the footsteps outside fade away. Finally they left him alone.

Sleep would not come, and he did not want it. He still saw thousands slaughtering each other under the hot sun. He had lost all reckoning of whose cries were those of his enemies or his allies. He lost fury and even fear this day upon the plain.

Countless furred, scaled, or dark- to light-skinned faces fell before his spear and arrows, and yet they kept coming. One mutilated body blurred into another . . . except for the last rabid goblin, dead at his feet when it all ended. Its long tongue dangled from its canine mouth into the blood-soaked mud.

Sorhkafâré heard a shout and then a moan somewhere outside in the camp, and then another.

The wounded and dying were given what aid could be rendered, but they only suffered the more for it. Who would want to live another day like this one?

More shouts. Running feet. A brief clatter of steel.

Someone fumbled at the canvas flap of his tent.

"Leave me," he said tiredly and did not get up.

The tent ripped open.

Camp bonfires outside cast an orange glow around the shadowed figure of a human male. Sorhkafâré could not make out the man's face. The light glinted dully upon the edges of his steel-scaled carapace. His skin seemed dark, like that of a Suman.

Sorhkafâré's senses sharpened.

By proportions, there had been as many humans among the enemy's horde as among his alliance forces. Most with the enemy had been Suman. Had one slipped into camp unseen? He sat up quickly.

The man's arm holding aside the tent flap was severed off above the wrist. His other hand was empty.

No one walked about with such a wound. Sorhkafâré heard another cry somewhere out in the camp.

The crippled skulker rushed in with a grating hiss, guttural and full of madness.

Sorhkafâré rolled to the tent's far side and pulled his war knife. His attacker fell upon the empty bedroll. As the man turned upon the blanket, Sorhkafâré drove his blade down.

It sank through the man's dark-skinned neck above the armor's collar, and he slumped, limp.

Sorhkafâré rushed from the tent. He searched the night camp for any officer to chastise over the failure of the perimeter watch. The few remaining cries died away one by one.

The nearest fire had been doused, and only smoking embers remained. Many of the torches were gone, and darkness had thickened in the camp. The moon was not yet high enough for his elven eyes, but he thought he saw figures moving quickly from tent to tent. Now and then came strange muffled sounds or a short cry.

"Sorhkafâré . . . where were you?"

A figure approached, slow and purposeful, between the rows of tents. He knew that voice. It grated upon his nerves every time the man spoke.

Kædmon, commander of the humans among Sorhkafâré's forces—or what were left of them.

Sorhkafâré had no strength for another argument. It was always Kædmon who challenged him. He pushed his men too hard and kept demanding night strikes after his people had marched all day.

Kædmon drew closer, and Sorhkafâré saw the dark rents in the tall man's chain armor. He had not bothered to remove it, but Sorhkafâré could not blame him. There was no point in doing so, as they would only ride hard with the dawn, either in flight or to face an endless enemy once more.

Someone stepped from a tent beyond Kædmon, dragging a body.

Sorhkafâré had no more sorrow to spare for those who succumbed to wounds. But the shadowed figure dropped the body in the dirt and turned away to the next tent.

"Didn't you see them come?" Kædmon said. "Did you not hear us cry for help as the sun dropped below the hills? Or was it only your own kind . . . your wounded that you culled from the dead today?"

Sorhkafâré turned his eyes back to Kædmon. He barely made out the man's long face and square jaw below a wide mouth.

"What venom do you spit now?" he answered. "We left no one who had even a single breath in them! All were carried in, even those with no hope to see tomorrow."

The man's ugly square jaw was covered in a few days' growth of beard. Stubble on his neck looked darker still. His steel coif and its chain drape were gone, exposing lank black hair hanging around his light-skinned face. His bloodthirsty human eyes glittered.

"You didn't bring me," Kædmon hissed back and his words grew awkward as if he had difficulty speaking. "I still breathed when they crept across the dead, looking for those you forgot . . . when the sun vanished from sight."

A dark patch at Kædmon's throat glistened as he stepped to within a spear's reach.

Sorhkafâré stepped back.

A gaping wound in the side of Kædmon's neck had covered his throat in blood mixed with some black viscous fluid. His lips and teeth looked stained as well.

Kædmon's eyes were as colorless as his pallid skin.

"I can't stop myself . . . they won't let me stop."

Kædmon shook with clenched muscles as his crystal eyes scrunched closed for an instant. He took a jerking step. All tense resistance vanished, and he charged with open hands.

Sorhkafâré set himself but did not raise his knife.

Kædmon had seen too much in these long years of battle. They all had. The man's mind finally broke under the strain. No matter their differences, he was an ally who had fought hard beside Sorhkafâré's own people. Kædmon had lost his own father when their settlement was overrun before alliance forces arrived to defend it. But still the man fought on, and his loyalty had never wavered.

Sorhkafâré sidestepped, ready to slap away Kædmon's grasp. He barely drew back his hand before Kædmon's grip latched around his throat. Too sudden and too quick for a wounded man.

Kædmon closed his fingers.

Sorhkafâré could not breathe. He tried to break the man's grip. Kædmon's features twisted in agony as his mouth opened.

"Don't fight," he whispered. "Please don't make me . . . make you suffer."

Sorhkafâré almost stopped fighting for air.

Within Kædmon's mouth he saw malformed teeth stained with blood. A human mouth with sharpened fangs like a dog or short-snouted goblin. He slashed the knife across the back of Kædmon's forearm, but the man did not even flinch.

Sorhkafâré's chest convulsed, trying to get air, and his sight began to dim. He rammed the blade into the side of Kædmon's neck.

Kædmon's head snapped sideways under the blow. He gagged once before his face turned back, now little more than a blurred oval of white in Sorhkafâré's waning sight.

"It won't help," Kædmon sobbed. "I'm sorry . . . it never does."

Air seeped in through Sorhkafâré's nose.

He heaved, filling up his lungs, then gagged and coughed as he tried to suck more air. He lay on his side upon the ground, not even knowing he had fallen. A blurred form appeared above him and reached down. Sorhkafâré twisted away in panic.

"Get up, sir!" it said, and the words were in his own Elvish tongue. "The horses have been slaughtered . . . we must run!"

Vision cleared, and Sorhkafâré saw one of his commanders. Snähacróe reached down for him, but Sorhkafâré only looked about for Kædmon.

The man lay crumpled on his side, off to the left. The shaft of an elven spear rose from his torso. Its silvery tip protruded from Kædmon's rib cage, and black fluids ran from the bright metal to the ground.

Sorhkafâré stared at the gaping wound, not truly aware of Snähacróe until his kinsman pulled at him, trying to make him follow.

Kædmon rolled onto his face and braced his hands upon the ground. He pushed up and lifted his head. Snähacróe halted in shock to look at the human.

Kædmon began to shake. Once more his whole body seemed to clench. His fingers bit into the earth as if he sought to hold on to it and keep from rising.

"Run," he whimpered.

Sorhkafâré still hesitated. The man could not be alive. The spear point dripped more black fluid from his body and the same ran from the knife wound in his neck. The broken stream of fluid vanished as it struck the earth, but Sorhkafâré heard the slow patter continue.

"Run . . . while you can!" Kædmon shouted.

Snähacróe wrenched Sorhkafâré around and they fled.

Grim silhouettes closed in behind them with pounding feet. The more that came, the more Sorhkafâré saw one here and there from the ranks of both sides that day in battle. Their faces seemed too pallid in the dark.

All around were figures with glittering eyes.

Sorhkafâré . . .

The name clung to Magiere's thoughts like her own, as she came slowly back to consciousness.

"Sgäilsheilleache, hold off!"

It was Brot'an's voice, but Magiere only saw moving blurs around her. She felt and smelled moss against her face.

She began panting hard.

"She is unnatural," Sgäile snapped. "Undead . . . in our forest!"

"No," Brot'an barked. "She is something else. Now do as I say!"

Magiere took three rapid breaths before her thoughts cleared in realization.

Brot'an had never told the others about what he had seen of her in Darmouth's crypt. He had kept her secret.

It didn't matter anymore. She'd lost all control, and they'd all seen her.

Magiere's sight cleared slowly. She lay on her side, one hand limp upon the moss before her face. There was blood on her fingernails.

But her hand was not long-boned and tan as it had been in the dream . . . the vision . . . whatever she should call the sights and sounds that had taken her. She saw only her own pale hand, not that of the elven man she had become . . . *Sorhkafâré.*

Why? She hadn't touched the remains of any victim, trying to see through the eyes of its undead killer at the moment of death.

Magiere flopped onto her back, trying to find the faces of those around her. She looked at the birch that she'd backed into and touched before the world turned black. She began to tremble.

The tree's trunk bore the mark of her hands. Where she'd touched it, the bark had darkened and dried dead. Brittle pieces had already fallen away.

"Leesil!" she cried out.

"Here . . . I'm here!" he answered; and then, "Get out of my way!"

A wet nose grazed her neck, and Chap's head pressed into her face.

She dug her fingers in his fur and hung on. Leesil dropped to his knees beside her.

Magiere latched on to him, thrashing around to bury her face in the chest of his hauberk and hide from all eyes.

"It's all right," he whispered.

She still felt the lingering shock in her body and saw in her mind the marks of her hands upon the birch. Nothing was all right anymore.

Magiere closed her fingers on Leesil's hauberk until its leather creaked in her hands and its rings bit into her palms. The name she'd been called still echoed in her head. Her . . . his allies came in the dark with colorless eyes and teeth stained with the blood of their own.

Sorhkafâré.

"I said keep back!" Leesil growled, and pulled Magiere closer. "It's over."

He knew better than to touch Magiere until she recognized him. But when she fell and cried out for him, he knew her dhampir nature had already retreated.

Brot'an stepped around to wave Sgäile off. Osha finally released Wynn.

Én'nish was on her feet but still hunkered from Brot'an's strike. Her one remaining companion aided the other that Magiere had thrown into the trees. They both emerged, but the latter man was limping badly and the front of his tunic was shredded.

Nein'a glared at Leesil in shock. Any hint of fearful and angry denials she'd cast at him were gone. There was only wary revulsion as her gaze drifted from him down to Magiere hiding in his arms.

"It is not over," Fréth said coldly, and the white majay-hì shifted silently in her way. "You have brought an undead into our midst. I do not understand how this is possible, but this thing you coddle will not remain."

Leesil's anger rose again, but he couldn't leave Magiere.

"Chap," he said quietly, "kill anyone who takes a step."

Chap didn't answer in any fashion. He simply paced around Leesil to stand before Magiere and glanced once at the white majay-hì blocking Fréth.

"Enough," Brot'an insisted. "If she were undead, the forest never would have allowed her to enter. There is nothing Léshil could have done to change that."

Leesil wasn't certain about the shift in authority taking place. Both Sgäile and Fréth were reluctant, but it seemed Brot'an took charge. For the moment, it served to protect Magiere from the others—but still, Leesil didn't like it.

Brot'an's pale scars stood out like white slashes on his lined face. "We are all fatigued from a night of running with no food. We will rest part of the day in the outer forest."

He gestured toward the fern-curtained passage.

"Fréthfâre, please report to Most Aged Father. Tell him all is settled, that we have found the human woman and will return soon. Sgäilsheilleache, you and Osha find food, and Én'nish . . ."

Brot'an spun toward her, and now Leesil couldn't see his expression.

"You and those serving your purpose will keep well apart from Sgäile and his charges. Or you will have more to answer for upon our return."

Én'nish picked up her fallen blade as she hobbled past Brot'an. Her face dark with malice, she joined her two companions and headed out through the woods' passage.

Leesil tried to get Magiere on her feet. When Brot'an approached, Chap lunged, and his teeth clacked shut on air as Brot'an leaped away.

"No more," Sgäile said quickly to the dog. "No more fighting . . . let him pass."

Brot'an betrayed subtle surprise at Sgäile's words. "It seems there are some things you have not told me."

Sgäile sighed but didn't answer.

"It's all right, Chap," Magiere said.

Leesil's uncertainty grew. Brot'an might have pacified further conflict for the moment. But it was still Brot'an, the one who'd used him. Leesil would never sink to a hint of gratitude, but he let Magiere step forward to follow Brot'an.

Leesil looked back into the glade. Nein'a watched him, but he no longer saw anything recognizable in her cold eyes.

An abomination in his land.

Most Aged Father—who had once been Sorhkafâré—quaked in his bower.

This pallid woman with blood-stained hair had fooled even Fréthfâre.

In that long night, running beside Snähacróe and the others, he had heard the cries behind him. Each dawn that followed, fewer remained in his company.

There had been humans and dwarves as well as his own kind. The dwarves had been the first to fall. Unable to keep the pace with their short legs and heavy bodies, fewer and fewer of those stout people were present at dawn when his meager forces fell prostrate upon the ground. They foraged for water and food by day, slept what little they could in shifts, and before dusk each night they fled inland toward Aonnis Lhoin'n.

Not long past each dusk, they heard the shouts and running feet of abominations closing upon them. Each night they were closer, as he and his forces grew more weary and worn with flight. More than once he glanced back to see dozens of sparking eyes, perhaps a hundred, in the dark.

Then humans and elves began to fall behind as well, and no one could turn back for them. Along their harried passage, they found desolate and shattered towns and villages. And more than once, pale figures erupted from the dark ahead of them. They slogged their way through, but more of his fleeing band were always gone when they halted at the next dawn.

Most Aged Father could not shake the memories from his mind.

Cuirin'nên'a and her hidden dissidents no longer mattered. Long ago, he had brought his people here to safety. Now this woman—this abomination— appeared among them. A human-spawned thing. The Ancient Enemy stirred sooner than he had feared. It was the only explanation he saw to account for this new tool of bloodshed and devastation. One that could breach his people's land, the only haven that had saved them in those long lost days.

Most Aged Father lifted his wrinkled hand from the bower's wood, but his fingers would not stop shaking.

CHAPTER FIFTEEN

Fréthfâre ran from the glade with her heart pounding. She fled far into the forest before daring to find a place in which to speak with Most Aged Father. How could she tell him what had happened, what she had seen? Where would she even begin? An undead entered their land and walked freely among the people—and was now protected by Brot'ân'duivé.

She glanced up at the sun caught on the edge of drifting dark clouds. Within moments, the morning light faded. The forest darkened around her. An omen.

She dropped to her knees beneath a tall elm's branches and pressed the smooth word-wood to its bark. Her reluctance to report such disturbing events fell before her need for Most Aged Father's guidance.

"Father . . ."

I am here, daughter.

His voice in her thoughts brought some relief. "I do not know where to begin . . . I have failed—"

I know all. I was there as you faced this horror. Destroy it! Tell Brot'ân'duivé my wishes, and dispatch the smaller human woman as well. You and Sgäilsheilleache first restrain Léshil. Disable him if need be, but he is not to be permanently harmed.

Perhaps Most Aged Father had not seen everything.

"Brot'ân'duivé protects this undead woman," Fréthfâre answered, "and allowed Léshil to speak with Cuirin'nên'a. Even with Én'nish's assistance and those with her, I do not think we could overcome the Greimasg'äh if he refuses. And Léshil and this woman would side with Brot'ân'duivé."

The tree was silent for a long moment, and then . . .

Give Brot'ân'duivé my instructions. He will obey.

For the first time, Fréthfâre doubted Most Aged Father's wisdom. Perhaps he had not seen Brot'ân'duivé's face as the elder anmaglâhk stopped Sgäil-sheilleache from going after the wild woman.

"Father, the situation is untenable. Osha is untried and in service to Sgäil-sheilleache's guardianship. I do not believe they would submit even to Brot'ân'duivé in conflict with that purpose. And the Greimasg'äh is . . ."

She faltered at casting aspersions upon one of her caste's eldest.

"Brot'ân'duivé is a stranger among us. Forgive my doubts, but would it not be better to lead this undead back to Crijheäiche? With those of our caste waiting, we could take her easily, especially if Léshil is to remain unharmed."

Again the tree went silent.

Yes . . . your wise counsel gives me great pride. Bring them to Crijheäiche.

Fréth breathed easily again. "In silence and in shadows."

The morning sun slipped behind thick clouds, and the promise of a fine day vanished. The sky turned gray, and the air grew chill.

Brot'ân'duivé knew what Fréthfâre would tell Most Aged Father—what she had seen and what he had done—but it could not be helped. He needed Léshil, or all the frail plans of Cuirin'nên'a and the long lost Eillean would lead to nothing.

In the crypt of Darmouth, it was clear how much this tainted woman, Magiere, meant to Léshil. Perhaps dangerously more than the half-blood understood. Brot'ân'duivé could not allow her to be harmed, or Léshil would suffer and be lost from the purpose that awaited him. Brot'ân'duivé stayed close to Léshil and Magiere and made certain that Én'nish and her companions remained far off.

It had been eight years since Brot'ân'duivé had seen Cuirin'nên'a, not since the night she had been banished into permanent isolation by Most Aged Father. There was too much risk in meeting with Cuirin'nên'a—for her, for himself, and for the few who supported all that Eillean had begun long ago. But the sight of Cuirin'nên'a's face with its hints of Eillean had put him off balance.

Though he had never spoken of it, perhaps the daughter suspected how much he had loved the mother. He had sacrificed so much to keep his promise to Eillean. He had sacrificed Eillean herself. Soon he would sacrifice yet more.

Léshil had good reason to hate him. But Brot'ân'duivé had no choice in bringing Cuirin'nên'a back for judgment. One of them had to remain free of Most Aged Father's confirmed suspicions, and Cuirin'nên'a had already fallen from their leader's goodwill. It remained imperative that Brot'ân'duivé not fall with her. She understood this.

He had manipulated Léshil into finishing his own mission and assassinating Darmouth. Again, he had seen no other option. What he did, he did for his people rather than the goals of Most Aged Father.

Sgäilsheilleache and Osha returned with walnuts and berries. Sgäilsheilleache looked ill and would not raise his eyes to anyone. Brot'ân'duivé pitied him. Sworn guardianship or not, Sgäilsheilleache would not rest easy in Magiere's presence—nor would Fréthfâre.

Neither would Brot'ân'duivé.

He reached out and took walnuts and berries with both hands. "Both of you stay with Én'nish and the others. Fréthfâre will return soon."

Sgäilsheilleache finally looked up. Before he objected, Brot'ân'duivé gave his assurance.

"I will serve your guardianship as if it were my own. Take your ease for a time. When we return to Crijheäiche, Most Aged Father will advise us wisely."

These last words stuck in his throat, but the pretense was necessary.

Sgäilsheilleache glanced toward Magiere, and a hint of revulsion resurfaced. He nodded and turned away with young Osha following.

Brot'ân'duivé stepped off through the trees toward the separate gathering of Sgäilsheilleache's charges. He had not met the small one called Wynn, who now sat against a large cedar, bare of branches at its base. She had torn a strip of cloth from some garment to make a bandage for the shallow slash on Léshil's forearm. Beside her was the majay-hì, Chap, who Sgäilsheilleache and Léshil had both spoken to in the clearing—a strange moment.

Majay-hì and human stared off through the forest, and Brot'ân'duivé caught a glimpse of the pack among the trees. Now and then, a white female ranged closer.

The fact that the pack and a *clhuassas* had aided a human in finding

Cuirin'nên'a was perplexing. Against their long-standing protection of this land from outsiders, they found nothing to fear from this little one called Wynn.

Brot'ân'duivé did not believe in portents, yet it was a strange sign. The doubts he had harbored over the years for Eillean's plan lessened a little more. The touched creatures of his people's land appeared to find Most Aged Father's ways unacceptable.

Magiere lay upon the ground away from the cedar's far side, looking weary and spent from her sudden fury. Léshil now crouched beside her.

Brot'ân'duivé knelt at Magiere's feet and began splitting the walnut shells with a stiletto.

"Do not strain Sgäilsheilleache further," he said plainly to Léshil. "Your actions thus far have placed him in a difficult position. Fréthfâre will now seek any reason to execute Magiere."

Léshil stared at him. Wynn shifted around the cedar's side, followed by Chap, to listen in.

Magiere did not move. "Wynn, what were you thinking? Running off like that?"

The little human frowned. "How else would we get around Most Aged Father's coercion? Or should we just let him dangle Nein'a in front of Leesil?"

Chap nosed Wynn with a growl, and she put a hand on his head.

"I am sorry, Magiere," Wynn continued but without a hint of regret. "Chap was leaving with the majay-hì, and I . . . knew where he was going. There was no time to tell you."

Brot'ân'duivé remained silently attentive.

Most Aged Father tried to bend Léshil to his will—but for what? Aside from the custom to never spill the blood of their own, the only reason the patriarch had for keeping Cuirin'nên'a alive was to learn of any others who aided her. The purpose for Léshil's safe passage became quite clear.

Brot'ân'duivé turned to Léshil. "You cannot free your mother . . . not without Most Aged Father's consent. He holds sway over the place of her confinement. If you still wish to free her, then you must return to Crijheäiche and bargain for it."

Magiere rolled up onto one elbow with a frown.

"What do you care?" Léshil spit out. "She's here because you dragged her back!"

"If I had not," Brot'ân'duivé replied, "then another of my caste would have done so . . . or worse."

"I thought elves didn't kill their own," Magiere said.

"Their own . . . are not always a matter of blood or even race," Brot'ân'-duivé returned. "I was Eillean's confidant and friend. Yes, true. So who better to assure Cuirin'nên'a was returned unharmed?"

He turned back to Léshil. "You know our word . . . *trú?*"

"It means 'traitor,' " Léshil answered coldly.

"Simplistically, yes. It also means outcast, outlawed, beyond the protection of a society. Our law against spilling the blood of our own is based in custom and tradition, not words or decrees as written down by humans."

"How convenient," Magiere said. "So much easier to twist."

Brot'ân'duivé ignored her and kept his attention on Léshil. "There are those who consider a traitor beyond the shield of custom and society—and not one of their own. As did Grôyt'ashia when he tried to take your life for interfering with my mission in Venjètz."

It was only half of the truth, but it served his purpose.

"And what about Léshil . . . Leesil?" Wynn asked. "What happens to him for killing one of yours? It was self-defense."

The young one eyed Brot'ân'duivé with a studied interest that left him wary.

"I will bear witness in Léshil's favor," he answered. "I know the truth of it, should it come to that."

"Truth?" Leesil spit. "In your mouth? Have any more sick jokes?"

"That, and the safe passage of humans in our land, is why the elders gather in Crijheäiche. Now Fréthfâre will give them something of greater concern to my people."

Brot'ân'duivé turned his eyes upon Magiere.

Magiere hurt for Leesil, despite her own pain. For all the trouble Wynn had caused, finding Nein'a had done little good.

She had lost control in front of their enemies, revealing her nature. They didn't truly understand what she was—but an explanation wouldn't gain her much. The child of a vampire would be viewed as little better than an undead.

Even worse, after all of Leesil's efforts, the loss and bloodshed, Nein'a wouldn't even speak to him.

Magiere avoided looking at the trees. Every time she did, they conjured images of the blotched dead marks her own touch had left on the birch. The ones no one else seemed to have noticed. Her vision of undead slaughtering an encampment still plagued her.

Elves, short and stout dwarves, and humans had fought side by side as allies, though it didn't seem possible. Certainly not in any part of her world. Wynn spoke at times of elves near her homeland who were far different from those here.

If it were real—if it had happened—then where and when? And how and why had she seen it upon touching the birch?

Wynn shivered in the cooling air and clutched at Chap for warmth. Even Leesil huddled up as if chilled.

"We should start a fire," Magiere said. "Brot'an . . . help me find firewood."

"I'll go," Leesil demanded, though he kept his eyes down, unwilling to look at Brot'an. "You need rest."

Brot'an seemed about to object to either option. Magiere shook her head slightly at him, and then tilted it toward Leesil. Brot'an remained silent in puzzlement.

"Stay here," she told Leesil. "Have Wynn tell you about trying to walk Nein'a out of the clearing. Maybe there's something we've missed."

She got up and started off, and Brot'an followed. When they were far enough away not to be heard, he spoke up first.

"What is on your mind?"

"You saw me change when we fought in the crypt, but you didn't tell your . . . kind about me?"

After a pause, he replied, "It was not their concern."

"Does anyone else know that Leesil killed Darmouth?"

He stopped walking, forcing her to face him. "I reported my purpose as complete. No questions were asked, so I did not elaborate."

"Yet you did tell them he killed Grôyt?"

"A body does require explanation," Brot'an replied passively. "I returned Grôyt'ashia to his family and kin. He was Anmaglâhk, and his throat had been slashed open. Only the truth . . . only another trained in our way, was a believable explanation."

Magiere hated it when any of these butchers referred to Leesil as one of them.

"Whatever you want from Leesil, forget it," she warned. "We're leaving, and—one way or another—we're taking Leesil's mother. Your people have put him through enough. He'll live as he chooses, and I'll see to that. Understand?"

A strange weariness, or maybe sadness, washed over Brot'an's scarred face. "You have mated with Léshil."

Magiere was so taken aback that she lost her voice for an instant. "Don't try meddling in my life. What's between Leesil and me is none of your concern."

"It is his concern, more than he may know," Brot'an answered. "I understand your intention, but you do not understand all that is involved . . . because of Léshil's heritage."

Magiere flinched at this, though she didn't understand all that Brot'an implied. Except perhaps that her connection to Leesil might be one more weight upon him in the coming days. She changed tactics.

"Then do me one favor," she said.

"If I am able."

"I need to speak with Nein'a alone . . . just for a few moments."

The wary Brot'an reappeared, and he shook his head.

"The others won't see or know," she went on. "I have questions for her before I decide what to do next. And I . . . I will owe you in return."

Being indebted to this man was almost more than Magiere could stomach, but she had to know what Leesil risked his future for. If she could go back in time and save her own mother, she would at any price. Magelia was worth the cost—but was Nein'a?

"Do not think for a moment," Brot'an warned, "that Fréthfâre will forget what she saw this day."

Brot'an's steady gaze made Magiere's persistent quiver all the more unsettling. He headed for the barrier woods, and she followed. When he stopped before the passage through those tangled trees, he held her off a moment longer.

"Remember your debt the next time I must have Léshil's cooperation for his own sake."

Magiere nodded, though it made her flush with resentment. She hoped Leesil would remain distracted by Wynn for a little while longer.

The passage through the woods had grown as dark as dusk beneath the clouded sky. As Magiere pushed aside the tall ferns and stepped into the open clearing, she wasn't certain how she would handle this meeting. She ended up waiting, lost in thought, until Nein'a appeared from around the domicile tree.

Nein'a carried the saffron cushion left beside the brook and headed toward her home. She stopped at the sight of Magiere, dropped the cushion beside the tree, and stood waiting.

As Magiere approached, Nein'a studied the two majay-hì still present. One lapped at the brook's water while the other curled upon the moss to wash. The sight seemed to bring the tall elven woman satisfaction.

"You risk the moment of peace Brot'ân'duivé created, but Sgäilsheilleache will be the one to pay if your absence is discovered."

Magiere had bargained blindly for this meeting, and now her tongue was tied as she looked upon this apparition of Leesil's past. Lovely, deadly Nein'a. Brot'ân's hint at Magiere's intimacy with Leesil suddenly left her uncertain in facing Leesil's mother. Magiere wondered—out of all others, why had Leesil chosen her?

Magiere wore her emotions on her face. She had no wiles and no ways with feminine mystery.

"Don't you miss him?" she asked quietly. "Aren't you glad to see him?"

It wasn't what she'd planned to say. But if anyone had taken Leesil from her, had parted them for eight years, the sight of him again would've broken her into tears.

"You are . . . his?" Nein'a asked, though it wasn't really a question.

Neither insulting nor as bitterly sad as Brot'ân's statement, and yet it intimidated Magiere.

"Yes. We own a tavern . . . in the town of Miiska on the Belaskian coast. But he has wanted to find you ever since Sgäile came at him in Bela and hinted that you might still be alive." Magiere found a touch of her own bitterness. "Even after everything you've done to him."

Nein'a stared directly into her eyes. "And what have I done to him?"

Magiere's hesitant bitterness became anger again. "You trained him—used him—forced him to murder in your footsteps. He drank himself to sleep every night just to forget the things you taught him to do."

"And would he have survived in your company without his training?" Nein'a asked.

"Survival, of course," Magiere hissed. "That is why you trained him. How unselfish!"

It was cruel, rather than just her usual bluntness. But did Nein'a bear any real love for her son?

"I know nothing of you," Nein'a returned. "Less even than you know of Léshil, who may yet serve a necessary purpose, and not just to my people alone. Only time will see if that comes to pass, and in part, I hope it does not. He must leave this land and get beyond Most Aged Father's reach. If you care for him, take him from this place."

She turned away and vanished inside the elm, not even stopping to retrieve the cushion she had dropped.

Magiere couldn't tell if it was rage or the forest's influence that made her tremble. The pieces of this game were still unclear to her.

Nein'a had trained Leesil without love—without a conscience. She had birthed him for a "purpose," as the Anmaglâhk called all their missions and dark tasks.

Chap had suggested that Nein'a and others among the Anmaglâhk wanted to thwart Most Aged Father. Or at least choose their own way to deal with some forgotten adversary their leader feared would return. For their own reasons, they wanted a half-blood for this. Perhaps they needed someone outside of their people as well as their caste. Leesil's mother had secretly trained him against the rules of her order.

Nein'a didn't love Leesil as a son, though he loved her as his mother.

Sorrow welled in Magiere as she swatted the ferns aside and strode out through the woods' passage. She would love Leesil enough to make up the difference.

Leesil glanced up as Brot'an returned with an armload of firewood and small dead branches for kindling.

"I cannot see what else to try," Wynn was saying.

"Where's Magiere?" Leesil asked Brot'an.

"Gathering more wood. She will return shortly."

Leesil rose to his feet and looked toward the elves' camp. He counted them and made certain all were present. They were, and relief from fear unleashed his anger. About to bark at Brot'an for stupidity, he held his words a moment longer. It didn't make sense that Brot'an would leave Magiere unattended.

How long had he been distracted by Wynn's experiences with Nein'a? His stomach churned each time he thought of his mother's greeting—or lack of it. He started off to find Magiere.

"She will return directly," Brot'an said. "Help me start the fire."

Leesil didn't wish to share even such a simple task with this man. But he crouched down, looking about repeatedly for any sign of Magiere.

The air grew damp, and the kindling was no better. Brot'an struck flint to a short stub of steel he produced, but it took a while to get decent flames started. Wynn fell to peeling bisselberries and cracking walnuts left beside the tree. Finally, Leesil heard footfalls crunching in the forest mulch. Magiere appeared but carried only three branches.

"Is that all you found?" Wynn asked.

Magiere didn't answer. Leesil took the branches and dropped them beside the fire.

"She's tired," he said, and pointed Magiere toward a large redwood a dozen paces off. "We're going over there to rest. Wynn, stay with Chap. Try to get some sleep."

"But you will be away from the fire," Wynn argued.

Leesil expected a challenge from Brot'an, but the man didn't even stand up.

"We should all rest," Brot'an said. "Find what comfort you can, but stay within my sight."

Leesil pushed Magiere on. Within sight, indeed. He wasn't about to leave Wynn alone in the scarred elf's company. He only wanted to be out of earshot. When he went to settle against the redwood, Magiere pulled back.

"Let's just sit in the open," she said and dropped down, waiting for him.

The forest grew darker with scant daylight, but she didn't seem to care. So he crouched and dropped to his haunches beside her.

"This isn't what you expected, is it?" she whispered. "You thought she'd be grateful to see you after all this time—no matter what happened when you escaped from Venjètz."

Is that what made her so quiet and withdrawn—worry for him? No, there was something more. He could sense it.

"No, not what I expected," he answered. "Nothing we do turns out as we plan. It's like my childhood never happened, and she doesn't even know me."

Magiere's face grew tense and thoughtful, and she seemed reluctant to look at him. She had exposed her dhampir nature. The elves' reactions would cut her deeply, and she'd become the focus of their hatred more than he. He didn't care what she was. She was still Magiere. But was he what or who she would really want?

A thing—a tool—a weapon. She deserved more than that. Even his own mother rejected him as anything more.

"You're my blood, Leesil," Magiere whispered, "my family . . . all that I need."

Leesil's mind went blank, caught between her words and the fear of losing her. He looked at the black locks of hair hanging around her pale face.

"Marry me," she whispered, quick and sharp.

Leesil braced a hand upon the ground between his legs. He grew almost faint as the weight of the day and everything that had happened vanished and left him light-headed.

In this place, surrounded by so little hope and so many threats for the future . . .

He couldn't think straight, her two words echoing over and over in his emptied mind.

"No," he blurted out.

Magiere lifted her head, her eyes round with shock.

"Yes, I mean . . . no," he fumbled. "I mean . . ."

Any other time he'd made an ass of himself, she'd turned livid, ready to club him for his stupidity. But Magiere just sat there in startled pain.

As if he'd struck her.

Leesil grabbed Magiere's face and pressed his mouth hard to hers. She wrestled free, nearly shoving him over. Confusion mixed with a hint of her old ire.

"Yes," he said quickly. "I mean yes . . . but no, not here and not now."

Oh, how he had botched things again. But Magiere's brows softened quickly.

"Can't you see?" he rushed on, and grabbed both her hands, holding them tightly. "I don't want it like this, not among enemies. Not until we're home again with Karlin and Caleb and maybe Aunt Bieja. That's where it should happen. Where it can be the right day—a celebration. The finest day of our lives."

Two tears slid down Magiere's face. "A celebration?"

"With dancing," he added.

She slipped her arms around his neck, clutching him so hard he couldn't breathe.

Chap stayed with Wynn, eyeing Brot'an, though he knew Leesil would not move out of sight. He tried to understand Nein'a's unexpected behavior.

Unlike Leesil, Chap had never anticipated an open welcome. The Nein'a that he remembered was cunning and cautious. So much so that Chap had always had difficulty in dipping even one memory from her thoughts. Brot'an and even Eillean were much the same. All three were adept at keeping their minds clear of triggered memories that would interfere with their focus upon what must be done. But Nein'a should be doing everything in her power to help free herself. Her refusal to leave perplexed Chap.

Wynn scooted closer to the fire and tried to stuff her small hands up her tunic's opposing sleeves. Brot'an appeared to be rearranging his own attire beneath his gray-green cloak. Chap heard clinking metal and wondered what the elf was doing.

He would not trust Brot'an, but his estimation of the man grew less certain. Brot'an served his own agenda, but he had placed himself between Magiere and his caste. He had also managed to keep Leesil under control, without letting their past conflict boil into the open.

Brot'an glanced across the low flames at Wynn and stripped off his heavy cloak. The sleeves of his green tunic were pulled down, but Chap caught no signs of weapons on his wrists. Brot'an stepped around the fire and draped his cloak over the small sage. Wynn jumped slightly.

"Sleep," he told her, and he slid down to sit against the tree behind the sage.

"Thank you," Wynn said, formally polite. "I left Chane's . . . my cloak back in Crijheäiche. Will you not be cold?"

"Sleep," he repeated.

Wynn lay back and, after a moment, closed her eyes.

Chap dropped his head to his paws, still watching Brot'an.

He should rest with Wynn and keep her warm. This day had been no better for her than the others. In some ways, far worse. The Fay knew of her gift—or curse—of sensing when they manifested nearby.

A soft blur of white appeared near the edge of a far cedar. Lily poked her head around and whined.

Chap stifled his eagerness to go to her, not wanting to leave Wynn and Magiere alone and subject to so many threats. When he turned from Lily with a sigh, he found Brot'an watching him, and wrinkled his jowls at the man.

"Go," Brot'an said.

Leesil kept watch from an open space between the trees. Magiere lay with her head upon his thigh, her eyes closed. Still, Chap would not leave.

He glanced at the group of Anmaglâhk gathered at another fire off through the forest. They huddled about the flames as Fréthfâre stood over them, but he could not hear their voices clearly.

"Enough!" Sgäile said too loudly and stood up.

Chap heard no more, though it appeared Sgäile defended whatever Fréthfâre had said to all there. Én'nish turned away where she sat, and the conversation ended.

Lily came up beside Chap, surprising him with a lick on his ear. He didn't look at her but kept his eyes on the gathering of enemies.

"No one will disturb your companions," Brot'an said.

The words broke Chap's concentration as he tried to catch any memories in the minds of the Anmaglâhk. He rumbled softly.

He did not care for so many having discovered how truly aware he was. First Sgäile—and now Brot'an spoke to him in full sentences, as if knowing he understood.

"We should all take what time is left to be with our own kind," Brot'an added.

The tall elf leaned his head back against the tree and stared into the fire's small dancing flames.

Chap got up slowly as Lily headed off. He shivered, but not from cold.

Though he was uncertain why, his thoughts slipped back to the phantasm he had suffered in the forests of Droevinka—Magiere's homeland. He had seen her, mad and feral, standing in the dark at the head of an army. Among the twisted creatures of the living walked those of the undead. He shook the memory off—it was a lie induced by sorcery.

Chap loped after Lily until she paused and circled around in a mulch-filled hollow between three close fir trees.

Her fur was warm and soft against him. He pressed into her as they turned about each other. There was relief in her gentle presence. For a little while, he was not so alone. He had kin of flesh, kin of living spirit, if not those who had betrayed him and taken his memories. And when he finally lay quiet beside her, it was with memory and not words that they spoke in whispers.

CHAPTER SIXTEEN

Leesil sat quietly with Magiere's head upon his leg. He expected rain to come, but the sky never broke open, so he saw no need to disturb Magiere and move to better cover.

Past what he guessed was noon beneath the dark clouds, Osha approached Brot'an. The young elf's gaze drifted to Wynn sleeping soundly in Brot'an's cloak.

"It is time," Brot'an called to Leesil.

At the sound of his voice, Magiere's eyes opened. She hadn't slept either and only rested.

Leesil's leg had gone numb beneath her head. He struggled to his feet, pulling Magiere up as his leg tingled with returning feeling. When Brot'an went to gather the others, Leesil left Magiere with Wynn and snuck off toward the barrier woods. Halfway there, he heard steps behind him, and turned to see Sgäile following.

"I won't be long," he said. "Unless you're fool enough to try to stop me."

"Then I will go as well," Sgäile answered. "Or you will not go at all."

Leesil was too weary to argue. He had no idea how soon another chance might come to see his mother. So he turned toward the passage through the woods with Sgäile close on his heels.

They emerged in the clearing, and Nein'a was outside her tree waiting. Leesil glanced back at Sgäile.

"Go," the man said with a sigh. "I will wait here."

Leesil had thought long on his mother while Magiere rested in his lap. Eight years in this glade, seeming so easy to leave and yet not, would drive anyone to odd ways. If he'd been thinking more clearly at their earlier meeting, he might have realized this. Stepping close before her and looking up into her calm yet disquieted face, he couldn't think of much to say besides the obvious.

"I can't free you by staying here. I'm going back to Crijheäiche to find a way to make your people listen." He lowered his voice. "Then you are leaving with me and Magiere."

She reached out and gripped his wrist. The action held no affection, and he almost pulled away.

"Forget me and leave this forest," she whispered, and then her tone grew soft, more like the lyrical voice he remembered from youth. "Please . . . my son."

All of Leesil's resentment melted in his mother's sudden warmth.

"You may trust Sgäilsheilleache's guardianship," she whispered. "But in all other things, trust only Brot'ân'duivé."

He jerked free of her grasp. "I will be back . . . and you should trust only me."

"Léshil," Sgäile called, sounding strained. "Come."

Leesil turned away from his mother.

By midafternoon, Wynn worried about keeping the pace Sgäile set. She still wore Brot'an's hopelessly oversized cloak over her baggy elven clothing, and the combined raiment was heavy and cumbersome. But she was still too cold to remove the cloak.

The few times she took her eyes from the others around her, the forest shifted in unsettling ways. With the sun hidden behind thick clouds, all the world was caught within a lingering dusk. Her spirits low, she struggled to keep up—but not only because she was exhausted and worried.

She felt cut off and alone.

Leesil and Magiere were silent except for brief glances and touches they exchanged. Wynn thought she saw Leesil smile briefly, just once, at Magiere.

Chap ranged in and out of their procession, sometimes coming back to Wynn's side. Not once did he speak into her head, and after only a short distance, he ran off into the trees once again. Even Osha rarely looked at her or Magiere. Brot'an was considerate in his actions but otherwise as distant as the rest of the Anmaglâhk.

Wynn had no one to turn to for a soft word or a look of comfort, and thoughts of Chap and her encounter with his kin returned often. This forest proved a terrible place that fed her loneliness.

Sgäile's demeanor worried her most. He had changed since witnessing Magiere's savage side. Wynn always found him daunting—occasionally frightening—but she had been certain he would protect her or Leesil or Magiere. Now his amber eyes were glazed, and any concern he showed was mechanical. Twice, he seemed about to speak to her, but then looked away.

He also appeared determined to rush them back to Crijheäiche as quickly as possible.

Somewhere behind Wynn, a strange chirp floated through the forest. She tried to slow and listen, but the procession's pace was too quick. She was left to wonder if it was the same kind of bird she had heard on their first journey in Crijheäiche.

Wynn had had enough of silence. All right, so she had brought much of this on herself. Or rather Chap had gotten her into it by running off without telling anyone. But compared to the encounter with the Fay, she should feel lucky to be alive.

She quick-stepped up behind Osha, trying to think of something to ask. Something useful—or not. Anything to break the silence for just one breath. She tugged on his cloak as she stumbled over the hem of her own.

Osha glanced over his shoulder with a frown.

"What is . . . *Greimasg'äh*?" she asked quietly. "A grasp-something? I heard the others use it to refer to Brot'an, and once for Urhkar. Some title or rank?"

Timid Osha looked ahead at Sgäile yet again. But Sgäile pressed on behind Brot'an's lead and did not appear to hear.

"Oh for goodness' sake, Osha!" Wynn snapped in a harsh whisper. "I am not trying to get some great secret out of you!"

Sgäile glanced back once.

"Shadow-grip . . . gripper . . . keeper . . . ," Osha said with difficulty, as the word seemed troublesome for his limited Belaskian. "Masters beyond our caste ways, beyond what our teachers know and teach us. Many say Greimasg'äh grip shadows, pull them in to . . . to hide them. No one see them until they want. It is great honor if Greimasg'äh accepts you for . . . to teach you. I am not lucky for this."

When Wynn looked ahead at Brot'an's back, she caught Magiere listening to Osha's words.

"There were . . . once five," Osha added. "Now are four . . . when we lose Léshil's great-mother."

For an instant, Wynn thought he meant Nein'a. "You mean 'grandmother' . . . Eillean?"

Osha nodded and went silent. Wynn was back to struggling to keep up.

"Halt for rest," Brot'an called.

Wynn expected Sgäile might argue, but he crouched by an evergreen, poised for the moment they resumed. She was grateful for any reason to pause and braced a hand on a silver birch to steady herself.

A shadow crossed Wynn, and she looked up.

Sgäile stood close enough that she could have counted the white hairs of his feathery eyebrows. His handsome face was lined with tension.

"All that happened this last day and night," he said quietly in Elvish, "was because you did not heed my words. You remain under my protection, but disobey again and I will do whatever is necessary to assure your safety . . . no matter that you will dislike my methods. Do you understand?"

Wynn bit back her retort.

If his kind had not imprisoned Nein'a, Leesil would never have needed to come here in the first place. She and Chap would not have had to break Most Aged Father's attempt at coercion. But Sgäile's tone was so serious.

"Yes," she answered stiffly.

He headed back to his resting place, and Wynn turned and found Leesil standing right behind her.

"What was that?" he asked.

"Nothing," she answered. "Just . . . nothing."

Leesil grabbed her hand and pulled her along toward where Magiere crouched. "You stay near us. And let's see if we can't tie up that cloak."

Wynn gripped down on Leesil's fingers, feeling a little less alone.

Forest scents intoxicated Chap, and still he returned often to look in on Magiere and Leesil and Wynn. The majay-hì shadowed the procession from out in the trees as they all headed toward Crijheäiche. But Chap believed the pack only made the journey because Lily stayed with him.

The dogs fell behind to sniff, and even to hunt. More than once, one of them chased down the silver yearling who had wandered off. Some ran ahead, but in the end, they always ended up back near the Anmaglâhk and Chap's companions.

He pressed his nose against Lily and drew in her warm scent. But as they returned again to the procession, he caught brief words in Leesil's memory, spoken in Magiere's hushed voice.

Marry me.

Chap paused, ears cocked.

And Leesil now dwelled in embarrassment upon his fumbled response.

How strange and surprising that it had happened in this place, in these dangerous times. But when Chap dipped Magiere's thoughts for her memory of that moment, his wonderment vanished.

He saw through her eyes the dead bark upon the tree she had touched. He heard the name spoken in her mind as she had blacked out.

Sorhkafàré.

It was not familiar to Chap at first, until he saw tangled pieces of what Magiere experienced the moment she fell prone.

He knew the encampment, and remembered that long-ago night in an ancient elf's fearful memories. The two became one.

Sorhkafàré . . . Aoishenis-Ahâre . . . Most Aged Father.

Magiere had touched a tree. She had seen a vision she did not understand—one of Most Aged Father's oldest memories.

Chap looked wildly about the forest, wary of every quiver of leaf.

Nein'a had looked about the clearing in the same way, easing only when the majay-hì appeared peaceful and settled in their surroundings. And Lily had tried desperately to keep Chap from going into Most Aged Father's home.

Somehow the withered old elf, impossibly long in his years, had been in Nein'a's glade. He had been in the tree Magiere had touched. It was the only thing Chap could reason.

Magiere had touched a tree . . . and eaten a piece of its life without knowing it. Chap remembered his delusional vision of her at the head of an army upon the edge of a dying forest.

He paced quickly through the trees, watching Magiere from a distance as his fear rose.

He wanted no more of this. He wanted only to be alone a while longer with Lily. But he kept seeing Magiere in his own remembered delusion and the dark shapes of others waiting upon her to enter the trees.

Lily yipped as a brown hare raced out from under a bed of mammoth coleus.

Chap did not follow her.

Welstiel headed south as dusk turned to night. He led their remaining horse packed with their gear while Chane's new familiar loped ahead of them.

He noted how gaunt Chane appeared. They would need to melt snow later, perhaps use the last crumbles of tea taken from the Móndyalítko, and replenish their bodies' fluids. For the most part Chane looked tolerable, all things considered. Even in his used cloak and scuffed boots, there was still some trace of a young nobleman, tall and arrogant. No one who saw him could doubt his heritage—at least the one that Chane once had in his living days.

Welstiel feared that he could not claim so much at present. He fastened his tattered cloak more tightly, and tried to smooth his filthy hair.

He had not dreamed these past days. Why would his patron show him the castle, its inhabitant, and the very room of the orb, only to fall silent? He clung to one hope.

The Móndyalítko had been clear in their directions. It was possible that Welsteil's patron felt no further assistance was needed. Yes, that must be the case.

Barren rocks and patches of snow and ice vanished as his thoughts drifted into the future.

He wore a white silk shirt and charcoal wool tunic. He was clean and well possessed, living alone on a manor estate in isolation, perhaps somewhere on the northern peninsula of Belaski, still within reach of its capital of Bela or the shipyards of Guèshk. The manor's entire first floor was given over to a library and study, with one whole room for the practice of his arcane artificing. He could create ever more useful objects and never need to touch a mortal again. For somewhere in the cellars below, safely tucked into hiding, was the orb—his orb.

The horse tossed its head, jerking the reins in Welstiel's hand, as the animal's hoof slipped on a patch of snow-crusted stones. It righted itself, and Welstiel looked up the barren mountainside at his companion.

Chane never wavered from his desire to seek out the sages. Why—to study histories and fill his head with mountains of broken pieces culled from the past? Ridiculous.

Welstiel shook his head. Only the present was useful. Let broken days of the Forgotten History remain forgotten, once he acquired what he needed. A solitary existence with no distractions.

But still . . .

"Have you ever tried your hand at artificing?" he asked, his own voice startling in the night's silence.

Chane lifted his eyes from his trudging steps. Conjury—by ritual, spell, or artificing—always stirred Chane's interest.

"Small things," he answered. "Only temporary or passive items for my rituals. Nothing like . . . your ring or feeding cup. I once created a small orb to blind interlopers. I conjured the essence of Light—a manifestation of elemental Fire—and trapped it within a prepared globe of frosted glass. When tripped, its light erupted, and it was spent."

Welstiel hesitated. "You developed notable skill for one who had no instructor. I wonder how you would fare with a more studied guide to teach you."

Chane stopped walking, forcing Welstiel to pause.

"Have you fed without telling me?" Chane asked.

"No, why?"

"You are different tonight . . . more aware."

Welstiel ignored this bit of nonsense. A series of loud barks sounded from ahead.

Chane dropped to the ground and folded his long legs.

Welstiel struggled to be silent and wait as his companion closed his eyes.

Chane would reach out to connect—spirit to spirit, thought to thought—with the wild dog he had enslaved. He would learn through the dumb beast's senses what it had found. Far more efficient than racing after the animal and wasting remaining energies before knowing if it was worth the expenditure.

Welstiel stood tense, fighting for patience.

The castle could be just ahead. The end of his repugnant existence might be that close.

CHAPTER SEVENTEEN

Night wore on as Magiere traveled beside Leesil and kept Wynn close. She cautiously allowed her dhampir nature to rise just enough to widen her vision. It accomplished little with the moon hidden from sight.

Leesil said no more about his mother. Wynn was near physical exhaustion, so her bursts of babbling were few. All the Anmaglâhk, especially Sgäile, were withdrawn and driven by their purpose. Only in one place in the world did people accept Magiere for who, rather than what, she was—Miiska. But home was far away.

She tried to shut out the vision she'd had in Nein'a's clearing, the marks her hands left on the tree, and whatever lay ahead in Crijheäiche. She tried to focus on Leesil.

Leesil was the imaginative one, not she. After facing Nein'a's coldheartedness, all Magiere wished was to make him feel wanted—and to let him know he would at least have her for the rest of his days. He reminded her that there was a place for them in this world, where others waited to stand up with them on the day they swore their oath. Annoying as Leesil was at times, he was right.

His words painted a picture in her mind of celebration with Karlin, Caleb, little Rose, and perhaps Aunt Bieja. Magiere imagined Leesil with his hair tied back and wearing a clean white shirt—one he hadn't mended and patched beyond its time.

Yes, she wanted this too.

The surrounding forest began to look familiar, and Magiere caught the soft glow of lanterns among the trees. They passed an enormous oak swollen into a dwelling.

"We're close," she said.

"Oh, for a bath and clean clothes," Wynn grumbled.

Fréth traveled just ahead of Leesil, but she slowed and dropped to the rear near Én'nish.

Magiere found this odd. Then she saw someone running toward them between the domicile trees, flashing in and out of pools of lantern light or the seeping glow from under a curtained doorway.

Leanâlhâm's yellow shirt stood out in the dark. She smiled and ran straight for Sgäile with her light brown ponytail swishing. Sgäile pulled her against his chest, and Leanâlhâm's eyes wandered about the group until they found Wynn.

"I am so glad you are found," she said with the relief of a lifelong friend. "Urhkarasiférin said you were lost in the forest, but I knew Sgäilsheilleache would find you."

Wynn smiled briefly over her exhaustion.

Magiere waited for Leanâlhâm's rush of questions. But when the girl tried to go to Wynn, Sgäile's arm tightened. He held her back, turning slightly away. Magiere knew it wasn't Wynn who he kept the girl from—it was herself.

Sgäile spoke harshly in Elvish to Leanâlhâm, and the girl's mouth dropped open with a flash of hurt in her eyes.

"*Bârtva'na!*" Sgäile half-shouted, cutting off her rising protest.

Magiere understood the word from the little Elvish that she'd heard Wynn translate. Sgäile commanded the girl to stop and obey. Leanâlhâm stared at him with open resentment.

"He ordered her back to their quarters," Wynn said quietly. "She is not to speak with us."

"What?" Leesil asked. "Why?"

It wasn't right for Sgäile to deny the girl so harshly. He didn't want his little cousin anywhere near the unnatural thing discovered among them. But for all the man's fear, he couldn't possibly believe Magiere would harm Leanâlhâm. She'd given her word to watch over the girl whenever possible.

Sgäile's distress ran more deeply than Magiere had guessed.

She glanced carefully about at the other Anmaglâhk. Most remained expressionless, except for Én'nish's venomous glare and Fréth's smoldering silence. But Brot'an now peered about the trees with a strange uncertainty.

Magiere wanted no more confrontations with Sgäile, and hopefully Leanâlhâm would do as he asked.

Leanâlhâm backed away, her features fading in the deeper black beneath a tree in the darkness.

"*Shiuvâlh!*" Sgäile snapped.

That word Magiere didn't know, but his tone made her tense. A shadow appeared behind Leanâlhâm, followed by another to the right. Magiere whirled around to find more closing on the left and from behind.

"Leesil . . . ," she hissed in warning.

He turned, watching dark figures move in the night.

Osha stepped closer to Wynn. Sgäile pulled a stiletto, as did Fréth. Brot'an turned about more slowly, the puzzlement in his steady gaze becoming cold displeasure. The first shadow stepped into plain sight.

Urhkar stood calm and passive. Another anmaglâhk came in behind him, and another from beyond Sgäile, and then another. All but the elder anmaglâhk held shortbows drawn with arrows notched, their gleaming heads resting over bow handles of silver-white metal.

Magiere found herself ringed in on all sides with Leesil and Wynn by at least twenty Anmaglâhk. No wonder Sgäile pushed them all so hard, knowing what waited upon their arrival.

"You split-tongue son of . . . ," Leesil started, his gaze on Sgäile.

Magiere grabbed Leesil's wrist and squeezed hard in warning as she glanced back at Wynn. A wrinkle of the sage's brow hinted at something more beneath her fright—a tinge of anger in the once-timid sage. Magiere saw no course of action that wouldn't end in all of their deaths.

Fréth and Sgäile faced inward toward Magiere. Sgäile kept his blade low, but Fréth did not.

"What are you doing?" Leesil demanded.

Brot'an gave Urhkar a slow shake of his head, but the other elder returned no reply.

"All of you pull back and allow us through," Brot'an called out.

Not one anmaglâhk retreated, and Fréth came straight at Magiere and Leesil.

"You will come with us."

Magiere heard Leesil's foot slip back, and the grinding of sod as he an-chored it and shifted his weight. Six Anmaglâhk stepped in with bows raised. Two were aimed straight at Wynn.

"No!" Magiere whispered. "Too many for a fight."

And then Brot'an sidled into the path of the bows aimed at Wynn.

"She is correct," he said plainly. "We must wait to find another way to re-solve this."

Leesil turned his head side to side, his eyes moving even quicker as he studied the spread of all those surrounding them. None of the elves lowered their weapons.

"Go!" Fréth ordered.

Uncertainly, Leesil moved up beside Magiere, and they followed Brot'an. They were swept away into the heart of Crijheäiche. Magiere grew more un-certain as they entered a wide clearing encircled by domicile trees.

Near to each tree's curtained doorway, she saw more of the Anmaglâhk. At the clearing's center rose a massive oak that dwarfed any tree she'd seen since entering these lands.

"They're taking us to Most Aged Father," Leesil whispered.

Wynn stayed close to Magiere as they faced Most Aged Father's dwelling. She looked about for any sign of Chap, but he was nowhere in sight. Neither was the pack or Lily. Sgäile pulled the doorway's curtain aside.

"Down the stairs!" Fréth ordered.

Wynn looked up anxiously at Brot'an. He nodded once and stepped through the entrance after Sgäile. Leesil went next, then Magiere, and Wynn followed with Fréth close behind her.

Inside, candle lanterns lit the wide barren chamber. A stairway of living wood along the left wall led down into the earth. Wynn reached the bottom, stepping off the last stair of embedded stone, and found herself in an earth-walled chamber. At its center was a root the size of a small domicile tree.

Glass lanterns hung from stone-packed earth walls and cast hazy yellow light upon massive roots arching through the ceiling overhead. Wynn was not certain why they were here, but this underground chamber disturbed her. No elf that she knew would choose to live this way.

"Move!" Fréth ordered and shoved Magiere from behind.

Magiere stumbled forward awkwardly, pulling her hand back from catching herself on the center root. She wobbled, and Wynn grabbed her arm, feeling the uncontrolled shudders running through Magiere.

Leesil whirled about, and Fréth raised her blade.

"You wouldn't even try," he said. "Your sickly master still needs me."

"Enough," Brot'an warned, but his eyes were turned toward Fréth.

"And Chap wouldn't let you," Leesil whispered at Fréth.

Wynn's attention was pulled in too many directions. Magiere quaked in a way Wynn had never seen before. She did not usually frighten this easily—and her fear led to fury, not weakness.

A flash of gray on the stairs caught Wynn's attention.

Chap descended, his jaws already open.

Sgäile tried to reach over the stairs and grab the dog. Leesil slammed his shoulder into Sgäile's back, shoving him aside as Chap lunged off the stairs with a rabid snarl.

Fréth barely caught sight of the dog before Chap's jaws snapped shut on her wrist. She dropped the stiletto with a startled inhale and jerked her arm free as the blade hit the chamber floor. Chap's snarls rang off the stone-packed walls as he drove Fréth backward.

Leesil snatched the fallen stiletto before Sgäile could dive for it. All Wynn could do was try to keep Magiere on her feet.

Fréth scrambled over the bottom stair, braced herself against the wall, and kicked out. Her foot struck Chap's chest, tossing him away. Chap twisted back at her so fast that Fréth gained no ground. He lunged at her, jaws opened wide.

Brot'an slipped between them, and Chap's teeth closed fast on his forearm. Chap thrashed his head and dragged Brot'an to one knee.

"Chap, stop it!" Wynn cried out.

Brot'an did not strike back. He crouched there, rigid and waiting as Chap settled to rumbling stillness.

"No more!" Brot'an said sharply.

Leesil held off Sgäile with the stiletto, but his eyes shifted toward Fréth. "There's little I wouldn't pay to kill you. Don't ever touch me or mine again."

"Chap . . . you let him go . . . now!" Wynn commanded.

Chap unclamped Brot'an's arm with clear reluctance, rumbling as he backed toward Magiere. His gaze remained fixed on the tall elf rising to his feet. Dark stains spread through the gray-green felt of Brot'an's torn sleeve.

He spotted the blade in Leesil grip, and held out his hand. "Please."

"Give it to him," Magiere whispered and straightened herself.

Leesil flipped the stiletto, catching its blade, and slapped the hilt into Brot'an's palm.

"Fréthfâre . . . ," Brot'an warned, tossing the stiletto to her, "keep your distance—and your conduct."

"And you too," Wynn said to Chap, though relieved to see him. "Where have you been?"

Chap ceased rumbling and the leaf-wing rose in Wynn's mind. *Watching.*

"This way," Sgäile said as he circled the chamber.

Wynn did not understand until she spotted the opening in the center root. Sgäile stepped through, and Wynn followed ahead of Magiere.

In the shining candlelight, Wynn at first saw only teal and saffron pillows on the floor, but her mouth went dry as she took in the rest of the small chamber.

Curled in a cradle of wood growing from the far wall and floor was the oldest elf she had ever seen. Only vague hints remained in his withered form to mark his race.

An emaciated face surrounded sunken eyes that had lost most of their amber color. Those old eyes never blinked, and patches of scalp showed through thinned hair. He shuddered with either fear or rage when he saw Magiere.

"Why are we here?" Leesil demanded.

"To be judged," Fréth snapped from the doorway.

Brot'an's broad frame stood in her way. Sgäile stepped close to the frail form in the living bower and proffered a deep, respectful nod. The old one did not even glance at him.

"Judged?" Wynn said.

Most Aged Father's thin, reedy voice filled the root chamber as he spoke in Belaskian.

"No undead will poison this forest. Destroy it at once."

Sgäile did not answer or look up.

"You'll be bleeding before anyone touches her," Leesil warned.

"She is not undead," Wynn blurted out.

"Truth," Brot'an added, and moved closer to the old one. "And this is not the way judgment is rendered . . . especially when guardianship and safe passage have already been given. Do you now break your word as well as that of Sgäilsheilleache?"

"You are Anmaglâhk," said Most Aged Father, and finally turned his attention on Brot'an. "You are sworn to protect the people. Would you leave an undead in their midst? I do not know how this one could even enter our land."

"Her heart beats," Brot'an returned. "I know little of the humans' walking dead . . . but enough to know she is not one of them."

Most Aged Father's eyes narrowed upon Brot'an.

Fréth pushed through into Wynn's sight. "Do you question Most Aged Father? Do you deny what we saw in the traitor's clearing?"

"The forest accepts her," Brot'an answered. "And the majay-hì do not hunt her."

"Until she showed herself for what she is," Fréthfâre argued.

"She is not undead," Wynn repeated straight at Most Aged Father. "She hates them as you do. She is only half of what they are, and it makes her their natural adversary."

Brot'an glanced at Wynn, as did the other elves, each with their own mix of suspicion and doubt. Magiere grabbed Wynn's hand with a sharp shake of her head.

Most Aged Father's voice screeched in Wynn's ears. "Half undead is more than enough!"

"Truly?" Brot'an asked. "Is a half-blood a human or an elf, let alone an'Cróan? And what would that make a three-quarter-blood?"

Sgäile lifted his head at the reference to Leanâlhâm, and Brot'an let the question hang. And it left Wynn wondering if the girl's status among her people was not yet determined. She watched all four elves present, waiting for someone to speak up.

They were not presenting arguments to sway Most Aged Father, for at least Fréth and Brot'an spoke from some equal authority here. It was their people's customs and cultural rule versus Anmaglâhk authority that was being called into question, as well as anyone's status of mixed heritage. In the end, Magiere's welfare alone might not be all that was at stake, though she would likely be the first weighed in the outcome.

"And still, this is not our decision," Brot'an continued. "As Most Aged Father has wisely stated, we are sworn to protect our people . . . to serve them, not to rule them or decide for them. We are not a clan."

"You overstep yourself," Fréth cut in. "Neither does a Greimasg'äh make decisions for the caste, nor define what it is."

"Yet another truth, Covârleasa," Brot'an answered agreeably. "The people determine what we are . . . have determined it. We serve them. We are defined by their will—not by ourselves or the purpose we serve. The clan elders are the voice and will of the people. They already gather to address any judgments—as is proper."

Sgäile finally spoke, in a ragged voice. "Usurp our people's ways, and there remains nothing for our caste to protect, preserve, or serve. Father . . . you would agree?"

Most Aged Father's old eyes were fixed upon Magiere. Wynn's panic rose as she realized that he wanted Fréth to murder Magiere where she stood.

"Wise as always, my son," Most Aged Father replied to Sgäile. "The elders will see this woman for what she is. But I withdraw my protection—the outsiders are no longer my guests."

Sgäile straightened and stiffened, staring at Most Aged Father as if some breach had occurred. Brot'an's features clouded. Both men were about to speak, but Most Aged Father held them silent with a frail wave of his bony hand.

"She stands formally accused," he continued, "as does Léshil for bringing her into our land, knowing what she is. All three interlopers will remain under guard. That is within the purpose and service of the Anmaglâhk. Do you not agree?"

The final question was aimed at Brot'an. Wynn waited for a denial, some argument that might get Magiere out of danger.

Brot'an nodded polite. "Yes, and I thank you for the reminder. I will escort them."

Sgäile looked ill. Perhaps he had never disagreed with Most Aged Father before.

Brot'an placed a hand on Wynn's back. "Go."

She hurried out to find Fréth waiting at the stairs, blade in hand.

Leesil hooked the doorway curtain with a finger and peered out of their living cell. Four armed anmaglâhk stood outside the domicile elm, gripping shortbows with arrows notched. Urhkar was among them, but not Osha. Leesil let the curtain fall back into place.

Magiere slumped upon one bed ledge in the tree's wall, her arms folded across her chest as if she held herself together. Wynn sat with Chap, spreading parchments of Elvish symbols on the dirt floor.

"We have to find a way out of this," Wynn said. "I do not believe Magiere will be given a fair trial. These people are paranoid about humans, let alone a . . ."

She didn't finish, but Leesil knew what she meant. Let alone an undead, half or otherwise, though even that wasn't the truth.

"We wouldn't get six paces out the door," Leesil said in frustration. "What's this council like? What kind of trial laws do the elves have?"

"How should I know?" Wynn snapped. "I have never seen one, even in my land. Chap may know more."

Chap swung his head from side to side and huffed twice for "no." Wynn sighed, sat back, and ceased spreading out the parchments.

Magiere had hesitated upon entering their quarters and remained silent thereafter. Leesil crouched before her and placed his hands on her thighs.

"I never should have brought you here . . . any of you."

Magiere didn't answer, but Leesil felt a quiver in her legs.

"I am guilty," she finally said. "At least of what they think I might be."

"Don't talk like that!" Leesil said. "You're not some undead."

She raised only her dark eyes to him—the same look she gave him when she thought he was being thickheaded or purposefully evasive. But her face was more weary than annoyed, as if she'd already given up.

"Do not do that!" Wynn snapped. "Not unless I am expecting it. I have had enough of getting sick for one day."

Leesil pivoted to find Wynn shoving Chap away. The dog growled and then clawed at the parchments. But he wasn't tapping out symbols for Wynn to read. He just scattered them in a tantrum as the sage tried to grab the sheets away from him.

"Stop it!" Wynn shouted at the dog. "We are talking the old way, whether you like it or not."

"Keep your voice down," Leesil warned. "What's going on?"

Both of them ceased fighting over the parchments. Chap growled at the sage, barking once for "yes."

Wynn took a long breath, frowning. "I did not want to distract you from more immediate concerns."

"Spit it out," Leesil demanded, and Chap barked agreement.

Wynn rubbed her knees where she knelt, and then crawled closer to Leesil.

"I can hear Chap," she said.

"What?" Magiere asked, her voice hushed.

"And I hear when he communes with his kin," Wynn added. "Although it may never happen again. They used him—as much as anyone has used either of you."

Leesil couldn't even form a question. The more Wynn whispered of all that had happened, from hearing Chap with the silver deer to the assault of the Fay, the less he wanted to know. As the sage finished, he stared at her and the dog.

Chap watched him silently in turn.

Leesil understood being an outcast in this world. He'd been alone but for Chap, without a place of his own, until he'd stumbled into Magiere—with Chap's meddling, of course. But now it seemed the dog didn't know everything concerning his own purpose.

Chap had been played by his own kind—one more unwitting tool manipulated by the Fay. Leesil wanted to sympathize with his oldest companion, but right now the last thing he needed to hear was that Chap was almost as ignorant as the rest of them.

And Wynn could hear him?

"The mantic sight," Wynn went on, "which I invoked by ritual in Droevinka to help you track the undead sorcerer . . . it returns at times. Whatever Chap did to take it from me, something went wrong, and it is getting worse. I was able to call it at will, but then Chap had to lick it away again."

"But you still hear him, even without the sight?" Magiere asked.

Wynn nodded, and then she flinched with a gag and uttered one word. "Sorhkafâré."

Magiere's leg muscles knotted under Leesil's hands.

Wynn balled up her little fist at Chap. "I told you—not until I am ready!"

Chap ignored her and focused on Magiere, and Leesil turned his eyes on the woman he loved.

That word—or name—did it mean something to her? Magiere's pallid skin made it hard to be certain, but she looked suddenly ill.

"Where did you hear that name?" she whispered.

"Not me," Wynn said. "That was Chap."

Leesil followed Magiere's rapt attention back to Chap, as Wynn slumped in resignation, speaking for the dog and turning a bit sickly herself. For every word Chap spoke through Wynn, Leesil saw his own dread echoed in Magiere's brown eyes.

Most Aged Father had been alive during the war in what the sages called the Forgotten History. How long ago wasn't clear. Even his own people didn't remember where or when he had come from.

The sages still argued over when this war took place, and even Chap couldn't guess, for his memories didn't give him any measure of time. However long ago, Sorhkafârê had not been old. Now he was the decrepit leader of the Anmaglâhk and impossibly ancient.

What Leesil heard still didn't explain the man's fanatical hatred of humans, strong enough to teach generations of his people to fear them. But how had Magiere known his long lost name?

"What else haven't you told me?" he asked her a little too harshly.

Magiere didn't answer.

Wynn flinched in fear, over and over, at the words Chap poured through her. As the tale swept on to the night following the battle, Leesil saw strange recognition in Magiere's face. More than once she mouthed a name before Wynn even spoke it aloud.

"I know them," Magiere whispered. "I was there . . . I was him that night . . . when I blacked out in Nein'a's clearing."

"How?" Leesil asked.

Magiere's voice carried none of its old bite as she glared at Chap. "You've been in my head again."

Leesil remembered the first time she'd had a vision. In Bela, she'd held cloth from a victim's body. She had walked the place where the corpse had been found and relived the moment that an undead had slaughtered the woman, a nobleman's daughter. Nothing like that had happened in Nein'a's clearing.

Magiere slowly shook her head. "All I wanted was to kill anything that got in the way of finding you. I touched the tree, and I was there . . . inside Most Aged Father . . . or his memory, at least."

"You saw undeads?'" Wynn asked. "Vampires . . . in the form of risen soldiers?"

Magiere looked at her. "He . . . they didn't know what was happening. They just ran inland toward On-nis Lo . . . Lon . . ."

Wynn sat upright. "Aonnis Lhoin'n?"

Magiere nodded. "I don't know if they made it, though obviously Sorhkafârê . . . Most Aged Father is still alive."

"You are certain you heard it right?" Wynn demanded. "Aonnis Lhoin'n?"

Magiere lifted her head. "Why? Have you read of it somewhere?"

"No," Wynn answered. "It still exists."

The sage looked as if she'd uncovered something astonishing. Her brown eyes wandered, growing doubtful, until a scowl spread across her round face.

"Wait," Leesil said. "You've seen this place . . . and it still bears the same name?"

Wynn shook her head. "It is what the elves of my continent call the centermost place in their land—First Glade—but no one in my guild knew it was that old."

She blinked rapidly, lost for an instant somewhere other than this moment.

Leesil wasn't certain what all this meant. "Perhaps the war wasn't as long ago as the sages think."

Wynn started at his voice. "No, we have long tried to determine when the war occurred. Some do not believe it ever happened, that it is all myth and legend spun out of proportion. But I have seen old scrolls and parchments, stone carvings and other things . . . from centuries back. Malourné, my country, goes back more than four centuries. The king's city of Calm Seatt is even older. And what we've found was much older still."

"What does that have to do with this . . . First Glade?" Leesil asked.

"Because my order has been deceived!" Wynn answered sharply. "There are three branches of the Guild of Sagecraft. The first was in my Malourné, decreed by our own kings of old. Shortly thereafter, the elves established their own to match ours. And one is in the Suman Empire along the eastern coast of my continent. It was all to help preserve civilization, present and past . . . should the worst ever come again."

Wynn turned to Magiere.

"If you heard right, a piece of what was lost has been within reach all along. Its past and history could never have been forgotten—not by the elves. It lay right before our eyes . . . and they said nothing of it!"

Leesil didn't care for this one bit. It was enough they had to deal with the secrets and lies that had tangled them among the elves of this land. How long had Wynn's far-off elven neighbors kept this to themselves, an ancient place hidden in plain sight?

"They were taken unaware, unprepared," Magiere whispered. "They didn't even know what to do . . . with what came at them in the night."

Leesil frowned until he caught up. Magiere's thoughts had turned back to her vision in the glade.

"No name," she whispered, as if searching for one, then her dark eyes settled upon him. "They didn't have a name for what they saw."

"I don't understand," Leesil said, sounding exasperated even to himself.

She grabbed his arms, fingers biting in. "Most Aged Father—Sorhkafâré—didn't have a name for what he saw. Undead, vampire, or anything in his own tongue. None of his comrades did. He didn't know . . . their own dead coming to feed upon them that night."

More disjointed pieces of a past that didn't matter here and now. None of it would help Magiere face the council of the an'Cróan.

"They had never seen or heard of an undead?" Wynn whispered. She paused, and then exclaimed, "There were no undead . . . until the war?"

"Dead history can wait!" Leesil snapped. "It's no good to us now, so enough—"

Chap snarled, and Wynn flinched as if her head ached. She looked at the dog and said, "Yes, a good question."

She held up one finger at Leesil before he could argue, and she turned to Magiere.

"I want no more secrets between us," Wynn said pointedly. "I told you, remember, as we sat at the campfire outside Venjètz? You nearly collapsed when we entered Most Aged Father's home. You tell me now—what is happening to you?"

Leesil waited tensely. Wynn had grown far less timid in the moons they'd spent together, but Magiere didn't take kindly to challenges. The last thing he needed was these two going at each other. Magiere dropped her head until Chap snarled at her again.

"I haven't slept in eight . . . maybe nine nights," she said quietly. "And not much before that . . . since we entered this land."

Leesil knew she was having trouble, but he'd had no idea it was this bad. He hadn't had many restful nights himself.

"But do I look it?" Magiere added, almost as a challenge. "I'm not tired, but I can't stop shaking. It gets worse when I'm inside these trees. I have to force myself to eat because I'm never hungry, not in any real way. Did you see the tree in Nein'a's clearing, the one I touched?"

Leesil shook his head, but Wynn sucked in a sharp breath.

"Your hands. Chap saw in your memories . . . they marked the tree."

Magiere faced Leesil. "Before I slipped into Sorhkafâré's memory, the shaking sharpened. Something ran through me as I backed into the tree, and then I was there, in his past. I didn't know what it was, and only guessed afterward, when I called for you."

She heaved a deep breath.

"I saw marks in the bark, like blight or as if part of it had died . . . shaped like my hands. I am guilty, though not for the reasons Fréth and the others think. A piece of that tree's life ripped away . . . into me. I think that's what's been happening to me . . . in this land. I'm not hungry or tired . . . because I'm . . . feeding on everything here."

"We keep this to ourselves," Leesil said quickly, hiding the panic he felt. "We can't let anyone know. Not with this council's judgment in the balance."

The doorway's hanging pulled back, and Brot'an peered in. He held a tray with several bowls and a pitcher.

"May I enter?" he asked politely.

"Do we have a choice?" Leesil answered.

"Leesil!" Wynn snapped. "Yes, Brot'an. We need to know what will happen next?"

Brot'an's large form filled the entrance as he stepped in. He set down four steaming bowls of stew. He reached back through the curtain and produced four clay cups that someone handed off to him. Crouching down, he poured water for them all, including Chap. But when he offered, no one touched food or drink.

He had changed tunics, and a white cotton bandage was wrapped on his forearm.

Brot'an eyed Chap thoughtfully. "It is safe for us to speak . . . so long as your majay-hì does not sense any presence that would hear us."

Leesil understood. Magiere's stolen memory hinted that the decrepit old elf had a way of moving about the forest without leaving his home. And Leesil remembered the strange way the majay-hì pack had acted just before Magiere lost control.

Brot'an settled cross-legged on the floor. "Have you finished with my cloak, little one?"

"What? Oh . . . yes." Wynn crawled to the chamber's far side and returned with Brot'an's heavy green-gray cloak. "Thank you."

He nodded slightly and turned to Magiere. "Are you well?"

"No," she answered.

"What's going to happen?" Leesil asked, though he wished Sgäile had come instead.

"In two days there will be a gathering," Brot'an began. "It has been a long time since a majority of the clan elders came at the same time. Word of your presence spread quickly, and they began traveling here once they heard. There is concern that Most Aged Father took it upon himself to give humans safe passage. This has never happened in anyone's memory. Some believe he overstepped his position. No one outside of certain Anmaglâhk have even seen Most Aged Father in nearly fifty seasons."

"Fifty seasons?" Leesil repeated. "How is that possible?"

Brot'an paused, as if deciding how to answer. "Most Aged Father is revered as the protector of our people, and his word weights heavily with many of our leaders. But the Anmaglâhk are not a clan, and therefore Most Aged Father is not a representative of the people—he is not a clan elder. At most gatherings of the elders, he has had no reason to be present. But he will be there this time.

"He might have appeared to defend his decision in giving you safe passage, or he could have sent Fréthfâre in his place. That issue will no longer be the primary concern of the council. He is now Magiere's accuser, and a judgment must be made. He must make his claim against Magiere before the council or withdraw it entirely."

"You want them to see him, don't you?" Magiere asked.

"I wish for them to hear him," Brot'an said. "His mind . . . is not what it once was. It may work in your favor to bring his judgment into question, but in turn may show he was not of sound mind in letting humans into our land."

Leesil sat up straight. "You planned this . . . to use that old elf's accusation against Magiere as a way to alert your people?"

Brot'an shook his head. "No, I never foresaw this. Though I knew your presence would raise issues to be addressed. That is now of little advantage."

"What do you mean by that?" Leesil demanded.

"Magiere has a choice to make," Brot'an answered, ignoring Leesil entirely as he gazed only at her. "Most Aged Father will likely choose Fréthfâre as his advocate. You must choose your own for the coming proceedings."

"Wynn can do it," Leesil answered. "She's a scholar, speaks fluent Elvish, and she knows Magiere."

"Leesil, I . . . ," Wynn stammered. "I am not certain I could—"

"That is not permitted," Brot'an interrupted calmly. "As a human, her presence is still in question—and she is not an'Cróan."

Leesil flushed with rising anger. "You're saying she has to choose one of you . . . an elf? As if there's even one of you we could trust to—"

"You do it," Magiere said. "I choose you, Brot'an, for advocate . . . if you're willing."

"No!" Leesil snapped.

"It is not your decision!" Brot'an barked at him. "Only the accused can choose, unless of unsound mind."

"Then she's unsound," Leesil countered. "She's a raving madwoman! What happened in Nein'a's glade is enough to prove that. And I choose Sgäile!"

"Leesil, stop this!" Wynn shouted at him.

"That is not how mental fitness is determined," Brot'an said. "And you are suspect as much as your companions. Your involvement in any capacity would draw further suspicion and work against her."

Chap stalked over to Magiere. He sat down before her and cast a narrow-eyed sneer at Bro'tan, then lifted his snout to Magiere and barked once for "yes."

Magiere put her hand on Chap's neck.

"Can you clear me?" she asked Brot'an.

"I accept your selection as advocate," Brot'an replied. "I will serve your interests to my fullest ability. I know you are innocent . . . of the claim made against you."

Magiere fell silent, as did Wynn, but Leesil was about to explode.

Brot'an turned on him in harsh voice. "There is more at stake here than Magiere's survival. . . . There is your mother's freedom."

Leesil tensed. "You'd better start making sense."

"Most Aged Father is the one who imprisoned Cuirin'nên'a, though it was never argued before the council."

"She was never given a trial?" Wynn asked.

"The clans accepted this," Brot'an replied, "as it was a matter internal to the Anmaglâhk. The elders respect that we serve to protect the people, and anyone accused of undermining our efforts puts all of them at risk. As I have said, Most Aged Father's word carries much influence."

"They don't even know what she did," Leesil said. "They just took his word that she was a traitor."

"The elders still believe him competent," Brot'an added. "More than competent—the wisest of us all, and the eldest of our people. In placing ourselves in service, the Anmaglâhk not only answer to the laws of the people but also to the rule of our caste. We have one leader—Most Aged Father. If he is seen as having faltered in one judgment, then the elders may find reason to examine other decisions he has made. That bears directly upon Cuirin'nên'a's freedom."

Brot'an waited for further argument. When none came, he turned again to Magiere.

"Trust me."

Chap barked once.

"Yes," Magiere whispered.

As Chap watched Brot'an leave, he second-guessed his own advice.

In spite of everything Brot'an said, his flickering memories never once strayed to Magiere—only to Leesil, Nein'a, or Eillean. Chap even caught words spoken when Eillean had given him as a pup to Nein'a.

Leesil was Brot'an's true interest, not Magiere.

Still, Chap believed that Brot'an might well succeed. Exposing Most Aged Father's reasoning as questionable could dismiss his claim against Magiere, and his judgment of Nein'a as well. And Chap saw no way to accomplish either of these feats himself.

Magiere still sat shaking upon the bed ledge. He nosed her hand until she ran it across the side of his face.

"I wish you could talk . . . for yourself," she whispered. "I would have chosen you instead of Brot'an."

Chap desperately wished the same.

Leesil took up one bowl and wooden spoon and brought them to Magiere.

"Try," he said. "Not just for pretense . . . perhaps eating something might dull whatever you're suffering."

Chap agreed in sentiment. The meat smelled savory, but for once, he wasn't hungry either. Instinct and not intellect nagged him with strange notions. Somewhere in the forest beyond Crijheäiche, his Lily ran with the pack.

CHAPTER EIGHTEEN

Wynn heard footsteps approach outside the elm.

Sgäile leaned in around the doorway curtain. "It is time."

Wynn was partially relieved. Trapped inside with Magiere and Leesil for two solid days had been trying. With little to occupy them, the days crawled by, broken only by meals, Brot'an's infrequent visits, and Leesil's incessant sniping at the tall anmaglâhk.

Sgäile glanced at Magiere's attire but said nothing.

Over the previous days, Brot'an had decided upon her appearance for the hearing. Magiere argued, of course, but he won in the end, and Wynn privately agreed with Brot'an's suggestions. Appearances meant much to elves, but Magiere was still grumbling moments before Sgäile arrived. She now wore a clean, light tan elven tunic with a square-cut neck and breeches to match.

Wynn had braided Magiere's hair so that not a strand would fly free, and she looked like a simple human woman. Far less dangerous in appearance, but there was nothing to be done about her pale skin and blood-tinged black hair.

Leesil changed into his oversized muslin shirt—complete with stitched rents—chocolate-brown breeches, and his own boots. He still looked a bit ragged with his hair hanging free about his shoulders. Chap was the only one who caused no grief, sitting quietly for once as Wynn brushed out his fur.

But all of their busy preparations could not dispel Wynn's fear. If Magiere was found guilty, she would be executed, and there was nothing any of them could do to stop it.

Wynn closed her eyes for a moment, trying to push such thoughts away. But she failed, and her mind wandered in directions more morbid. How might the elves decide to kill Magiere? If they believed her undead, beheading or fire were the only options . . . and Sgäile had once expressed revulsion at the prospect of dismembering the dead.

Wynn opened her eyes and steadied herself. No, it would not come to that. They still had Brot'an.

He had explained only the barest bits of the coming proceedings. Most Aged Father had made a claim concerning Magiere's true nature. Until this was settled, there would be no direct trial before the elders. Instead, the claim must first be substantiated as a dispute between opposing parties. Wynn grasped only scant nuances, and Chap had been no help. Instead he had filled her head with questions that Brot'an never answered.

"Where is Brot'an?" she asked, for he had not returned this day to escort Magiere.

Sgäile ignored her. "It is time. Come."

Leesil headed out, and Wynn fell in behind Magiere and Chap.

Osha was among the Anmaglâhk escort waiting outside. His face filled with concern as he met Wynn's eyes. Sgäile led the way, his guards flanking and following. Chap trotted along outside their retinue.

Wynn did not see Lily or any other majay-hì. She stayed close behind Magiere as they headed inland through Crijheäiche. She had no idea where they headed, but in her mind, she pictured some mammoth oak nurtured by elven Shapers into a council hall.

Cultivated trees and brush passed by in a blur until they came to an open area and were herded between two wide oaks where many elves waited. They had reached the gathering of the elders, but there was no council hall, and the number of those gathered was greater than she had guessed.

Ancient oaks surrounded a long and gently sunken clearing covered by a lawn. Lower branches were as thick as a normal tree's trunk and grew together in bridges from one tree to the next.

Onlookers, dressed in varied attire, sat or stood upon those bridge-branches and gathered in masses between the wide trunks. Those closest turned their eyes on the newcomers, the interlopers, the humans in their midst.

One elderly woman with filmy eyes sat in a wood chair of tawny grain. All of the chair's flowing curves, from its head-high back to its armrests and legs, were made from a single piece, like the rain barrels of Gleann's home. The woman wore a maroon cloak of raw-spun cotton over a matching robe, and she held a rolled parchment on a walnut spindle in her lap. Two younger men in similar cloaks stood at her sides, and others close by shared aspects of their attire.

Their glances were more studied than others, though Wynn did not find that a relief as she stepped by them. She was gripped by an impulse to grab Magiere's hand and offer comfort, but knew she should not.

Among the crowd gathered around every inch of the clearing, many were elaborately dressed. Wynn saw hair ornaments of wood rings for tails, circlets garnished with wildflowers, sparing jewelry of polished wood and stone, and a few crystals or gems that sparked in the bright sun. Few sported metal accoutrements of any kind, although one cluster of elves wore strangely shaped broaches of copper and brass. Everywhere Wynn looked, large amber eyes watched her from within dour caramel and triangular faces.

Partway around the clearing's far side was a cluster of short figures crouched upon the grass—the Äruin'nas. Shirtless, exposing their elaborate body paintings, and with their hair shaped into spirals and curls by dried mud, two of their elders sat cross-legged on the depression's lip. Wynn squinted, trying to make out the blue-black markings on their skin. Something about those symbols reminded her of the sigils and diagrams of thaumaturgy and conjury she had seen in the guild's library in Malourné.

Clan elders were not difficult to pick out, due to their age. Each was accompanied by attendants, though many had larger retinues.

Then she caught the yellow and russet of the Coilehkrotall, Sgäile and Leanâlhâm's clan, but she did not see an elder sitting before them.

Chap crept in beside Wynn, and there was more than one curious glance over his presence. She dropped a hand on his back, curling her fingers in his thick fur.

At either end of the clearing's floor were oval oak tables. Brot'an stood behind the nearer one, sifting through scrolls among leather-bound sheaves of paper. He looked up, his expression passive but for those severe-looking scars skipping over one eye.

Sgäile led the way downslope, and Wynn lost all self-confidence. She stepped out into full sight of the council of the an'Cróan.

"Well met," Brot'an said.

He looked solid and distinguished in his green-gray, though he wore no cloak. Without it, his shoulders seemed too broad for his tall frame. A forest-green ribbon held back his silver-streaked hair. Sgäile and his guards retreated to the slope's base.

"What are we waiting for?" Wynn whispered.

"Most Aged Father," Brot'an answered. "It should be a quietly dramatic entrance."

Wynn raised one eyebrow. Was that sarcasm?

"Who's the prosecutor?" Magiere asked in a low voice.

"The council has not chosen one," he answered, "as the claim against you must be settled first. Fréthfâre is 'advocate' for your accuser. Sgäilsheilleache serves as 'adjudicator' of proceedings."

Leesil sighed.

From the depression's upper edge and bridge-branched trees, a swarm of amber eyes looked down upon Magiere—and Leesil. Those behind Brot'an's table were close enough for Wynn to see their curiosity, anger, and baleful fascination. The elder elven woman and her companions displayed only cold interest.

As a child, Wynn had attended a livestock fair with Domin Tilswith. A calf born with three legs was on display at a center stall. Everyone stopped to stare and point. Wynn felt like that calf, though she guessed Magiere suffered far worse.

Caramel faces among the crowded turned, one by one, and then more. Wynn followed the wave of shifting focus.

Fréth came down the far slope, dressed the same as Brot'an, with her hair pulled back. Four anmaglâhk followed behind her, bearing the ends of wooden bars over their shoulders.

Between the bearers, Most Aged Father sat upon an ornate chair with rounded sides that cradled his frail body. He was wrapped in a blanket or long shawl of the gray-green, the color of his Anmaglâhk. Whispering murmurs filled the clearing at his entrance.

Most Aged Father's face was overshadowed by a fold of his wrap, but Wynn thought he squinted against the bright sun. His emaciated features and pale skin were worse to look upon than in his root chamber's dim candlelight. The bearers settled him beside Fréth's table, and he turned his head slowly, examining the crowd.

Sgäile stepped to the clearing's center and lifted his face to the gathering, calling out in clear Elvish, "I welcome the people and their clans, as represented by their elders, to hear the claim in dispute."

Not a breath passed before Fréthfâre's voice rose. "Brot'an'duivé, you are already in breach of our ways. Only the accused may stand at your side. The others will be removed immediately."

Brot'an stepped around his table past Magiere. For all his calm ways, his voice thundered across the clearing.

"Léshil is involved by implication and has a right to be present. And I choose the one called Wynn"—he pointed to her for all to take note—"to serve as Magiere's translator."

All eyes turned to Wynn, and she shrank from them, stepping halfway behind Leesil.

"The accused has the right to hear all that is said," Brot'an continued, "as it is said and not thereafter. I will not allow the accuser's advocate to complicate matters by requiring me to be Magiere's translator as well as her advocate! That would be a breach of courtesy . . . if not law."

Sgäile cut off Fréth's retort with a hand raised toward Brot'an.

"The accused's advocate is within custom and law. The advocate for the accuser"—and he turned toward Fréthfâre—"has no further grounds for this challenge."

Fréthfâre scowled and went to crouch beside Most Aged Father.

Wynn quickly translated all that was said for Magiere and Leesil, though a few nuances of dialect frustrated her. The night before, Brot'an had advised them that proceedings were conducted in Elvish, the proper language, and few clan leaders spoke any other tongue. He told them little else, claiming there was no time to understand more. Too much preparation might work against Magiere, if Fréthfâre tried to trip her up amid rehearsed responses.

Wynn was uncertain how much of this was just Brot'an's own scheming. Undoubtedly he risked alienating Most Aged Father and his own caste in standing as Magiere's advocate.

Brot'an stepped further into the clearing. "I thank the council for being present to render judgment, but I fear your time is not well spent."

Fréthfâre stood up. Both she and Most Aged Father turned rapt attention on Brot'an as he gestured toward Magiere.

"Most Aged Father gave this woman and her companions safe passage and sent Sgäilsheilleache under oath of guardianship to escort them to Crij-heäiche. Now, her own host claims that she is one of the humans' undead—something unnatural, returned from beyond death to this world. A human without a guide would have succumbed to the forest, left to wander until captured or dead. An undead could not have entered at all, as none have ever been seen in our land. Yet she walked among us for many days and in the company of a majay-hì. The claim of the accuser is shown false by Magiere's very presence."

Wynn hurried her translation, but as Brot'an paused, her gaze slipped to Most Aged Father. She unconsciously shifted back half a step at the steady hatred upon his face. The ancient elf appeared about to erupt, but Brot'an resumed in a forceful voice.

"Look upon the accused in the full light of day. Human, without doubt. For as little as we know of their kind's . . . 'undead' . . . our land and the spirits of our ancestors have never tolerated such before. By both these ancient authorities, the claim against her should be dismissed as superstition."

Wynn heard dissenting voices, high-pitched in anger, and her attention swung to their source—the Äruin'nas. One of their elders shouted to a nearby elven clan. Wynn could not follow their strange language, though its sound and cadence was akin to Elvish. Clearly they came only to see a human put to death.

Brot'an returned to his table as Wynn finished translating.

Leesil smoldered with satisfaction—perhaps surprised and pleased by the strength of Brot'an's statement. But this was only the beginning. Wynn knew the claim against Magiere could not be dispelled with words.

Most Aged Father leaned toward Fréth, whispering, and she crouched briefly to listen.

Fréth shook her head emphatically, and Most Aged Father squirmed in seething frustration. She stepped around her table, but Most Aged Father shouted out before she reached the clearing's center.

"Twister of truth!"

The wizened old elf jabbed a bony finger at Brot'an.

Brot'an dropped his eyes to the table, and Wynn faltered in her translating.

Murmurs faded among the gathering as Fréth turned in shock to Most Aged Father.

"She is undead!" he shouted weakly. "I know her kind, as the rest of you do not. My caste witnessed her change with their own eyes. Sgäilsheilleache was present, and who among you would doubt his word?"

"Do something," Leesil hissed at Brot'an.

"Be quiet," Wynn warned.

Brot'an did not look up. Neither did he seem affected by the old elf's words.

Several elders around the clearing turned to attendants and companions. Some called out to each other, while others sent companions weaving through the crowd to nearby clans. There were too many low voices for Wynn to catch anything that was said, but she noted surprise mixed with concern on many faces.

Brot'an remained placidly silent, which only made Wynn more nervous by the moment.

Fréth looked hesitantly at Sgäile, as if waiting for him rather than Brot'an to say something. She backed away as Sgäile stepped out.

"The accuser . . ." Sgäile's voice faltered. "The accuser will leave his claim in the hands of his advocate and remain silent until called upon. And as all are aware, the adjudicator is not permitted to witness for either side of a dispute."

When Brot'an lifted his head, he showed neither reluctance nor satisfaction —only cold poise.

Sgäile, standing within Most Aged Father's plain sight, was an obvious choice for support. Even Wynn understood that choice, for what she knew of Sgäile, but he had a rigid adherence to his people's customs, as well as the hidden codes of his caste.

Brot'an's blunt opening had been a goad thrust at Most Aged Father. The old one could not contain himself, and his outburst had served Brot'an. But Wynn realized still more.

If Most Aged Father's claim was proven true, then he was accountable to the elders for having given Magiere safe passage in the first place. If proven false, the elders might see him as senile and erratic for claims against one under his own protection. And either way, he might be held presumptuous for allowing humans into this land at all. The council grew unsettled by his inappropriate action.

Wynn turned a suspicious eye on Brot'an.

The tall and scarred anmaglâhk played a dangerous game with his leader—with Magiere caught between them. Yet who better to stand against the claims of a patriarch of assassins than a master among the Anmaglâhk?

Wynn slipped her hand around Magiere's wrist and squeezed lightly.

Fréth reclaimed the clearing's center and began in a calm, clear voice.

"Do not be fooled by this woman's appearance. As Brot'ânduivé says, we know little of the humans' undead. Who among you could swear to know one upon sight? Three days past, I saw her eyes turn black, her teeth and nails like a predator's, and her strength grow beyond any human's. She attacked my caste like a feral beast. Any acceptance by our land or the majay-hì was achieved through trickery. She is dark-begotten and must be destroyed . . ."

Fréth pointed around at the ring of clan elders. ". . . Before one of yours dies at her hands."

Wynn hesitated to translate those last words. As she did so, Leesil blew a sharp snort through his nose, but Magiere and Chap remained silent.

Sgäile stepped forward. "The accused's advocate will present first arguments."

Brot'an picked up a parchment to take the field, but a rustle among the crowd made him halt and turn. Wynn looked back as someone pushed through and descended the slope behind Brot'an's table.

Medium height and slight of build, even for an elf, he wore a cloak of dull yellow over a russet shirt. When he pulled back the hood, steel-gray hair stuck out in an unkempt mass.

Gleann of the Coilehkrotall approached Brot'an with an owlish smile. "I see I am late, but my barge only just arrived."

Magiere's wide eyes mirrored Wynn's own surprise.

"It is pleasing to see you once more," he said to them in Belaskian, then returned to Elvish. "Brot'an'duivé, have you not stopped growing yet? How you do not knock yourself senseless on the forest's low branches is beyond me. Hmm . . . now, where am I sitting?"

Gleann gazed about but his eyes settled at the clearing's far end.

"Aoishenis-Ahâre, well met," he said and raised a hand. "And still alive, I see. Sgäilsheilleache—or adjudicator, is it—where *am* I sitting?"

His entrance brought the proceedings to a standstill, though Magiere looked relieved. Brot'an's mild frown did not hide his subtle amusement. Wynn was about to point out the other Coilehkrotall when Sgäile hurried over.

"Grandfather, why are you here?"

"Do not be dull-witted," Gleann answered. "I represent our clan. Hui'u-väghas could not attend, but one of ours should hear and judge this claim."

Sgäile was openly distressed. It occurred to Wynn that Gleann had arrived a little too quickly compared to her own long journey down the river, and apparently he had more than a passing acquaintance with Brot'an. Why would a wry humored old healer have anything to do with a master assassin?

Across the clearing, Most Aged Father—who never replied to Gleann—looked both offended and anxious as he gestured Fréth to his side.

"Can we continue?" Fréth called out.

Sgäile rushed Gleann upslope to their clan. Brot'an waited politely until the elder was settled before addressing the gathering.

"I call no witnesses at present. Rather, I begin with a test, as it will require time."

Even Most Aged Father grew attentive.

"In the burial ground of our ancestors," Brot'an continued, "reserved for those first in this land, rests the ancient ash tree that began all things here—Roise Chârmune, the Seed of Sanctuary. Those who come of age seek it out and take the true name they bear for life. Most all here have done this . . . have felt the strength of hallowed ground beneath their feet . . . felt the presence of our ancestors close upon them. But Magiere is human and not allowed to attempt what I propose."

He let his pause hang until all curious eyes were cast his way.

"A proxy must go in her place to Roise Chârmune—and the ancestors—to plead for a branch."

A rumble spread quickly around the clearing. Brot'an raised his hand but had to shout over the crowd.

"What greater counsel is there than that of our first blood? No one can approach the Seed of Sanctuary without just cause, and a branch would only be given if the cause served our people. That would settle any claim against this human woman."

Wynn translated as fast as she could. Leesil stepped out before she even finished. Both she and Magiere tried to grab him before he could unwittingly commit some breach of custom, but he slipped out of their reach.

"I'll go," he demanded. "I'll do it."

"Leesil, no!" Magiere hissed, but he ignored her.

Most Aged Father crackled something at Fréth, and she called out, "Léshil does not know the way—and should not. He is not pure of blood, and he is not an'Cróan."

The crowd's rumbling grew uneven.

Brot'an's voice hammered the gathering into silence. "Do you now speak for the ancestors as well? Do you wish to raise claim concerning Léshil at this time?"

Fréth hesitated for a long moment. "He will not survive," she said finally. "He will not be allowed in, as he is not one of us."

"That is a decision for the ancestors, not you," Brot'an replied. "But if Léshil returns, and the accused takes hold of the branch without harm, then neither of them could be a threat to us. Or would you, Fréthfâre, care to tell how some 'human trick' could fool the spirits of our first blood?"

Leesil stood too far off for Wynn to tell him what was said. He looked about, at a loss, and Brot'an did not translate his words.

"What's happening?" Magiere whispered.

Wynn told her and then grabbed Magiere before she went after Leesil. "Do not say anything!"

Fréth made no reply to Brot'an's final barb. Stranger still, Most Aged Father watched the elders around the clearing with concern.

"A guide must be chosen for Léshil," Brot'an added. "Someone acceptable to the people by their elders."

Osha stepped forward. "I will take him."

"No!" Sgäile shouted, too loudly. "I am adjudicator . . . I am the impartial here . . . I will guide Léshil."

Soft murmurs grew slowly, but no voice lifted in dissent. Wynn caught a flicker of surprise on Brot'an's face before he regained stoic composure.

"Sgäilsheilleache, it shall be. As Most Aged Father said, no one would doubt his word. I ask for adjournment until he and Léshil return—or for three days as the limit."

All around, elders rose amid their clans in implied consent. The gathering broke into smaller clusters, talking among themselves in a low-voiced cacophony that filled the depression between the encircling oaks. Across the clearing, Fréth and Most Aged Father were lost in conspiratorial whispers.

As Leesil returned, Magiere grabbed his arm. "What did you do?"

"You do not know what is involved," Wynn added.

Leesil didn't answer either of them.

"Sgäilsheilleache will lead you," Brot'an said in Belaskian. "I do not know why, but he is a better choice than I had hoped for."

"Hope?" Magiere snapped. "You hoped? That's all you've got?"

"No one will doubt his word," Brot'an assured her.

Wynn tried to calm Magiere and then noticed Sgäile.

Anmaglâhk were difficult to read—except the plain-faced Osha—and Brot'an and Urhkar were the hardest of all she had met. Wynn could not take her eyes off Sgäile.

Osha approached him with open worry, but Sgäile did not react. He seemed weary, and flinched when Osha touched his shoulder. Sgäile turned his head, watching an oblivious Leesil.

Fear passed across Sgäile's narrow features.

Magiere pulled away from Wynn, closing on Brot'an like a wolf.

"What have you gotten Leesil into?"

"How could you blindly agree to this?" Magiere ranted.

She paced the open space of their domicile elm, watching Leesil shove the last of the grapes and a blanket into a canvas pack.

"You don't know the forest," she went on. "You don't know what you're facing!"

When Leesil looked up, Magiere went numb at his familiar expression. Cold and hard desperation suggested he would try anything without a thought for the danger.

"I'll face an ash tree," he said flatly. "What's so dangerous about that?"

"Didn't you hear Wynn? Ancestors . . . spirits! You don't know what that means." Magiere ran a hand down her face. "I can't believe I trusted Brot'an."

"Did you think this would be settled through persuasive oration?" Wynn asked. "The elders must see that you are not what Most Aged Father claims. I do not understand it, but if this branch provides disproof of the claim, then we will use it."

Magiere turned angrily on the sage, but her voice failed.

For the first time, she understood how Leesil felt in Venjètz. While she'd moved freely about, he'd remained trapped inside Byrd's Inn. But the thought of two or three more days in this tree, with him far beyond her reach, was almost more than she could bear.

Chap lay dejected on the floor, staring toward the curtained doorway.

"And you," she snapped at the dog. "Don't you have anything to say?"

He lifted his muzzle to her and then returned to his strange vigil. Magiere looked to Wynn for any response the dog offered, but the sage just shook her head with a shrug.

"Brot'an is doing better than I expected," Leesil said. "If I bring back this branch, it looks like that will settle it. Hopefully there'll be no following trial. Fréth and her withered master will have nothing left to counter."

He got up and grabbed Magiere's hand.

"This is my fault for bringing you here. It's a sick twist that Brot'an is the one to give me a way to fix this, but I'll take it anyway. It's time I woke up and did something. Please, just wish me luck."

He was desperate for her support. All Magiere could do was hang on to his fingers.

"I do," she answered, her voice breaking. "But I can't stand that you're doing this alone. I should be with you, not Sgäile."

As if called, Sgäile stuck his head through the doorway curtain. "Léshil, are you prepared? We should begin."

Leesil leaned in and kissed Magiere, quick and soft. "I'll be back in a couple days at most, and everything will be all right."

He let go and headed for the door. Chap got up to follow, but Leesil stopped him.

"No, you stay with Magiere and Wynn. We can't leave them alone among the elves."

Chap barked sharply twice in denial, and Magiere knew exactly how he felt. But the dog turned his eyes on her and then Wynn. He whined and flopped back down. There was nothing else to say, and Magiere sank to the floor beside Chap.

The curtain fell into place as Leesil left, cutting him off from her too abruptly.

CHAPTER NINETEEN

Leesil spoke little with Sgäile as they jogged through the forest. They headed northwest for the morning, but by early afternoon, Leesil grew less certain of their course. The sky clouded over. With only hazy light and no sun, the forest changed in small degrees.

There were fewer flowers and more wet moss. Patches of it clung to tree trunks and branches overhead. The trees were older and gnarled, with bark darkened by moisture thickening in the air. For a while, a drizzle pattered against the leaves.

Sgäile cast off whatever weight crushed him upon volunteering for this task. He returned to his earlier self from their first journey to Crijheäiche. Perhaps, like Leesil, Sgäile was relieved to have anything to do besides wait in frustration for others to do something.

The forest grew ancient as they traveled, its trees taller and thicker and wider, blocking out most of the sky. In the lingering false dusk beneath their leaves and needles, the forest seemed aware it had a pair of trespassers.

Leesil grew less aware of where he was—as if here the forest's manipulations pressed harder upon his wits. He often turned his head to look behind and couldn't recognize anything that he must have just passed.

Sgäile's shoulder brushed through a spider's web, glistening with dew. An eight-legged shadow scurried down the back of his cloak.

Leesil slapped it off, but when he looked down, there was nothing scurrying across the mulch into hiding. He wondered about their final destination as daylight faded even more.

Sgäile slowed and looked about. "If we keep on, we will reach the grounds well past midnight. Or we can camp and continue at dawn."

Sleeping in this dank and dark forest was less than enticing.

"Let's take rest and food," Leesil said. "Then move on."

Sgäile nodded and swung the small pack off his shoulder. "I have water, flatbread, and a little walnut oil."

"I have grapes."

They sat on a rotting log, sharing out what they'd brought. Leesil fidgeted as the damp soaked through his breeches. Sgäile removed a leather lid from a small clay pot, tore off a bit of flatbread, and dipped it in. He set the vessel between them, and Leesil did the same.

"This is good," he said, and held out the grapes. "I wanted to . . . to thank you for doing this, for trying to help Magiere."

"I care nothing for helping Magiere." Sgäile paused, shaking his head. "Pardon, I did not mean to sound . . . I do this for my caste. Brot'ân'duivé on one side and Fréthfâre on the other—this is not good. I serve my duty as adjudicator in the hope of bringing this gathering to a close, so my caste will be as one again."

Leesil kept quiet. If Sgäile really believed that ending Magiere's hearing—regardless of the outcome—would seal the rifts in his caste, he was blinder in his devotion than Leesil had first thought.

"We should focus on our task," Sgäile said, and once again his expression grew uneasy.

"Why the worry?" Leesil asked. "What's at this place with the special tree?"

Sgäile scowled at the casual reference. "The first of our people were buried there long ago. All an'Cróan are descended from them. We go there alone to seek guidance in choosing our name for life, when we come of age."

"How old is that?"

"When parents and child agree it is time."

"You did this? So you had some other name before Sgäile?"

"Sgäilsheilleache," he corrected. "It means 'In Willow Shade, or Shadow.' "

"And that's what your ancestors said you should call yourself?"

"We do not see or hear the ancestors," Sgäile answered. "It is something I saw . . . in the presence of Roise Chârmune."

"So there was a willow somewhere nearby?"

"No. It was . . . something far off, far from this land . . . in the shade of a willow."

"Then what—some kind of vision? And that's all you saw . . . just a willow tree?"

Sgäile let out a sharp sigh.

Leesil knew he was somewhere close to the mark. Superstitious nonsense—and here these elves thought themselves so much better than humans.

"So, you call yourself by whatever you see. You're stuck with whatever comes up."

It was Sgäile's turn to be disdainful. "We are free to choose any name we wish, from whatever comes—in part, in whole, or not. Though what is experienced at Roise Chârmune remains, just the same."

"Then what's got you so worried about all this with the branch?"

"As I said . . . we go alone. It is not proper for anyone else to be present. We do not even care to speak of our experience to others . . . but for the name we choose."

"I'm not going for any name, so stop dodging the question."

Sgäile covered the walnut oil and got up to tuck the jar into his pack. He stared a long while through the darkening forest before looking down at Leesil.

"You are half-blooded. None but my people go to Roise Chârmune . . . and the ancestors."

Was that it? Leesil sighed. "So they reject me, and I go back. I'll find some other way to get Magiere and my mother away from your people."

"You must first gain hallowed ground before the ancestors accept or reject your plea."

As much as Leesil preferred Sgäile over the rest, there were moments when he'd had enough.

"Oh, dead deities!" Leesil got up, weary of cryptic answers. "Just say what you mean for once."

Sgäile's jaw twitched. "I would tell you more if I knew. But unless you reach hallowed ground . . . I do not believe you will come back."

Wynn sat on the floor trying to jot down the day's events. From the customs and proceedings to what she remembered of clan distinctions, she scribbled out everything that came to her. Later, when more time permitted, she would rework it into something comprehensible.

Magiere halfheartedly groomed Chap's long fur but kept glancing toward the curtained doorway. Chap lay with his head on his paws. Wynn could think of no words of comfort for either of them.

She was thankful for the strange quill gifted her by Gleann. The bulbed grip above its silver-white head was awkward in her small hand, but in her rush, she did not have to stop as often to replenish its ink.

The doorway drape swung aside, and Leanâlhâm peeked in. "May we enter?"

"Yes, please," Magiere answered, and paused in grooming as Chap lifted his head. "Who's with you?"

"Osha," Leanâlhâm said. "No one but your advocate may see you without a guard."

Leanâlhâm carried in a tray of grilled trout with wild onions and two steaming mugs. She held a canvas bag tucked under one arm. Wynn smelled tea mingling with the scent of food. Osha stepped in behind the girl and set down a bowl of water for Chap.

Osha eyed both Wynn and Magiere, as if uncomfortable with his formal role here. Or perhaps like others who had been in Nein'a's clearing, he believed Magiere some monster of the dead and did not care for close proximity. Either way, Wynn had no patience for it.

Leanâlhâm set down the tray and dropped to the floor before Magiere and Chap. The girl reached slowly for Chap's head. Before her touch landed, he flicked his tongue through her fingertips. She let out a startled, giggling gasp and then looked back at Osha, who fidgeted nervously.

"Oh, please," Leanâlhâm said in Elvish. "They have been alone all day. It is impolite to deliver their supper and just leave."

Osha's mouth fell open and then closed again with the barest grunt. His gray-green cloak was slightly askew on his shoulders. He crouched by the doorway and looked at Wynn.

"How do you fare?" he asked.

"I am all right," she answered and set down her quill. "Though it would be more polite to speak Belaskian among those who do not understand your language. And you need the practice."

Osha was caught somewhere between embarrassment and confusion at her tone. Or perhaps he had had enough of being chided. Wynn sighed, rolled her eyes, and forced a smile.

He relaxed sheepishly, realizing she jested. When his gaze flicked to Magiere, that hint of a smile vanished. Leanâlhâm showed no such concern.

"Sgäilsheilleache will keep Léshil safe," she said.

Magiere nodded. "Thanks . . . it's good of you to come."

"Do not worry," Leanâlhâm continued. "No matter what they face, Sgäil-sheilleache never fails. Brot'ân'duivé and Grandfather will do the rest, and you will soon be free."

Osha grew uncomfortable. He understood enough of what was said, and shared another doubtful glance with Wynn.

Leanâlhâm's words rolled in Wynn's head. This was the second time she had noted some casual connection between Gleann and Brot'an. Poor Leanâlhâm was as blind as Leesil, if she thought these proceedings would end any time soon—no matter this quest's outcome. Whatever Fréth and Most Aged Father would throw at Magiere, it would be unexpected and ugly.

Wynn took the mug of tea the girl offered her. "How did Gleann arrive so quickly? It took us nearly eight days to reach Crijheäiche."

"Grandfather said that he left shortly after we did, but he did not tell me why." For the first time, Leanâlhâm hesitated and then leaned forward. "But he has the faith of our clan and our other elders. His vote will be counted, and his voice will be heard."

A simplistic view, judging by what Wynn fathomed so far.

"You should eat," Osha said, "and we should not talk of the gathering."

"Yes, Osha," Leanâlhâm answered, and did nothing to hide her exasperation.

She served trout and onions onto polished wood plates, and the savory aroma grew each time she portioned the fish.

"Here," she said, placing one plate before Chap. "A whole boned fish just for you."

Chap's tail switched the floor twice as he sniffed.

Wynn was glad to see his interest. Since facing down his kin, for her life, he had been so withdrawn.

Leanâlhâm pulled an oblong tawny box from the canvas bag, its top stained in light and dark squares.

"I brought a game we call Dreug'an. It will help pass the time."

"Dreug'an?" Osha coughed out, well past uncomfortable, and stumbled in his Belaskian. "Sgäilsheilleache question where come from. He think me lax in duty."

Leanâlhâm ignored him and removed small white and black river stones from a drawer in the box's side. "He will know exactly where it came from. It belongs to him. Grandfather brought it for me."

Osha's dark skin seemed to pale as he sagged. Then Brot'an ducked through the doorway curtain, startling everyone.

Magiere's expression hardened. She dropped her plate, and the two-tined fork clattered on it. Before she snapped a word at him, Brot'an pulled the curtain aside again. His silver hair glowed with the darkness behind him.

"I will speak with Magiere alone. Osha, you will attend Wynn outside. Leanâlhâm, return to your quarters."

Osha immediately got to his feet.

Wynn did not like having only Osha as a familiar face to look upon among the guards outside. As much as this tree was little more than a prison, it did provide limited safety. Brot'an merely stood by the doorway.

Leanâlhâm lightly touched Magiere's leg as she got up and quickly headed out. Osha stood waiting upon Wynn.

"Please," Brot'an said pointedly and looked down at Chap. "And you."

Chap rose slowly to all fours. For a moment, Wynn readied to pounce on the dog should he lunge at Brot'an. Chap turned his eyes upon Magiere.

"Go on," she said. "You stay with Wynn."

Chap trotted out. Wynn followed and found herself amid Osha and two other anmaglâhk. She wondered what Brot'an had to say to Magiere that no one else should hear. Leanâlhâm already headed off under the escort of another anmaglâhk. The girl looked back long enough to wave in parting before fading among the night trees of Crijheäiche.

Something more occurred to Wynn. When Leanâlhâm had said, "No matter what they face," she referred to Roise Chârmune.

The nametaking rite of the an'Cróan was unfamiliar to Wynn. She had never heard of such among the elves of her land. All here went to hallowed ground when they came of age to be given—or was it "to take"?—a name other than what their parents chose at birth. Leanâlhâm was about sixteen, if Wynn remembered right. Old enough to have gone herself.

But by the way the girl spoke of this sacred place, Leanâlhâm had never been there.

Leesil stopped behind Sgäile near a dank oak. The silence was wrong.

He should hear something—bugs, maybe a cricket, or even leaves shifting in a breeze. But he heard nothing, now that their own footfalls had ceased.

The forest thinned ahead, and he saw an open space screened by branches. It was so dark, the masses of leaves and trailing moss were little more than black silhouettes. Yet beyond them was soft light, like what a full moon might provide.

Leesil glanced up. He wasn't certain, with the forest canopy thick overhead, but the rest of the forest was too dark for a moon, full or not. He tried to make out what was hidden beyond in the clearing. He only caught a hint of glistening ocher limbs behind surrounding gnarled oaks draped in moss.

"Do not move," Sgäile whispered. "Do not look for it."

He glanced at Sgäile, uncertain what this meant.

Something slid wetly across the forest mulch. Faint and soft, it carried from directly ahead.

Leesil did look. He saw nothing but the glow of the clearing beyond the black shapes of the oaks. Sgäile's final words after their meal echoed in Leesil's head.

Unless you reach hallowed ground . . . I do not believe you will come back.

For the first time since starting this task, fear tickled the back of Leesil's neck—not of death but of failure. What if he didn't return to Magiere? What would happen to her? He clenched one hand, ready to face whatever this place threw at him.

The sound grew subtly louder, closing off to his left, as if something circled around the clearing instead of passing through it. A wet dragging sound came between pauses in slow rhythm.

"Repeat my words," Sgäile whispered quickly, "exactly as I say them."

Leesil barely heard him, still searching for whatever came. He was prepared for a fight, not a speech. Then he glanced at Sgäile.

The elf stood frozen in place, staring straight at the silhouette trees. His eyes twitched once to the left toward the sound and then quickly turned back ahead.

"*Ahârneiv!*" Sgäile began. "*Œn päjij nävâjean'am le jhäiv . . .*"

The dark base of one oak bulged near the ground.

The swelling rolled and flowed across the forest floor toward Leesil. It turned into the path toward the half-hidden clearing.

The soft glow beyond the silhouette oaks caught on the piece of slithering darkness, and its surface glinted to iridescent green.

A long body, as thick as Leesil's own torso, was covered in fist-sized scales. Their deep green shimmered to opalescence as it came closer. Leesil caught the yellow glint of two eyes that marked its approaching head, like massive spiral-cracked crystals in an oblong boulder pushed along at a hand's-breadth above the ground.

A snake . . . no, a serpent, too large to be real.

Leesil reached slowly down his thighs, but his blades weren't there. He slid one foot back to retreat.

"No!" Sgäile whispered. "Do not move! Repeat my words . . . quickly!"

The serpent's body knotted and coiled, gathering into a mass. Its scaled and plated head rose to hover before Leesil, swaying gently. A long forked tongue whipped at his face with a hiss.

Slit irises in its yellow eyes watched him steadily.

The serpent's jaw dropped open. Fangs as long as Leesil's forearm glistened in the dark maw of its mouth. It could swallow half of him at once.

"Léshil!" Sgäile whispered. "If you would save Magiere, you must speak my words."

The serpent undulated as its head swung toward Sgäile's voice.

Leesil heard the man's shuddering breath as he felt some part of the serpent's scaled body scrape across his leg. He was still prepared to fight his way past this thing if he had to. He glanced quickly at Sgäile, and the sight was like ice pressed into his eyes, feeding its chill into his body.

Sgäile averted his gaze, anywhere but at the serpent's massive head. He closed his eyes tightly. He was shaking, his muscles rigid.

An anmaglâhk was frozen in terror, and Sgäile's fear bled rapidly into Leesil.

"I . . . I can't," Leesil whispered.

But if he died here, Magiere would die too. The serpent swung back, yellow eyes centered on him.

"I can't speak your language," he said, despair mounting. "I won't get it right."

*   *   *

Magiere wanted to beat answers out of Brot'an's scarred face. She had trusted him, and Leesil might pay for her mistake. Brot'an spoke before she uttered her first demand.

"There is more at stake than just your freedom. Even if Most Aged Father's claim is dismissed, neither you nor Leesil will leave this land alive. You are interlopers, humans, so do not be naïve. Am I clear so far?"

Magiere's ire held beneath her uncertainty.

"Very well," Brot'an added quietly, and settled upon the chamber floor before her. "All balances on whether Léshil steps onto hallowed ground . . . as much as whether or not he gains the branch of Roise Chârmune."

Magiere wasn't certain what this meant.

"To be elven, as you call it," Brot'an said, his voice tainted with distaste, "is not an'Cróan. We are our heritage, our blood, more than whatever race you see us as. Only as an'Cróan can Léshil plead for Cuirin'nên'a before the elders."

"If he's elven," she snapped back, "then he's got as much right as anyone, under your laws."

"No, he does not," Brot'an countered, quiet and sharp. "Do you think an outsider could demand Cuirin'nên'a's freedom? To be an'Cróan—to be of the blood—is all that matters to my people."

Magiere looked away. The last thing Leesil—or she—wanted was to be snared even deeper among these people and their ways. What arrogance, what nonsense and superstition!

"What are you talking about?"

"I mean you no malice," Brot'an said. "And only wish you to understand what is truly at stake. There was no time to waste in arguing this, so I chose not to give you that chance. The only way Léshil will be seen as one of us is if he can step onto hallowed ground. That is as important as the reason he goes there."

"If?" Magiere snapped.

"Sgäilsheilleache will guide him . . . teach him the words to ask entrance. There is no other way."

"Ask who? The ancestors?"

Brot'an shook his head. "None of us have seen what guards Roise Chârmune, as no one has gone there before but a full-blooded an'Cróan. And none have been rejected, to my knowledge. Leesil must gain entrance before he reaches it or the ancestors."

Gain entrance? What did that mean?

"What did you see at this Roi-say . . . this Seed of Sanctuary?" she demanded. "What's guarding it? Just tell me what you know."

"A sound," he answered, "something moving in the forest surrounding hallowed ground. I know no more than that. When I spoke the words my father taught me, all was silent again. I stood a long while before I tried to walk in. Even when I left, I neither saw nor heard anything more."

"What did you say?"

Brot'an hesitated. "A formal plea in my language. Nothing that would tell you more or ease your mind."

But it implied that if Leesil did not make it into the burial ground . . .

"For what it is worth," Brot'an added, "I believe Léshil will return."

"What did you . . . experience when you went for your name?" Magiere asked. She tried to remember what Wynn had said Brot'an's name meant. Something about a dog.

"That is an impudent question."

"Does it look like I care?" she hissed. "You think you'll walk out of here without answering?"

"I see that you love him," Brot'an said, "in some fashion, though I do not know if that is better or worse for him. I ask you again. Have you mated with Léshil?"

"That's still none of your business."

"No more than my naming is yours. I know the answer, but I would hear it from your own lips . . . now!"

Magiere saw Brot'an was as determined as she was to get answers.

"Yes," she said bluntly.

Brot'an slumped ever so slightly. "What do you know of Leanâlhâm's mother?"

"She was never happy or at home here. She ran off when her husband abandoned her and Leanâlhâm."

Magiere didn't care for the way Brot'an studied her.

"We have more than one word," he said, "for the degrees of what humans so casually call love. Only at its deepest do we bond . . . mate . . . for life. It is why we observe a period of *bóijt'äna* before bonding, as Én'nish did for Grôyt'ashia."

"Grôyt brought on his own death!" Magiere countered.

"I agree, though you are not following my meaning. Én'nish may look upon Léshil as the murderer of her 'betrothed,' you would say. But her obsession has taken her reason. Even Léshil's death may not end her suffering. My people bond for life."

Magiere knew of others who'd lost a loved one because of Leesil. "Grief never ends. It's just something you learn to live with."

Brot'an slowly shook his head. "Not for some . . . not for an'Cróan. Mating is life—and death—and overwhelms all else. It is rare that we ever mate outside of bonding for that very reason. Do you not remember Léshil's words to me in Darmouth's crypt . . . when I stepped too close to you at the end?"

Magiere could never forget. *Touch her, and I'll kill you and everything you love.*

Brot'an went on. "It was then I first suspected what lay between the two of you."

He had purposefully chosen not to kill her that night in the crypt. Magiere now suspected the reasons were more complex than some slip of compassion.

"Leanâlhâm's mother did not flee this land," Brot'an said. "That is what the girl chose to believe. Gleannéohkân'thva and Sgäilsheilleache chose not to correct her . . . to let time bring her more slowly to the truth with the maturity to face it. Her mother ran mad into the forest. Though her body was never found, I do not believe she survived."

Magiere tried to shut out mounting fear. "What of Leanâlhâm's father?"

"He lives," Brot'an added coldly. "Life is not always lost in such matters. The young are the most vulnerable. He did not love the girl's mother, by your definition of the word, though he will still suffer. Gleannéohkân'thva was rash in bargaining to take Leanâlhâm's father under tutelage . . . in exchange for a bonding he thought might ease the suffering of Leanâlhâm's mother."

Brot'an got up, heading for the door. "Léshil is only half-blooded, with more years than Leanâlhâm's mother had when she bonded and mated with the girl's father. Léshil knows none of what I have told you. It is important that you comprehend exactly what you have done with him."

He said this with no spite, but Magiere didn't wish to discuss her relationship with Leesil further.

"You still owe me an answer," she said quickly. "Your name . . . Wynn said something about a dog."

" 'Dog in the Dark,' in your tongue," Brot'an corrected. "Though 'mastiff' would be more precise. Not wild but domesticated, like the ones humans use in war."

"Is that what you saw when you went for your name?"

Brot'an remained halfway to the door, his back still turned to her.

"It came in silence out of the night, straight from the shadow of Roise Chârmune. It tore off its iron-spiked collar with its paws and bared its teeth, as if tuning upon its master."

He finally looked back, and Magiere's own spite faltered for an instant at the discomfort in Brot'an's lined face.

"At the time, I thought it a resentful shadow of arguing with my father over what I should do with my life. He did not wish me to take up service. Then later, when I joined Eillean, I thought it an image of the coming war. But I lost my taste for omens and portents over so many years. When Eillean died, it was a name and nothing more . . . until you appeared in our land."

Brot'an turned away to the door. "And now I stand before my people to pull down Aoishenis-Ahâre for the sake of a half-blood and a dark-tainted human woman."

He was gone, leaving Magiere alone with mounting anguish growing upon an old forgotten fear.

Her memory slipped back to a tiny inn outside of Bela. She had waited there for Leesil. It had seemed almost better—safer—to let him go, before he fell prey to her dhampir side. In spite of all her fears, she wanted him too much.

What had she done to him?

Chap laid a ways off and watched the elm where Brot'an spoke privately with Magiere. Osha tried to occupy Wynn in learning to play Dreug'an. The sage relented but showed little interest and watched the curtained doorway.

Try as Chap might, he could not hear what was said. And without line of sight, he could not dip for memories surfacing in either Brot'an or Magiere. He snarled at one Anmaglâhk guard just to see the man flinch.

Chap's ears stiffened when Brot'an finally emerged and walked on into the dark, not even stopping to tell Osha to return Wynn to confinement.

Osha quickly packed up the Dreug'an board and pieces and ushered Wynn off with the other two Anmaglâhk close behind. Chap stayed a moment longer.

He reached out for Brot'an's memories.

Whatever the man discussed with Magiere had left him unsettled, for his mind was not the blank slate Chap had found upon other occasions. Memories flashed in his mind so quickly that Chap had to focus hard to keep up.

A mastiff stalked out of the shadow of a strange barkless tree amid a wet and barren clearing. It snarled silently at Chap as he watched it through Brot'an's memory.

Brot'ân'duivé—the Dog in the Dark.

This was the moment when Brot'an had gone to the ancestors for his name.

As the memory faded, Chap saw an image of Leesil traveling in the forest. And then again the image of the dog that appeared when Brot'an stepped onto hallowed ground.

The memory vanished. Brot'an's mind was as hidden as before.

Chap traipsed back to the elm, trying to fathom what he had glimpsed. He turned as Brot'an's tall form slipped away between the trees.

A naming—and Leesil.

Chap stood there . . . long enough that he grasped the connection.

Leesil was traveling to the place where all an'Cróan took their true name, or so they believed. If he gained hallowed ground, it would be to plead for a branch from Roise Chârmune. But Brot'an hoped Leesil might gain more.

Why would Brot'ân'duivé want this to happen? Why did an Anmaglâhk master want to know Leesil's true name?

"I can't speak your language. I won't get it right."

Sgäile's throat closed at Léshil's panicked words. He stood shaking, and still could not open his eyes to this thing no one had ever seen, nor did they know where it came from or why it stood vigil over this hallowed ground.

His people only knew it by a name and the oath that spoke of its deadly nature.

"*Ahârneiv . . . ,*" he began again, and then faltered as he felt its hissing breath upon his face.

Would it understand in any other tongue? And if it did, would it let him live, coming here with Léshil? All who came to Roise Chârmune must come alone!

Sgäile began the litany once again, this time in words Léshil could understand.

"Father of Poison . . ."

He waited in tense silence for Léshil to repeat it.

"Father of . . . Poison . . . ," Léshil whispered.

Sgäile took a quick breath. "Who washes away our enemies with Death . . ."

Léshil echoed him again.

"Let me pass by to my ancestors, first of my blood. Give me leave to touch the Seed of Sanctuary."

As Léshil repeated his words, the serpent's breath faded from Sgäile's face, and he waited long in silence.

He heard coils grating upon the earth . . . and then the softer wet sound of mulch beneath the trees somewhere ahead. Longer he waited with his eyes shut, until the sound nearly faded altogether.

Something dropped upon Sgäile's shoulder, and he opened his eyes, breathing so quickly he grew dizzy. He kept his eyes on the dark oaks ahead, afraid to catch even one more glimpse of Ahârneiv.

It was gone.

Léshil's hand slipped off Sgäile's shoulder and fell limply at his side.

"We . . . are free . . . to go on," Sgäile whispered.

He almost did not believe the words as they came from his lips. Sgäile glanced sidelong at the half-blood—who had just changed his whole world, and perhaps that of Leanâlhâm.

For more than two years, he and his grandfather had urged Leanâlhâm to wait, to put off her name taking, though their arguments grew weaker with each passing moon. They feared that she would not return from this place, not with human blood in her.

Still, Léshil did not move.

"You have gained hallowed ground," Sgäile urged. "You are accepted as blood."

Léshil slowly turned his eyes toward Sgäile.

"I'm here for one reason," he snapped. "For Magiere, caught among your kind because of me. I don't care how you or your ghosts see me."

Léshil stepped on toward the clearing. Sgäile hung back, stunned back into silence.

Human blood, by any degree, was a baffling thing.

Leesil stood before the tree at the bare clearing's center and stared up at its wild branches filling the air above him.

It wasn't shaped like the tall and straight ash trees he had seen. Stout branches sprouting from its thick trunk curved and wound and divided up into the night. A soft glow emanated from its fine-grained wood to dimly light the clearing.

Leafless and barkless—yet somehow alive. From its wide-reaching roots lumping the earth to its thick and naked pale-yellow body and limbs, its soft rippled surface glistened beneath its own glow.

"You must touch it," Sgäile whispered from behind. "Roise Chârmune will know why you have come, and the ancestors will decide."

Leesil shivered. The night was only cool, but it had suddenly grown crisp within the clearing.

This was what he'd come for, but after passing the guardian serpent, he wavered at touching this tree. He quickly slapped his hand against its bare trunk, just to be done with it, and shivered again as the temperature dropped sharply.

"Sgäile . . . ?" he said.

The man looked anxiously about and folded his hands under his arms against the mounting cold. Whether from fear or frigid temperature, he shook where he stood.

"I do not know," Sgäile whispered.

Someone stepped around the naked tree's far side.

The figure wore the gray-green of an Anmaglâhk, cloak tied around its waist and cowl pulled forward. But it was short for an elf, no taller than Leesil himself.

Leesil began to pull back.

"Do not move!" Sgäile warned. "Do not take your hand from Roise Chârmune!"

Leesil didn't believe this was a vision. Surely one of Sgäile's caste must have followed them.

The figure raised a hand and held it up before Leesil's eyes. In that closed fist was an Anmaglâhk stiletto, silver-white blade pointed downward from its round, plain guard.

Leesil snatched the figure's wrist with his free hand.

The clearing lit up as if under a burning noon sun.

Where there had been cold, now sweltering heat choked the air in Leesil's lungs. Within the figure's cowl he saw a face . . . his face.

Leesil stared into his own reflection within that cowl.

There were the faint scars on his own cheek from where Ratboy had clawed him. His own amber eyes stared back at him, somewhat too small for an elf's, above a chin not quite tapered enough for a full-blood's.

His reflection looked older, somehow. And tears began running down his—its—face.

Leesil stood there, gripping the wrist of his reflection.

Heat made his double, his twin, or whatever it was ripple before his eyes. A shift in the land beyond the surrounding oaks tugged at his attention.

He thought he saw barren mountains beyond rolling tan hills that were too smooth and perfect. High peaks rippled in the distance as those hills radiated heat. Sgäile hissed out one word.

"Ancestors!"

Darkness filled the clearing. The cold bit again at Leesil as his gaze shifted back. His breath caught as one puff of vapor rushed from his lips.

He saw no reflection of himself anymore. His grip was closed on a slender translucent wrist that glowed like the naked ash. And he looked into . . . through . . . the transparent face of a tall elven male.

The man's eyes turned stern as he looked back at Leesil. His face was broader at the cheekbones than other elves'. An ugly scar slanted from his forehead to his right temple and another marred the left side of his jaw below his peaked ear. He had seen battle during his life; his hand around the stiletto appeared toughened and calloused.

No, not a stiletto . . . the elven warrior held a branch of naked pale wood like that of the ash tree. Long and straight overall, the wood showed gentle wavering throughout its length like any natural branch stripped of its bark.

Pale glimmers erupted in the darkness behind the branch's bearer.

Leesil remembered the ghost horde of the Apudâlsat forest, all hideously wounded in the moment of their death. These were different.

They appeared as in life, dressed as they must have been long ago, though their transparent forms held no color but that of the ash tree's wood. A third were male, the rest female, and not all appeared old. Leesil counted at least a dozen.

Their attire varied. Some were clothed no differently from the elves Leesil had seen around the council clearing. But others wore hauberks and bracers of hardened leather, either plain or covered in overlapping plates and scales of metal. Two wore helms of triple crests with scrollwork spirals engraved in their sides, as did the one Leesil still gripped.

They carried spears, some as long as pikes, and quivers and bows slung upon their backs. Not the short ones the Anmaglâhk disassembled to hide away, but longbows capable of great range. One middle-aged female with scars down her left upper arm had thick triangular war daggers on her wide studded belt. They looked more like a human weapon than those Leesil had seen among elves. The spear in her grip was shorter than her height. Its thick shaft appeared to be metal instead of wood, and its head was wide-bladed and nearly as long as a short sword.

And that one, with wild eyes full of fury, smiled at him beneath narrowing eyes.

But there were none among the spirits dressed as Anmaglâhk.

An elder woman in a robe approached behind the tall warrior holding the branch. Her face was slender and lightly lined with age. Long hair waved and floated as if she moved through water.

Take the limb of Roise Chârmune . . . and guard it as it will guard you . . . as you will guard life, Léshiârelaohk.

Leesil heard her voice, though her lips never moved.

Tell Sorhkafâré we wait for him.

A different voice. Male, tired but purposeful, like a sigh of relief after long burden.

Leesil turned his eyes back on the scarred and wide-cheeked warrior in his grip. The man's gaze shifted toward Sgäile then flickered once to Leesil. He seemed puzzled by something between the only two living people in the clearing. Then the spirit looked deep into Leesil's eyes.

Tell Sorhkafâré that Snähacróe still waits for his comrade . . . when he is finally ready to rest. Tell him . . . Léshiârelaohk.

Leesil knew the first name from Magiere's vision—the long-forgotten name of Most Aged Father. The second might be this one holding out the branch. But that final name he couldn't place, though it was close to what his mother and her people called him.

Léshil . . . Léshiârelaohk.

He wasn't sure he could repeat it aloud, but its sound vibrated in his head, as if spoken again by both the elder woman and the dour warrior.

The tall spirit opened his fingers, and the ash branch began to fall.

Leesil released his grip and snatched it from the air.

When he looked up again, the clearing was empty but for himself, Sgäile, and the soft radiance of the naked ash.

He saw no spirits. Not a one.

Leesil held up the branch of Roise Chârmune.

CHAPTER TWENTY

Midafternoon on the second day, Magiere ripped aside the elm's doorway curtain at the sound of running feet.

"Leesil?"

Six anmaglâhk stood outside, with Osha in the front, but there was no sign of Leesil or Sgäile.

"Is time," Osha said in his thick accent.

"Where's Leesil?" she asked. "How can the elves resume proceedings without Sgäile?"

"You come," he urged.

Wynn threw on Chane's cloak as Chap rose, and they followed Magiere out.

The guards flanked them as they hurried through Crijheäiche to the council clearing. Again Magiere grew uneasy as she stepped between the bridge-branched oaks and the closest onlookers backed out of her way. She took a slow calming breath at the sight of Leesil and Sgäile standing with Brot'an behind the oak table.

Leesil held his hand out. Magiere hurried down the slope. One anmaglâhk almost grabbed for her, but Osha waved him off.

Faint dark rings surrounded Leesil's eyes, but he smiled at her. His muslin shirt and cloak were damp and smudged. He and Sgäile had returned in half the time Brot'an had asked for, so likely they had pushed on all night. Their gear was piled beneath the table, but Leesil's punching blades rested on the surface—along with something hidden by a shimmering piece of white cloth.

"What are the blades for?" she asked.

Leesil shook his head. "They were here when I arrived. Brot'an must have sent for them."

Brot'an's hard glare told them both to be silent.

Across the clearing's depression, Fréth and Most Aged Father entered as before, his chair carried by four anmaglâhk. As he was placed beside Fréth's table, the old elf leaned forward and peered toward Leesil and Sgäile.

Wynn stepped in close to Magiere, ready to translate.

Sgäile looked as worn as Leesil as he stepped to the clearing's center. His hair was a mess, streaming down around his pointed ears in a white-blond tangle. He called out, "The review of the claim will continue. Advocate for the accused may proceed."

Brot'an stepped out as Sgäile backed away, and the crowd fell silent in anticipation. Magiere watched the faces around the clearing, and when she reached Gleann, he lifted his chin to her with a wry, subtle smile.

"I call on Osha of the Âlachben," Brot'an said.

Wynn whispered in Magiere's ear, "Osha of the Rock-Hills clan."

Osha approached, and Brot'an lifted Leesil's winged blades, still in their sheaths. He drew one, raised it for all to see, and then turned to Osha.

"Can you tell us what this is?" he asked.

"It is one of Léshil's weapons," Osha answered quietly.

Brot'an cocked his head toward those of the gathering. Osha cleared his throat and repeated with stronger voice.

"Unique blades," Brot'an continued. "Do you know where he found them?"

"I believe he designed these himself," Osha answered.

"And what are these used for?"

"To destroy undead, or so he said . . . by taking their heads."

"Irrelevant!" Fréth shouted. "Léshil is not accused and these weapons have no bearing on the claim in dispute. The accused's advocate will keep to relevant testimony."

"Relevance will be addressed," Brot'an replied calmly. "If the opposing advocate will refrain from further interruptions. As Sgäilsheilleache is not permitted to witness for either side, I have turned to another in this matter."

Magiere followed Brot'an's seeking look toward Sgäile.

"Objection noted and rejected," Sgäile proclaimed. "But the accused's advocate will be expedient in making this line of questioning relevant."

As Wynn translated, Magiere wondered about the proceeding's rules. Brot'an seemed to have some freedom in questioning, but she wasn't certain why he was concentrating on Leesil's weapons. It seemed that Sgäile's limitations as adjudicator now worked against Brot'an, for Sgäile was the most familiar of all with Leesil and herself. Sgäile had been present in Bela when they hunted undead in its streets and sewers.

Fréth whispered in Most Aged Father's ear. He glowered but kept silent.

Brot'an turned back to Osha. "How did you learn the use of these weapons?"

"Léshil told me and the others who escorted him to Crijheäiche."

"Did he work alone?"

"No, he said Magiere and the majay-hì"—he pointed to Chap—"hunted with him. Destroying undead was their vocation."

Brief and broken murmurs sifted through the crowd. Magiere remained tall and straight, with crossed arms, and tried not to meet anyone's eyes.

Brot'an held both his arms wide. "Her vocation was to destroy the undead. And why would one so-claimed undead"—he turned toward Most Aged Father—"hunt its own kind?"

"Hearsay!" Fréth shouted. "And conjecture. Your opening statements are concluded. Keep to the presentation of what is verifiable . . . or be done!"

Sgäile cut in before Brot'an could reply. "Objection upheld. What was heard by the witness from another is not direct testimony unless the original speaker is not present."

"A valid point," Brot'an replied. "Then let us hear it directly . . . I call Léshil as witness."

"He is not one of us," Fréth shouted. "He is not an'Cróan and may not speak before the council."

Brot'an paced back to his table. He ripped aside the shimmering cloth, and lifted what hid there into plain sight.

It was a smooth branch, glistening bare of bark.

"Once again, you presume to speak for the ancestors," Brot'an called to Fréth. "And yet here is a branch from Roise Chârmune. How is he not one of us . . . if he was given this?" He pointed the glistening branch at Sgäile. "I call upon the ajudicator to confirm."

Sgäile nodded slowly. "In my presence . . . the ancestors gave it freely to Léshil."

"They gave it to him directly?" Brot'an asked. "He did not procure it with their implied blessing?"

The hiss of whispered voices surrounded the clearing. Magiere looked down at Wynn in confusion, but the sage only translated the words and shook her head, looking about with uncertain worry on her round face.

"Yes," Sgäile finally answered. "They appeared to Léshil and one gave him the branch of Roise Chârmune."

Brot'an and Sgäile were the only ones who didn't look stunned. Murmurs among the elders and clans grew until the noise drowned Sgäile's shouts for silence. Across the field, Fréth stood silent. She looked back at Most Aged Father, but the old man only stared at Leesil. Even his spite was masked in surprise.

Leesil scowled with his eyes on the ground.

Magiere was so lost. If Leesil had the branch, why had Brot'an waited to reveal it like this? It seemed one more trick he played on his patriarch, perhaps to keep Fréth and the old man off balance. Magiere wished she could risk asking Leesil questions in the middle of all this.

"Not enough," Fréth called, though it lacked her usual sharp conviction. "Even among our own, only those who've taken their full place as one of us can speak before the elders when in council."

"Another true point," Brot'an answered, and Fréth looked wary, as if she'd stepped into a trap. "Blood is not enough. A name is needed to be an'Cróan . . . to be recognized as one of us."

"Léshil does not have . . . ," Fréth began, but the last of her words had no voice and were only marked by the movement of her lips.

"He does," Brot'an answered, and turned upon Leesil. "Speak your true name for all to hear and recognize your rights."

Magiere looked at Leesil.

"It doesn't mean anything," he whispered to her. "Whatever it takes to get you out of here . . . I don't care what they believe."

"The witness will refrain from speaking," Sgäile called loudly. "Except as directed by the council, an advocate, or the adjudicator."

Magiere wanted to grab Leesil and make him tell her what had happened.

Leesil took a long breath. "Leshi . . . Le . . . shi-air . . ." He sighed in frustration. "I can't pronounce it."

Sgäile frowned, the tan lines of his face creasing, and he shouted out,

"Léshiârelaohk! And it was not chosen by him . . . it was given by the ancestors themselves."

All sound in the clearing faded instantly. Then a low thrum of voices grew and erupted into a deafening chaos.

Magiere spotted Gleann leaning forward upon his small stool. He was silent, staring down to the field at Leesil. But unlike the shocked disbelief or outrage of others, his expression was eager—and even excited.

Leanâlhâm stood behind him with confusion on her young face. She touched Gleann on the shoulder, whispering in his ear. He reached up and patted her hand with a satisfied smile but said nothing in return.

Whatever the name meant either it wasn't clear or the meaning had raised disturbing questions among the council. Or maybe it was that Leesil had acquired any name at all. Magiere looked to Wynn for help.

The little sage wrinkled her nose and then whispered, "Something about 'grief' and . . . maybe 'tear'? I cannot fully decipher. Its construction seems older than even the dialect spoken here."

Brot'an stood erect with the branch gripped at his side, ardent and determined pride in his eyes as he looked upon Leesil. Clearly he knew what the name meant and it pleased him. This worried Magiere most of all.

He raised the branch, turning before the crowd, until the gathering's noise settled enough for him to be heard.

"Tell us of what happened on hallowed ground," Brot'an said to Leesil.

Fréth offered no further objection.

Leesil recounted briefly, and Brot'an translated for the gathering.

Not all of it made sense to Magiere. Leesil was reluctant and spoke simply, like the times she caught him in some foolishness and forced him to confess. By her guess, he wasn't telling everything. But he offered enough to bring all voices to full silence as the elders and others listened in rapt attention.

"And what is the use of your weapons?" Brot'an asked. "How does this use relate to the accused?"

Leesil spoke more forcefully this time, expanding upon Osha's earlier answers. He even told of their first encounter with Sgäile in Bela, and of Chap's own part in their efforts to hunt undead. The crowd listened with interest.

"Now the people may question the truth of these words," Brot'an said. "Do the elders question the naming of . . . Léshiârelaohk?"

His gaze slipped to Fréth and Most Aged Father. Neither said a word, though Fréth seethed visibly in frustration.

"The ancestors granted Léshiârelaohk's request." Brot'an lifted the branch once more. "Magiere, come forward. You may bring your translator."

She tried not to hesitate as she stepped out, and Wynn came with her, a little more cautious.

"If the accused is truly undead," Brot'an called out, "no tricks or arcane practice will serve her. This branch, gifted by the ancestors from Roise Chârmune, is their bond to our land by which no enemy of the life here could walk our forest."

He held the branch out to Magiere.

She stood frozen. Inside, she trembled—not just from the affliction the forest had pressed upon her. What if the branch did something to mark her as an undead after all? Or worse, what if it drained of all remaining life at her touch?

Magiere couldn't breathe. She reached out and grasped the branch in her bare hand.

It felt smooth but not slick or wet, as it appeared to be. At first it was cool, even cold, then it warmed gently in her grip. It felt alive, and her panic sharpened.

For some reason, her eyes met and held Sgäile's. She waited for the wooden symbol to wither or to burn her . . . or something.

Nothing happened.

"If she were undead," Brot'an called out, "this could not happen. Not one sign of rejection. No strike against her flesh by the ancestors through the very emblem of our land and bloodline of old."

Magiere began to breathe again. Brot'an walked an arc around her and around the clearing as he spoke.

"She is unusual, yes, perhaps as suited to her calling. In battle, she appears fierce . . . even predatory, as some have said, and I have seen this myself more than once. But the ancestors have not marked her as a threat to us. Whatever issues some might take with her, the current claim is false."

Brot'an waved Magiere and Wynn back to the oak table.

"I rest for now," he said, "and yield to the address of the accuser's advocate."

Magiere approached the table, watching Leesil. He reached out and grasped her pale hand. She quickly dropped the branch on the table and turned to look across the field.

Fréth remained by her table, locked in uncertainty, but Most Aged Father didn't look shaken a bit by Brot'an's presentation. Magiere quivered inside, wondering what the old man would try next.

Wynn leaned in close between Magiere and Leesil, translating quietly for them.

Fréth strode to the clearing's center, wasting no time as she addressed the gathering in a clear, light voice.

"The accused's advocate has not addressed all possibilities. This human does not merely 'appear' fierce in battle. Her body takes on more literal attributes . . . by which she turned upon the living around her. We accept the testimonies presented so far without challenge, but even her companions do not fully understand her nature."

Wynn detected the slight falterings in Fréthfâre's voice.

Not uncertainty, but more like a speech too quickly memorized, repetitious and glib. Wynn studied Most Aged Father, wondering if Fréth served as his advocate or just his mouthpiece.

Fréth strode back to her table and flicked a summoning hand at the crowd behind her. Én'nish pushed into view through a cluster of anmaglâhk and came downslope with something cupped in her hands. Fréth took it and proceeded across the clearing. As she approached Brot'an's table, Wynn saw a sacred white flower in Fréth's hand. The same as the one that Sgäile had warned her not to touch.

White velvet petals shaped like leaves gathered the sunlight that struck them and returned it in a soft glow. The base and stem of the flower were a dark green, close to black.

"We saw some of those on our way here," Leesil whispered.

Fréth held it up for the clan elders to see.

"*Anasgiah*—the Life Shield. Prepared by a healer in tea or food, it sustains the dying, so they might yet be saved from death. It is vibrant with life itself, and feeds the life of those who need it most."

Anxiety grew in Wynn's stomach. By all she had heard, the ancestors were thought to weigh and render judgment according to an'Cróan needs. This flower was an inert thing, void of such intelligent consideration—whatever its use might be in these proceedings.

"The accused will come out," Fréth ordered.

Magiere approached in an echo of Fréth's own self-confidence. Wynn trotted after, uncertain if protocol allowed it, but no one stopped her.

Without warning, Fréth slapped the white petals across Magiere's face.

Wynn gasped as Leesil tried to rush out. Brot'an pulled him back and then walked up behind Magiere.

"What is the meaning of this?" Brot'an demanded, as Sgäile moved quickly to join them.

Wynn grabbed hold of Magiere's arm, fearful of what she might do in return.

Magiere barely flinched, but her dark eyes locked on Fréth's amber ones. Then she began to shake uncontrollably. Fréth watched her with a startled satisfaction.

Wynn wrapped her arm around Magiere's waist. Fréth raised the flower for all to see.

The white petals darkened. First to dull yellow, and then ashen tan as they withered. The flower died in Fréth's hand, and crumpled petals fell away to float to the ground.

Rumbling grew among the gathering. The shrill voices of the Äruin'nas shouted above all.

"Only an undead could cause this!" Fréth cried. "*Anasgiah's* potency is such that an undead does not have to consume the petals to consume what it offers. For that is what an undead truly feeds upon—life!"

In horror, Wynn craned her head around up at Brot'an.

His face was tight and hard, but he was caught as unaware as anyone else by this trick Fréth played. At the field's far end, Most Aged Father watched with ardent eyes, and the barest smile stretched his shriveled mouth.

Wynn tried to force calm as she held on to Magiere, but she found none. Fréth could know little more of the undead than anyone present. She could not have known how the flower would react to Magiere. This was Most Aged Father's doing.

The old one's test challenged Brot'an's—perhaps even canceled it out.

Brot'an motioned Magiere and Wynn to return to his table. Wynn walked Magiere back, steadying her until she grabbed the table's edge. Sgäile had to shout for silence again, but one of the Äruin'nas elders rose to his feet, screaming back at Sgäile in his strange tongue.

"Do not throw another demand upon these proceedings!" Sgäile replied. "No vote has been called. You will hold for deliberation."

The short old one spit one more vicious utterance. Sgäile did not answer, and stood waiting until the Äruin'nas elder settled cross-legged upon the depression's edge.

Fréth stalked back to her table as the crowd's rumble settled. She removed three stilettos and a shining garrote wire from her sleeves and belt and dropped them all upon the table.

Most Aged Father did not look at her. His ardent satisfaction remained focused across the clearing upon Magiere.

"Brot'ân'duivé sought the ancestors' judgment," Fréth cried out. "I do so as well. But words and tests will not settle this. I disarm and call for trial by combat. Let the ancestors guide my limbs in the old ways. Let them decide who speaks the truth."

The gathering's murmurs rose into a cacophony. Most Aged Father sat back in his chair, milky eyes glittering.

"Confer!" Brot'an shouted.

Sgäile nodded in discomfort and barely contained his distaste as he looked at Fréth.

Brot'an turned to Magiere as Wynn hurried to catch up in translating. She faltered and staggered as Chap shoved in beside her.

"What's happening?" Leesil asked.

"Old ways," Brot'an sighed. "All but forgotten. When a dispute cannot be settled through deliberation, trial by combat may be called, though it has never been sought in my lifetime. And it must be sanctioned by the elders. The victor must put the opponent down, or the opponent must verbally yield. It is believed that the ancestors support the victor's truth."

"That is not all she wants," Wynn said. "She goads Magiere into revealing her nature. Fréth wants them all to see Magiere transform, and if she cannot defeat Fréth without calling upon her inner nature . . ."

Either way, Magiere could lose, and she was still shaking.

Magiere's eyes shifted back and forth. "I might . . . might control it long enough . . . still win . . ."

"No," Leesil snapped. "You're not going out there!"

Magiere was barely able to speak between shudders, and Wynn knew she could not hold her dhampir half inside if a fight ensued. In Nein'a's clearing, Magiere had lost herself in this same shaken state.

"Most Aged Father told Fréth to do this," Wynn said. "She reported everything she saw in Nein'a's clearing, but only he would know how the flower would affect Magiere."

Brot'an turned hard eyes on Wynn, likely wondering how she knew this, but she gave him no chance to question her as she rushed on.

"He knows Magiere may not be able to hold back. The instant she succumbs, she will be finished. This has nothing to do with Fréth putting the outcome in the hands of her ancestors."

Magiere leaned back, half-sitting on the table's edge, and closed her arms tightly about herself. All Leesil could do was stand before her, holding her steady by the shoulders.

"A vote must still be taken," Brot'an said.

He pushed off the table and headed toward Sgäile. Fréth joined them. An unknown anmaglâhk came out as well and handed Sgäile two small baskets.

"Let us hope the vote fails," Wynn whispered as Leesil turned to watch.

"A vote on challenge is called!" Sgäile shouted.

It started slowly at first. Wynn saw stones being tossed by the elders. Black or white, they tumbled downslope or arched directly to the clearing's floor. Gleann's black one cleared the slope completely and thumped upon the turf. He gave her a smile, and Wynn understood.

Black to decline, and white in favor of combat.

Wynn did not need to look to know what color the Äruin'nas elder threw.

Brot'an and Fréth followed as Sgäile gathered and separated the stones into the two baskets. They returned to the clearing's side, where he poured them into two piles. Both appeared equal. He began counting.

Before he shouted the results, Brot'an already headed back toward Wynn. Chap growled beside her.

"Trial by combat has been granted," Sgäile called.

Brot'an began pulling stilettos and blades from his wrist sheaths and boots, slapping them on the oak table.

"What are you doing?" Wynn asked.

He ignored her and turned to face the field. "I call the right of proxy, as the accused's advocate."

Halfway to her own table, Fréth spun about. Even from the distance, Wynn saw her eyes widen.

"No!" Most Aged Father screeched. "That would prove nothing! The human is an abomination, and you would challenge your own caste for her sake?"

Wynn grew dizzy, trying to translate amid the noise rising from the onlookers and still follow all that was happening. Nausea surged in her stomach under Chap's leaf-wing voice.

Too quick a denial! He is eager for this.

She looked down to find Chap with ears flattened, glaring across the field at Most Aged Father.

For all the old elf's accusations, and his attempt to deny Brot'an, the Anmaglâhk patriarch appeared to quiver with anticipation. Chap spoke again in Wynn's head.

Brot'an's intercession fuels the old one. He sees opportunity . . . he wants Brot'an to fight.

Most Aged Father tried to stand and failed, slumping into his chair. He lifted his frail face to all those around the clearing.

"Do you see what this thing has wrought? She has poisoned us and driven our own people to violence against each other!"

Brot'an turned to Sgäile. "By law, this is my right."

Sgäile was slow to respond. He said something Wynn could not hear over the crowd. But his answer was clearly a confirmation to Brot'an, and he hung his head.

Wynn did not know Sgäile well, but she knew where his loyalties lay. The last thing he would want was for his own caste to turn upon itself.

This is no longer just about Magiere, Chap said.

Wynn saw Most Aged Father's shouted denial for what it was—a calculated misdirection. If Brot'an won, it would shake his own caste's faith in him and might even lead to claims that he sided with enemies of the people. If he lost, though that seemed so unlikely, all that remained was the council's final judgment for what to do with Magiere. Either way, Most Aged Father would have his way in some part.

Wynn could do nothing but wait and watch.

Brot'an stood relaxed but erect upon the clearing's turf as he looked to Fréth. "Whenever you are ready."

Chap knew Brot'an grasped for the only option he had left, but Most Aged Father spoke one truth. At any violence among the elves, Magiere would be seen as the cause. Even if found innocent in Brot'an's victory, it would only settle the immediate claim. In the end, it would weigh against all three of Chap's charges when it was time for the council to consider the human interlopers in their land.

He did not care what the Anmaglâhk did to each other, but he would not allow Magiere to be used anymore.

Chap bolted across the clearing, not caring about any attention he called.

"What are you doing?" Wynn shouted after him.

There was no time for explanations. He raced for the clearing's far slope and lunged up the incline straight at Gleann and his clan.

The old healer's jaw dropped halfway open. Chap let out a snarl. It was the only way, the safest place, to break through. Only Leanâlhâm stood transfixed with fright. Before Chap had to swerve to get around the girl, Gleann jerked her aside. The rest of his kinsman scrambled out of Chap's path.

He shot through to the open forest beyond.

Even his own presence as a majay-hì no longer counted for Magiere. He had felt the doubt and suspicion behind those who watched him from around the clearing. They saw a puzzle they could not unravel in a majay-hì who kept company with humans, and most believed that he was wrong— deviant and twisted by a life no majay-hì would choose.

They did not know how close to the truth they were—for all the wrong reasons.

If the Anmaglâhk and the elders wanted battle to find truth, he would give them one.

Chap cut through brush and trees, until he broke into a wide alley created by a deep brook. He leaped up a smooth boulder overhanging the rippling water. In the distance behind him, he heard the crowd in the clearing.

Their sounds drowned from Chap's ears as he ripped the forest's peace with a howl.

Sgäile felt as if his heart would rupture. He no longer knew what was right or wrong. He knew only the ways of his caste and of his people. He had followed both with such devotion and conscience. But since the humans' arrival, one had been continually pitted against the other. Now two of his own turned on each other over an outsider.

Brot'ân'duivé and Fréthfâre. Greimasg'äh and elder of caste against Most Aged Father's chosen Covârleasa. Two of the caste's most honored.

At its worst—if neither yielded—one would die.

Brot'ân'duivé had right of proxy for Magiere, and Sgäile could not help but agree with his decision. It was proper, for what he saw of the woman's sudden failing condition. He did not understand why the healing *Anasgiah* had done this to her, nor did he care for the manner in which it was done.

Fréthfâre's only goal appeared to be forcing Magiere to transform before the gathering. Perhaps they should see this. Perhaps Fréthfâre was not wrong either.

Sgäile's mind spun as Brot'ân'duivé stood waiting upon Fréthfâre's response.

And then Chap raced away across the clearing and through the crowd.

That instant of distraction left Sgäile uprepared. Every muscle in his body clenched as Fréthfâre rushed at Brot'ân'duivé.

All Sgäile could do was wait for one to yield—or one to die.

Leesil stood speechless as Chap vanished through the crowd. Then Fréth struck out at Brot'an.

Her palm strike never landed. Brot'an spun away low with a sweep of his leg. Fréth hopped back into a crouch. Before her feet touched earth, Brot'an was already up.

Leesil only cared that Brot'an won. That hope didn't even grate upon him in this moment.

Brot'an didn't close on Fréth but stood his ground, waiting as she circled. When she charged again, even Leesil was startled. It all happened before he could blink.

Fréth's lunging foot slid forward along the ground. Brot'an took a wide step left, and upon the twist of his torso, drove his right fist for her face.

She hit the ground in a hurdler's straddle, and Brot'an's strike passed over her head. She struck out for Brot'an's bent knee with her momentum. He shifted quickly into his other leg, but the change put him into Fréth's path. She pushed off with her rear cocked leg and shot upward for his abdomen with straightened fingers.

Brot'an twisted away, dropping to his back, as Fréth rose into her forward leg. She speared her hand downward at his exposed throat.

Leesil felt Magiere's hand close tight on his arm.

Sgäile took two quick steps forward before stopping.

Brot'an pulled his head aside, and Fréth's ridged fingers embedded in the clearing's earth.

"She's trying to kill him," Magiere hissed.

Leesil already knew this. Fréth would know she couldn't win unless she threw everything she had at Brot'an. Or maybe there was more to this than just Magiere's life—maybe a way to get around their custom of not spilling the blood of their own.

Most Aged Father watched without the slightest flinch at the way Fréth went after Brot'an. However it ended, Leesil feared that Magiere's fate would still be left dangling.

Brot'an swung his leg to the side, and the force rolled him over onto his face. As Fréth pulled soiled fingers from the earth, Brot'an's second leg shot out into her chest.

It was almost the same move Leesil used himself when trying to catch an undead from below while on the ground. Sgäile had once called it by some strange name that meant "Cat in the Grass."

Fréth wasn't fast enough to get out of the way.

Leesil heard the impact, and Fréth's body arched.

Her feet left the ground as she shot backward, headfirst. Her shoulders hit the earth a dozen steps away. Impact and momentum whipped her legs over her head. Leesil thought for certain her neck would snap under the fast folding curl.

She flattened on the ground, facedown, and then pushed herself up and got to her feet. She didn't waver, but struggled quietly to regain her breath.

For all Brot'an's size and age, he was nearly as fast as Fréth. And any slim advantage she might have in that wouldn't be enough to counter his experience.

"Yield," Brot'an demanded, circling around her.

A thin bloodied line marked the side of Brot'an's neck. Fréth had grazed him with her fingernails.

"Why is he holding back?" Wynn whispered.

Leesil swallowed any response, as Fréth went at Brot'an again.

Brot'an stamped hard against the earth with his right foot. An instant later he was turning fast in midair. His other leg whipped toward her at a downward angle.

His knee struck her forward arm, but his foot smashed her hip.

Fréth toppled under the impact. Her lighter body didn't have the mass to endure it. She slammed down sideways into the ground and somehow managed to kick out. She caught Brot'an's other foot just before it settled to the earth.

Brot'an spun sideways in the air. As he fell, he flattened one hand against the ground, but he crumpled and his right shoulder struck. He rolled away into a crouch, shaking his head. Fréth tottered as she got up, and then she stumbled to a halt as a howl echoed over the clearing.

Leesil looked about for the sound. The gathering broke into startled cries. Elves on the forest side of the clearing scattered downslope.

Chap lunged out through the crowd, tearing up sod as he charged straight at Brot'an and Fréth.

CHAPTER TWENTY-ONE

Magiere didn't know what to think when Chap charged into the council clearing, but shock followed an instant later. He wasn't alone. An entire pack of majay-hì spilled through the crowd in his wake, including the white dog she'd seen with Chap more than once.

Chap bolted straight at Brot'an and Fréth. He cut between them with a vicious snarl and bared teeth. Without pause, he ran to Magiere. Even Wynn backed up as the dog dug in his front paws and lurched to a stop.

Majay-hì of all shades, all with crystalline eyes, ran one by one through the clearing. The white female came directly to Chap. The dark one with grayed muzzle who'd charged Magiere in Nein'a's clearing circled in on Brot'an, cutting between him and Fréth.

Fréth backed up several steps, but Brot'an looked about in open confusion. Sgäile tried to step in then froze before the maniacal snapping of a tall steel-gray dog.

Wynn grabbed Magiere's hand, pulling her forward toward Chap. "Come on! You have to go with him—now!"

"What are you doing?" Leesil asked.

"Chap says she must come," Wynn answered.

Magiere stepped out in a daze. In three breaths, all but two majay-hì closed on her. The remaining pair paced like guardians before Brot'an, Fréth, and Sgäile. Leesil ducked around in front of Magiere to face any dog that came too close. Only the dark one with the gray muzzle growled as he approached.

More cries and shouts erupted in the crowd behind Magiere, and she looked back with Leesil and Wynn.

Another pack wormed through the gathering above. The only elf who stood her ground, watching without surprise, was the elder female in maroon holding a scroll. This second pack spread around the clearing's side slopes, pacing before the wide-eyed gathering of elves.

A third pack burst out, upslope behind Most Aged Father. These gave the old elf a wide berth as they circled around the clearing's side. As the packs met, they spread, bordering the clearing floor on all sides.

Those with Chap stayed close around Magiere, and the white female nosed her way nearer. Leesil set himself in her path, but Wynn pushed him aside as she knelt by the female.

"Stop it," she said. "Her name is Lily, and she will protect us."

Chap barked once.

Everyone, including Brot'an, Sgäile, and Fréth, looked about in shock. At least three dozen dogs ranged within the clearing, long legs trotting, long fur bouncing up and down. Four of the dogs gathered around Magiere to form some sort of vanguard. She watched them in wonder. What did it mean?

Gleann called out in Belaskian from where he stood above the dogs pacing the clearing's slope. "I think they try to tell us something." His lined face held a hint of amusement. Then he spoke in Elvish to the others around him.

"This settles nothing!" Most Aged Father shouted. "Disperse the dogs and end this interference."

"He's right," Magiere said at Wynn's translation. "We're not getting out of here this way . . . not without bloodshed."

"Stay where you are," Wynn ordered. "Chap, make that old man be quiet!"

Chap turned toward the patriarch but held his ground in front of Magiere.

Wynn flinched sharply, glanced at Chap, and then turned wide eyes upon Leesil.

"What?" Magiere asked. "What did Chap say?"

A handful of Anmaglâhk came out of the crowd in answer to Most Aged Father's demand. But any attempt to descend into the clearing was cut off by snarling dogs charging. One anmaglâhk drew a blade.

Magiere grabbed Wynn's tunic shoulder, shouting at Chap as much as the sage. "Stop this, now! It's not going to work."

"What else have we got?" Leesil argued. "I'm not letting them take you."

"Leesil, go with Chap," Wynn said suddenly. "Now . . . and when he barks once at you, only you, give Most Aged Father his message from the ancestors."

Magiere had no idea what this meant. Confusion and frustration made her shudder harder. She'd never turned from a fight. But if Leesil, or even Chap or Wynn, came under threat, she wouldn't be able to control herself in this state.

Leesil glared at Chap. "You've been in my head again!"

"Shut your mouth and do it!" Wynn snapped at him.

Magiere grabbed Leesil by the shirtfront. "This is Chap's game now. Follow his lead."

Chap stalked forward across the clearing, and Leesil followed, looking worried.

A shrill whistle like a rushing song carried above the noise of the gathering.

Chap and Leesil were only partway across the field, and even the majay-hì turned confused circles at the sound. A clan elder in a dark brown cloak raised a hand and pointed high beyond Magiere.

Leesil turned, and Chap did as well. Brot'an lost his stoic self-control for an instant as he stared beyond Magiere. She turned around.

From the upper reaches of one bridge-branched oak, something launched from the thick leaves into the air. It spread wings longer than any bird Magiere had ever seen, and spiraled downward in wild arcs. The closer it came, the more Magiere doubted its shape. The majay-hì scattered away as it landed beyond Leesil and Chap. Magiere sucked in a breath and held it.

Not a bird, for—she—had arms and legs. She looked only at Magiere, as if she saw someone familiar.

Her wings were immense, and their combined span was at least three times her height. They folded behind a narrow and slight-boned torso of subtle curves like that of an adolescent girl. She was no taller than an Äruin'nas, and perhaps less. From pinion feathers to the downy covering on her body and face, she was a mottled off-white. Instead of hair, larger feathers combed back like a headdress and were matched by the same on the backs of her forearms and lower legs.

Two huge oval eyes dominated her face, pushed slightly to the sides by a long narrow nose that ended above a small, thin-lipped mouth. Her eyes were like polished stones, dark at first but turning as red as a dove's where they caught sunlight. She cocked her head like a crow, studying Magiere.

This frail creature stepped toward Magiere, rocking slightly upon the earth as if walking wasn't quite natural for her.

"Úirishg," Wynn said, the word exploding on her exhale.

Magiere couldn't take her eyes from this winged female. The majay-hì pulled farther aside to give her passage. A dry female voice from somewhere behind said, *"Séyilf!"* The word rattled in Magiere's empty mind until she heard herself try to numbly repeat it. But the closest she got out was "silf."

"The Wind-Blown," Wynn translated.

The silf drew closer and reached up with a hand of narrow fingers. She parted her lips as if to speak, and between them, in place of teeth, were ridges like the edge of a bird's beak inside her mouth. The sound that came out of her throat was somewhere between the cry of a hunting hawk and a sparrow's song.

Gleann came down and stopped beside Wynn. Most of the majay-hì descended to the clearing floor. Even Chap returned with Leesil close behind. Fréth headed for Most Aged Father, who now watched in silent suspicion. Brot'an and Sgäile approached behind Leesil.

The silf looked about, growing agitated or nervous, and flexed her wings.

Gleann waved everyone off before they came too close. From behind him, one of the Äruin'nas stepped out.

"This is Tuma'ac," Gleann said in accented Belaskian. "He may be able to translate."

Tuma'ac looked up at Magiere with a vicious twitch of his eye that made the strange markings on his sun-wrinkled face seem to dance. He nodded once to Gleann but looked to Sgäile.

Sgäile regained himself, perhaps remembering his place as adjudicator. "Yes, proceed."

Tuma'ac approached the silf, and indeed she was shorter than he. He motioned with his hands toward himself and spoke to her in his strange tongue. The odd cry erupted from the silf again, sounding much the same as before to Magiere. Tuma'ac blinked twice as he looked sidelong at Magiere, but his sudden shock faded in disgust. He barked something at Gleann.

Gleann's high eyebrows rose even higher. "He says the séyilf called you 'kin' . . . or blood of her kind."

Magiere looked to Leesil, who only shook his head, and then to Wynn.

The sage was horrified. She gave Magiere a quick shake of her head. Not in confusion but more that she couldn't speak her mind here and now.

It was enough to bring Magiere to her senses, enough to call up memories of a hidden room beneath the keep of her undead father.

One of the decayed bodies there had rotted feathers among its bones. Wynn called them Úirishg, the five mythical races, of which the elves and dwarves were the only known two. Five beings had been slaughtered in that hidden blood rite to make Magiere's birth possible.

Magiere turned cold inside, looking back into the silf's dark eyes.

It cried again, and the chain translation passed once more to Gleann.

"She says you are not to be harmed . . . her people will not tolerate any violence against one of their own."

"That cannot be true!" Most Aged Father shouted. "'You translate incorrectly. And even so, how could she know?"

Again the chain of words passed, but this time Gleann stumbled and spoke one elvish word to Wynn. The sage seemed to have difficulty.

"Something like . . . ," she began and shook her head. "She is . . . a spiritual leader of some kind. 'Spirit-talker' is the closest I can think of."

Gleann turned toward Most Aged Father. "If you wish to call Tuma'ac or the séyilf a liar, then do so for yourself and not through me. Do we now reject the word of those we promised to protect and hide in our mountains?"

Wynn shifted close to Magiere with a whisper. "The feather and berries in the mountain passage. It was one of them . . one of the séyilf."

The silf turned away. Her flurried thrash of wings sent majay-hì scattering, as she half leaped and flew to the piles of stones that Sgäile had left at the clearing's edge. She grabbed a black one and tossed it across the clearing.

It tumbled to a halt before Most Aged Father, and he shook visibly as his expression turned livid.

The silf screeched again, and Tuma'ac grunted in satisfaction before speaking to Gleann.

"She calls us to vote," Gleann said, pointing to the stone, "and gives that of her people . . . against the claim of Most Aged Father."

"Do the advocates have anything further to present?" Sgäile asked quietly.

Brot'an shook his head once. But Most Aged Father clutched at Fréth, whispering harshly. Fréth kept shaking her head in denial.

"Your answer, advocate!" Sgäile called with more force.

Fréth stood up, and her head dropped as she shook it slowly. "No . . . nothing."

Sgäile stepped to the clearing's center. "The Advocates have retired. We ask the elders to deliberate and render judgment on the claim presented."

Gleann didn't return to his clan. Instead, he simply cast a stone—black—and gave Magiere a curt bow. It was a kind gesture, but not enough to make her hopeful.

Another black stone arched out from behind her and tumbled across the ground. Magiere looked back.

The tall female in maroon stood halfway down the slope, the one Sgäile had called Tosân . . . something on the night they searched for Wynn. Her calculated study of Magiere turned suddenly upon Leesil, and then she walked back up to her chair between her like-clad attendants. How her filmy eyes saw anything was disturbing.

Magiere wasn't certain how long it would take the others, or whether a quick or protracted vote worked more in her favor. She tried not to meet the silf's steady stare, for its strange face was too difficult to read. She didn't want to think about her own past, her birth, and why this creature had mistaken her as kin.

One at a time, then in twos and threes, black and white stones fell into the clearing.

Magiere closed her eyes. She felt Leesil's arm slip around her shoulders and tighten.

She didn't watch Sgäile gather the stones, but after long moments she heard their clatter as he poured them into piles upon the ground.

Gleann's voice rose so loud it startled her, and her eyes snapped open as Wynn translated.

"As the claim against her is now dismissed, Magiere's companions cannot be held in blame either. They came here as guests of Most Aged Father and under oath of guardianship. No reason has been given to breach either. They must be released, and their property returned. Then other matters require our collected attention"—he glanced toward Most Aged Father—"concerning Anmaglâhk ways in conflict with those of the people."

"It's over," Leesil whispered.

Magiere couldn't see any difference between the stone piles at Sgäile's feet. He seemed to understand her confusion and nodded to her.

"It is over—for now," Brot'an added. "I will take you back to quarters, so you may rest."

"Not quite," Leesil returned. "I still have a claim to make for my mother."

"It will be addressed," Brot'an answered. "The rest will be settled without either of you, and should cause you no more concern. Do not press the matter when it is not yet necessary."

Leesil glanced at Magiere, caught between concern and stubbornness.

Magiere put a hand on his chest. Both looked up as a rush of wind around Magiere whipped Leesil's loose hair wildly about.

The silf dropped upon the table behind Magiere and reached out too quickly, startling Leesil into the defensive. Magiere grabbed his wrist.

The tiny female flexed her wings and raised her hand more slowly this time. She lifted the side of Magiere's hair, letting its strands slide between narrow fingers ending in roan-colored nails that curved slightly like talons. The silf cocked her head, watching the hair fall bit by bit.

Magiere pulled back at the thrash of her wings as she lifted into the air and flapped away beyond the treetops.

Leesil exhaled. "As if we haven't had enough for one day."

"There is one more thing," Wynn said. "Brot'an, would you please wait with Magiere?"

The sage grabbed Leesil's arm, pulling him along as she followed Chap toward Most Aged Father.

Chap had no idea what this séyilf—silf—truly wanted. Like Magiere and even Wynn, he was confused as to why it mistook Magiere for kin. Somehow the small winged female sensed the blood of its own used in Magiere's conception.

He had tried reaching for its mind to catch any memories, but he found nothing besides images of himself and his charges climbing downward through the mountain. The female had been the one to leave them a trail . . . the one who had called out to him amid the blizzard. This was all he gathered from it. He was left wondering why it had twice interceded on their behalf and how long it had watched them from hiding.

Chap had planned for a fight, even wanted it in part. Or at least enough distraction to take the one person who mattered—Most Aged Father.

He had watched the an'Cróan shaken by how the majay-hì cast their "vote" in this matter. Lily had likely strained her place among the pack in convincing them for him, but they all shared some strange animosity for the leader of the Anmaglâhk, a being too old for natural life and yet making claims against Magiere as an undead.

Perhaps his rejected kin were correct—flesh and heart made him reckless. He did not care anymore.

Most Aged Father's bearers had not come for him. Even this did not matter to Chap. He wanted answers, and he would take them.

Fréthfâre stepped in his way as he closed on the old one.

"We only have a message for Most Aged Father," Wynn said.

Chap barked once, not turning his eyes from the patriarch.

"Snaw . . . hac . . . ," Leesil began, then sighed in frustration.

"Snähacróe," Wynn pronounced for him.

At the name, Most Aged Father's milky eyes widened and he sat up as straight as he could.

"He said to tell you . . . ," Leesil called out clearly, "that he's waiting for his comrade to join him . . . when you're done."

Chap lunged into the old one's mind, waiting for whatever might come.

Sounds and images rose, led by the face of a tall elf with wide cheekbones. Chap let go of all else, even anger, and sank into Most Aged Father's rising memories.

Sorhkafâré stood amid the night-wrapped trees surrounding Aonnis Lhoin'n, First Glade.

It had been the longest run of his life to reach his people's land and what now seemed the only sanctuary in a blighted world. He led his dwindling group to this place hoping to find other survivors, hoping to find help. But he could still hear the grunts and weeping and madness of the night horde ranging beyond the forest's edge.

All through his flight home, every town and village, and even every keep and stronghold, was littered with bodies torn as if fed upon by animals. The few living they encountered joined them in flight from the pale predators with crystalline eyes, always in their wake.

The numbers of their pursuers grew with each fall of the sun.

Fewer than half of those who fled Sorhkafâré's encampment with him reached the forests of his people. Not one of the dwarves made it on their stout legs carrying thick heavy bodies. Thalhómêrk had been the last of their people to succumb, along with his son and daughter.

In a dead run through the dark, Sorhkafâré had heard the dwarven lord's vicious curses. He looked back as Thalhómêrk submerged under a wave of pale bodies. He shuddered at the sound of bones cracking under the dwarf's massive fists and mace. And still the horde flowed toward Sorhkafâré and over Thalhómêrk's son and daughter. He could not tell which one had screamed out, as Hoil'lhân's voice smothered it with a visceral shout. She whirled to turn back.

Her hair whipped about her long face as she swung the butt of her thick metal spear shaft. It cracked through a pale face. Splattering black fluids blotted out the creature's glittering eyes and maw of sharp teeth.

Sorhkafâré did not understand Hoil'lhân's preference for dwarven and human company, nor her restless and savage nature. Perhaps she had been killing for too long.

Hoil'lhân spun her spear without pause as three more pale figures closed on her. The spear's wide and long head split through the first's collarbone, grinding into its chest. She jerked her weapon out as the other two hesitated, and she screeched at them madly, ready to charge.

Sorhkafâré grabbed her, pulling her around as more of the horde rushed at them through the dark.

"Run," he ordered.

Even in renewed flight Hoil'lhân tried to turn on him with her metal spear. Snähacróe snatched her other arm, and they dragged her onward.

"You cannot save Thalhómêrk," Snähacróe said in a hollow voice.

The endless running took its toll. Two more of Sorhkafâré's soldiers dropped in their tracks before any saw the forest's edge. All he could do was hope they died of exhaustion before . . .

In the clearing of First Glade, humans and elves now huddled in fear. Sorhkafâré could no longer look at their gaunt faces.

So few . . . and in the distance, beyond the forest's limits, carried the shouts and cries of dark figures with crystalline eyes. A part of him found that easier to face than to count the small number who still lived.

A small pack of the silver-gray wolves came out of the trees. They moved with eerie conscious intent. At first their presence had frightened all, but they never attempted any harm; quite the opposite. They wove among the people, sniffing about. One stopped to lick and nuzzle a small elven girl holding a human infant.

These wolves had eyes like crystals tinted with sky blue, and neither he nor his troops had ever seen such before. But during his campaigns against the enemy, Sorhkafâré had heard reports and rumors of strange wolves, deer, and other animals joining allied forces in battles in other lands. Which made these wolves a welcome sight.

The survivors in First Glade ate little and slept less. If sleep did come, they cried out in their dreams. Every night, Sorhkafâré waited for the pale horde to surge in upon them.

But they never came.

On the sixth night, he could stand it no more and walked out into the forest. Léshiâra tried to stop him.

Youngest of their council of elders, she stood in his way, soft lines of coming age on a face urgent and firm beneath her long graying hair. She pulled her maroon robe tight about herself against the night's chill.

"You cannot leave!" she whispered sharply. "These people need to see every warrior we have left ready to stand for them. You will make them think you abandon them."

"Stand against what?" he snarled at her, not caring who heard. "You do not know what is out there any more than I. And if they could come for us, why have they not done so? Leave me be!"

He stepped around her, heading into the trees, but not before he caught Snähacróe watching him with sad disappointment. In days past, his kinsman's silent reproach would have cut him, but now he felt nothing.

Sorhkafâré followed the sounds of beasts on two legs out beyond the forest, wondering why they had not come for the pitiful count of refugees. These things on two legs . . . things that would not die . . . blood-hungry with familiar faces as pale as corpses'. He heard them more clearly as the trees thinned around him, and he stopped in the night to listen.

The noise they made had changed. Screams of pain were strangled short beneath wet tearing sounds.

Sorhkafâré stumbled forward, sickened by his own curiosity.

Through a stand of border aspens before the open plain, he saw three silhouettes with sparking eyes. They rushed, one after another, upon a fourth fleeing before them.

Still, he kept on, slipping in behind one aspen.

In days past, Sorhkafâré would have leaped to defend any poor victim. But not now. It did not matter if anyone out there on the plain still lived. He peered around the aspen's trunk.

The three hunkered upon the ground with lowered heads, tearing back and forth. Beneath them, the fourth struggled wildly, its pain-pitched voice ringing in Sorhkafâré's ears.

The sound of such terrified suffering ate at him.

He lunged around the tree, running for the victim's outstretched hand. Halfway there, the figure thrashed free and scrambled across the matted grass with wide, panicked eyes . . .

Glittering, crystalline eyes.

Sorhkafâré's feet slid upon autumn leaves as he halted.

Out on the plain, dark silhouettes chased and hunted each other with cries of fear and hunger. The moon and stars dimly lit shapes tearing into each other with fingers and teeth. With nothing else to feed upon, the pale creatures turned upon each other.

These things . . . so hungry for warm life.

One of the three lifted its head.

Sorhkafâré made out a pale face, its mouth smeared with wet black. Its eyes sparked as if gathering the waning light, and it saw him. It rose, turning toward him as the other pair chased the fourth through the grass.

Sorhkafâré heard his own breath. He retreated a few paces, just inside the forest's tree line.

This pale thing he saw . . . a man . . . was human.

His quivering lips and teeth were darkened, as if he had been drinking black ink. He sniffed the air wildly and a ravenous twist distorted his features. He began running toward Sorhkafâré.

This one smelled him, sensed his life.

Sorhkafâré jerked out his long war knife and braced himself.

The human came straight at him, its feral features pained with starvation. Perhaps it gained no sustenance in feeding on its own. But he no longer cared for anything beyond seeing these horrors gone from his world.

It ran straight at him like an animal without reason.

When it stepped between the first trees of the forest, it stopped short, hissing and gurgling in desperation. Sorhkafâré saw the man clearly now.

Young, perhaps twenty human years. His face was heavily scratched, but the marks were black lines rather than red. His flesh was white and shriveled, as if it were sinking in upon itself. The thing cried piteously at Sorhkafâré and took another hesitant step.

Why would the horde not enter the forest, if they were starved enough to turn on each other?

Sorhkafâré raised his knife and cut the back of his forearm. He swung his bloodied arm through the air.

"Hungry?" he shouted. "I am here!"

The sight of blood drove the man deeper into madness. He charged forward with a scream grating up his throat. Sorhkafâré shifted backward, feeling blindly for smooth and solid footing.

As the pale man lunged between two aspens, he grabbed his head with a strangled choke. He turned about and cried out—but not in anguished hunger. This was a sound of fear and pain as he whirled and wobbled. The man stumbled too near one aspen, and he clawed wildly at the air, as if fending off the tree.

Sorhkafâré watched in stunned confusion. A howl carried around him from within the forest.

It was like nothing Sorhkafâré had ever heard—long and desperate in warning. Two of the silver-furred wolves burst through the underbrush and out of the dark, their eyes glowing like clear crystals tinted with sky blue.

The first slammed straight into the screaming man and latched its jaws around his throat, ripping as it dragged him down. The second joined in, and their howls shifted to savage snarls as they tore at their prey.

The man's scream cut off in a wet gag, but still he thrashed and clawed.

On instinct Sorhkafâré ran in to help the wolves, but they kept snapping and tearing at the man's throat.

One of them shifted aside. It pinned the man's arm with teeth and paws. The other did the same, and they held him down as the first one looked up at Sorhkafâré.

The wolf waited for Sorhkafâré to do something—but what?

The man's throat was a dark mass shredded almost to the spine—yet still he writhed and fought to get free. Black fluids dribbled from his gaping mouth and blotted out his teeth. A mouth that either snarled or screamed with no voice.

He could not still be alive. No one could live after what these wolves had done to him . . . tearing at his neck as if . . .

Sorhkafâré dropped to his knees and snatched the man's hair with his free hand. With so little sinew left on that neck, it was easy to hold the head steady. He pressed the long knife's edge down through the mess of the man's throat until it halted against bone.

In a quick shift, he released his grip on the hair and pressed on the back of the blade with all his weight.

The blade grated and then cut down through neck bones.

The pale man ceased thrashing and fell limp as a true corpse.

Sorhkafâré sucked in air as he lifted his gaze to the first wolf, its muzzle stained with wet black like his own hands. He stared into its eyes as his mind emptied of all but two truths.

The forest would not allow the horde in. And if one got through, these wolves sensed it and came.

He climbed to his feet, still breathing hard, and crept back to the forest's edge to look out upon the rolling plain.

Dark forms rolled, ran, leaped, and crawled in the grass. Others barely moved, little more than quivering masses choking in the dark. Pale figures chased each other—slaughtered each other.

Sorhkafâré stood watching, unable to look away. Every figure that came close enough for his night eyes to see was human.

He saw not one elf. Not one dwarf. Not even a goblin, or the hulking scaled body of a reptilian locathan, or any of the other monstrosities the enemy had sent against him.

Only humans.

He turned and stumbled back toward First Glade. The wolves paced him all the way to his people.

He found Snähacróe kneeling behind an injured human youth, bracing the boy up while Léshiâra worked upon the boy's leg. In the past days, these two shared company more and more.

Léshiâra closed her eyes, and a low thrum rose from her throat. She lightly traced her fingertips around the boy's deeply bruised calf, over and over, and then went silent. She opened her eyes and rebandaged the boy's leg.

When she stood up and found Sorhkafâré watching her, she frowned.

"Come with me," he said.

Snähacróe looked worried and followed as well.

They walked into the center of the glade.

In the open space stood an immense tree like no other in this world. Its trunk was the size of a small citadel tower, and high overhead its branches reached out into the forest.

Sorhkafâré saw where those limbs stretched into the green leaves and needles of the surrounding trees and beyond. A soft glow emanated from the tree's tawny body and branches, bare of bark but still thriving with life. Massive roots like hill ridges split the clearing's turf where they emerged from the trunk to burrow deep and far into the earth.

Sorhkafâré laid a hand upon the glistening trunk of Chârmun, a name that humans would translate as "Sanctuary."

"We must take a cutting from Chârmun," he said to Léshiâra. "Can you keep it alive over a long journey?"

She grew pale and did not answer.

"What are you planning?" Snähacróe asked, moving closer to Léshiâra.

Sorhkafâré looked at his one remaining commander. "The horde turns upon itself. They have nothing else left within reach to feed upon—but it does them no good. In perhaps days, there may be few enough left for us to slip away."

"No!" someone snapped sharply.

Sorhkafâré knew the voice before he turned his head.

Hoil'lhân stood at the clearing's edge, and around her paced three of the strange tall wolves. All four were spattered and dripping in black fluids. All four watched him with equal intensity. Hoil'lhân stabbed the long, broad head of her spear into the earth, and Sorhkafâré watched more black fluid run from its sharp edges to the grass.

"Where have you been?" he demanded.

"Where do you think?" Hoil'lhân spit out at him. "The enemy's minions range upon our very borders . . . and you wish to run?"

"We cannot stay here in hiding within this blighted land," Sorhkafâré returned.

"I said no!" Hoil'lhân shouted, running a hand through her white, sweat-matted hair. "I will not let the enemy take what is ours! I will not leave any more that I cherish . . . fleeing with their screams at my back!"

"Enough," Snähacróe warned.

"It was not a request," Sorhkafâré said firmly. "I am still your commander."

Hoil'lhân breathed hard, twisting her hand around the upright shaft of her spear.

"And since when do you alone speak for our people?" Léshiâra said quietly, stepping toward Sorhkafâré. "You do not sit in the council of First Glade, and we no longer follow the old ways of divided clans. Such decisions are the province of myself and the others of the council."

"There is no council left!" Sorhkafâré shouted at her. "You are the only one that remains . . . so do you alone choose for our people, like some human monarch?"

"That is not my meaning," she snapped back. "There are too many here who need us."

Sorhkafâré shook his head. "What if they are the very ones by which the Enemy can still reach us? Out beyond our forest . . . those dead things that move and feast . . . they were once humans, like those still among us."

"You do not know how this was done to them," Hoil'lhân growled. "Or if the Enemy's reach could find any who shelter here!"

Snähacróe turned, staring off through the trees, as if trying to see the forest's edge. Léshiâra fell silent and closed her eyes, seeming to grow older and wearier before Sorhkafâré's eyes.

But he could not relent.

"We will take our own people. Perhaps the wolves will join us as well. We will get as far from here as we can reach. We will plant our cutting from Chârmun and create a haven for our people far from the Enemy's reach."

"Our people?" Snähacróe asked.

"Not the humans," Sorhkafâré answered.

"The outsiders are dismissed!"

Chap didn't know who spoke those words, but they jerked him to awareness. His legs trembled as he pulled free of Most Aged Father's memories.

Leesil dropped to one knee beside him, but Chap regained his own footing.

Several anmaglâhk came in around Most Aged Father. Under their threatening encouragement, Chap turned away with Leesil and Wynn. Magiere joined them as they were all ushered out of the council clearing.

Chap struggled to follow but could not stop trembling. He looked up at Magiere's black braid swinging as she leaned against Leesil while they walked.

He knew why Most Aged Father feared Magiere so deeply, though the old man did not fully understand what she was. He saw only some new shape of those among the pale horde of his memory. She was far worse than even the old man could imagine.

Magiere was human, born of the undead. Yet she walked freely and unfettered into this land. Chap's mind raced back to his fear-spawned delusion in the Pudúrlatsat forest—of Magiere as the general at the head of an army . . .

No, a horde—one that could not enter a shielded land without her.

If only he could tell Magiere alone, without the need of Wynn to speak for him. Magiere deserved at least that much privacy, but there was no way to achieve such.

Chap blinked but could not keep the old elf's memories from casting ghost images across all things around him. A war had devoured the living at the end of a time known only as the Forgotten . . . the Forgotten History of the world. On the plain beyond the elven forest surrounding First Glade, Most Aged Father had watched the waves of undead sent by the Enemy.

All of them—every last one—had been human.

CHAPTER TWENTY-TWO

Once Leesil had delivered the ancestors' message to Most Aged Father, they were all escorted back to quarters. Most Aged Father's claim had been dismissed, and thereby Magiere was cleared by council vote, but the elders remained to debate as they left. Leesil had no idea what would come next. The look on the old elf's face still lingered in his mind, but he felt no sympathy for the fear and festering pain he'd seen there. His mother was still imprisoned, and he'd had no chance to plead for, or demand, her freedom.

Magiere huddled on the dirt floor at the elm chamber's center, as far from the tree's inner walls as she could get. Wynn sat lost in thought upon one bed ledge with Chap sprawled at her feet. The day wore on in a lingering crawl as Leesil paced around with Magiere watching him.

She no longer visibly trembled, but her face was still weary and drawn. He finally fetched her some water, along with a few nuts and berries left for them. He reached out and stroked her black hair.

"Please," he insisted. "Try a little."

What relief he'd gained from the dismissal of Most Aged Father's claims wasn't enough. He had to get to his mother. He had to get Magiere out of this land and away from the elven forest.

The doorway curtain bulged aside, and Brot'an stepped in. He immediately settled on the floor with a long slow breath. He looked so openly distressed, it unnerved Leesil.

Leesil would never understand this man's ever-twisting motives, but Brot'an had stood up for Magiere when no one else would or could. Grudgingly, Leesil was grateful, though he'd never say so to Brot'an's face.

"What's wrong?" Leesil asked.

"I have failed," Brot'an said flatly.

"Most Aged Father lost, and Magiere is safe," Leesil said.

"Safe?" Brot'an shook his head. "They did not even suggest replacing him, after seeing him . . . hearing him. The elders gathered to question why he allowed you safe passage, but he told them his decision was an internal matter directly related to the safety of our people."

He paused, as if not believing his own words.

"Some are still troubled that he allowed humans into our land, but they will not consider that he is unfit. Age is too much a virtue among my people."

A low throaty chuckle escaped Brot'an's lips. It sounded wrong coming from such a man.

"You mean Most Aged Father?" Magiere asked.

"All of you will be forced to leave tomorrow," Brot'an continued, running a hand over his scarred face. "Be ready by first light. At least Gleannéohkân'thva had the foresight to speak up and gain you a barge downriver to Ghoivne Ajhâjhe. From there, you will be given safe passage by sea—the first humans to step foot on one of our ships. You will not need to cross the mountains again."

Leesil crouched down. "What?"

Brot'an looked at him with a saddened expression. "The elders are resolved. The claim against Magiere may be dismissed, but your presence will no longer be tolerated."

Wynn came closer, settling near Magiere.

"We can't leave," Magiere said. "Leesil hasn't even spoken for Nein'a. If he's now recognized as one of you, he has a right to—"

The doorway curtain lifted again, and Sgäile peered inside. He looked harried and exhausted. Leesil's cloak was draped over his arm.

"Léshiârelaohk," he said. "Your property is—"

"Don't call me that," Leesil warned. "It's not my name."

Sgäile sighed. "Your property is restored. I have brought your gear and blades . . . and Magiere's sword and dagger."

"Come in," Leesil said a little less sharply.

He didn't care for how that name implied he was one of them, but Sgäile only followed custom in using it, the same as with all of his people. And

Leesil wanted to hear another view on what had happened at the council. Of anyone he'd met in this land, Sgäile was the most trustworthy.

Sgäile shook his head, his tangled white-blond hair swaying. "I cannot stay. Grandfather and Leanâlhâm leave at dawn. There is much to do, but if you would, come tonight to the third oak upriver from the docks and say your farewell. Leanâlhâm has been comforted in meeting you."

Leesil chose not to press for his views on the council. Sgäile clearly believed this entire matter was finished.

"Tell Leanâlhâm that I'll try," Leesil lied.

Sgäile set the gear inside the door and was about to depart.

"Send Leanâlhâm for naming," Leesil said. "If that's something she still wants. There's no reason to keep her from it anymore. She can reach hallowed ground, if I did."

Sgäile didn't reply and slipped out. Leesil picked up his blades and began strapping them on.

"What are you doing?" Brot'an asked.

"I'm going to have a talk with Most Aged Father." He tossed Magiere her falchion. "Care to join me?"

She caught the sword and stood up.

"No more brash foolishness!" Bro'tan said. "Any threats, and you will be killed. I have been considering another tactic . . . though it may cause unpredictable changes for my caste."

"What tactic?" Wynn asked. "What more could you do?"

Brot'an's eyes shifted several times in indecision. "Remain here until I return."

"What are you up to now?" Leesil asked.

"I will speak with Most Aged Father myself. It should not take long."

Leesil locked eyes with Magiere, and she nodded at him.

"All right," he agreed.

Dusk settled as Brot'ân'duivé headed for the massive oak. He did not call out for permission to enter and descended the stairs. Before he could enter the central root chamber, Fréthfâre stepped out and grew angry at the sight of him.

"Father has not sent for you."

"Leave," he whispered, stepping straight at her.

Fréthfâre's eyes narrowed.

He did not try to push past her but stopped short, waiting before the chamber's doorway so that Most Aged Father could see him.

"I would speak with you alone," Brot'ân'duivé called. "Please send your Covârleasa away."

The ancient leader reclined limply in his cradle of living wood, still shrouded in the same wrap he had worn to the gathering. His eyes were half-closed in weariness, but they opened fully at the sight of Brot'ân'duivé.

"I have no interest in the demands of a traitor," Most Aged Father said. "I will deal with you soon enough."

"Send Fréthfâre out," Brot'ân'duivé repeated. "You will have interest in what I say . . . to you alone."

Most Aged Father stared at him long, then slightly raised one hand. "Leave us, daughter."

"Father—" Fréthfâre began in alarm.

"Go!"

Fréthfâre turned a warning eye upon Brot'ân'duivé before she stepped around him. Brot'ân'duivé waited until her soft footfalls faded upon the stairs, and then he stepped into the ancient patriarch's root chamber.

"What worthless excuses do you offer for your conduct?" Most Aged Father asked, his voice cracking.

"No matter this day's outcome, the elders were disturbed by your behavior and demeanor. I expected them to replace you."

"With you, perhaps?"

Brot'ân'duivé ignored the question. "The ground you stand upon crumbles. If the elders learn what you have us do in the human countries, how long before they do as I hoped?"

"Manipulation . . . and open challenge?" Most Aged Father displayed only mock astonishment before he chuckled softly. "No surprise in this. I have long suspected you, deceiver."

Brot'ân'duivé shook his head calmly. "I serve my people, as our caste was intended from long-forgotten times . . . as all Anmaglâhk believe when they take oath of service. It is we, as well as our people, who are deceived by you. Yet we have kept faith, just the same. Turning humans upon each other serves no purpose but to salve your own fears. They are not this enemy you speak of so sparingly, whatever or whoever it might be."

Most Aged Father's hands went limp. "You had my trust, my love . . . how long have you been a traitor among your kind?"

"I have never been a traitor to my people, though I no longer believe in your ways. And neither is Cuirin'nên'a. The elders may turn a blind eye for what you do to her, because she is one of us. They see it as an issue of the Anmaglâhk. But I would now barter for her release."

"Barter?" Most Aged Father returned. "Why, when you will soon join her?"

Brot'ân'duivé's voice grew cold. "You will release her tonight. Or I will tell the elders how you use the Anmaglâhk to set the humans on each other."

Most Aged Father's dried features stretched in mounting fury, and Brot'ân'duivé stepped closer.

"I will break my silence before the council," he said. "I will tell them all that I know of what you have done. As yet, you have nothing to hold against me. Release Cuirin'nên'a, swear to her safety . . . and I will swear my continued silence."

He watched Most Aged Father and waited.

The ancient elf would cling to power at any cost, even for just a little longer. Whatever he feared was coming would drive him to it. He would accept this bargain, and once Cuirin'nên'a was free, Léshil would leave this place and have no reason to return. If not safe, he would at least be beyond the old one's reach, until it was time for him to serve his purpose.

"I . . . accept your exchange," Most Aged Father croaked, his eyes stark with madness. "But this changes nothing. The loyal Anmaglâhk will continue to serve our people."

"Is Cuirin'nên'a released?"

Most Aged Father finally closed his eyes and placed his withered fingers against the walls of his bower for a long moment.

"She is released, so go to her, if you wish. But send Sgäilsheilleache and Fréthfàre to me at once."

Brot'ân'duivé turned away, his heart pounding.

They both knew the half-truth of all this. For now, it served Brot'ân'duivé's own ends and left him time to plan. Whether first he betrayed—or was betrayed—had yet to be seen.

But he was no traitor to his caste. He protected their future, for he still believed in the old one's fear of an enemy yet to show itself. He would do what he must to keep the Anmaglâhk whole and sound. Until they were needed no more, when it all finally ended on the stroke of the blade in Léshil's . . . in Léshiârelaohk's hand.

"In silence and in shadows," Brot'ân'duivé whispered as he left.

Magiere tried to keep Leesil calm, but he kept pacing the elm's chamber, and she finally set to cleaning her falchion. It wasn't necessary, but handling the blade kept her from snapping, between the tension of lingering and the vibrant shivers within her.

Wynn sat on the floor, writing with her quill.

"What are you recording now?" Magiere asked.

"The end of the gathering. My guild will find it of interest in comparison to elven culture elsewhere."

"I'm glad I could offer them some diversion," Magiere sniped.

"Magiere, that is not what I—"

"Sorry . . . forget it."

In Magiere's mind, she kept pondering the silf's sudden appearance, and the idea that it or one of its kind had saved them from the blizzard. Why had it chosen to appear only before the council? How long had it been following her?

The chained translation of its belief that she was somehow of its blood still haunted her. She hoped it didn't know how she'd come by such mistaken heritage.

The doorway curtain folded aside, and Brot'an stepped in. He did not look tired, but he was panting lightly.

Leesil rushed at him. "What happened?"

"Your mother is free," Brot'an answered without warning. "But she does not know it herself, so we must go to her now. I will explain the delay of your departure later and arrange for another barge."

Magiere was dumbstruck, like Leesil, but Chap lunged to his feet.

"Brot'an . . . ," Wynn began, with confusion in her eyes. "How?"

Magiere wondered the same thing, but she slammed her falchion back into its sheath as Leesil snatched up his blades and strapped them on.

"I don't care how," he said.

Chap barked once in agreement and was out the door faster than the rest of them could follow.

*   *   *

In the root chamber beneath the vast oak, Fréthfâre scarcely believed what Most Aged Father told her.

"Released?" she repeated.

Sgäilsheilleache stood silent beside her, his expression unreadable. She knew him better than he realized. Recent events had left him in turmoil. Today had been the worst in her life, defeat after defeat in humiliation.

"Yes, daughter," Most Aged Father said. "Cuirin'nên'a's time is served, and she is released."

"Why?"

Anger crept into his voice. "Do you question me?"

"No, Father," she answered quickly. "I only . . ."

Something was wrong. Brot'ân'duivé had demanded a private audience, and now a traitor was released among the people.

"Will that be all, Father?" Sgäilsheilleache asked. "Do you require anything?"

Fréthfâre wondered at his calm acceptance, as if it were all part of a normal day. Sgäilsheilleache rarely questioned anything, unless faced with the unforeseen. And this was certainly unforeseen.

Most Aged Father squinted at Sgäilsheilleache, and his milky eyes grew soft. "No, my son. Do not be troubled further. Go and rest. We all need rest."

Clearly, Most Aged Father placed no blame upon Sgäilsheilleache for this day's outcome. And why should he? The blame lay with Brot'ân'duivé, and sooner or later, Fréthfâre would find the proof of it. A Greimasg'äh had betrayed his caste, and this could not be left unattended.

Sgäilsheilleache turned and left, but Fréthfâre could not bring herself to go just yet.

"Father, pardon me, but what does this mean? Should I go to inform Cuirin'nên'a?"

He shook his ancient head. "Most likely, Brot'ân'duivé will go tonight and take Léshil with him."

The chamber seemed to grow dim around her as she tried to reason through Most Aged Father's words. Nothing made sense.

"Go now, daughter," he said.

She climbed the steps out of the earth, lost in her tumbling thoughts, and then ran outside, not stopping until she reached the elm where Léshil and his humans were kept. Before she reached the doorway, she knew the elm was empty. Still, she peered inside.

All were gone . . . gone to free Cuirin'nên'a.

Fréthfâre stood in uncertainty. Why had Most Aged Father called her in tonight to tell her this? He was exhausted, and if there was nothing for her to do, then why not leave the news until morning? Why such urgency followed by so little explanation?

She stared off through the trees as her turmoil mounted.

Father had tried to tell . . . to ask her something without putting it into words. For some reason, he could not give the order himself.

Her stomach churned at the thought of Léshil, his traitorous mother, and those humans escaping. Not after they had found a way into this land. Not after all the discord they had sown among her caste. And not after what they had done to Most Aged Father.

She had been at his side for long years . . . long decades. Whatever the reason that he could not ask her outright, she knew what he expected of her.

Fréthfâre ran toward the river and the docks. In the full of night, the trees blurred by. She fled to the sixth birch upstream and fell to her knees by its doorway, pulling back the cloth hanging.

Én'nish sat alone inside on the floor. The cup of tea before her must have sat a long while, for it no longer steamed. She stared blankly ahead, and then turned her sharp face toward the doorway.

"Fréthfâre?" she said, taken back. "Are you well? What is wrong?"

"We go north immediately. Brot'ân'duivé takes Léshil and the humans to free Cuirin'nên'a. They must be stopped." She hesitated before adding, "This is the wish of Most Aged Father."

Én'nish cinched her cloak's trailing corners across her waist, and then her sudden eagerness wavered.

"I do not understand, Covârleasa," she began, respectfully. "If the Greimasg'äh is with them, why are we sent behind him?"

"Brot'ân'duivé is a traitor. You heard and saw him today."

Én'nish still hesitated.

Fréthfâre was not certain how to deal with Brot'ân'duivé, but she understood what must be done this night. A traitor escaped punishment, and humans would leave knowing the way for others to return to her people's land.

"We will not spill the blood . . . of our own," she said, firm and slow.

She let the words hang.

Longing hardened Én'nish's eyes as she understood Fréthfâre's meaning.

No, they would not spill the blood of their own, but the outsiders must be dealt with.

Én'nish blinked slowly with a deep exhale, as if finally releasing long-harbored pain. She followed Fréthfâre out like one who finally saw the salve for her wounds within reach.

Chane struggled through the heavy snow. Wind pelted his face with large flakes that clung to his hair and cloak. He could only see a few paces ahead and followed the mute shapes of Welsteil and their one remaining horse.

"We must find shelter," Chane rasped. "We cannot locate the passage until this blizzard has passed."

"No," Welstiel answered. "We keep looking. It cannot be far."

The Móndyalítko had told them to seek a passage along a deep ravine. Once they passed through, they would be able to see the castle.

Only three nights past, Chane's wild dog familiar had found the way, though calling it a ravine was an understatement. It was a deep and jagged canyon impossible to climb down, and its bottom was filled with snow-blanketed rocky crags. After its discovery, Welstiel behaved like an obsessed madman, driving them hard up through the mountains.

Chane halted. Going on was useless if they could not see. He was about to insist they pitch the tent when a long howl and yammering barks carried on the wind from somewhere ahead.

"The dog!" Welstiel shouted over the wind.

Chane was in no mood for Welstiel's premature elation. "Wait!"

He dropped to sit in the cold snow and closed his eyes, reaching out for his familiar's thoughts. When he found his way into its limited mind, he saw through the dog's eyes.

At first, his sight was obscured by snow slanting through the dark as the dog scrambled forward. Then the animal halted at the edge of a precipice. Chane looked down through its eyes into a gorge at the canyon's top end, and vertigo overwhelmed him. The dog stood on a flat rock overhang, digging through loose snow.

"What has it found?" Welstiel asked desperately.

"I do not know . . . something." He opened his eyes reluctantly and stood up. "Upward . . . ahead."

Chane took the lead, holding the dog's thoughts to sense the way. When he spotted the animal's tracks already fading under the blizzard, he released the connection and picked up his pace. Ahead he thought he saw where the canyon's upper end spiked downward into the rocky range. Upon its near side, something dug wildly in the snow.

Chane trudged quickly up and dropped beside the dog. He looked down with his own eyes to where the canyon opened into a deep gorge too wide to see its far side. He began digging by hand, clearing snow from the ledge until he exposed a piece of flat slate that did not match the ledge's basalt stone. The piece was half the length of his body and smoothly fitted to the ledge's edge—except for a hole to one side just large enough for a hand. Chane cleared the opening with his fingers and lifted the slate panel.

Welstiel hovered above him as they looked down.

Snow-covered ledges—wide steps—were carved into the gorge wall, though Chane could not be sure in the blizzard if they went all the way to the unseen bottom.

Welstiel examined the piece of slate. "This was intended to hide the passage?"

"I do not think so. More likely a marker to find it or perhaps shield the first steps from erosion. This path is used regularly by someone, for it took much work to carve it out, crude as it is. Let us hope it leads somewhere useful, though we will have to abandon the horse."

Welstiel stared into space. "The Móndyalítko said we would step out to see the castle. It has to be down there somewhere . . . it must be."

Between the darkness and the storm, Chane had no way of telling if this was true, and he was sick of blind optimism. "Do we try tonight or wait until we have more time tomorrow?"

"Now," Welstiel answered instantly, and pulled their packs from the horse. "Move on. We leave the dog as well."

Again, Chane had no voice in their decisions, and his anger seethed quietly. But he held his tongue. Perhaps they were close to Welstiel's coveted orb, and once they found it, Chane might give Welstiel a surprise or two of his own.

Chane braced a hand against the steep rock wall and took two steps downward, peering below. He saw nothing through the blizzard—not even the gorge's bottom, nor its far side. Snowflakes slanting across the night seemed to materialize out of the dark. The lower he went, the more the wind lessened, until the snow drifted lazily downward.

Behind and above him, Chane heard Welstiel's boots scrape the steps.

Sgäile headed for the third oak upstream from the docks, eager to be with his family once more and away from all others. He pulled the doorway drape aside, and there sat his grandfather, Gleannéohkân'thva, upon an umber felt throw as he wrote with quill on parchment.

"Where is Leanâlhâm?" Sgäile asked.

"She went to find a few things for our journey," his grandfather replied. "It will be an early start. Will you come with us?"

Sinking down, Sgäile untied his cloak and lifted the clay teapot from its tray.

"I must first see Léshil and his companions safely off, then I will come home for a while. I wish to bring Osha with me—with your consent. Except for his training, I am considering a request to be relieved of duties for the remainder of winter . . . perhaps longer."

His grandfather looked up, puzzled, but merely patted his shoulder. "Osha is always welcome. And it would be good to have you home for a while."

Sgäile poured tea into one of the round cups and turned its warmth slowly between his palms.

Indeed, to have a little peace once again, even into the spring. Time to reflect on many things he had not been aware of before today. Strange animosity existed between Brot'ân'duivé and Most Aged Father—a revered Greimasg'äh and the founder of their caste. A rift that apparently had grown silently over time. Fréthfâre as well had some part in it, for her ardor in challenge had raised Sgäile's awareness in the worst of ways.

He sipped the tea slowly, but it brought him no comfort.

Leanâlhâm fell through the door, breathing hard. "Sgäilsheilleache! Come—quickly!"

He set the cup down, grabbed her hand, and pulled her inside. "What? Are you injured?"

"No . . ." She gasped in another deep breath. "Urhkarasiférin gave me dried figs for our journey, and in returning, I saw Fréthfâre outside Én'nish's quarters. They did not see me, but I heard part of what they said. They go north after Léshil and Brot'ân'duivé."

Sgäile sat back, whispering to himself. "Léshil has gone to tell Cuirin'nên'a."

"Tell her what?" his grandfather asked.

Sgäile came back to himself. "Most Aged Father has released Cuirin'nên'a. She is forgiven. Léshil and his companions must have gone to tell her." He looked at Leanâlhâm. "Brot'ân'duivé is with them, and Fréthfâre follows after?"

"Yes," she cried. "And Én'nish. But I do not believe Brot'ân'duivé knows they follow."

Sgäile carefully set down his cup.

"They spoke of not spilling the blood . . . of their own." Leanâlhâm's voice quavered. "But why would they need to? And something in Fréthfâre's voice . . . she only mentioned Brot'ân'duivé—not Léshil or his companions! Why would she say this to Én'nish?"

Sgäile stood up, rapidly tying the corners of his cloak. His first instinct was to go directly to Most Aged Father, but if Fréthfâre acted on her own, this would only cause more discord.

"I will find Léshil first," he said. "I will uncover what is happening."

"I am coming with you," Gleannéohkân'thva said.

"No, I must run."

"Are you suggesting that I cannot keep up? Your caste is at odds with itself. You need a clan elder, and I am the closest you have." He turned to Leanâlhâm. "Do not leave our quarters, and do not tell anyone where we have gone. If asked, we have gone to gather supplies for the trip."

Leanâlhâm nodded quickly. "Hurry!"

Gleannéohkân'thva donned his cloak, not waiting for Sgäile's agreement.

"Stay behind me," he told his grandfather. Perhaps he would need the voice of an elder.

They left the oak, running along the river to the open forest, rather than through Crijheäiche.

CHAPTER TWENTY-THREE

Magiere ran beside Leesil, and a part of her still doubted such sudden good fortune. Their journey into her own past in Droevinka had uncovered horrific circumstances surrounding her birth. Their passage through the warlands and Leesil's past in Venjètz had only led to anguish and murder.

She'd hoped the journey into the Elven Territories would be different, and now it seemed Leesil would have what he wanted. The outcome was better than she had dreamed possible. Nein'a had been released with no bloodshed, and they were all promised safe passage out of the elves' lands to any destination they chose.

All they had left was the issue of Welstiel's artifact, though Magiere had little idea where to begin. Then they could go home.

Brot'an and Chap led the way, with Wynn in the center. Leesil and Magiere brought up the rear. Magiere wasn't certain how she felt about Nein'a's company, but she pushed the doubt away. Only Nein'a's freedom mattered now—or rather Leesil's relief from his long years of guilt.

"Do you know where you are going?" Wynn called to Chap and Brot'an.

Chap yipped once and tossed his head without slowing. Magiere saw a flash of white in the brush to her right, and then two more of silver-gray among the trees.

"How long have they been with us?" she called out.

No one answered, and they jogged onward at a pace meant for Wynn's short legs.

"How do you think she'll take it?" Leesil asked. "Finally being free?"

"What?"

"My mother. She's been trapped here so long . . . I wonder if she'll even believe it at first."

"Leesil—" Magiere began.

A hissing in the air broke her attention as Brot'an turned and started to duck.

A darting pale shaft struck the back of his head. He pitched forward and crashed limply to the earth.

Magiere dodged the other way, as Leesil grabbed Wynn's cloak and pulled her behind a tree. Magiere peered back the way they had come. Leesil jerked out one winged blade as she pulled her falchion.

Chap had vanished, but Magiere knew he'd be close by. She watched for movement but saw nothing in the forest.

"He's been shot," Wynn whispered, and started to crawl toward Brot'an's prone form.

Leesil pulled her back.

Magiere couldn't see Brot'an's face, but he wasn't moving. Beside him lay an arrow on the ground. It hadn't sunk in on impact—good fortune perhaps, but that didn't seem likely.

She hesitated at letting her hunger rise, but she did it. As her night sight widened, she focused upon the fallen arrow.

In place of a narrow pointed head was a blunt gray ball of metal. Whoever had fired it wanted Brot'an left alive.

"Is he breathing?" Magiere whispered.

Wynn craned her head. "Yes."

"Äruin'nas?" Magiere asked, and looked back down the path.

"I don't see anyone," Leesil answered.

A soft thud. Magiere whirled back.

A figure clad in gray-green stood between her and Brot'an, with a stiletto in each hand. Amber eyes fixed upon Magiere. Even with the wrap across the figure's face, Magiere recognized those eyes.

Fréth charged straight for Leesil before Magiere could move.

Leesil was forced to duck into the open to get clear of the tree, and Fréth lashed out a booted foot into Wynn's head.

Magiere heard a snapping sound at the impact. "No!"

As Wynn twisted and fell into the brush, Chap leaped through the leaves above her and closed on Fréth.

In the corner of Magiere's vision, someone dropped from above behind Leesil.

Én'nish crouched with her overlong stilettos in hand.

Magiere halted in hesitation over whom to go after.

Good fortune was nothing but a fool's faith. If it wasn't the undead, it was the Anmaglâhk coming at them from the dark.

Leesil sucked in a sharp breath as Fréth's foot collided with Wynn's jaw. The little sage topped into the brush. He heard either the crossbow or the quarrel case on her back crackle under her weight. Then Chap lunged out over the top of her, charging at Fréth as Magiere skidded to a halt, looking in his direction.

A glint of bright metal flickered in the corner of Leesil's vision. He whirled to see Én'nish coming at him from him behind.

Leesil twisted away.

Her long stiletto pierced the shoulder of his cloak. She turned sharply, her body like the handle of a twin whip. The movement drove her lead arm onward as the other came under and up. The first blade tore free of his cloak, passing his head. The second arced upward for his throat.

Leesil swept his winged blade upward, catching Én'nish's rising stiletto on its top edge. As he brushed her thrust up and away, she seemed to ride his momentum into the air.

Her foot touched a tree trunk, and she pushed off. Leesil spun around as she came down behind him, his blade on guard. Én'nish's long, narrow stiletto screeched along the wing of his punching blade.

She was sweating. Her face was twisted with rage, and the suffering in her eyes was too familiar.

He'd seen it before, as he crouched upon the frozen ground outside of Venjètz, clinging to the skulls of his father and what he'd first believed was his mother. Only the face he saw then was Hedí Progae, who sought vengeance for her father, Leesil's first kill for Darmouth.

He was tired of killing. He didn't want to be anyone's weapon anymore.

Én'nish rushed him, twisting like a cat to get inside his blade's reach and strike for his chest or throat.

Leesil spun with her, letting her lower blade skid over his hauberk as he parried the upper one. He slammed his empty hand into the side of her ribs.

Én'nish tottered off balance as she swept past, but she pivoted with a scissoring slash of both stilettos to fend him off.

Behind her, Leesil saw Chap raging and snarling after Fréth.

"No!" Magiere shouted. "Guard Wynn!"

Her voice was thick, her words awkward, and Leesil caught the black disks of her irises expanding. But he feared she might not best Fréth even in a full dhampir state.

And Én'nish stood in his way.

Leesil swallowed fear into cold dispassion, as his mother had taught him. He had to put Én'nish down to get to Magiere—and killing was what he'd been made for.

Hunger rose in Magiere's throat and rushed through her body. This time, she welcomed the ache spreading through her jaws.

Her eyes burned as her sight widened, and the night lit up before her. She swung the falchion with all the speed and force she had. Not an effective attack, unless Fréth was stupid enough to think she could block it.

Fréth quickly slid back out of the sword's arc and further from Wynn and Brot'an. That was all Magiere wanted from her first strike.

Before Fréth could come behind the falchion's swing, Magiere reversed, bringing its dull backside straight around.

Fréth winced as it smashed into her shoulder. She bent and turned with the impact, but the falchion's tip tore through her tunic.

They both froze, eyes locked on each other.

All Magiere saw was another murdering anmaglâhk with a bloody tear across her tunic's shoulder.

Fréth flinched once at the sight of Magiere, and then her gaze fixed with determination.

"Dead thing," she hissed. "You belong in the dirt, buried and forgotten."

"You . . . don't know," Magiere grunted out, "how to deal with undead . . . and I'm much more."

Fréth darted sideways, heading for the nearest tree.

Magiere had seen Brot'an use the same move on a column in Darmouth's crypt, stepping up to spring over her head, and drop behind her.

She chopped downward as Fréth lifted a foot.

Fréth jerked her foot back in midleap, and the falchion hit the tree's trunk. Bark and wood slivers sprayed off it. Fréth extended her foot again, but it landed too high. All she could do was push off and roll back across open ground.

Magiere whirled, blade up, facing off with Fréth.

Chap charged from the other side but stopped short, planting himself between Fréth and Wynn. He had fought at Magiere's side enough to know when to attack and when to stay out of her way.

She feinted low and left, shifted right, and turned the falchion in an upward slash for Fréth's midsection. The stroke missed, but Fréth failed to get within arm's reach. They spun away from each other again.

Fréth was far enough away this time that Chap tried to close in.

Wynn groaned, and Magiere couldn't help but look. The sage rolled weakly in the brush, but the crossbow on her back caught on something.

"No!" Magiere shouted to Chap. "Guard Wynn."

The instant cost her. When her eyes shifted back, Fréth was gone.

Blinding pain shot through her side.

Chap dashed toward Wynn thrashing feebly in the brush. Blood ran from her mouth and spread through her teeth. She could not get free of the crossbow tangled in the bush. He bit into its strap, tearing at it until it snapped.

Wynn rolled onto her face, trying to push up to her hands and knees.

Load and fire! Chap shouted into her mind.

He was about to turn and pick an attack of his own, when Wynn faltered and fell to the ground again. Her olive face twisted in pain.

Chap dipped into her mind, calling up her memories of contented moments. Quiet nights sleeping by campfires or in the quilt-covered bed of an inn. Two kittens purring in her lap. Hot mint tea and spiced lentil stew. The smell of fresh parchment and the feel of a quill in her hand. Her fingers curled in his fur.

Wynn lifted her head, clutching at the crossbow.

Chap pulled an unbroken quarrel from the quiver with his teeth and dropped it beside her. She rolled onto her knees, heaving the crossbow's string back with both hands. With the string locked in place and the lever cocked, she grasped and set the quarrel.

Wynn looked up and hesitated, gaze shifting between the two conflicts. Chap turned about.

Leesil fended off Én'nish as she slashed madly at him. He did not fight with the same quick instinct and brutality that Chap had seen in the past.

Then Magiere stumbled as Fréth stabbed her from behind. They were too close together now for Wynn's questionable aim.

Chap panicked, shouting into Wynn's thoughts: *Én'nish!*

He heard the crack of a quarrel leaving Wynn's crossbow as he charged at Fréth's exposed back.

Magiere felt Fréth's arm wrap around her neck and jerk tight. Then the blade slipped out of her side.

Hunger ate away the pain. She rammed her elbow back, but it never connected.

A bloodied stiletto came over her shoulder for her throat.

Magiere wouldn't release her sword. Unable to whip it back, she tried to grab Fréth's wrist before the stiletto touched her skin.

Fear should have taken Magiere as she struggled for air. Instead, rage whipped hunger into fury. She would not let Fréth win . . . or she would make her pay dearly for it.

Fréth's weight increased sharply as if her whole body lurched and slammed inward upon Magiere. The arm around Magiere's throat loosened as she toppled forward under the sound of snarls.

Magiere hit the ground face-first. Fréth's weight rolled off with an angry scream. Her voice was quickly drowned in growls and tearing cloth. Magiere spun on her hip, pulling her legs under as she twisted to a crouch.

Chap darted away from Fréth's wild slash, his teeth parted in a shuddering growl and fur bristling on his neck and shoulders. Fréth scrambled to regain her footing. The back of her cowl was shredded, and she ripped it off, sidestepping to keep her two opponents in sight.

Magiere rose up, her mind hazy with the heat welling in her body. Hunger fed on the tingling shiver the forest pressed upon her.

Instinct drove her to attack . . . to stop at nothing until Fréth was dead. This one had come at her and those she cherished, time and again, and now brought Én'nish, who served only one purpose—to kill all of them where no one would see.

Magiere held her place. A little reason remained and stirred inside her.

Each time she swung, Fréth came in behind the falchion's passing. The woman closed to advantage for her shorter blades and hampered Magiere's use of the longer and heavier weapon.

Magiere didn't need a weapon.

She could mangle this bitch with her bare hands. All she needed— wanted—was for Fréth to come in one more time. Magiere made the barest feint with the falchion's tip and then loosened her grip, ready to drop it.

Fréth's attention remained on Magiere, but she didn't come. Her left hand whipped to the side—and flung a stiletto straight at Chap.

The shudder in Magiere's body sharpened. Her grip clenched tight on the falchion. She lunged as Fréth took her first charging step.

Magiere caught Fréth's other stiletto in her free hand. She felt nothing as she wrenched the blade aside and rammed her falchion straight in. The sword didn't even jump in her hand as its tip sank into Fréth's gut.

It happened too quickly. Fréth's eyes didn't even widen until Magiere clamped her bloody hand around the woman's neck.

She squeezed until she felt Fréth choke, and then shoved hard.

Fréth's body arched backward, sliding off the falchion as Magiere jerked it loose, and Fréth hit the earth, writhing on her back.

Magiere raised the falchion to finish her.

A shout vibrated through her bones. "Stop!"

Én'nish lurched and stumbled before Leesil. A quarrel seemed to sprout suddenly from the back of her right shoulder. She didn't cry out, and only dropped one stiletto as her right arm went limp.

Leesil spotted Wynn kneeling in a flattened bush with the crossbow still against her shoulder. The little sage dropped the weapon and crumpled.

Én'nish lunged at him with her remaining blade.

Leesil slipped aside, again and again, staying beyond reach. Then he saw Fréth fling a blade at Chap, and the dog tried to duck away.

The blade missed his face and the handle clipped his ear as the weapon tumbled across his back. He snarled sharply.

The next thing Leesil saw was Fréth on the ground, holding her belly. A dark stain was spreading quickly through her tunic and between her fingers.

Magiere raised her falchion.

Én'nish lunged at Leesil again, throwing her whole weight to take him while distracted. He tried to deflect and brought up the punching blade on instinct.

Its edge sliced the back of Én'nish's hand and down her forearm, splitting her sleeve open. She cried out, jerking away, and tried to swing again.

Sgäile appeared, folding her tightly in his arms from behind and pinning her.

Sgäile ran hard toward the sounds of screeching steel and voices.

Brot'än'duivé was on the ground, attempting to push himself up. A bludgeoning arrow lay near him. Blood dripped from Wynn's mouth down her chin. Én'nish, with a quarrel in her shoulder, still kept at Leesil.

And Magiere ran Fréth through with her sword.

Sgäile didn't hesitate. He folded his arms tightly around Én'nish from behind, pinning her up against his chest, and shouted at Magiere. "Stop!"

She wavered.

"Léshil, do not let her take Fréthfäre's life."

Léshil was already running around Magiere to stand in her way. He spoke too softly for Sgäile to hear. Magiere slowly lowered her sword.

Gleannéohkân'thva caught up, trying to get his breath. He faltered at the sight before him.

"Grandfather, see to Fréthfäre first," Sgäile blurted out.

Én'nish still struggled in his arms. He thrust his knee into the back of hers. When her leg buckled, he threw his weight on her. She dropped, and he held her down.

"Enough!" he barked, pressing hard on her until she finally lay still. "What is this? What have you done?"

"Most Aged Father ordered us to dispatch them," Én'nish snarled. "And you interfere in our purpose! They deserve to die!"

"And Brot'an as well?" Sgäile snapped. "No! Father would never . . ."

He looked at Fréthfäre, blood-stained and curled upon the earth. He did not believe Én'nish.

Sgäile had seen the way Fréthfäre went after Brot'än'duivé before the council, all for a challenge of truth as Most Aged Father's advocate. But the patriarch of his caste would not violate his word. No, this had to be Fréthfâre's doing—and hers alone. Why else would she bring only Én'nish, in the woman's anguished state, in coming after so many with Brot'ân'duivé?

He went cold inside.

"Sgäilsheilleache!" his grandfather snapped, untying Fréth's cloak. "Question Én'nish later. Fréthfâre's wound is severe, and the others need attendance. Assist me—now!"

"I can see the bottom," Chane said.

Welstiel trembled but did not answer. After two decades and more of preparation and searching, the end was close. Never would there be another night of hunger, feeding upon the wretched and filthy masses. Only eternity filled with peace and contemplation, with the orb in his possession.

Welstiel gave silent thanks to the patron of his dreams.

He might not be able to enter the castle without Magiere. But still his patron guided his steps. He would find a way to bring Magiere to serve his need.

Welstiel was in control once more.

"Careful," Chane rasped. "These lower steps are much worn, and do not look solid."

Welstiel set his palms firmly against the gorge wall. He was still eager to lay eyes on the six-towered castle of his dreams—to see arched metal gates, the black ravens, and every detail that was engraved upon his mind.

Chane slid down the last few steps and trotted out onto the gorge's bottom filled with rough boulders and stones coated in snow. Welstiel hurried down and strode past when he reached solid footing.

At first there was nothing to see, and he scrambled recklessly over the gorge's floor, until coming upon a cleared path coated in light snow. He heard Chane behind him, but he could not wait and raced on, slipping more than once. The path turned, closing again toward the right face.

Welstiel looked about in the dark. He saw nothing but snow gathered on the craggy bottom of the gorge's expanse. He lifted his gaze, searching.

Switchbacks were carved into the gorge's more gradually sloping face, and the path led upward part of the way.

"No," he whispered, stumbling two more steps.

Chane's harsh whisper filled his ears amid the slow-falling snowflakes.

"What is wrong?"

Welstiel gazed up, unable to answer.

He looked upon a small construction chiseled out of the gorge's rock face.

A glowing torch or lantern, mounted upon a pole before its small single door, lit up wood-shuttered windows. The building seated deep into the rock face, no higher than two floors tall, was some kind of ancient and forgotten barracks or a long-lost stronghold in the middle of nowhere.

There was no castle. There were no gates. No ravens. No courtyard. No magnificent ice-fringed spires.

"No," he whispered again.

Cold numbness melted under sorrow and began to burn away in outrage. Welstiel spun around, raising his face to the dark sky.

"For this?" he shouted.

All the nights of trudging hopefully through snow and rocks and cliffs, dragging half-dead horses, and pushing Chane onward. Was his patron amused? Did it sleep, laughing, waiting for him to return to hollow dreams?

He had fallen under his own father to wake from death in a vile existence. And for more than two decades he had searched for release with only his patron's teasing whispers in his slumber. More than once he had grown weary of it, and turned to potions and arcane drugs to keep him from dormancy. But in the end, he had always relented and gone back to the scaled patron of his dreams.

This was the end of it.

He would dream no more . . . listen no more.

"Do you hear?" Welstiel called out to the stars.

They shone down upon him, distant and unconcerned. So much like an unseen light glinting upon the scales of massive coils turning in the dark.

Chane stared at him. "Who are you talking to?"

Welstiel barely heard him.

"No more!" he cried out to the sky, and grew more spiteful at the anguish in his own voice. "I am finished with you! Go back to where you hide. Find another toy . . . to cheat!"

Somewhere in the still night he heard a scrape of footsteps echo softly through the gorge.

Another small flicker of light wormed up the last switchback before the stone structure with its decrepit wood shutters. Welstiel's anger broke his self-control, and hunger widened his sight.

A figure stepped out the structure's narrow door. Dressed in a pale blue tabard over a dark robe with a full cowl, it lifted a torch high, as if calling the other light rising up the path.

That other light reached the narrow level shelf before the structure, and below it came two more figures wearing similar attire. The two met the one, and all three figures went inside.

Welstiel could not remember where he had seen such clothing before. A monastery, perhaps? It did not matter. Here was opportunity for his outrage.

How many years had he listened to his patron's mocking words?

The sister of the dead will lead you.

Very well then. But he no longer put faith in such things. She might lead, but he would not need her in the end. There would be others to serve him.

"Lock them in . . . ," he whispered. "All of them."

Chane stepped around into his sight, glancing up to the stronghold before looking into Welstiel's face. He cocked his head as if not certain of what he had heard.

"Lock them all in," Welstiel repeated. "Feed if you must, but leave them alive . . . for now."

Chane's eyes glinted in anticipation.

Welstiel just stood there.

The sister of the dead will lead you.

Yes, she would still do that. But he would not be alone when he came after her—the puppet of his deceiver.

Leesil reluctantly assisted Sgäile in holding Én'nish down. Gleann severed the quarrel's shaft and pushed the remainder through.

Fréth was more fortunate than she deserved. Magiere's falchion had not damaged any vital organs, but Most Aged Father's pet anmaglâhk would be weakened for a long while. Maybe for life, unless Gleann had tricks and skills beyond what Leesil had seen.

Magiere had taken a stiletto through the side, but Gleann claimed it wasn't serious. He scowled suspiciously at the wound, which had already stopped bleeding.

He dressed everyone's wounds with leaves and a strange lemon-yellow moss, and he hummed softly with eyes half-closed as he traced fingertips around Fréth's bandaged injury.

Wynn's jaw wasn't broken, but the inside of her mouth was cut and her gums still seeped blood. She grimaced each time she flushed her mouth with cold water, and made a sour face when Gleann forced her to chew some of the moss. She hoped that the abrasion of Fréth's boot wouldn't leave scars on her face.

Brot'an complained of dizziness and bore a large lump at the base of his skull.

Leesil waited until he was certain his own companions were well cared for, but then all he could think of was pressing onward. His mother still waited. Magiere got up, dark eyes full of understanding.

"We'll get there," she said quietly.

Leesil looked to Brot'an. "Can you still lead? If not, Chap can take us."

"No," Sgäile said. "Brot'ân'duivé and my grandfather will make a litter for Fréthfâre. Her wound must be sewn. They will take her and Én'nish back to Crijheäiche. I will take you to Cuirin'nên'a." He turned and looked down at Fréth. "Speak of this to no one outside our caste. There will be no more discord among us, and you will be dealt with accordingly, Covârleasa!"

Brot'an rose and nodded to Leesil. "Return soon. I wait to see Cuirin'nên'a as well."

Sgäile bowed slightly, and Brot'an headed off to find makings for Fréth's stretcher.

It seemed Leesil's return to his mother was finally under way again when Gleann began walking north after Sgäile.

Sgäile halted. "Grandfather, you should return with the wounded."

"There are others who can tend them upon their return," Gleann answered. "As much as it may slow him, Brot'ân'duivé is hulkish enough to drag Fréthfâre's litter by himself. And Én'nish can do no more than follow in her present state. I am coming with you."

Sensing an argument brewing, Leesil cut in. "Magiere and Wynn may still need him, as it will take us a lot longer to return."

Gleann smiled at Wynn. "Come, child. And do not remove that moss from your mouth until I tell you."

To Leesil's relief, Sgäile just grunted. They headed north once again at a slower pace.

Leesil wasn't certain of the distance, but the journey would likely take the rest of the night. They continued until the forest began to lighten with the dawn and they emerged in a shattered clearing of broken branches, torn flowers, and one large uprooted birch.

Chap stopped in sudden weariness, glanced up at Wynn, and took a few steps into the clearing. The sage joined him, placing her hand on his back. Leesil was about to call them back when Chap turned away with Wynn at his side. The dog stalked on through the trees with his head hanging.

They all moved on, and Leesil saw the edge of the barrier woods.

He wanted to run but held back, not wishing to leave Magiere or the others behind as they entered the woods' passage. When he broke through the ferns at the far end, Leesil emerged in the familiar glade.

"Mother?"

He didn't see her at first. She came around from behind her domicile elm and stopped.

"Léshil?"

The hem of her ivory wrap dragged across the grass as she walked closer. Her silken hair spilled down her shoulders and disappeared behind.

Leesil looked at her for a long moment, the sight of her washing through him.

"You're free," he said bluntly. "You're leaving with me."

He reached back for Magiere—who had stood by him and fought for him, even against his own destructive obsession. She clasped his hand.

Favoring her swollen lip, Wynn smiled as Chap trotted up to Nein'a.

Sgäile and Gleann politely remained by the ferns, but Sgäile confirmed Leesil's words.

"You have been released. Most Aged Father told me this himself."

Leesil didn't know what to expect as his mother stared at him with anxious doubt. She glanced about the clearing's border trees. For an instant Leesil saw a vicious glower spread across her elegant features.

"Free," she whispered.

Leesil wanted to take hold of his mother, but he simply stood near her. "Yes . . . finally."

"What will I do?" she asked.

There was a strange loss in her voice, as if doubt would never fade completely.

Nein'a had been a skilled assassin and spy, a wife then widow, a mother and a daughter . . . and Anmaglâhk. She had also been trapped alone in this glade for eight years. Leesil reached out slowly to take her fingers.

"Come with Magiere and me."

Anxiety grew in her large eyes.

"Into the human world again?" She shook her head. "No . . . too long, too many years there."

Leesil felt as if he'd been dropped over a precipice. Then his thoughts traced backward through what life he'd had with her.

She had been ordered to Venjètz and lived there for over twenty years, had birthed and cared for him, trained him, and all the while held Most Aged Father's bloodlust at bay. Then imprisoned and alone, without Gavril. How long had it been since she'd lived as she wanted? As much as it hurt, Leesil tried to understand.

But what else could she do? She had no home here—only enemies. Leesil looked at Magiere in deep concern. The two of them could not stay.

Gleann stepped cautiously forward. "Cuirin'nên'a, do you remember me . . . Sgäilsheilleache's grandfather? I have a granddaughter who is . . . not unlike your Léshil. I fear she grows tired of being the only woman of the house. Our settlement is small and simple, but there is always room for one more."

Nein'a looked at him. "Gleannéohkân'thva? Yes, I remember you."

Her words came evenly, and Leesil thought he caught something more than passing recognition within them. When he glanced at Gleann, he remembered how quickly the old man had arrived for Magiere's trial before the gathering, and how familiar he'd been with Brot'an.

Brot'an and his mother—both dissidents among the Anmaglâhk, both acquainted with Gleann. Had Sgäile ever noticed this?

"Do us this honor," Gleann said to Nein'a and then turned his owlish gaze upon Leesil. "If that is agreeable to both you and Léshil."

Nein'a's serious and exquisite face twisted in pain.

It was clear to Leesil that she wanted to accept Gleann's offer of a small quiet place in her own world where she might find some normal life of her choosing. Yet a part of Leesil grew anxious at the thought of leaving her among those who'd imprisoned her . . . and perhaps others who'd plotted with her over so many years. But if he trusted anyone among those he had met in this land to help her, it would be Gleann.

Nein'a gripped Leesil's fingers, and Magiere moved up, still grasping his other hand. He stood there caught between the two women of his world.

When Leesil looked at Magiere, he thought of the wedding to come . . . someday. He would swear fealty to her before their friends and, he hoped, her aunt Bieja. Shouldn't his own mother be present as well?

"You must continue," Nein'a said. "The ancestors will guide you. Do not let anything sway you when the path becomes clear."

It never occurred to Leesil before how much she was like her people, down to their fanatical superstitions. He'd seen the ghosts at the naked tree beyond the serpent and heard them call him by a name he didn't want. But he'd seen a ghost or two in his own life. Most were somewhere between an annoyance and a threat to be banished. They weren't worth this kind of blind faith.

Leesil saw how much Gleann's offer meant to her. Perhaps she would be safe and could come back to herself—to the woman he preferred her to be, his mother.

"All right," he said. "Come back to Crijheäiche with us, and we'll talk."

"Crijheäiche?" she repeated.

"Be at ease," Gleann said. "You will not see anyone you do not wish to."

Sgäile stepped forward, stripping off his cloak. "Put this on and over your head."

Of all the things Sgäile had done, for this Leesil felt most grateful.

"Do you have things to gather?" Wynn asked in her sensible way. "Anything here you wish to bring?"

Nein'a looked about the clearing, and her eyes sparked with the smoldering anger Leesil remembered so well.

"Only what once belonged to me," she said, and turned away into the tree.

When she reemerged, she held the bundled cloth with the skulls of Gavril and Eillean.

Leesil breathed in with difficulty, as Nein'a took her first faltering steps toward the ferns. He walked beside Magiere, not knowing what more to say. She linked her arm with his as they began the journey back.

CHAPTER TWENTY-FOUR

The return to Crijheäiche left them all exhausted, even Nein'a, who looked wary of her surroundings. Sgäile settled her in a small domicile tree by the river, close to Gleann and Leanâlhâm. When he offered to sit in vigil for Nein'a, Leesil insisted upon doing this himself.

Magiere understood, and so she took Wynn and Chap back to their own quarters.

Chap had been behaving strangely since the end of the trial—from the moment he and Leesil went for a final word with Most Aged Father. His crystal blue eyes shifted continually. Magiere suspected that the strain of the past days affected him as much as any of them.

In all honesty, she'd have much preferred to sit with Leesil, but if Nein'a wished to speak to him, they would need time alone. Poor Wynn looked quite a mess with her swollen jaw and tangled hair. The young woman had been abused too much over their travels.

"You sleep now," she said, guiding Wynn to a cushioned bed ledge inside the elm. "Save the bath for when you wake up."

Chap whined loudly.

Some might think it difficult to read a canine's face. Not so for Magiere, after all the time she'd spent with him. She could read his agitation in the bristled fur and twitch of his jowls. He prowled toward Wynn in halting steps.

Wynn rolled over on the bed ledge to sit up. With dark circles under her eyes, she glared at Chap.

"Not until I am ready!" she grumbled. "Get that through your thick head!"

Lately, her temper had grown shorter, but this was perhaps for the best.

"What now?" Magiere asked.

"He wants to talk to you," Wynn said tiredly. "As if that is all I am good for anymore. Chap, just go to sleep, and let me do the same!"

Chap stalked closer to the sage, his eyes locked into hers. Wynn let out a sigh and slid off the ledge to the chamber floor.

"He says he is afraid . . . of showing me something, but you have to know the truth, and this is the only way."

She wavered, looking small and young to Magiere.

Too many times Chap had revealed something that made Magiere wish she had a way to speak alone with the dog. Wynn might have grown hardened in the last two seasons, but there were still things the sage was not prepared to face. Things that Magiere herself didn't care to think on, and it made her dread what Chap might pass to her through Wynn.

Magiere sank down, the three of them in a huddle, and ran a hand over Chap's silver-gray ear.

"What is it?" she whispered.

The dog glanced with concern at Wynn, but then fixed his eyes on Magiere. She stared back, growing more unsettled by the moment. Until Wynn whimpered.

The sage pulled up her knees, hiding her face in her hands, and began to sob.

"Wynn?" Magiere's fear sharpened. "Chap, whatever you're doing, stop it now!"

As she reached for Wynn, the sage cringed away, then clutched Magiere's wrist tightly.

"Once we leave elven land," she said, her voice low, "never come back . . . you must never set foot here again!"

As much concern as Magiere had for Wynn, she glared at Chap. He dipped his muzzle, flinching under her watchful eyes. Whatever he said to the sage, he didn't stop. Wynn's fingers tightened on Magiere's wrist, and the sage began to whisper Chap's words.

The longer Chap spoke through Wynn, the more numb Magiere became, until all she felt was the same shudder in her flesh that grew each time she stepped within a domicile tree.

"You were made to breach these lands . . . to breach any last refuge of the living," was the last thing Wynn said.

Magiere's mind rolled in a tangled mess as Wynn crawled back into bed, hiding her face.

Magiere sat upon the chamber floor with Chap.

She kept hearing words in her head spoken in pieces. Some from the last memory Chap had stolen from Most Aged Father. And more from what she'd heard others say. The worst was the missing piece from Chap's delusion spawned by sorcery.

No undead existed . . . before the lost war of the Forgotten History.

No undead rose . . . but humans.

No undead walked elven lands . . . but her.

In the forest of Pudúrlatsat, far south in Droevinka, Chap had fallen prey to a phantasm cast by the undead sorcerer Vordana. Magiere and Leesil had suffered the same, each experiencing a delusion fed by their worst fears—and perhaps something more hidden within each of them.

Chap had never told Magiere or anyone of his delusion until now.

He had seen her with an army, its ranks filled with creatures and beasts driven by madness for slaughter. She stood at the head of those forces in black-scaled armor, fully feral with her dhampir nature cut loose. Among the horde were the shadowed and gleaming-eyed figures, as in Magiere's own delusion and nightmares. The undead waited for her to lead them into a thriving forest. Everything died in her wake . . . under their hunger.

In Most Aged Father's memory, the undead horde hadn't breached the elven forest. Those who fled to that final refuge huddled together, listening to the sounds of starving undead legions tearing each other apart.

Magiere cowered on the elm's chamber floor. She had been imbued . . . infected with the nature of a Noble Dead, and yet was still a living thing. This had been accomplished with the blood of the five races, the Úirishg. By their blood used in her conception, and the life within her, Magiere could go wherever she wished.

The undead could not breach First Glade or the forest it touched. Not until the war came again to cover the world—and Magiere was born.

This was the reason she had been made.

Chap's understanding of all these pieces, much of it hidden or stolen by his kin, was the worst thing he could have done to her.

That wasn't the end of what was grinding Magiere down. Chap knew what Leesil's strange name meant. He heard the name of the female elder in Most Aged Father's memory, the one called Léshiâra—Sorrow-Tear.

Leesil . . . Léshil . . . Léshiârelaohk . . . Sorrow-Tear's Champion.

Magiere leaned on both hands, trying to draw in breath. Chap crept in, brushing his muzzle against her face, but she barely felt it.

Nein'a and her confederates envisioned their own way to deal with this unknown enemy that Most Aged Father feared would come again. Leesil had been conceived as their instrument, made for the need of the living with the skill for killing that the Anmaglâhk knew so well.

And Magiere? She had been born tainted by the undead to breach all last refuges of life.

Each of them made for opposing sides of a war yet to come.

She couldn't stop the tears slipping from her eyes.

Small hands gripped her shoulders. Wynn knelt down, and Magiere collapsed into the sage's lap.

"I am sorry," Wynn whispered, trying to pull Magiere closer. "For what I said . . . the way I said it. You are not what they tried to make you. You do not have to be this."

But Magiere only thought of one thing.

Outside in the dark was the half-blood she loved, made for a purpose to counter her own . . . created to be her enemy.

In two days, Magiere stood on the riverside docks beside Leesil. Of all inappropriate times, Wynn struggled with a brush to clear tangles from Chap's fur. Brot'an, Sgäile, and Leanâlhâm watched her efforts with amusement.

"Hold still!" the sage snapped in exasperation.

Osha kept his eyes on Wynn as well, but his expression held no humor.

In the middle of them all, Nein'a stood quietly distracted near Leesil, and he fell into his old habit of babbling whenever nervous or upset.

"Remember what I said—there are elven ships that sail the Belaskian coast. Just send a letter to Counselor Lanjov at the bank in Bela, and he will get it to us straight away. We have some things to finish before going home to Miiska. But you can come there just the same, whenever you wish."

Nein'a nodded, her eyes drinking in her son's face. She, Gleann, and Leanâlhâm had delayed their own departure to see the "visitors" off.

"You may have more than one task," she whispered.

Magiere hoped when they finally returned home that her aunt Bieja would be there waiting. She wondered what the blunt, gruff Bieja and the sly, watchful Nein'a might think of each other.

Gleann had handled any dissatisfaction among the elders at the delayed departure. Now they had to leave—for more reasons than just the council's decree.

The market up from the docks bustled with activity. Tall elves in bright clothing bargained over goods from smoke-cured fish to beeswax candles to bolts of the elves' strange shimmering white cloth that look much like silk or satin.

The barge arrived to take them down the river, and pulled up to the docks. Leanâlhâm stepped out from behind Nein'a. Her face filled with alarm at the sight of it.

"Oh, Léshil . . ."

"I'll try to send word of how we fare," he said.

Most likely, that wouldn't happen, but Magiere kept quiet. The girl would miss him, and Leesil had never been one to write letters. Then again, he'd never had anyone to write to, if such a letter could make it into the elven lands.

Sgäile and Brot'an boarded the barge.

"What are you doing?" Magiere asked in confusion.

"We come down the river with you," Brot'an answered. "It is best, considering . . . It is best. We can arrange passage for you at the coast." He gave Nein'a a long look. "Léshil must be kept safe."

For the first time since her return, Nein'a almost smiled.

Chap whined and gazed down the riverbank. Lily roamed there with her pack.

Wynn kneeled beside him. "Do you wish to run with them for a while?"

He hesitated, then licked her face and bolted off.

It was time to leave, and Magiere hurt for Leesil, watching him look one last time at his mother. Magiere agreed that Nein'a should remain here for now, to rest and gather herself. But knowing this didn't make the parting any easier for Leesil.

Nein'a reached out with her slender tan hand to Leesil's cheek. "Good hunting, my son."

Magiere found this an odd farewell, but Leesil just turned and stepped onto the barge, and she followed with Wynn.

Wynn held a hand up to Osha. She didn't speak. From the dock, he held up his own in response, but his expression was impossible to read.

"Good-bye," Magiere called to Gleann and Leanâlhâm. "I won't forget you."

Gleann smiled sadly as the barge pulled away.

Wide silver birch trees and hanging vines rushed past once again, and the docks of Crijheäiche vanished behind them.

Eight peaceful days later, Chap stood beside Lily gazing down a gentle slope toward the coast. He clearly saw the Hâjh River and his companions' barge near its mouth spilling into a expansive gulf. An azure ocean stretched beyond it to the horizon.

After all Chap's time in the immense forest, it was strange to see a city at the far edge of these wild elven lands. Small, thatched dwellings spread around higher structures at the middle and along the shore. He was surprised that coastal elves did not live in trees like those of the inland. Lily followed as he loped down the hill through the thinning trees and headed for the city's outskirts.

As the distance closed, he saw a few shops and stalls and scattered domicile trees on the fringes. One larger structure was composed of multiple floors built around the towering trunk of a redwood. Its upper branches spread wide like a second leafy roof over the building. Judging by the windows and small specks of people about it, it appeared to be an inn or its equivalent among the an'Cróan. He kept on, looking ahead to the far docks barely visible between the shoreline structures. The barge would be tied off there soon enough.

Lily whined and stopped.

Chap spun about and pressed his head against hers, showing her memories of his companions who waited. Lily backed up. He looked into her crystalline eyes, tinted with yellow flecks.

She would not come with him.

They had left the other majay-hì beyond the last hill, for the pack would go no further. Lily pressed her head to his and showed him images of inland elven enclaves and her kin running through the forest. Perhaps her kind did not approach the coastal people.

He did not want to leave her, and barked as he bounded a few steps forward and then spun about. But she held her ground. Chap looked to the coastline with its faint white lines of waves curling into the shore.

He had broken with his kin, the Fay. He had tangled and thwarted Most Aged Father's attempt on Magiere's life and his plans to use Leesil to ferret out dissidents. And now that Brot'an had revealed himself, Chap would do whatever was necessary to keep Leesil from the man's reach.

He would resist anyone who sought to use Leesil or Magiere. He would find his own answers for what lay ahead of them all.

Chap went back and pressed his nose against Lily, breathing in the rich earthen scent of her fur. It made him feel heavy and weak with sorrow.

But Leesil and Magiere and even Wynn still needed him.

Chap turned from Lily and ran for the coast. He could not bear to look back, even when he heard her howl fade into the forest.

EPILOGUE

The dreamer fell through boundless night, frigid wind ripping past.

The night sky began to undulate.

Rippling mounds arched within the darkness like black desert dunes and then sharpened into clarity. Stars became glints of reflected light upon black reptilian scales the size of small battle shields. Those scaled dunes shifted into mammoth reptilian coils, each larger than the height of a mounted rider. They turned and writhed on all sides of the dreamer, with no beginning, no end, and no space between.

The scales vanished, but the dreamer still fell. A coastline appeared below, fringed by high snow-packed mountains.

Here, a voice whispered above the roar of rushing air. *It is here.*

The dreamer tumbled downward, until high mountain peaks of perpetual ice rose like a jagged-toothed maw on all sides. Within that snowbound canyon stood a six-towered castle bordered by stone walls. The dreamer, in rapid descent, caught only a glimpse of high arched gates.

A white snowfield beyond rushed up.

Then impact.

No pain or darkness came, only shudders of fear, as to a child lost in the wilderness. The dreamer lay in crusted snow, staring up at twin gates of ornate iron curls. They joined together at their high tops in an arched point. Mottled with rust, the gates were still sound in their place. Beyond stood the castle's matching-shaped iron doors atop a wide cascade of steps.

A carrion crow sat upon the gates, watching the dreamer expectantly.

The castle dimmed from sight into darkness. Reptilian coils rose all around, their twisting and churning increasing in speed.

The orb is yours . . . I now give it to you alone . . . take it!

The dreamer tried to scramble across the snow, but then only the black coils remained, closing in, tighter and tighter.

Sister of the dead, lead on.

Magiere's eyes snapped open, as she gasped for breath and thrashed out of the bed. She scrambled across the floor and huddled naked and shaking in one corner of the elven inn's tiny room. She tried to scream, but all that came out was a harsh whisper.

"Leesil!"

He sat up quickly in the bed.

Black coils seemed to move in every shadow of the dark room as Magiere reached out for Leesil hurrying toward her.